MR CAMPION'S COVEN

Also by Mike Ripley

Margery Allingham's Albert Campion

MR CAMPION'S FAREWELL *
MR CAMPION'S FOX *
MR CAMPION'S FAULT *
MR CAMPION'S ABDICATION *
MR CAMPION'S WAR *
MR CAMPION'S VISIT *
MR CAMPION'S SÉANCE *

The Fitzroy Maclean Angel series

LIGHTS, CAMERA, ANGEL
ANGEL UNDERGROUND
ANGEL ON THE INSIDE
ANGEL IN THE HOUSE
ANGEL'S SHARE
ANGELS UNAWARE
Etc.

Other titles

DOUBLE TAKE
BOUDICA AND THE LOST ROMAN
THE LEGEND OF HEREWARD *

Non-fiction

SURVIVING A STROKE
KISS KISS, BANG BANG

** available from Severn House*

MR CAMPION'S COVEN

Mike Ripley

First world edition published in Great Britain and the USA in 2021
by Severn House, an imprint of Canongate Books Ltd,
14 High Street, Edinburgh EH1 1TE.

Trade paperback edition first published in Great Britain and the USA in 2022
by Severn House, an imprint of Canongate Books Ltd.

severnhouse.com

British Library Cataloguing-in-Publication Data
A CIP catalogue record for this title is available from the British Library.

ISBN-13: 978-0-7278-9083-2 (cased)
ISBN-13: 978-1-78029-781-1 (trade paper)
ISBN-13: 978-1-4483-0519-3 (e-book)

All Severn House titles are printed on acid-free paper.

Typeset by Palimpsest Book Production Ltd.,
Falkirk, Stirlingshire, Scotland.
Printed and bound in Great Britain by
TJ Books Limited, Padstow, Cornwall.

For Margaret and Joe Maron, who took me to Harkers Island where we drank Margheritas, made red-eye gravy, ate hush-puppies, saw horses walking on water and sat out a hurricane.

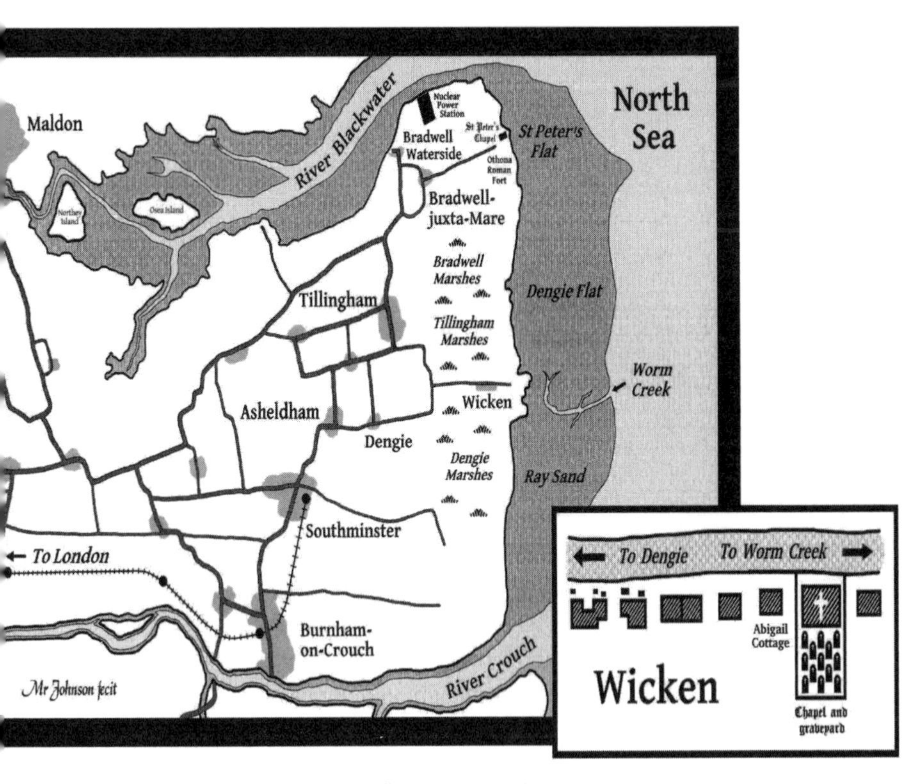

A fairly accurate map of the Dengie peninsula in the County of Essex, including the hamlet of Wicken.

CONTENTS

ONE
The Hoi-Toiders

The East Coast of America, 1963

It was Rupert, son of Albert, Campion who started the hare running, though he was in no way to blame for what happened eight years later and four thousand miles away. This did not, however, stop Mr Albert, father of Rupert, Campion from suggesting, with tongue firmly in cheek, that it was so.

'Can I try your beer, mister?'

'Now just you hush, Lucinda, you know you're not allowed beer, so leave Rupert alone. I'll tell you when you get to the legal drinking age.'

'Awww, Mom . . .'

'Just what is the drinking age in North Carolina?' Rupert asked his hostess.

'As far as my daughter is concerned, it's fifty-five, but you're okay as far as beer goes. You might have trouble buying hard liquor though. Cheers.'

Professor Kathryn ('with a k and a y') Luger showed her companion a perfect set of teeth and held up her long-necked bottle of beer, its sides glistening with condensation, to toast him.

'It's far too hot to think of drinking spirits,' said Rupert Campion once their bottles had been formally chinked.

'It is a foolish Yankee indeed who comes to the South in July.'

'Do you mean the South, or the Confederacy, because I would point out that I am an Englishman, not a Yankee.'

'But you go to a Yankee school.'

'That I cannot deny,' grinned Rupert.

It would have been foolish for him to try and do so, as it was at Harvard that he had met Professor Luger, or perhaps the better way of putting it would have been ambushed by the woman at a sherry party thrown to welcome students from outside the United States. Whether or not he was of legal sherry-drinking age under American law had not occurred to him at the time, though he did notice that almost all faculty members were sipping lethally concentrated martinis. He was a guest in the country, however, and so quietly sipped his sherry as though to the manner – if not the manor that Americans expected all Englishmen to own – born.

He had been fending off some rather aggressive questioning about the current craze for British pop music from a senior, white-haired faculty member with a pronounced *mittel-Europa* accent whose name he had heard but quickly dismissed as too difficult to either pronounce or remember. He smiled and nodded appropriately as good manners dictated but gradually found himself backed literally into a corner of the high-ceilinged, white-painted, brightly lit room (so white and bright it hurt the eyes). It seemed as if the entire crowd standing, drinking and munching canapés, had conspired to avoid making eye contact with him.

'Dr Heydenrych, you old goat! Leave that young man alone, we have important business to discuss. I've had him in my sights since I got here, but I had to wait for them to release their secret supply of decent bourbon.'

The voice which announced Rupert's escape, and immediate recapture, was a deep, mellifluous Southern drawl, though Rupert thought 'drawl' a particularly crude adjective for something so sensuous. It belonged to a tall blonde woman perhaps twice his age, though it was so difficult to tell with Americans as they were all so disgracefully healthy, dressed in a two-piece pink cotton suit which fitted smoothly on every angle and curve. A well-manicured set of fingers waved a crystal tumbler brimming with brown liquid and tinkling with ice cubes in the face of Rupert's inquisitor as an FBI man in the movies might flash a badge. It seemed to be all the identification required.

'But naturally, Professor Luger . . .' said the old man, nodding to Rupert and backing away, already scouring the party for his next victim.

'You'll have to forgive Heinrich,' the woman said through a dazzling smile. 'Well, you don't *have* to, but being an Englishman, you surely will. Now that I've rescued you from that old bore, you are, if not my prisoner, then my indentured servant, at least for the next fifteen minutes.'

'How did you know I was British?'

'Your suit is Jermyn Street, London, rather than Brooks Brothers, and your tie is tied, not clipped on, plus the way you were arguing with Dr Heydenrych.'

'I hardly said a word to him!' protested Rupert.

'Exactly. A hip, cool American boy would have told him to take a hike. You were so polite it was toothache painful.'

'So you decided to rescue me?'

'Not specifically. I came here to seek you out to talk about Essex,' she said, making the 'Ess' slow and sibilant, then snapping out the final syllable.

'I beg your pardon?' gulped Rupert, mishearing.

'Essex, the place,' said the woman, smiling at the pink dots of embarrassment blooming on Rupert's cheeks.

'The one in England, or here in Massachusetts?'

'The English one, though I'm glad you've noticed the link.'

'Difficult not to. It was quite a shock to see signposts to Braintree here in Boston, not to mention Cambridge and then Suffolk and Norfolk counties. Made me feel quite at home.'

'Good. You could be just the man I need. Your father would have been ideal, but you'll do.'

'My father?' Rupert had exchanged embarrassment for confusion. 'You know my father?'

The woman finished her drink and casually handed the glass to Rupert while she delved into a leather clutch bag for a packet of cigarettes.

'I knew him, all too briefly, during the war.'

'The war?' Now confusion was being elbowed out by disbelief. 'Surely . . .'

'Why thank you, kind sir,' she said, her Southern drawl more pronounced than ever. 'I *was* exceedingly young during the war, a mere snip of a gal, but I was doing my duty in Washington as a very junior typist at the War Department when we met.'

Rupert examined his glass and, to his despair, found it as empty as the one he had been handed. Now the flames of confusion and bewilderment were being fanned by awkwardness. He was saved by a passing waitress with an empty salver on which he deposited the glasses and, in what he fancied to be a quick-draw motion as seen in the better cowboy movies, produced a shiny new Zippo lighter from his jacket pocket and ignited the cigarette which was firmly encased between two scarlet lips patiently waiting for a flame.

'Thanks. I'm Kathryn Luger,' said the woman, exhaling a stream of smoke above Rupert's head. 'Would you like a cigarette? They're menthol.'

'I'm Rupert Campion and no thank you, I don't smoke.'

'But you carry a cigarette lighter in case you come across a lady in distress. That shows you are Albert's son.'

Rupert decided to pull himself together. 'It's Professor Luger, isn't it? But you're not one of my professors, are you?'

'I'm in anthropology, which is far more fun than the antiseptic stuff they feed you in the business school. Did your father approve of your choice?'

'To be honest, I think he wanted me to go to Cambridge, England rather than Cambridge, Massachusetts, and read something frivolous like archaeology or . . .'

'Anthropology. That sounds like the Albert I knew.'

'But just how did you know him, Professor? He's never talked much about the war, but from what I gather, he was mostly active in the European theatre.'

'I can assure you that Albert Campion experienced the war on at least two continents, though I quite understand why he has not spoken about it. We both worked for organizations known only by initials – he used to call it a real alphabet soup – and the most important one was S for secret.'

'Fascinating,' breathed Rupert, 'you must tell me more.'

'Not a chance, sonny, but give your pop my regards when you see him next. He might remember me as Kathryn Masteller as I was back then, though he always called me Kate; Luger is my married name.' She chuckled as she exhaled smoke. 'Most of the GIs shipped over to help you guys in Europe went looking for a Luger as a souvenir. I got mine after the war, by marrying one.'

'Is your husband here?'

'No fear. He's a dedicated scientist, an astrophysicist; very boring, very awkward in social situations. He works for NASA at the Langley Aeronautical Lab in Virginia.'

'That doesn't sound boring at all,' Rupert protested politely.

'Space exploration probably isn't,' said Professor Luger, putting her head on one side as if considering the proposition carefully, 'but Clyde, that's my husband, is; though I guess he feels the same about anthropology, so that kinda evens things out.'

Rupert was beginning to regret that he did not smoke and was also craving more alcohol. 'I'm still not clear, Professor . . .'

'Kathryn, please; and that's with a "k" and a "y".'

'Kathryn . . .' Rupert continued uncertainly. 'I'm not clear what it is I can actually . . . do . . . for you.'

'You can come with me on a little expedition, young Rupert. You're a Campion, after all, and Campions are always up for a challenge.'

The winning smile, the perfect teeth and a large portion of pure femininity all came into play.

Rupert, now nervous, and guilty for feeling so, spoke almost plaintively. 'What sort of expedition?'

'Think of it as academic research. Have you ever been to the Outer Banks of North Carolina?'

'I wasn't aware there were *Inner* Banks in North Carolina, let alone Outer ones. I take it we are not talking about the places where one can cash a cheque or stage a robbery, are we?'

'We are talking offshore islands, mostly mud but some with spectacular lighthouses on them and some with more horses than people. I want to take you to Harkers Island. It's a long drive, but it'll be fun. You can bring your swimming trunks and we can make a long weekend of it.'

Rupert's eyes flicked across the room until he located a glass ashtray and he scurried off to claim it, using the time to think furiously. When he was back in place in front of the invitingly mysterious Professor Luger, and decidedly uncomfortable about just how disturbingly attractive he found the woman, Rupert stood like a good soldier, or at least a diligent batman, and concentrated on holding the ashtray steady.

'What exactly will I be doing on this . . . expedition?' he asked, trying to keep his voice as steady as his hand.

'I need you to listen to someone,' said the professor, tapping ash from her cigarette without looking, simply assuming the ashtray would be in range. 'You could say I need your ears.'

'My ears?'

She tossed back her hair dramatically and struck an imperious pose. '*Friends, Englishmen, scholars, lend me your ears!* I need your ears to help in my research.'

'Why mine?'

'Because they're English ears! And also because, as you are a Campion and here at Harvard, I'm assuming there is something of a brain between them.'

'And what will I be hearing?'

'An accent, an old English accent or dialect. One that hasn't changed much in over two hundred and fifty years. All you have to do is tell me if you understand what's being said. Don't look so worried – the local yokels are fairly harmless and you'll be perfectly safe with me.'

Of that, Rupert was far from sure. 'Will your husband be joining this expedition?'

'Good grief, no! The very idea of being stuck on an island with nothing to do but lie on a beach, drink beer and converse with the natives, would horrify Clyde. No, he'll be hard at work trying to get a monkey into space and, if he remembers, back to Earth.'

Young Rupert, who had (clearly) neither his father's years nor experience of the ways of the world, totally failed to spot the mischievous twinkle in the professor's eyes.

'How do you feel about children, Rupert?'

'Well . . . I . . . I . . . hadn't considered . . . I don't really . . .'

'You don't hate them? You're not allergic to them?'

'No, of course not.'

'Good, because my daughter Lucinda, known as Lulu, will be going with us and she can be a bit of a handful.'

As the previous autumn, or fall, as Rupert was learning to call it, had been a harum-scarum time of nuclear brinkmanship, it was a relief to be sitting on the beaches of an island off the American coast which had not been planted with Russian missiles and pushed on to the front pages of newspapers worldwide.

Not that Harkers Island was very far off the American coast, merely the length of a wooden bridge, and its inhabitants, from the original Coree tribe onwards, had never shown any enthusiasm for Marxist philosophy. They did, however, share sunshine and sandy beaches with those more strident islanders in the Caribbean and, within minutes of arriving at what Professor Luger described as her 'beach house', Rupert found himself with trousers rolled up to his knees, paddling in the warm shallow surf, being dragged along by the hand of a small but deceptively strong five-year-old girl.

After the long drive down from Boston, which had begun in pre-dawn darkness, Rupert was grateful for the chance to stretch his legs, feel the grit between his toes and appreciate the vista over a flat calm sea out towards a line of low sandbanks over which swooped a squadron of unidentifiable seabirds.

Kathryn Luger, who had insisted on driving her large station wagon the full distance, despite Rupert's protesting that he had a perfectly legal driving licence albeit for driving on the wrong side of the road, had ordered him to take Lulu 'for a splash' in the late afternoon sunshine while she 'freshened up' in the beach house. It was not, as Rupert had half-expected, a colourful beach hut of the sort found at Southwold or Frinton, but a three-bedroomed bungalow of wooden construction which would have passed for a luxury executive home in any new town in England.

When she emerged, waving an arm to signal the two beachcombers, she was wearing a one-piece swimsuit in blue with large white polka dots, a wide-brimmed straw hat and the large round sunglasses favoured by America's first lady. She had a blanket draped over her shoulders and carried an ice bucket chinking with glass bottles. Rupert and his temporary charge joined her as she stretched the blanket on the sand and received, respectively, an ice-cold beer and something he was learning to call a 'soda'.

'We have food in the refrigerator and a fully stocked bar,' said Kathryn, 'and the sun is shining. Welcome to Harkers Island.'

'It's quite a place,' said Rupert, shielding his eyes with a hand and peering over the water at the sandbanks out towards the horizon, 'and positively magical, unless my eyes are playing tricks. Are those *horses* out there, walking on the water?'

'Yes, they are, but where they're walking, on the mud banks, the water is only a few inches deep. It's rather unsettling to be in a rowing boat out there and to have a couple of ponies splashing by. They're totally wild and descended from the horses carried by Spanish explorers after their ships were wrecked. There are more shipwrecks out there' – she pointed out to sea with the neck of her beer bottle – 'than there are people on the Outer Banks, from pirate galleons to Civil War fighting ships and blockade runners, to merchant marine and quite a few U-boats. It's sometimes called the Ghost Fleet.'

'Fascinating,' said Rupert, 'but you haven't brought me here on a hunt for sunken pirate treasure, have you?'

'Pirates!' yelled young Lucinda, doing an impromptu and rather violent war dance in the sand. 'Let's go pirate! Yo-ho-ho!'

'Lulu loves coming here,' said her mother by way of explanation, 'and though it's historical treasures we're looking for, they have nothing to do with pirates.'

'So we're not going scuba-diving and fighting sharks, then?'

Lulu picked up on the word and her dance increased in frenzy. 'Sharks! Sharks!' Thankfully, they had the beach to themselves, so no innocent bathers were panicked.

The professor stretched out her long – and, Rupert noticed, quite shapely – legs. 'Nothing so dangerous, not even a giant squid to wrestle.'

'Squid! Squid! Giant squid!'

'Take it easy, Lulu, or ice cream's off the menu. And all I want you to do,' she said to Rupert, clearly the second child on the beach, 'is lend me your ears. I mean it. The guy who looks after my beach house when we're not here, which is most of the year and especially hurricane season . . .'

'Hurricanes?' blurted Rupert.

'Blow! Blow! Blow the man down!'

'Lulu, *please*! Big people talking here. Anyway, the guy who looks after our property and who stocks the larder for us when we visit, is a local, born and bred here on Harkers, a genuine Hoi-Toider.'

'A what?'

'Hoi-Toiders, High-Tiders – that's what they call themselves here. He's a good old boy called Nathaniel, or Natty, Whybrow, and he'll be calling on us after dinner to make sure we've got enough supplies for the weekend and so I can pay him for the groceries. I want you to meet him.'

'For any particular reason?'

'Just one. I want to know if you can understand a single goddamned word he says.'

If he had been expecting a grizzled old sea dog with a wooden leg and an optional parrot, Rupert was sorely disappointed. From his ruddy complexion, Nathaniel Whybrow had clearly led an outdoor life, but the red chequered shirt and faded blue overalls he wore suggested an agricultural rather than seafaring career. A stalk of wheat or rye grass hanging from the corner of his mouth would not have looked out of place, but then neither would a lobster pot tucked under one arm.

They had dined early, as Americans do, on hamburgers topped with melted blue cheese, a delicacy Rupert was growing dangerously fond of, just as he was gradually, if uneasily, becoming accustomed to seeing televisions in kitchens and dining rooms. Then with only minimal precociousness, as it had been a long day, little Lucinda had agreed to take a shower and get ready for bed and a story read by her mother. While this operation was taking place, Rupert turned off the television, thinking it the polite thing to do as a guest in the house, and from his overnight bag took a copy of *America's Wealth* as a sop to his academic conscience.

He was beginning to come to grips with the economics of colonial America when he heard a distinct tread on the boards of the porch and then the rapping of knuckles on the door of the house. From a bedroom Kathryn had yelled, 'Get that, will you?'

Their visitor was short for an American. Rupert had been warned by his father that he would soon get a stiff neck, looking up to Americans of the same generation who seemed to have put on a massive growth spurt in the post-war years. Natty Whybrow was of a different generation, though exactly which one was difficult to determine as, to Rupert's eyes, he could have been anywhere between fifty and eighty years old. But, he remembered, he had been brought to Harkers Island to use his ears not his eyes, and when Natty began to speak, he realized he would, as his hostess might say, have to earn his corn. The thing was, Natty Whybrow did not say a word, simply stood there in the doorway looking at Rupert as if he had landed by flying saucer, despite the latter's attempts at civility.

'Hello there, you must be Nathaniel. We were expecting you.'

When that failed to provoke any sort of response, even in facial expression, Rupert added: 'Professor Luger – Kathryn – said you would be joining us this evening.'

It was only when Lucinda, somewhere behind Rupert, said loudly, 'Natty's here and you said I could get him a beer!' that the caller's weather-beaten face cracked into a broad grin aimed firmly at a point over Rupert's shoulder. It was to that point he strode with a bow-legged gait, gliding by Rupert as if he wasn't there, in order to grab Lucinda by the arms and whirl her twice around, the girl squealing in delight.

Without waiting for an invitation, Natty climbed aboard one of the high stools by the 'breakfast counter' – as Rupert was learning to call that peculiarly American innovation – and thanked his junior hostess profusely for the bottle of beer she selected from a cavernous refrigerator both she and Rupert could have taken sanctuary in.

'Hi there, Natty,' said Kathryn as she joined them, having changed into tight-fitting blue jeans and a white man's shirt knotted at the waist. 'This is Rupert. I told you about him. He's here from England.'

Nathaniel Whybrow raised his beer bottle in a toast before applying it to his lips without waiting to be offered a glass – another trait of Americana which Rupert was having to come to grips with.

'So you be the 'fessor's poopil, that roight?'

Out of the corner of his eye, Rupert saw Kathryn's face contort into an expression partly of amusement, but mostly of challenge, as if defying Rupert to answer. Being brought up correctly, Rupert ignored her and spoke to the visitor. 'Not exactly, but we are at the same university. Kathryn tells me you're a native Harkers Islander.'

'She told you crackly. Born 'n bred here.'

'Then I suspect you've seen a few hurricanes in your time.'

'Oh aye,' Natty nodded sagely, 'but you'll be safe for another month Oi reckon, the hooge ones come mostly in August and September. Don't suppose you get 'em in Lunnon, but we've had some big blows here. I remembers when . . .'

And the visitor, who had at first seemed reluctant to open his mouth to anything other than the lip of a bottle of Schlitz beer, spoke almost without drawing breath for a good half-hour, using the stool at the kitchen counter as his personal pulpit. His verbal river was only diverted when Lucinda announced with a loud yawn that as she had her pyjamas on and the television was off, she might as well go to bed.

Kathryn smiled indulgently as she shepherded her daughter to her bedroom, and when she returned asked Natty Whybrow how much she owed him for groceries and general expenses incurred in looking after her property. A figure was mentioned quietly and Rupert had the good grace to avert his gaze as Kathryn opened her purse and counted out a certain number of dollars.

Wishing all a good night with a fulsome smile, Natty Whybrow took his leave, but was probably no more than twenty feet from the beach house before Kathryn just had to ask.

'So what did you make of that? How much did you get?'

'Almost all of it,' said Rupert breezily, feeling rather proud of himself, 'even the story of how his wife put her shoulder out "wrenching wet towels on laundry day" but fortunately she'd already cooked his dinner.'

Kathryn Luger studied her houseguest carefully, nodding appreciatively. 'I'm impressed, young Campion. I must admit, "wrenching" threw me for a while, I suppose it means wringing the water out of the towels, which makes sense as the Whybrows don't have a dryer. That was a good spot. What else caught your ear?'

'Well, "Lunnun" for London was a dead giveaway, as did "that don't argefy" when he meant something was indisputable,' said Rupert, trying to avoid sounding like a cod Sherlock Holmes, 'but also how "u" sounds became double-o sounds. "Stupid" came out as "stoopid", "pupil" was "poopil", and at one point he said something had happened at the "opportoon" moment, which made me smile.'

'And your conclusion?'

'He seems a charming man, a local character.'

'I meant about his speech, his accent. Did you place it?'

'Traditional Essex,' said Rupert casually. 'That's Essex, England, of course.'

'You don't seem surprised.'

'Should I be? If the descendants of Spanish horses can survive out there on the sandbanks for three hundred years, why not the speech patterns of the original settlers who no doubt came from East Anglia? I've read somewhere that there are people in the Appalachians who speak Shakespearean English, though perhaps not with the dramatic heft of a Laurence Olivier. You find these quaint old traits surviving in mountains and on islands.'

'Can you pinpoint Natty's accent any more specifically back to the old country?'

'I'm sure it's Essex, though it could be Suffolk or even north Kent. I'm no expert. Is it important?'

'It's interesting,' said the professor, 'at least to me, because I've asked and no one seems to know for sure, which is weird as Americans are usually very keen to claim their origins. Scots-Irish, Italian-American, Irish-American, that sort of thing. Did you know there are more Caledonian Societies running more Highland Games here in North Carolina than there are in Scotland?'

Rupert hoped he looked suitably impressed rather than horrified at this information. 'So you don't know where the original Hoi-Toiders came from?'

'Oh yes, they came from Massachusetts in 1693, according to local legend, not long after landing there from the old country; only a matter of months after landfall, so it's said.'

'Is that a problem? It's feasible, isn't it?'

'Certainly, but why did they leave Massachusetts – an established colonial settlement – to come all the way down here to a godforsaken island surrounded by mudbanks?'

Rupert shrugged his shoulders. 'They didn't like the look of Massachusetts? They preferred somewhere warmer? I'm no colonial historian. I have no idea,' he pleaded, then noticed the twinkle in the woman's eyes, 'but I suspect you have.'

'I have enough ideas for a postgraduate doctoral thesis.'

'You already have a PhD,' Rupert pointed out.

'Yes, but this could be a fascinating subject for someone else, because you've got to take the date into account.'

'I have?'

'Your father would have spotted it immediately. The settlers of Harkers Island landed in, then left Massachusetts in 1692 or '93, which was quite a significant period in a place called Salem.'

'Salem? You mean the Salem witchcraft trials?'

'Exactly. I think the original Hoi-Toiders sailed from Essex in England to find a new life in Massachusetts, but when they got there and found the witch trials going on, they changed their plans and came all the way down the coast.'

Rupert gave another shrug. 'Well, who can blame them? Who would want to get caught up in the middle of a witch-hunt? You don't pack up your family and your worldly goods and cross the Atlantic in a leaky wooden ship only to be accused of witchcraft.'

Professor Luger smiled the smile of she-wolf. 'Especially not if you actually *are* a witch . . .'

TWO

Letter from America

The east coast of England, 1971

'Who do we know in Georgia, darling?' asked Mr Campion, selecting a light blue airmail envelope from the morning's bundle of post.

'The one in America, or the one where those rather sturdy red wines come from, and Stalin as well, didn't he?' answered his wife, without looking up from the pages of that morning's *Eastern Daily Press*.

'Oh, the American one to be sure. The University of Georgia at Athens, presumably not the one in Greece, to be specific.'

'Interesting, but I'm no wiser,' said Amanda. 'Why not open it and read the letter rather than just the return address? If it's blackmail or a death-threat, they're unlikely to put a return address, and I believe the Inland Revenue uses brown envelopes, so you should be safe.'

'I have always admired your practical streak, darling, and now that I have Georgia on my mind, as the songsters say, let us see what this missive from the colonies contains.'

Campion sliced open the letter with a butter knife, extracted two thin sheets of typed airmail paper and began to read, seemingly engrossed in its contents, for what his wife considered was a deliberately unreasonable length of time. A series of long pointed sighs and a loud rustling of her newspaper indicated her mood of growing impatience and her husband knew better than to prolong that particular tease.

'It's from a gentleman called Mason Lowell Clay, whoever he is, writing at the behest – note that, behest – of a Professor Kathryn Luger, whoever she is.'

'Does it become clear?'

'Only that she seems to be an old chum of Rupert's from his

time at Harvard, which is presumably how this Mason Lowell Clay got our address.'

'Has Rupert ever mentioned a Professor Luger?'

'Not that I can recall offhand. No, wait, I can.' Campion removed his spectacles and tapped the end of one of the arms against his teeth. 'Rupert sent me a very rude letter when he was a student, telling me how he'd run into an old girlfriend of mine from the war years.'

'Really?' asked his wife calmly. 'How rude?'

'Not rude, cheeky. The lad was deliberately adding two and two together and making twenty-two, just to get a rise out of me, a rise in his allowance that is. Of course, I told him to publish and be damned.'

'Quite right, darling. One should not be blackmailed by one's children, only by one's wife. So this Professor Luger was a wartime conquest?'

'Hardly. She was Kathryn Masteller . . . or something like that . . . when I knew her, and she was a secretary in Washington. She was assigned to me for the duration of my posting over there.'

'As what? As translator?'

'I certainly needed one at times,' chuckled Campion. 'Quite often the only time I could make myself understood was by doing a very embarrassing impression of John Wayne, but Kathryn was actually my secretary and communications officer, a very bright, attractive young thing.'

'How young?'

'Young enough to see me as no more than an eccentric uncle, a Nick Charles sort of figure, though without a Nora or an Asta.'

'How attractive?'

'Very. She was constantly surrounded by clean-cut, freshly pressed American officers swarming over her like bees in the lavender fields. It would seem that she married someone called Luger and became an academic.'

'So why is she rekindling an old flame after all of – what – twenty-six, twenty-seven years?'

'Hardly a flame, darling, no more than a small spark, a glimmer, of adulation. After all, I was the dashing English diplomat – well, that's what she thought I was – and no doubt I reminded her of Robert Donat or Leslie Howard.'

'Who?' Amanda asked innocently.

'I shall ignore that. You are younger than I, but you are not that young. Anyway, Kathryn is neither here nor there, she is merely a conduit for young Mr Mason Clay, who appears to be some sort of student, and students being what they are these days he is unlikely to offer any adulation at all to an old buffer like myself.'

'So what does Mr Clay want?'

'What do students always want? A world without nuclear weapons? An end to apartheid? Peace in Vietnam? Lower prices in the Students' Union bar? No, I must curb my cynicism, which is brought on solely by the jealousy of youth by the old and decrepit. It appears that Mason Clay is a student of history and anthropology and is researching the origins of a group of settlers who decamped for a better life in the New World nearly three hundred years ago. It sounds as if he's doing a mass genealogical study for his doctorate on a particular bunch of religious dissidents from Wicken-juxta-Mare in Essex. Professor Luger, who seems to be mentoring him, gave him the idea and assured him that the Campion family were experts in all things Essex, though I can't think how Rupert gave her that idea.'

'You must remember to ask him at the weekend, or had you forgotten that he and Perdita are coming to visit?'

'Of course I had not forgotten, and I have made sure the larder is fully stocked because I know that unemployed actors are always hungry. Why do they call it *resting*? They never rest when they're not working, they're very active, eating and drinking to put on fat for the lean months, or in some cases, years.'

Amanda peered disapprovingly over the rim of her newspaper. 'You can't begrudge your son and his wife a square meal or two.'

'Or four, or five.'

'They have both chosen theatrical careers and we must support them. They are trying, you know. It wasn't Rupert's fault that the play at the Criterion folded after two weeks. Perdita is very excited about getting a callback after her audition for *The Benny Hill Show* with Thames television.'

'I'm not altogether sure about that one,' said Campion ruefully.

'Neither is Rupert,' his wife agreed.

'Perhaps, as he's resting, Rupert could look after Mason Lowell Clay, who intends to come to London, and within the next few days too, to bury himself in dusty old records and census returns, but also wants a 'field trip' – whatever that is – to this place Wicken-juxta-Mare, which I have to say I'm not familiar with.'

Mr Campion turned to the second page of the letter and giggled as he read. 'Mason Clay, however, is nothing if not thorough, and has even supplied not only directions but a geographical location. It appears to be situated 52 miles from London at a frighteningly precise latitude of 51.62 degrees and a longitude of 0.87 degrees, which would put it slightly to the right and above Greenwich in my schoolboy atlas.'

'It's on the Dengie Peninsula,' said Amanda, still concentrating on her newspaper. 'Out beyond Maldon and south of the Bradwell nuclear power station.'

'I am so impressed with your navigational skill, darling. I would have had to resort to a globe, a sextant and possibly an abacus to work that out.'

'I just read about it,' Amanda flicked the newspaper with both hands, making it snap, 'here under "all the news that's fit to print".'

'And Wicken-juxta-Mare has made the news?'

'It seems to be just known as Wicken these days and, technically, it is the mudbanks off the coast near there that have made the news.'

'And how did the Wicken mud demand the headlines? Do they contain oil? There's supposed to be quite a bit of it in the North Sea. Or is it an unexploded bomb from the war, or a lost aircraft? Things like that often get burped up by the mud on that coast.'

'No, nothing like that, but a mystery, that's for sure. The classic maritime mystery in fact, a real *Marie Celeste* puzzler. A luxury yacht, it says here – but is there any other sort so far as the press is concerned? – has been found abandoned and stuck on a mudbank off the Dengie Peninsula and Wicken just happens to be the nearest inhabited spot to it inland.'

'I am guessing that the use of the word "inland" explains why Wicken is no longer "juxta-Mare".'

'I would think that a fair assumption, given that part of the coast, though nothing has been called "juxta-Mare" for centuries. "Next to the Sea", as in our own dear old Wells Next-the-Sea is the nearest you would get these days.'

'So it is no longer a port, if it ever was one, that is?'

'Why? What are you thinking, Albert?'

'I was merely surmising – or ruminating – that there are so many little places on the Blackwater and the Crouch where sailing and yachts are quite the thing, that a yacht, unknown and unloved, could have become possessed, slipped its moorings on a high tide and floated off to a life of freedom roaming the seven seas as a ghost ship.'

'Except it didn't get beyond the mudflats and, anyway, Wicken is inland, not next to the sea any more and, besides that, the yacht wasn't unknown or unloved.'

'Pray give me the full SP, as Lugg would say.'

Amanda shook the newspaper again, as if it was a burden to hold it while extracting further details to satisfy her husband's curiosity and found the story she had previously only skimmed.

'The yacht was called the *Jocasta* and was named after her owner, Jocasta Upcott. Even you may have heard of her, my dear. Rupert and Perdita certainly will have.'

'*Dame* Jocasta Upcott,' said Mr Campion, 'star of stage and screen, though mostly stage. I don't think they give damehoods to film stars per se.'

'Don't be snobby, Albert, even though you may be correct. You said her Lady Macbeth and her Volumnia were both excellent when we saw her that season at Stratford. Plus, she does a lot for charity and is always making appeals for the RSPCA, the PDSA and Guide Dogs for the Blind, *and* she has a drama school named after her. Rupert tried to get in there but failed the audition.'

'I knew there was a reason she was on my naughty list.' Campion sniffed haughtily. 'Serves her right if she's misplaced her yacht.'

'She hasn't misplaced it; it's been found abandoned. Dame Jocasta's captain was sailing it back from her holiday home in France to Brightlingsea where she berths it over winter. The yacht made it as far as the Dengie Peninsula mud, but it seems the captain didn't. There has been absolutely no sign of him. The yacht was empty, devoid of human life.'

'Gosh, how spooky! I'll bet there was a steaming mug of Ovaltine and a half-eaten meat pie on the captain's table.'

'Not quite,' said Amanda, in what her husband thought of as her best governess voice, 'something even more mysterious. Apparently, fifty yards from the yacht, they found the captain's sea boots upright in the mud. No captain, just his boots.'

'Goodness me, how odd.'

'Yes, there's definitely a mystery there.'

'No, darling, I meant it odd that a place I had never heard of raises its ugly head twice before breakfast is over. Coincidence? Very probably. Is there any more tea in the pot?'

Later that day, Mr Campion tried to remember where he had read the maxim *once is happenstance, twice is coincidence, third time is enemy action*, and could not decide whether to attribute it to a Greek philosopher or a Roman general. He was sure it was a profound piece of wisdom; the sort of aphorism he would have loved to claim authorship of. It rattled around his brain, prompting him to curse the way advancing age allowed memories to be misplaced, particularly given that, as the morning progressed, the adage became more relevant.

If Mason Clay's letter concerning his researches was the initial happenstance mention of a place called Wicken, and Amanda noticing the item in her newspaper was the coincidence, then the call to action was prompted by a pair of perfectly innocent telephone calls by Mr Campion, the first to his son.

'I don't know Mason Clay, Pop, but if he's one of Kathryn Luger's students, then he'll need all the help we can give him. Does he say when he's coming over?'

'Well, there's the thing; next week it seems.'

'And where's he staying?'

'There's the other thing, he's asked me if I could recommend a reasonably priced hotel in London or, alternatively, arrange for him to have a set of rooms on a staircase in a Cambridge college of my choice.'

'You have to make allowances for Americans. He's probably looked at a map and seen that England is so very small and Cambridge and London are only half an inch apart.'

'It's not so much his grasp of geography, Rupert, it's that he is clearly naïve thinking that there are such things as reasonably priced hotels in London or that I would be cruel enough to recommend my old rooms at St Ignatius to anyone brought up with electric light and internal plumbing, let alone air-conditioning.'

'Americans are innocent, rather than naïve, Pops. They are also generous to a fault and often expect others to be generous to them, though I suspect they are often disappointed. Professor Luger was kind and generous to me when I was at Harvard, so I would like to help her student if I can. Perhaps he could come and stay with us.'

'Don't be silly, my boy, you and Perdita don't have room to swing a spare American. I'm going to offer him the run of the Bottle Street flat for a month. You are welcome to mentor him while he's here, take him to a chophouse in the City for lunch and a few pubs down the East End in the evening to give him the feel of modern London. Oh, and introduce him to a policeman because Americans can't believe they're unarmed . . . and make him go upstairs on a double-decker bus, that always amuses them.'

'I'll meet him, of course, I'm sure he's a charming fellow, but I hope I won't be resting for too long. Something might come up any day now and I have to be available for auditions. Wouldn't it be better if you asked Lugg to show him the ropes?'

'Lugg!' exclaimed Mr Campion, trying not sound like Lady Bracknell. 'If Lugg took him on a pub crawl down the Mile End Road, it could put Anglo-American relations back to Boston Tea Party days. But now you've put me in mind of the old recidivist, I must track him down and ask him to get the flat up and running, make sure the sheets are aired and there's a shilling in the meter, that sort of thing.'

'If you ring Bottle Street, you might catch him there,' offered Rupert. 'I ran into him last night in the West End outside the Palladium and we went for a drink in the Argyll Arms.'

'He wasn't doing his Stage Door Johnny act, was he?'

'I didn't ask. You know Lugg; if he wants you to know what he's up to, he tells you. If you have to ask, it's none of your business, but he did say he was spending all his off-duty hours at the flat waiting for a plumber to call to fix a leak in the central heating.'

'Yes, he mentioned that when he did his weekly whip-round

with the Hoover and I told him to get a *bona fide* tradesman in rather than rely on some distant relative of his who did a plumbing course as part of his probation. You're quite right, though, I ought to warn him or he might come upon Mason Clay, presume he's a burglar and defenestrate him.'

'Or he could offer him a few tips.'

'Indeed he could,' said Campion, smiling into the receiver.

Magersfontein Lugg, having been named after a British defeat in December 1899 during the Second ('as if one wasn't enough') Boer War, was forever linked umbilically with the nineteenth century. He had always bridled at this, claiming that by the time the London newspaper carrying a report of the battle reached his newly delivered mother ('wrapped around two-penn'orth of fresh cod'), the twentieth century had well and truly dawned. His mother, an impressionable woman, thought Magersfontein would be an exotic and distinctive name for her baby boy, which it was, and that it would celebrate yet another victory for the glorious British Empire, which it didn't.

His relationship with Mr Campion had baffled many an onlooker over the years. Those within Campion's social circle thought the big man, who was prone to mangle but never mince his words, was an odd choice for a manservant or valet, and a few, rapidly corrected, made the mistake of calling Lugg a butler. Lugg himself had never admitted to being more than a 'gent's gent' and had always maintained that his devotion to Campion and his family was his lifelong penance for a misspent youth attracting the attention of the forces of law and order. That this might embarrass Campion's coterie of friends and acquaintances never occurred to Lugg, who often claimed that Campion's persistent mixing with the lower, often criminal, classes was a constant embarrassment to him.

For his retirement, Mr Campion had secured him the position of beadle at Brewers' Hall, a position well-suited to his talent for looking impressive in ceremonial fur robes and wielding a tipstaff, as well as allowing him to follow one of his main hobbies in life. His duties, mainly terrorizing a small staff and personally supervising the victuals at formal banquets, were not onerous, and allowed him plenty of spare time in which, out of loyalty and a sense of duty, he could continue to serve the Campions. Keeping an eye on Campion's London flat at 17a Bottle Street was one of those duties, and always a pleasurable one, as the flat, situated above a police station in Piccadilly, appealed to Lugg's sense of both achievement and mischief.

'Regent 01 . . . I mean 743-1300,' Lugg answered when the telephone in the flat rang.

'Good morning, old fruit, having trouble keeping up? The old Regent Street exchange has gone the way of silent movies, farthings and National Service.'

'This is the Aphrodite Glue Works, how may we be of service?'

'That's more like it,' Campion chuckled down the line, 'the old ones are the best.'

'No, the old ones are just old, like me and you,' said Lugg wearily.

'Speak for yourself, chum, I have no intention of acting my age. Now grab a pencil and take copious notes, for I have instructions for you.'

'Instructions like what you would give to a lackey, or a paid h'employee, f'r instance?'

'Do I detect an air of Bolshevism? I meant to say I had a few suggestions which I hope a valued family retainer would take to heart, especially a family retainer who knows where the bodies are buried.'

'Go on then – what you letting me in for this time?'

'Nothing too arduous, just a bit of housekeeping and a spot of babysitting.'

'Babysitting? I saw young Rupert last night out on the town.'

'I know, I have spies everywhere, but I don't count treating my son and heir-to-not-very-much to a light-and-bitter down the Argyll Arms as babysitting. Anyway, it's not him, although it's thanks to him in a way. I'm going to offer the flat to an American postgraduate student for about a month, so I want you to keep an eye on him, show him the ropes.'

'Show him the fleshpots, you mean?'

'No! Absolutely not.'

'Just checking. What's he studying, this Yank?'

'Something historical, something anthropological, I think. Nothing you would approve of, probably. He'll spend most of his time in museums or records offices going through old documents I should think, but it all has to do with a place out on the Essex coast called Wicken, so our American friend will want to hire a car and rely on you for directions, plus handy tips like remembering to drive on the right side of the road, which is, of course, the left. His name is Mason Clay, by the way, and I'm sure he's an upstanding fellow and all-round good egg, so please don't corrupt him too much.'

'Did you say Wicken?' Lugg asked, catching Campion off guard.

'Yes, Wicken is the place he's interested in.'

''e's not the only one, is 'e?'

'What do you mean by that, O Enigmatic One? I do hate it when you do enigmatic.'

'That's the place where that yacht was found abandoned. Jocasta Upcott's floating gin palace.'

'Pure coincidence, but that's the place.'

'Oh so you 'eard, did yer?'

'I read it in the newspaper.' Campion risked a white lie. 'We do get newspapers out here in the sticks, you know.'

'I meant 'ad you 'eard *from* her?'

'No, why should I have?'

'She rang 'ere yesterday, the great dame 'erself, all posh vowels and ee-nun-sea-a-tion. Gawd knows where she was ringing from, but I swears I could have heard her without the phone. Talk about playin' to the upper circle . . .'

'She's a thespian; that's what she does. What did she want?'

'Wanted you, but o'course I said you was retired.'

'Why?'

''Cos she wanted to hire you to find somebody, somebody who's gone missing from that yacht of hers what ran aground. Naturally, I told her you don't do private narking and never had, as that would just be common.'

'And how did she take that?'

'Not well, but I wasn't havin' her waste our time.'

On the other end of the line, Mr Campion raised an eyebrow at the use of 'our'. 'That was a trifle harsh,' he said, 'as she must be upset. As I understand it, the captain of her yacht disappeared leaving only his sea boots sticking up out of the mud.'

'Oh, it wasn't 'im she was worried about; never mentioned *him,*' answered Lugg with relish, 'it was Robespierre.'

'Who on earth is Robespierre?'

'The most important person in the world, according to her, but then she's an actress and they do tend to get hysterical.'

'So is it her agent? Her hairdresser? Her make-up artist?'

'Nah – it's her dog, innit. She don't give a fig for the yacht or its captain, but she wants her dog back, an' I'll bet you anything it's one of those poncy French poodles.'

THREE
Dame Jocasta's Yacht

Detective Inspector Andy Hankin of Essex CID felt much more relaxed about leaving the familiar environment of the county's police headquarters in Chelmsford for a case 'out on the mudbanks' when he learned that Sergeant Thomas Trybull had been assigned to assist him. Relieved, as well as relaxed, for although the investigation process itself held no fears for him, the coastal location and the presence of a boat did, as Hankin had had an irrational fear of the sea since childhood and had never learned to swim. Acting Detective Sergeant Trybull, however, having spent his entire police career to date in Maldon on the Blackwater estuary, was well versed in amphibious craft of all shapes and sizes, and how to mess about in them. For his part, Trybull was happy with the proposed partnership as, although he had no knowledge of his superior officer's nautical phobias, he was always proud to display his knowledge of local waters in public and, in private, inordinately pleased with the title 'detective', albeit 'acting', and the chance to work in plain clothes.

There was another reason why Sergeant Trybull was happy to play the loyal subordinate to the younger inspector as, while he relished the roles of trusty guide, navigator, driver and even translator in the wilder, forgotten edges of the county, he was terrified at the possibility of having to confront, or in any way have to deal with, the owner of the *Jocasta*, the object of the case they were investigating. Not only was Dame Jocasta Upcott a thespian – and actors of any rank were notoriously difficult to deal with – but she was an aristocrat among thespians, honoured by the Queen and therefore as much a national treasure as Stonehenge or the Magna Carta, and just as impervious to police interference.

Hankin had an unnatural fear of open water which could have affected anyone; Trybull had a severe social inferiority complex of the sort which affected Englishmen more than others. Hankin knew his place was on firm dry land; Trybull simply knew his place.

'According to the initial Coastguard's report, there was nothing wrong with the *Jocasta* apart from the fact she was stuck on a mudbank,' Trybull said as he negotiated the maze of B-roads which formed almost a grid following the lines and banks of drainage dykes over the Dengie Peninsula as it bulged eastwards out into the sea, shouldered by rivers to the north and south. 'She's berthed at Brightlingsea, so that's her home port, so to speak, and it's presumed she was heading there.'

'Would it be normal for it to sail so close to the coast?' Hankin asked, noting roadside signposts to places named Cock Clarks, Roundbush and Cold Norton, and wondering why he had never heard of them.

'No one deliberately sails that close to the peninsula; there's no reason to. There's no place to put in unless you go round to Burnham, on the Crouch after Foulness Point, or into the Blackwater after rounding Sales Point. Neither takes you to Brightlingsea and, in any case, most people would want to give Bradwell a miss. Call it superstition, but most sailors give it a wide berth.'

'I think it's common sense to give a nuclear power station a wide berth, not superstition. They shouldn't be allowed.'

'You weren't one of the Ban-the-Bomb lot, were you, sir?' Trybull asked, wondering when Hankin had been a student, for there was no doubt in his mind that he was in the presence of a university graduate.

'No, not my line at all, but I do think that if nuclear power is so safe, why don't the politicians build a reactor in Whitehall instead of plonking one out here on the coast, spoiling the view from Mersea Island? And there's no need to call me "sir" while we're alone, Tom.'

'I'd feel happier if I could, sir, so's I don't slip up when it matters. Wouldn't look good in front of Dame Jocasta.'

'Oh, I don't think we'll have to bow and curtsey before Dame Jocasta,' said Hankin. 'I doubt she'll leave London to grace us with her presence out here in the wilderness. Probably send her press agent or her solicitor.'

Trybull exhaled with relief. Press agents and solicitors he

could deal with; the one could always be intimidated, the other usually needed a favour and such protocol was sometimes interchangeable. But a diva with a damehood, that was a different kettle of social and domestic problems; domestic because, had he actually met Dame Jocasta, his life at home, off duty, would have been made intolerable by Mrs Trybull's desire to know every conceivable detail of the actress's appearance, couture, mannerisms and, above all, *age*; and Mrs Trybull, as an interrogator, was as relentless as any sadistic black-clad Nazi screen villain.

'Or her insurance assessor,' Hankin continued, spotting another signpost pointing to Latchingdon and Snoreham, though wondering whether that was two places or one. 'Dame Jocasta might have a healthy bank balance, but even she can't afford to lose a yacht, can she?'

'It's not lost, sir. We know exactly where it is and the Coastguard boys have anchored it down. With a high tide she should be easy enough to pull out of the mud. I wouldn't mind helping out with that,' Trybull said dreamily.

'Fancy claiming a bit of salvage, do you, Tom? We could nip back to Maldon and you could sail your pirate ship round the coast and claim the *Jocasta* as a prize. I would insist that you fly the Jolly Roger, though.'

Trybull smiled politely, but thinly. 'My little sailing dinghy couldn't budge the *Jocasta*, sir, but I've got mates in the Blackwater Sailing Club with a motor launch which would do the job, and we'd do it for free because it would be a crying shame if anything happened to her.'

'You know the ship? It sounds as if you do.'

'She's a yacht, sir, not a ship, and yes, I know her. Well, I've seen her berthed up at Brightlingsea. She's a nice-looking craft: a forty-foot Bermuda yacht, sometimes called a Gentleman's Yacht, built by Whisstocks of Woodbridge up in Suffolk, in 1939.'

'Bit of an antique, then?'

'I'd say vintage rather than antique, but she wears her age well. Francis looked after her, made sure she was always seaworthy, even if sometimes he wasn't.'

'Francis?'

'Francis Jarrold, the skipper.' Trybull bit his lip and kept his voice calm. 'That's why we're here, sir, isn't it? We know where the *Jocasta* is, it's her captain that's gone missing.'

'I knew your mother, you know,' said the voice with regal authority. 'Not well, I admit, but she came backstage once to congratulate me on my Ophelia. Of course, that was years ago.'

'At least fifty,' said Mr Campion softly.

'What was that?'

'Nothing, Dame Jocasta, just clearing my throat. Please tell me how you think I can help you.'

'Firstly, I must thank you for telephoning me. When I spoke to your . . . your . . . *man* . . . at your London flat – he was your London man, wasn't he?'

'He's been called worse, believe me.'

'What? Do speak up! You really should enunciate better; I had enough trouble following your man bumbling on about you being retired or similar. People like us don't retire, Rudolph, they carry us off stage in a box draped in black to the sound of a muffled drum.'

Mr Campion cleared his throat for real this time and spoke up. 'A suitably dramatic image, but my vicar-on-Earth, or at least in London, was perfectly correct in that I am enjoying a blissful retirement out in the country. Oh, and by the way, I have been known as Albert Campion for so long now, I've got rather fond of the name.'

'Stage names have never bothered me, they have their place in the scheme of things, but I have never felt the need to hide my identity. Early in my career a film studio offered me a contract if I changed my name because they thought picture-goers would not find an affinity with a leading lady called Jocasta. I refused, of course, and said that if my name was good enough to appear on a playbill next to an Olivier and a Gielgud, then it was good enough for the marquee of a tawdry Ritz or Essoldo.'

'I always fancied Rock Hunter as a name, but Albert Campion came along and we've been joined at the hip ever since. What can Albert do for you, from his peaceful rural nursing home?'

'Good God, you're not immobile, are you?' Dame Jocasta declaimed in a stentorian voice which would have stirred the attackers of Harfleur into action. 'You do sound a bit doolally, but I'm told that's part of your *shtick*, as the old Yiddisher comedians used to call it.'

'My dear lady, I can assure you I am sound of wind and clear of mind, but I repeat, I am retired and not in need of employment, which is what I understood you were offering.'

'Employment? Who said anything about employment? I was hoping you would be able to do me a small . . . service. In return for which, I might be able to return the favour.'

'This service has something to do with your yacht being wrecked on the Essex coast, I take it.'

'Abandoned, not wrecked,' said Dame Jocasta firmly, 'and I'm not expecting you to sail round and throw a line on it to claim the salvage, but you're not a nautical man, are you?'

'Not at all. My sea legs extend no further than the Queen's Room on the *QE2*.'

'Thought not. I would have heard if you were a cloth-cap admiral.'

'A *what?*'

'Going a bit deaf, are we? First sign of ageing. Cloth-cap admirals are what we call weekend sailors down at the yacht club. Well, to be honest, I suppose I'm one myself, though they don't dare say that to my face.'

'Then they are both wise and diplomatic,' conceded Mr Campion.

'Of course they are. I'm their honorary president and they like having a title on the club's headed notepaper. That's why they put up with Francis; that and the fact that he contributed to ninety per cent of the bar takings.'

'Francis? I'm afraid, Dame Jocasta, you are losing me. In nautical terms I have struck the iceberg and am slowly sinking beneath the waves. Please throw me a lifebelt.'

The sigh which came down the line would have plucked heart strings in the cheap seats at the Old Vic.

'My dear Albert, you have a reputation for being discreet,' said Dame Jocasta, and Campion could almost hear her eyelashes fluttering down the line, 'and you do live in East Anglia, do you not?'

'Well . . . yes.'

'Then you are perfectly placed to do me a small service. It is not something I wish to trouble the police with, and I would certainly not wish the press to get wind of it.'

'And it's to do with your beached yacht? It hasn't exactly been washed up on my doorstep, you know. East Anglia is a big place.'

'But I can't be seen there; the newspapers would have a field day!' The ingénue had been replaced by the noble tragedian. 'I need someone I can trust on the spot for me.'

'To do what? Deal with the press?'

'No, I'm sending my press agent to do that and to supervise the refloating of the *Jocasta*. All you would have to do is take care of my darling Robespierre.'

'That would be your dog?'

'I prefer "faithful companion". He is very dear to me and I'm terribly worried about him. I would simply die if anything has happened to him.'

Spectacularly, thought Campion, and with encores.

'I'm not sure what I could usefully do . . .'

'You could go to this place Wicken, wherever it is, and find out what has happened to *mon cher* Robespierre and telephone me as soon as you have news. You can reach me at home here in Chelsea or leave a message at the Old Vic where we are rehearsing something modern and quite ghastly. I will make it worth your while.'

'I have told you I am seeking neither reward nor, indeed, employment.'

'But your son, Rupert, is a resting actor I believe, and he may well value my . . . shall we say "matronage", if that's a word.'

'I'm not sure it is in the sense you mean, but I understand the offer behind it. I cannot speak for Rupert, but he has always expressed the ambition to pursue his career as a thespian under his own steam, without fear or favour from family or friends.'

There was a moment of silence on the line in which Mr Campion felt that he had successfully claimed the moral high ground. Then Dame Jocasta gathered her forces.

'You did say he wanted to be an *actor*, didn't you? Have I misunderstood? Is he training for the priesthood? Acting is a hard profession, Albert; it's not who you play on stage but who you know who stages the play. A word from me in the ears of certain producers could get your boy an audition or two, I will say no more than that.'

'And I will do no more than mention your kind offer to Rupert and let him decide. In the meantime, I will go and look for your hound, for the white knight in me cannot refuse a request from a dame in distress, which sounds rather like the title of one of those farces they did at the Aldwych, doesn't it?'

'I have no idea what you mean,' declaimed a grand dame far from distressed. 'I restrict myself to the legitimate theatre, but thank you for looking after Robespierre for me.'

'I haven't actually found him yet,' Campion pointed out, 'but I will drive down to Essex this afternoon and sniff around for you, which is what dogs do, I believe.'

'There's no need for crudity. Poor Robespierre has been either wandering those marshes all alone or, even worse, has been kidnapped by one of the locals.'

'Have you received a ransom demand?'

'No, I have not, but I would happily pay a reward for his safe return. T.T. has my authority to meet any reasonable demands.'

'Who is T.T.?'

'Timothy Timms, Timmy to his friends – no, clients, because he doesn't have any friends. He's a very famous press agent, handles a lot of theatricals. I sent him down there last night. He's staying in a bed-and-breakfast called The Oyster Shack in a place called Tillingham.'

'If he's there, why do you need me?'

'Timmy deals with the newspapers and sucks up to the theatre critics, he's absolutely useless at anything else. He doesn't know that Robespierre is missing, he's just looking after my interests vis-à-vis the *Jocasta*. Use him if you have to, but otherwise don't count on him for anything.'

'Let me get this straight, Dame Jocasta – your dog was on board your yacht?'

'Oh, yes, Robespierre loves to go sailing. And he was company for Francis and would stand guard whenever Francis put in for . . . supplies.'

'Francis is, I take it, your captain or yacht master or driver, or whatever you call him.'

'Yes, he is.'

'And he's missing too?'

'You'll find him in the nearest pub probably. Robespierre's the one who needs looking after.'

'But doesn't it concern you that this Francis has run your yacht aground on a mudflat and disappeared?'

'He's done crazier things in his time. His trouble is he's too fond of the rum ration. Follow the trail of empty bottles and you'll find him, but don't worry about Francis Jarrold. He'll turn up; he always does.'

Francis Jarrold did indeed turn up that very afternoon. He was found lying face down and bootless, firmly stuck in cold, thick, coastal mud, and quite dead.

A visiting birdwatcher had been attracted to the body by the frantic scrabbling and occasional howling of the large and very muddy dog pawing at it.

FOUR
Peninsula

Detective Inspector Hankin had equipped himself not only with the latest *AA Book of the Road*, but also a 1930s' Ordnance Survey road map of the area, it being the most up-to-date detailed map in police headquarters. He did, however, suspect that it was a reprint of an earlier, nineteenth-century edition, as Bradwell was proudly designated Bradwell-juxta-Mare, but at least the older map showed, as a tiny black dot, the location of Wicken-juxta-Mare, a place in danger of slipping off the map both physically and metaphorically.

The narrow B-roads running along the lines of drainage-dyke banks were straight enough to falsely suggest a Roman heritage, something which surprised him, as did the hills outside Latchingdon. He had assumed a vista that would be as flat as a plate, offering wide spaces of sky coming down to merge with the reclaimed land, divided by the hedgerows which had the only trees visible running their length, almost as if they had been regimentally planted as telegraph poles. As the police car topped the hills he was given a brief sighting of the borders of the peninsula, or at least two sides of it, the River Blackwater to his left and, further away to his right, a glimpse of the River Crouch. As the car descended the hill, he lost sight of both rivers and now the land was flat; an expanse of fields and hedges stretching out to a horizon of marshes, mudflats and sea which would complete his watery entrapment.

In the next village, Hankin registered a more familiar sight, a white weatherboard pub belonging to Gray & Son, the Chelmsford brewery. As if by telepathy, Sergeant Trybull sensed his thoughts.

'Take a good look, sir, and remember where it is, 'cos there ain't any decent hostelries out where we're going.'

Hankin forced a laugh. 'No pubs at the seaside? You're having me on; be telling me there's no donkey rides on the beach either.'

'There ain't no beach, sir, not much of anything really, just mud and salt marsh. The only thing the peninsula is famous for is salt.'

'One of the county's most famous exports, Maldon sea salt. You should be proud, being a Maldon man.'

'Goes back a lot longer than the industry in Maldon,' said Trybull, trying not to lecture his superior officer. 'They say they were drying salt round here in Roman times, if not before. They used to make red clay bricks, more like baking trays to trap seawater, and then the sun would evaporate the liquid and leave the salt. They were called *briquetages*, I think, and where they were made or smashed to get at the salt, the debris formed mounds of rubble which were called "red hills". For years people thought they were natural freaks of geology until the archaeologists found they were really rubbish dumps.' He risked a quick glance at his passenger before adding, 'Sir.'

'Very interesting, Tom. I'm glad I've got you as a tour guide,' said Hankin without sarcasm. 'Now tell me what I can expect in Wicken.'

'Nothing much, sir. It barely clings to the map by its fingertips . . .'

The police radio crackled with their call sign to interrupt the sergeant and to inform them exactly what they were to expect.

Hankin no longer consulted the maps open on his lap as Trybull appeared to have no need of navigational aids, which was just as well, as – to all intents and purposes – they were about to drop off the edge of the civilized world.

The village of Dengie, from which, Hankin presumed, the peninsula took its name, was not much of a village, and did not even feel the need to add its name to a fingerpost which pointed them simply to 'St James's Church'. The small church, when they found it around a bend at the end of a narrow ribbon of road sparsely dotted with small weatherboard houses, clearly had some age. Having had considerable experience of dealing with church break-ins and their roofs being stripped of lead, the young inspector had become a reluctant expert; he recognized Roman brick and tile, flint nodules and fourteenth-century yellow bricks in its fabric. St James's also occupied a position of some height in the landscape, not that that was saying much in terms of feet above sea level, but it claimed enough high ground to offer a panorama over the lower grey-green flatlands eastwards to where – somewhere – the sea came up to the sky, and to the south where the River Crouch twinkled in the distance.

Trybull had turned off the metalled road and on to what was little more than a farm track, and completely unsuitable for overtaking, which as far as Hankin could determine put them on a direct line to the sea. Now he did consult his older map and tried to locate which track, or it might have indicated the line of a dyke, they were on. No indicator of habitation past or present was marked, but in minute type, surrounded by the symbol for marsh, reeds or saltings, was the word 'Wicken'. And beyond that the land gave way to the grey shaded bulge of sand or mudbanks marked as 'Dengie Flat' to the north and 'Ray Sand' to the south of a thin serpent of a meandering inlet or channel which struggled, but failed, to connect with the land.

'Welcome to Wicken,' said Trybull suddenly, and Hankin did a double take before he realized that the black building which had just flashed by the car window must have been a house and not the barn or cowshed he had first assumed. And then there were two more houses of brick and white weatherboarding and then three small thatched cottages in a row, and that seemed to be that. There was no post office or any other retail establishment, no telephone box, no street lights, no pub, a stone building which might be a chapel of sorts, and certainly no sign welcoming visitors to Wicken and asking them to drive carefully.

The single track continued into the unknown, beyond these paltry offerings in the name of civilization, and Hankin gave mental thanks that the police car had not met any vehicles coming the other way. Come to think of it, he had seen few vehicles of any description since Tillingham, and in Wicken itself perhaps only one car, an ancient Austin parked in the small front garden of one of the houses he had first thought was an agricultural shack, and a tractor parked off the track in a gap in the hedgerow.

As if to refute Hankin's musings about the dearth of modern transport, a white estate car materialized a hundred yards in front of them, stationary at an angle across the track.

'Roadblock,' said Trybull, decelerating and parking a few feet from the offending vehicle, which he identified as a Volvo 120, a car known as a 'Sturdy Swede', which would have undoubtedly come off best in any collision at speed with his Morris Minor police car.

'I put a couple of pairs of Wellingtons in the boot,' said Trybull as the two policemen climbed out of the car, automatically buttoning their overcoats against the sharp tang of the salty breeze which greeted them. 'We'll need them if we're going down there to join the festivities.'

Beyond the Volvo the track ended, and the land, if it was land, dropped away sharply, as if sliced by a giant cake knife, by some five or six feet. From there it stretched out flat and wide, a static sea of brown mud pockmarked by clumps of wiry stalks and grass. There was no sight or sound of animal life, but some fifty yards out on to the mud plain stood a copse of human figures, gathered in a rough circle. Beyond them, Hankin could glimpse water in the weak sunlight, but how far away the ocean was – if it was ocean – he found impossible to estimate.

'Quite a crowd down there,' said Hankin, stamping his feet into the boots he had exchanged for his brown suede shoes, silently giving thanks for Trybull's foresight.

'Looks like the locals have turned out to help the doc.' Trybull patted the roof of the white Volvo. 'This is Dr Harry's car.'

As Hankin walked around the car he noticed a rectangle of printed card bearing the words 'Doctor on Call' on the dashboard.

'Dr Harry?'

'Harold Fathoms, the local GP with a surgery in Southminster. He's done police work for us before now and, if he's here, you can guess what they're all gawking at.'

'Who are the rest? First-aiders from Wicken?'

'Looks like the entire population of Wicken, if you ask me,' grunted Trybull, 'turned out for a bit of entertainment. There's not much to do in Wicken.'

They stepped down from the track and strode out on to the mud, automatically following the crowded footprints of the half-dozen figures ahead of them. As they approached, the circle of figures, all clearly male, began to widen, and the policemen could see the object of their attention, a humped shape lying on the mud covered, incongruously, by a tartan picnic rug, as if anyone would choose this spongey, stagnant desolation as a suitable site for a picnic.

One of the circle began to march with some purpose towards the two policemen, clearly wanting to communicate something away from the madding crowd and, once in hand-shaking distance, the stocky white-haired figure introduced himself.

'Good to see you, Tom. It was getting a bit lonely out here.'

'Thanks for holding the fort. Dr Fathoms, this is Inspector Hankin from Chelmsford.'

'Good to meet you, Inspector. I was told you were on your way anyway.'

'We were coming about the boat,' said Hankin, 'and got the call about the body over the radio as we were en route. Did you find it?'

'Not me personally,' Dr Fathoms pointed out, 'but it was me who telephoned county headquarters.'

'So who called you?'

'A sweet young fellow called Graham Roberts who was on a birdwatching safari around the marshes. He spotted a dog howling over something out here on the mud and thought it was in distress. When he found what the dog had found, *he* was the one in distress, but he showed great presence of mind and used his belt as a lead, tied it to his bicycle and pedalled like fury until he found a telephone.'

'That couldn't have been easy around here,' said Hankin.

'The lad showed great initiative and fortunately he's one of my patients. He followed the telephone wires to Middlewick Farm, which is just before Dengie, and rang me. Graham and the dog are both there being looked after by the farmer's wife.'

'We'll have to have a word with him,' said Trybull.

'Naturally,' agreed the doctor. 'He won't run away, but I doubt he'll be of much help. It all seems clear enough what happened.'

Sergeant Trybull nodded wisely but Hankin was not deterred. 'It does?'

'Yacht runs aground in the night, stuck tight in the mud. The skipper, instead of waiting for the morning tide, jumps overboard and tries to walk ashore.'

'Dangerous in the dark,' said Trybull, lifting one Wellington boot so that it made a squelching sound, 'in this stuff.'

'Bloody madness, in my opinion, but maybe it seemed like a good idea at the time if you were as drunk as the late skipper, which I think we'll find he was when we do the autopsy. He was, as they say, fond of the bottle.'

'You know him, doctor?'

'Not personally, Inspector, but they do.' Dr Fathoms jerked a thumb over his shoulder, indicating the group of men still surrounding the body. 'They're from Wicken and say his name is Jarrold and he's from there originally but now lives up in Brightlingsea and ferries a yacht around for some rich film star. Or did.'

'Any idea how long he's been dead?'

'Hard to tell out here in these conditions, but at least twenty-four hours, probably more.'

'And cause of death?'

'Without having him on the slab, which I'm happy to say will be someone else's job, I would guess that the amount of mud and seawater he inhaled probably restricted his breathing to a largely fatal degree.'

Hankin ignored the jaundiced sarcasm which medical men always took with the police when they were asked for specifics before an autopsy, and knew it was useless to press the point.

'So where's the yacht, then?' he asked, scanning the empty terrain which he could only think of as a 'mudscape'.

The doctor raised his right arm and pointed in a vaguely northeasterly direction.

'It's about a quarter of a mile over there in a little inlet the locals call Worm Creek, though it's technically a channel through the mud, not a creek.'

'I can't see anything.'

'Well you can't from here, because it's lower and the yacht has tipped over on to one side so the mast isn't visible. You can see it quite plainly from the sea, I'm told. In fact the coastguard had already spotted it and there was something in the paper this morning about it.'

'How do we get to it?'

'Unless you know a secure path across the mudbanks, I wouldn't risk it. Your best bet would be to approach from the sea. You did bring a boat with you, didn't you, or perhaps a helicopter?'

Andy Hankin's stomach experienced a sudden chill at the thought of being either on the water in a small boat or hovering at some distance above it.

'You want to move the body?' he asked Dr Fathoms, being far more comfortable talking about corpses on less-than-solid land than anything to do with water.

'I was thinking of the yacht that poor man came from and presuming you would want to go aboard. There's an ambulance on the way to pick up the body, but it'll take them ages to find the place. Once you've had a look and are happy with things, these chaps will help me get the body up here on to the hard.'

'So you do intend moving the body.'

'We could leave him where he is until the tide comes in again and takes him out of sight and out of mind, or leave him overnight and hope the local wildlife don't get too peckish.' The doctor gave the policeman his best don't-tell-me-my-job-and-I won't-tell-you-yours look. 'In other words, yes, I do intend moving the body as I do not regard this as a crime scene. I will leave it to you to discover whether the yacht is one.'

Hankin's inners squirmed again. It was as if this country doctor could sense his phobia about all thinks nautical and watery.

'Getting a forensics team out here would be difficult,' said Hankin, establishing his authority, 'and a waste of resources if you are sure this was an accidental death, doctor.'

'A coroner might plump for suicide,' said Fathoms with a non-committal shrug of his shoulders, 'but in my opinion there was no sign of human intervention in this death.'

'There's still the question of formal identification, sir,' said Trybull, clearing his throat.

'No problem there, Tom,' said the doctor. 'I've got four volunteers down there on the mud willing to identify the deceased, and you probably know him yourself, being as how all you messing-around-in-boats chaps stick together.'

'So it is Francis Jarrold from the *Jocasta*?'

'You've got your sea boots on so you'd better come and make sure, Tom. Would that be good enough for you, Inspector?'

Hankin and Trybull followed Dr Fathoms as he picked his way off the track and down on to the damp mud plain. As they trudged towards where a dead body ironically signified the only evidence of life apart from a plaintive gull somewhere above them, the four pallbearers, as Hankin was beginning to think of them, turned their attention from the picnic rug shroud to the new arrivals.

Dr Fathoms performed the introductions, though three of the four men standing vigil above the corpse appeared completely uninterested in the new arrivals. The fourth seemed to welcome an increased audience.

Joshua Jarmin, George Bugg and Robert Barly were, according to Dr Fathoms, all residents of Wicken who had turned out to offer assistance when the body had been found by the birdwatcher. They had been alerted by his screams and cries for help as he had pedalled his bicycle furiously, with a large brown dog in tow, through the village in search of a telephone.

The fourth guard of honour was distinguished from the others not only by his dress – a large-check three-piece suit, pink shirt and green-spotted cravat protected by a flapping plastic raincoat and Wellington boots – but also his distinctly urban accent and the fact that he was not afraid to use it. He was also determined to stand out in his choice of headwear: a brown houndstooth deerstalker with the earflaps down and tied under a quivering chin.

'And I am Timothy Timms,' he said, and then paused as if waiting for the policemen to write it down. 'I am here acting for Dame Jocasta Upcott, the owner of the yacht which washed up here the night before last.'

'Are you from her insurance company?' asked Trybull.

Mr Timms recoiled in horror. 'I am Dame Jocasta's *theatrical agent*,' he said, brooking no argument.

'Then I fail to see why you need to be present here,' Hankin said sternly.

'Mr Timms has been most useful,' Dr Fathoms intervened. 'He was the first to positively identify the deceased.'

'You knew him?' Hankin had no qualms about using the past tense.

'I did indeed. He's Francis Jarrold, who was employed by Dame Jocasta to look after her yacht and to sail it to wherever the whim took her. I can't understand how the accident happened. Francis was an Essex man and an experienced sailor.'

'Which accident are you referring to, sir?'

'Him running the *Jocasta* aground, of course. I came down here to demand to know what he was playing at, but there was no sign of him until today.'

'Are you staying in Wicken, Mr Timms?' asked Sergeant Trybull, not taking his eyes off the three local characters, who had quietly edged away around the body, distancing themselves from the incomer with the London accent.

'In Tillingham actually,' said Timms, 'at a quite primitive bed-and-breakfast place, but I drove down to Wicken today to see if anyone could help me get to the *Jocasta*. I was trying to persuade these gentlemen here when the hue and cry was raised by that birdwatcher chappie and so we all waddled down here to play at mudlarks, and to see if we could help, of course.'

'And you are sure this is the body of Francis Jarrold?' Hankin reasserted command.

'Absolutely. He's worked for Dame Jocasta for nearly ten years. He lived in Brightlingsea up the coast.'

'Family?'

'None. He had a wife but she divorced him years ago, citing Johnnie Walker whisky and Lamb's Navy Rum as co-respondents.'

'Bit of a toper, was he?' said Trybull.

Timms snorted a laugh. '*There's* a word I never expected to hear out here in the boondocks, but yes, Jarrold was a drinker, a boozer, a bit of a soak. Never let it interfere with his job though, until now. Usually reliable when out on the water, bit of a loose cannon when he put into a port.'

'Knew him well, did you, sir?'

'My office paid his wages on behalf of Dame Jocasta. It's one of the services we provide to our favoured clients.'

'Well, if we're sure we know who he is,' said Hankin, pushing his hands deep into his overcoat pockets and pulling out a pair of thin leather gloves, 'and you, Dr Fathoms, are sure he's dead, then I think we can say the scene is secure for the moment. Can we turn the body over so I can go through his pockets? Gentlemen, if you wouldn't mind helping?'

The three Wicken residents exchanged glances before moving uneasily towards the body, one of them bending over to pull the picnic rug away and then the doctor helping to turn the corpse, which came free from the mud with a disturbing cross between a squelch and a slurp.

'While I'm doing this, Tom, would you mind taking the names and addresses of all here?'

Before Trybull could flip his notebook and lick his pencil, Mr Timms was reaching for his wallet. 'Let me give you a card, sergeant.'

'That won't be necessary, sir. Even out here in the boondocks, we can write.'

Timms's mouth pouted into a lower-case 'o' but whether it was in response to Trybull's gentle sarcasm or the sight of the body revealed face-up, was unclear.

Hankin sank on to his haunches and held his breath as he leaned over the mud-encrusted remains of Francis Jarrold. It was impossible to discern any distinguishing features apart from the fact that the face had a beard due to the thick layer of brown sludge adhering to it and, thankfully, the eyes were glued shut by the slime. The jacket he was wearing, a lightweight denim affair, had two breast pockets which contained nothing solid Hankin could discern and neither did his trouser pockets, though all his clothing was filthy, soaked and clamped to the contours of the body. Only when the body was stripped and hosed down might anything be revealed, but Hankin doubted much would be found. Far more revealing, perhaps, was what was obviously not present on his stockinged feet.

'He has no boots on. Where are his boots?'

'Near his boat, according to the newspapers,' said the doctor. 'Sticking up in the mud where he left them.'

'How did the newspapers find that out?'

'A Coastguard boat spotted the yacht yesterday and, though they couldn't get to it, they tried to hail it, and then got close enough to see a pair of empty sea boots. There was no sign of

Jarrold, but the empty boots added to the mystery and somebody just couldn't resist telling the press.'

'That's the sort of thing I have to deal with all the time,' said Mr Timms, keeping his eyes averted from the mud figure that had been Francis Jarrold, sure that he could see small things *moving* across it.

'For the moment, Mr Timms, there will be no communication with the press without clearance from me,' said Hankin, standing and stretching his spine. 'Is that understood?'

'Whatever you say, Inspector, but Dame Jocasta is a very newsworthy person. This is bound to bring the reptiles of Fleet Street sniffing around.'

'They may be already here,' said Trybull, standing tall and looking back to the raised track and beyond the police car and the doctor's Volvo as the sound of motor engines approached.

'It's the ambulance,' said Dr Fathoms, 'they've found us at last.'

'There's a car right behind it, following it,' said Trybull, 'but I don't think the reptiles of the press drive Jaguars, do they?'

'I'm terribly sorry,' shouted the tall, thin, white-haired figure emerging from the driver's seat of the Jaguar like a slowly opening penknife, 'I didn't realize we were about to run out of road. Let me get out of the way if I can do a three-point turn, though it might end up as a thirteen-point turn. Promise you won't laugh at my reversing skills.'

'Get rid of him, Tom,' Hankin hissed at his sergeant. 'We don't need any more rubber-neckers here while we're lifting the body. See him off the premises.'

'Tread softly, Inspector,' said Dr Fathoms. 'That's Albert Campion.'

'Who the hell is Albert Campion?'

That was the trouble with police work, thought Trybull as he picked his way through the mud to the slope leading up to the track, the inspectors were getting younger every day.

At the ambulance he spoke to the driver and told him to wait for instructions, then moved on to the Jaguar where the new arrival was standing on tiptoe, peering through large round spectacles at the figures below out on the mud.

'I do apologize if I am intruding, and I do not normally chase ambulances, unlike the denizens of Fleet Street, but as we were both heading in the same direction I thought it only civil to let it go first as there might have been an accident.' He turned towards Trybull his face expressionless but unthreatening. 'I came looking for a yacht, but you appear to have found a body.'

'Yes, we have, Mr Campion.'

'Once again, I have to say I am sorry, but have we met?'

'Not officially, sir. I'm Sergeant Trybull, Essex Police based at Maldon, and I'm well aware of your reputation.'

'That does sound ominous, Sergeant, and I promise you I will get out of your hair, but may I ask if that poor unfortunate down there in the mud is Francis Jarrold?'

Trybull flexed his shoulders and rocked back on his heels slightly, a move he knew was more impressive when in full uniform.

'You'd need to talk to my inspector about that, sir.'

'Quite correct, Detective Sergeant,' said Mr Campion, noticing the mixture of surprise and pride on Trybull's face at the addition of 'detective'. 'I take it he's one of those gentlemen down there. I had better go and introduce myself.'

'You'd need boots to get over there,' said Trybull, thinking practically rather than politically. 'The mud will suck those nice shiny brogues right off you before you've gone two yards.'

The elderly man smiled and looked down at his feet then stepped to the rear of the Jaguar and patted the lid of the boot.

'I'm a retired countryman, Sergeant, and never travel anywhere without a pair of Wellingtons.'

'You won't need them today, Mr Campion,' said the sergeant, remembering his inspector's instructions. 'Mr Hankin down there don't want any more spectators. We have to move the body and talk to the witnesses, so he hasn't time for . . . for . . . civilians, as you might say, beggin' your pardon.'

'No apology necessary, Sergeant, for I am indeed a fully paid-up, retired civilian and really quite proud of the title, for I have no official duties, few responsibilities and the freedom to fritter away my time as I please – subject, of course, to the draconian conditions laid down by my wife.'

Tom Trybull used all his police training to prevent a smile. He knew of Campion's reputation – had even read an article by him in the *Police Gazette* – and was delighted to find that here was a toff you could do business with.

'I have to ask you to move your car, sir, so the ambulance can get back to the road.'

'Of course, of course, but no sniggering at my manoeuvring. I will get out of your way, though I did rather want to see the *Jocasta*.'

'You'll need a boat to do that. She's down in a channel that cuts through the mud, and leaning over according to the coast-guards who spotted her yesterday morning. The locals call it Worm Creek, or just The Worm, and it cuts down deep enough that you couldn't see anything but her mast even at a full tide. You can't see her at all from down on the mud, but from up here you can just about make out the top of her mast, over there, due east, about a quarter of a mile.'

'I am impressed with your eyesight,' said Campion, screwing up his eyes behind his spectacles, 'and I will happily take your word for it. A pity, I did want to see her.'

'Why, sir?'

'Not out of idle curiosity, I assure you, but the owner asked me to check up on it and I've driven down specially.'

'You know Jocasta Upcott?'

'Doesn't everybody? Unfortunately, she claims to know me, or at least she once met my mother, and I was the nearest person she could think of to send here to get the lie of the land, or should that be mud?'

'Her agent, a Mr Timms, is already here,' said Trybull, 'down there with the doctor and my inspector. He's the portly gent with the Sherlock Holmes hat.'

'Oh good, he made it already, that was quick,' said Campion, keeping a neutral expression. 'And the other gentlemen . . .?'

'Local men from Wicken.'

'And they found the body?'

'No, they just turned out to help Doc Fathoms.'

'Harry Fathoms? I think I've had dealings with him, profes-sional rather than personal medical ones that is. Was he first on the scene?'

'He was called in as soon as the body was spotted.'

'Dare I ask by whom?'

'I'm not sure I should say, sir. We haven't taken a statement from him yet.'

'Taking statements would imply a crime had been committed here rather than a tragic accident.' Campion paused, taking no pleasure in Trybull's sudden discomfort. 'But I have no wish to put you on the spot, Sergeant. The truth of the matter is that I simply wanted to know if anyone had seen a lost dog around here.'

'A dog?'

'Dame Jocasta's pet dog. Apparently it enjoyed sailing and travelled regularly on her yacht. The great lady is terribly worried about her darling hound and she can be awfully *dramatic* when she's worried, if you know what I mean.'

'I think I understand, sir. The wife was once very attached to a Yorkshire Terrier. Nasty, snappy little thing it was, couldn't stand it myself, but she let it rule the roost.'

Campion nodded sagely, as if the two men were agreeing that wives were, and always would be, an unfathomable mystery.

'You'll be wanting to use a telephone, I expect.'

'Of course,' said Campion, catching on. 'Must report progress and all that.'

'The nearest one, I'm told, is at Middlewick Farm, just through Wicken and before you get to Dengie. You'll find a chap there who might be able to help. He's a birdwatcher called Roberts, I believe.'

'And he found the body?'

'As I understand it, he found the dog that found the body.'

FIVE

Give a Dog a Bone

A lone telephone pole bearing a single sagging wire indicated that Middlewick Farm was connected to the outside world, or at least a telephone exchange, and Mr Campion, having parked the Jaguar in the farmyard, strode up to the front door and knocked, prepared to demand the divine right of all lost travellers: the free public use of their valuable private instrument.

The door was answered by a short, middle-aged woman wearing a long flowery apron over a green shirt and brown corduroy trousers. The apron displayed two very large and conspicuous damp patches and there appeared to be soap bubbles in the woman's hair which drooped damply over her eyes. She pushed back her fringe with fingers encased in bright yellow rubber gloves.

'What is it now?'

'Good afternoon, my name is Campion. The police told me this house had a telephone. I wonder if I may use it? I am more than happy to pay for the call.'

The woman, whom Campion assumed to be the farmer's wife, stood back and pulled the door open wider, revealing a hallway which resembled a cross between a disorganized antique shop and a tack room. It was lined with boots with varying amounts of mud and other matter attached to them, an incredibly ugly elephant's foot umbrella stand holding a display of walking sticks and riding crops, a line of pegs from which hung various bits of animal-related leads and bridles, and a selection of outdoor clothing which would have graced the shop window of an Army and Navy store. At the end of the hall, Campion spotted a small octagonal table on which rested a grey-green telephone, an object which seemed strangely modern in such a location.

'Help yourself,' said the woman. 'You can leave the money

on the table when you're done. Gawd knows, it's open house here today.'

Campion bowed politely as he crossed the threshold. 'Yes, I heard you had an unexpected houseguest. Chap called Roberts, I believe.'

'Nice lad,' said the farmer's wife, bustling down the hall ahead of him. 'Come in the kitchen and have a word if you like; he's having a bath.'

Thankfully sparing Mr Campion's blushes, Graham Roberts was not having a bath but he was involved in a clearly titanic struggle performing ablutions on a large brown poodle in a tin bath laid on a rubber mat in front of the kitchen Aga. Shirtsleeves rolled up to the elbow, red in the face and sweating profusely, the young man was giving his all to the task, but from the state of his clothes, the kitchen floor and the enamel front of the Aga, the dog was either enjoying himself too much, or had put up a fight. It barked and shook itself free of a gallon of soapy water as Campion entered. Graham Roberts tightened his grip on the poodle's leather collar and accepted this most recent shower with good grace.

'Oh, please keep still, doggie, this is for your own good.'

Young Mr Roberts – Campion put his age at no more than twenty-one – was clearly losing the battle of wills with the dog, though he did seem to be winning the war against the outer coat of dried mud which caked the dog's fur, so much so that it was clear that the dog was a white, not brown, poodle and a large one at that.

'My, you are a dirty dog, aren't you?' said Mr Campion, and then beamed a smile at the young man kneeling by the tin bath. 'I meant Robespierre, of course, not you.'

Graham Roberts scooped water with cupped hands over the dog's ears, which had pricked at the mention of his name, just as a long pink tongue lolled out and tasted soap bubbles.

'Do you know this hound?'

'I know his name, though we have not been formally introduced, have we, Robespierre? My name is Campion, by the way.'

Campion held out a hand, palm down, and the poodle stretched his neck in order to lick it.

'Good boy, Robespierre. Now, sit!'

The dog did as ordered, planting his rear end with a splash into the murky water, then put his head on one side to observe the new arrival with quizzical but intelligent eyes.

'Don't get too close,' said the farmer's wife, arriving with a saucepan of clean water for Robespierre's final rinse, 'you'll ruin that nice suit.'

'He's calmed down now you're here,' said the bath attendant. 'I'm Graham Roberts. I found this poor chap out on the mudflats in rather distressing circumstances. He was caked in mud, as you can see. We've changed the water twice already.'

'You were out birdwatching, I understand.'

'I usually am on my days off, but today's experience has rather soured me.'

'When you found . . .'

'I didn't find anything; he did. Robespierre, did you say?'

The dog turned his head in response.

'That appears to be his name.'

'Wasn't Robespierre something to do with the French Revolution?'

'Yes, he was, but before you say it, it was Marat who was assassinated while in his bath, and we shouldn't really talk about that in the dog's presence, unless of course the lady of the house happens to be called Charlotte or Corday.'

'My name's Laverick, Mrs Laverick,' said the lady of the house, 'and if you know whose dog this is, you're welcome to him, and best you take him out of here before my husband gets back with our two lurchers. They'd have this scrawny animal for breakfast. Didn't know there was any dogs in Wicken, though.'

'Robespierre's owner doesn't live in Wicken,' said Campion, deliberately not offering a name, 'which is why I'm here, to claim him.'

'So what was he doin' on the flats? Not natural for dogs.'

'Actually, I think the Germans bred them as gun dogs for duck hunting, so Robespierre should be no stranger to splashing around in muddy water, as we can see from the state of your floor; but he came off a yacht, the one that ran aground the day before yesterday.' Campion glanced towards Graham Roberts, who was gently combing Robespierre's coat with a scrubbing brush. 'The man you found – he found – was the skipper, but Robespierre belongs to the dog's owner, who lives in London.'

'Lunnon?' said Mrs Laverick, as if she had received an electric shock. 'You're willing to take the dog to Lunnon?'

Campion wondered if her reaction would have been any less if he had said New York, or even Saturn instead of London. 'Once he's dried off a bit.'

The poodle snapped at a soap bubble which had floated into range. Campion took it as a sign that the dog approved of the idea.

'Right then, get him out the back door before he shakes hisself all over my kitchen,' ordered Mrs Laverick, opening a cupboard under the sink. 'I've got some old towels we can use and there's a horse blanket in the barn you can line your nice car with.'

'You are too kind,' said Campion. 'Robespierre and I are most grateful.'

'You'll need to put him on a lead as well,' the woman added. 'There are some hanging in the hall. My husband don't believe in throwing anything away, so take your pick.'

With Graham Roberts pulling at his collar, Robespierre jumped gracefully out of the tin bath and, before the young man could step back, slapped his wet flanks against his trouser legs. Even as he began to complain, Mrs Laverick had the back door open and was shepherding man and beast outside, where the dog braced his legs and shook himself violently, spattering the few remaining dry patches of the young man's clothing.

Towels were thrown over the dog and roughly applied, the dog's lolling tongue showing he was enjoying the massage and the attention. At least, thought Campion, the poodle had not been clipped like effeminate topiary, and with the mud sluiced from him was a sturdy and really quite handsome example of the breed. He seemed perfectly relaxed when Campion clipped a thick leather lead to the metal loop on his collar and reassured to hear that he was, indeed, a good boy.

'Are you sure the police won't mind you taking him?' asked Graham Roberts, dabbing more in hope than expectation at his shirt front with one of Mrs Laverick's towels. 'Dr Fathoms told me to stay here until they came and took a statement.'

'I think they will be along soon to do just that, but I doubt they will want to question Robespierre here. Unless you think he might add something useful to your account of things.'

Young Mr Roberts grinned sheepishly. 'I was out on the mudflats when I heard barking, and that frightens off the birds, so I looked for the dog. He was standing over the body and howling and I went over to chase him off as much as anything, but he didn't shift and let me get close enough to grab his collar. He was filthy with stinking mud and must have been rolling in it. I took my belt off and looped it through his collar and dragged him away. I saw there was nothing I could do for the poor man face down in the muck, so I got on my bike and set off to find a telephone. I spotted Mrs Laverick in the front garden and she kindly invited me – us – in.'

'That sounds like a perfect statement, just the sort the police love. Tell them all that and, if they ask about Robespierre here, say he is in my care until I can return him to his owner.'

Campion took out his wallet and selected a business card which bore his name and the Bottle Street flat address, handing it to Graham Roberts.

'That's me and that's where Robespierre will be tonight should anyone official want to speak to him, and if necessary I will ensure he has a solicitor to represent him. But first, I must take up Mrs Laverick's kind offer and use her telephone.'

Campion, with Robespierre walking neatly to heel on the lead, returned to the hallway and dialled Rupert's London number. Delighted, for once, that Rupert was 'resting' and therefore at home sitting by the telephone waiting for 'the call', Campion gave his son instructions which, he added mysteriously, might well result in something to his advantage.

In the kitchen Mrs Laverick offered him a grey horse blanket, folded as if it had been used as a cushion, explaining that her husband had used it on the metal seat of an old tractor he no longer drove and, though it smelled a bit, the dog wouldn't mind, and it offered a bit of protection for the car's upholstery.

'You have been exceptionally kind to put up with all this, Mrs Laverick,' said Campion, tugging out his wallet again. 'You must let me give you something for your trouble.'

'Not necessary,' said the woman. 'Can't bear to see an animal in distress. Mind you, he's bound to be hungry,' she added with a twinkle in her eye.

'You wouldn't have any dog food to spare which you could sell me?'

'Not as such,' said Mrs Laverick, bending over the Aga and opening one of the ovens from which she removed a large baking tin. 'But there's the remains of a roast leg of mutton we had the other day. Not much meat left on it, but he might appreciate the bone. I'll wrap it in newspaper for you.'

Robespierre had suddenly lost all interest in his damp pelt, his new master, or the prospect of a car ride, and was now concentrating intently on the meaty joint on offer.

'Please don't bother to wrap it, we'll take it as it is, and I hope this will provide a replacement.'

Mr Campion handed over a five-pound note which disappeared into Mrs Laverick's yellow-gloved hand, and in the same movement in the opposite direction, the leg bone found its way into Robespierre's jaw. A frantic wagging of the tail suggested he thought it a fair trade.

'You'd better take his toy as well,' said Graham Roberts, picking something off the floor by the tin bath.

'His what?'

'He had a toy he was playing with by the . . . the body. It was like a dog with a ball, wanting someone to throw it for him. Except it wasn't a ball, it was a child's doll. He wouldn't leave it and he only let go of it when we put him in the bath. It's still pretty filthy and chewed up, but it might keep him quiet.'

'He seems happy enough with his bone,' said Campion, 'but I'd better take it along. Perhaps he can't get to sleep without his comforter. I have an old acquaintance who feels much the same way about six pints of light ale.'

'Frankly, Mr Baskerville, I expected something larger.'

'Ha-ha, very funny. Actually, that was quite good for you, Lugg.' Campion closed the door behind him and released the dog from its lead. 'Go on boy, sic him, go sink your fangs into that more than ample flesh.'

A resolute Lugg stood his ground and held out a fist at dog muzzle height. It was a fist which had come that close to a human nose on more than one occasion, but had never before, by a human, been licked so lovingly.

'Who's a good boy then? Had your dinner? Feeling peckish?'

'He's enjoyed a substantial mutton bone on the way here,' said Mr Campion, shedding his hat and coat.

'I was talking to you,' said Lugg with a malicious grin.

'I take it Rupert has been in touch?'

'Yus 'e 'as, an' he'll be calling round shortly. I did the shopping and got a nice piece of braising steak for your supper if yer hungry.'

'That sounds fine, I could certainly eat.'

'I was talking to the dog.'

'All right, that's enough of the comic cuts. I could murder a drink, but you've probably got a bowl of water waiting on the kitchen floor.'

Lugg massaged the dog's ears and the poodle was wise enough not to resist. 'Matter of fact, I have, along with a selection of the finest tinned dog food and biscuits 'Arrods could deliver at short notice. Will our guest be staying long?'

'I'm hoping that Rupert will get him home either tonight or first thing in the morning. I don't think it would be fair on our American guest to find a four-legged roommate. His name's Robespierre, by the way.'

'Sounds French, not a Yank name at all.'

'Really, Lugg, what's got into you? Rupert said he saw you near The Palladium the other night. You weren't auditioning, were you? Has Mr Tarbuck gone for good? I would think carefully about treading the boards, old fruit, I'm not sure the boards could take your weight.'

Lugg cupped the dog's muzzle in his right hand and Robespierre's pink tongue flicked in and out in rapid, lizard-like movements, clearly savouring the experience.

'What a nasty, rude man, eh, boy? I'll bet he doesn't talk to you like that, does he? You know who your friends are, don't you, Robespierre?'

'Cut the act and wash the Bovril off your fingers – I know that trick – before you pour me an indecently large whisky with a positively meagre amount of water. I'm assuming you'll join me, if you're not already ahead of me.'

'Well, I may have opened a bottle of claret at teatime, but only to cook the beef with. There's some that would be grateful for a hot meal at such short notice, not to mention havin' a dog to contend with and Rupert will need victualling, I'll bet. Not that I 'ad any plans of me own for this evening. Not that anybody cares or even asked if I 'ad.'

Mr Campion furrowed his brow, as if concentrating on the fat man's diatribe. 'That reminds me,' he said, 'I must ring my wife.'

Rupert arrived at Bottle Street as both his father and Robespierre were enjoying their dinner and Lugg was testing the claret to see if it had 'gorn off'. Being an unemployed actor, Rupert was, naturally, always grateful for a free meal, and for the fact that Lugg had counted on that when out shopping.

'How's Perdita?' Campion asked his son, mentally crossing his fingers that his daughter-in-law's acting career was progressing better than his son's, or at least just progressing.

'Bubbly,' said Rupert, 'as usual. She's auditioning for a season in Rep and has a call-back on a TV commercial; for a well-known brand of dog food, funnily enough.'

'We are still expecting you for the weekend, are we not?'

'Absolutely, but there may be a spanner in the works, a small spanner, but it has disrupted our plans slightly.'

'You have found employment?' Campion asked with a smile.

His son ignored the question. 'After we spoke this morning, before you decided to become Dogcatcher General, I thought I had better check on our American friend Mason Lowell, as he had been rather vague about exactly when he was coming over here. So I rang him.'

'You rang America?'

'I popped round our agent's and used his office phone while he was out,' Rupert admitted sheepishly.

Mr Campion, who had met, and liked, the couple's agent, Maxim Berlins, produced a broad grin of approval. 'I'd love to see Maxim's face when he gets his phone bill.'

'He'll never notice,' said Rupert not altogether convincingly, 'and he'll convince himself he was ringing someone important in Hollywood, but it was worth the risk. Mason Lowell is super keen to get started on his research. Super keen, his exact words.

And he's convinced that you will have a list of reasonably priced hotels waiting for him when he arrives . . . on Saturday!'

'Saturday?'

'Yes, it was a surprise, but it seems his travel agent found him a last-minute cancellation at a very good price and he couldn't resist. I'm meeting him at Heathrow about eleven o'clock in the morning. I haven't told Perdita yet . . .'

'Well, I suggest you do that immediately, if not sooner. Bring your surprise American here from the airport and let him get settled and over the shock of meeting Lugg, whom you had better bribe in advance. Then why don't you and Perdita bring him up to us for what's left of the weekend. We can have Sunday lunch together if nothing else, and your mother can make up a spare bed and you can all head back first thing Monday. How does that sound?'

'Perfectly wonderful as long as "Mom" can put up with a precocious Yank whose table manners may not be up to much.'

Mr Campion glanced towards the kitchen where Lugg was noisily clattering pots and pans in between making reassuring noises to Robespierre, who had finished his main course and was hoping for seconds or possibly dessert.

'Don't concern yourself there. Your mother likes Americans; she works with them all the time. As for table manners, I doubt there is anything left to shock her on that front apart from you calling her "Mom" when you ask her to pass the gravy.'

'Then it's a deal, but I suppose only if I do your dog-walking mission,' said Rupert.

'Not dog walking, Lugg's already volunteered to take Robespierre for a stroll around the park before bedtime. Your task will be dog *returning*.'

'Returning to whom?'

'His owner, and I think you'll like this: a great theatrical dame.'

'Wot? Like Widow Twankey?' Lugg interrupted loudly from the kitchen.

'It's not the pantomime season,' Campion shouted back, then winced in anticipation of the inevitable response.

'Oh, yes it is!' Lugg returned, cackling with laughter.

'I am referring, Rupert, to Dame Jocasta Upcott, whose telephone number and address I will supply. I suggest you let

Robespierre catch up on his beauty sleep here and take him to Chelsea in the morning.'

Father and son glanced in unison towards the small sofa which Robespierre had claimed and, having extended his body to fill the space, had drifted off to sleep.

'Dame Jock herself . . .' breathed Rupert in admiration. 'Really?'

'Really, and as I would not dare call her that, I suggest neither should you.'

'It's what the back row call her, the extras in the crowd scenes, the spear-carriers, the angry village mob. No matter what the director decides about blocking a play, to wander in front of Dame Jock is a hanging offence. But of course she's a legend, one of the greats of the West End. How did you end up with her dog?'

'Long story, and one which can wait until the weekend, indeed should wait until Sunday lunch with our American visitor, as it will amuse him.'

'It will?'

'I think so. He said in his letter that he was interested in a place called Wicken in Essex, and he's clearly a bright chap as he knew how to find it on a map and even sent co-ordinates. I didn't know the place existed, but it does, although there's not much of it, just a few cottages along a road which isn't a proper road but doesn't have to be as it doesn't go anywhere except into the sea.'

'So it's a fishing village?'

'Not remotely, and "village" would be a wild exaggeration. Wicken might have once been known as Wicken-juxta-Mare, but it's not very "juxta" nowadays. It seems stuck between salt marshes and mudbanks which stretch out to the horizon. All in all a pretty empty landscape. The RAF used the mudflats for bombing practice during the war, and earlier, I think I am correct in saying, it gave H.G. Wells a smidge of the inspiration he needed for his *War of the Worlds*. It certainly is other-worldly and would be just the place they would film *Dr Who* if they wanted to show a desolate planet.'

'Sounds a terrible place,' said Rupert.

Again, there was a forthright contribution from the kitchen.

'Lamb!' bellowed Lugg.

'Are you making a comment or writing a shopping list?'

'Salt-marsh lamb, grazing sheep on salt marshes gives a lovely flavour to the meat. The area's famed for it, along wiv Maldon sea salt, and then there's oysters just along the coast, all good eating.'

'And thus spake our very own Galloping Gourmet,' said Campion, 'so it must be true.'

'I always thought of him as a bargain-basement Fanny Craddock,' said Rupert quietly. 'But what was Dame Jocasta doing out at Wicken?'

'She wasn't doing anything; what her dog was doing there is the better question.'

'What is it you're not telling me, Pop?'

Campion removed his spectacles, breathed gently on the lenses and began to polish them lazily with a bright white handkerchief the size of a blanket. 'Two things, actually. Firstly, I found Robespierre being cared for by a local farmer's wife after *he* had spent a day and a night splashing about in the mud. He had come from Dame Jocasta's yacht, which had run aground. The master of the yacht, a chap called Francis Jarrold, was found drowned in the mud this morning. He was actually found by Robespierre, but unfortunately he can't tell us exactly what happened. Either that, or he's got a very good solicitor who has told him not to say anything which might incriminate him.'

'I suppose the police are involved.'

'You know me so well, my dear boy, but it all *looks* like a tragic accident.'

'You're not sure?'

'I have a funny feeling about it, that's why you must be careful what you say to Dame Jocasta when you deliver her pooch.'

'But at the same time, find out what she knows?'

'That's my boy, but as subtly as you can.'

'Was that the second thing you weren't telling me?'

'Not exactly. I ought to warn you that when Dame Jocasta asked me to retrieve her poodle, she hinted that in *quid pro quo* she might put a word in the right theatrical ears with the aim of advancing your career as a thespian. Now I have no idea how such a thing might work, for I am blissfully ignorant of the back alleys and power plays of the acting profession, but I said that both you and Perdita were strongly independent and determined to make your way on merit in your chosen profession.'

Rupert leaned forward, his face a picture of eager anticipation. 'Did she really offer to help us? If she did, I'll walk her damned dog every day for a year, take it to the vet, enter it for Crufts, anything.'

Mr Campion sighed and was not comforted by Lugg's far from *sotto voce* observation from the kitchen doorway.

'Good lad.'

SIX

Captain Waudby's Log

Mason Lowell Clay Junior, to give him what Lugg would refer to as his 'full moniker', looked more like a trainee FBI agent or a junior insurance salesman rather than a student in his grey Brooks Brothers suit, white button-down shirt and plain black tie. His blond hair was cut short *en brosse* which may have suggested he was in the services or, the more cynical might claim, was a good disguise for a student studying abroad in order to avoid the American draft system and an unpleasant sojourn in Vietnam, for no casual observer would think such a clean-cut specimen was shirking anything.

That he was American was in no doubt, from his shirt having short sleeves and his tie being a clip-on, to the way he ate, carving his meal into segments then spearing them right-handed with a fork. He endeared himself to the senior Campions, however, when he declared, over Sunday lunch, that Yorkshire puddings were 'the best vehicle for conveying gravy from plate to mouth' he had ever experienced.

That he had already won over the junior branch of the family was clear enough, Rupert treating him as a long-lost drinking buddy from his student days (although Mason Lowell had made it clear that he did not partake of alcohol), and Perdita had appointed herself as his tour guide and cultural advisor, adding a new historical site or a West End show he simply had to see every five minutes to an already lengthy list.

'You have a lovely house,' said Mason Lowell as Amanda and Perdita gathered in empty plates, 'and that was a super lunch, Lady Campion.'

'It's Amanda, please, Mr Clay, and thank you for both observations.'

'And you must call me Mason Lowell, which may sound odd to you, but that's how I am called in my family, to differentiate me from my brothers Henry Lowell Clay and Clarence Lowell Clay.'

'Well, if you insist,' said Amanda, slightly confused.

'And I must thank Mr Campion for providing me with an excellent base at Bottle Street and the use of your manservant.'

Their American guest was clearly startled by Amanda's clashing of plates and Perdita's explosive laugh. 'I'm sorry, have I said something untoward? You must correct me if I do, this is my first time in England and I want to act correctly.'

'My dear Mason,' said Campion with a gentle smile, 'the only thing you have said which may be untoward is the word "untoward". You surprised us by referring to Lugg as my – or anybody else's – manservant, and you would have surprised, nay shocked, Lugg himself had he heard you.'

'And don't ever call him a butler,' said Perdita.

'Or a major-domo,' added Rupert.

'Or chamberlain, equerry or steward and certainly not liege-man, as somebody once suggested,' said Amanda, glaring affectionately at her husband.

'When he was officially in my employ, many years ago,' said Campion, making a tent of his long fingers, 'he preferred the term "gent's gent", but now he prefers "loyal family retainer", albeit unpaid and often unnecessary. If pushed, I introduce him either as my "henchman" or as a fellow member of the British Olympic tiddlywink team, depending on who is asking.'

Mason Lowell turned his confused face towards Rupert, seeking reassurance that he had not landed on some forbidden plant.

'Welcome to England, Mason,' said Rupert, 'and my father's famous sense of humour, which translates into all known languages, except German of course. Just think of Lugg as part of the furniture and don't let him lead you astray. We call him Lugg; mother likes to call him "Magers". Your best bet is to stick to "Mr Lugg". Keep it formal; he will respect that.'

Mason Lowell creased his brow and grinned. 'Is that a polite, English way of telling me to know my place?'

'Exactly,' said Mr Campion, 'because Lugg doesn't know his, never has, and yet we all trust him with our lives and our reputations, if not necessarily with our wallets and certainly not with the keys to the wine cellar.'

'As a non-imbiber, that will not be a problem,' said Lowell.

'Don't tell Lugg that,' said Campion, 'but do tell us about your current researches. Please give us a hint before my wife serves up one of her famous apple pies, after which no amount of coffee will keep us from nodding off for an afternoon nap.'

'I doubt my story will either, sir, but I am happy to share it.' Mason Lowell leaned forward in his chair, placed his forearms on the table and with a long forefinger began to gently push his dessert spoon and fork until they were perfectly parallel.

'I sort of inherited the idea for my thesis from Professor Kathryn Luger. I believe you know her, sir. I know Rupert does; she was, as they say, much taken with him.'

'Was she now?' said Perdita, stroking Rupert's arm. 'I can't think why.'

'She began the groundwork ten years ago,' Mason pressed on, 'but then she got promoted and distracted and too busy to pursue her pet project, so she handed it to me as a suitable topic for my doctorate.'

'Rupert has told us of her interest in the settlers of Harkers Island,' said Mr Campion, 'when he was a student in America. The inhabitants spoke with a pronounced Essex accent, which is remarkable but not an impossibility. The dialects, accents and speech patterns of immigrants can survive in a new country for centuries. I knew a chap once, he was a professor, but don't hold that against him, who taught at the University of Tromsø in Norway for many years then retired back to England. The only place he felt comfortable was north Yorkshire because, after years of talking to Vikings, he understood the local accent, which was a legacy from the Vikings who invaded a thousand years ago.'

Mason Lowell, sensing a sympathetic audience, warmed to his subject. 'The settlers on Harkers, who are known as 'High-Tiders', make a fascinating case study, partly because the sample is relatively small and therefore easy to study, and partly because a group of early colonists all came from the same localized area.'

'Which would be Wicken.'

'Yes, albeit via Massachusetts, which again is interesting. For some reason a group of settlers from Wicken moved to the Americas, landed in Massachusetts but then decided to pack up and move hundreds of miles down the East Coast to North

Carolina; a journey as dangerous as crossing the Atlantic in those days. What possessed them to do that, take that risk to keep their little community together, is the question I am trying to answer.'

'And why should the answer be in Wicken in our Essex, three thousand miles away from your Harkers Island?' asked Campion.

Mason's eyes glowed and his fingers danced over the tablecloth like pale spiders until they found more cutlery to rearrange. 'Because not all of them settled on Harkers. The journey from Massachusetts had been hazardous, to say the least. Their ship had to contend with thick fogs and no wind, which slowed them down. Their supplies of food and water ran dangerously low. When they put in at some point, which we think might have been in Delaware, to find fresh water, they were attacked by the native Indians and five men were killed. Further down the coast they stopped at a Swedish settlement where they were cheated over the purchase of barrels of salt pork. There was an altercation, two more men died, and three women – all of them indentured servants – jumped ship, preferring to stay with the Swedes despite their sharp practice. One of them was actually called Amanda.' Mason grinned at his hostess.

'Perhaps the Swedes were taller and more handsome than the Essex men they were travelling with,' said Amanda innocently.

'They almost certainly were,' said Mr Campion, 'but let Mason continue with his narrative.'

'Well, after all their trials and tribulations, when the *Abigail* reached Harkers Island . . .' Mason paused, seeing blank faces around the table, '. . . I should have said, their ship was called the *Abigail* . . .'

'The third wife of David and one of the few female Jewish prophets,' said Campion. 'Abigail, that is; and I realize that now I am interrupting you. Apologies, Mason, please . . .'

'By the time the *Abigail* reached Harkers, some of the passengers had had enough of the New World so, after a brief stay for refitting and replenishing supplies, they opted to return to England. Some stayed and became the High-Tiders. It's the other part of the company, the ones who made it back to England; they're the ones I want to find. Well, their descendants, of course, the ones who returned to Wicken.'

'Fascinating,' said Campion. 'May I ask what your source for this story is?'

'The log of Captain Charles Waudby, master of the *Abigail*.'

'The actual captain's log of a seventeenth-century ship taking colonists to the New World? My goodness, there's a rarity. It must be a very valuable document. I'd love to see it.'

'So would I,' said Mason Lowell, 'but it doesn't exist.'

The silence over the dining-room table could have been cut with the carving knife Mr Campion had used on the joint of beef they had consumed, and it was Campion who broke the silence.

'Enough suspense, Mason – we insist you reveal your sources or we will begin to suspect you are leading us on a wild-goose chase, something which, in this household, I reserve as an exclusive privilege.'

'Have you heard the name Joseph Hurrell?' Lowell asked enigmatically.

'No.'

'I'm not surprised,' said Lowell. 'He was a person of little consequence in the scale of things; a chancer, an opportunist, possibly a forger, certainly a dubious character of low morals.'

'Why do I not know this gentleman?' Campion wailed, slapping the back of a hand to his forehead. 'He sounds just the sort of fellow who would be blackballed from the same clubs as I am.'

Mason Lowell recognized that this was more British humour on display, but chose to carry on regardless. 'Joseph Hurrell died in 1740, having failed to achieve either fame or fortune from a novel called *Captain Waudby's Log*, only three copies of which are known to have survived. It was the story of a seafaring captain taking colonists – religious dissenters – to America in 1692, and details their crossing of the Atlantic and then a second journey down the East Coast and then a return to England. Hurrell's novel was called *Captain Waudby's Log* because it was promoted as a genuine account as written by Charles Waudby, the captain of the *Abigail*.'

'May I ask when this bestseller was published?' asked Mr Campion.

'In 1721,' said Mason, 'and it was anything but a bestseller. Both the author and printer lost money on it.'

'Because it had competition.' Campion beamed. 'Very stiff competition.'

'Albert, you're going to show off any minute now,' chided his wife, 'I can tell. Come on, put us out of our misery so Mason can get on with his story. And be brief, or there'll be no pie for you.'

'My dear, I simply recalled that the bestselling book of 1719, as any schoolboy should know, was Daniel Defoe's *Robinson Crusoe* which, if memory serves, was actually the story of a shipwrecked sailor called Alexander Selkirk, and it was the memoirs of a man called Woodes Rogers, the ship's captain who actually rescued Selkirk from his desert island, that became the talk of London and inspired Defoe to write his novel.'

'Quite correct,' said Mason Lowell, with a nod of admiration. 'Defoe's classic went into four editions in that first year and has been in print ever since. Joseph Hurrell was clearly trying to emulate, or should we say cash-in on, Defoe's success. Sadly, he failed on two counts: Captain Waudby's story was not nearly dramatic enough, and Hurrell was a lousy writer. However, it is safe to assume that Hurrell, being an unimaginative author, relied heavily on his source material, so what we get in his novel is probably the authentic log of Captain Waudby, or at least the best we can get. The details of the voyage do seem authentic and – as far as we know – Hurrell never left England, so he took it all from Waudby's sea journal.'

'Details of seasickness, disease, storms, scurvy, cannibals and pirates?' Perdita asked with mock relish.

'All of the above,' said Mason, 'though no pirates or cannibalism, but some fine detail such as the diet on board the *Abigail*: salt pork, ship's biscuits and burgoo.'

'Burgoo?' queried Rupert and Perdita together.

'Where I come from,' said Mason, in an accent which emphasized his origins in the Southern states, 'it's now a sort of stew made with whatever comes to hand meat-wise: pork, chicken, beef, even squirrel, but back in 1692 on board ship, it would have been a sort of oatmeal porridge.'

'Gruel!' said Mr Campion, with such enthusiasm that the entire table turned towards him. 'We had it at my prep school and we called it gruel. Sorry, Mason, please continue.'

'We have assumed,' the American persevered, 'that once we strip out Hurrell's florid prose and digressions, mostly on religious themes, trying to prove he was a man of greater intellect than he actually was, what is left is directly taken from Captain

Waudby's account of the voyage. Hurrell was no sailor, and from his rambling style did not have the education or imagination to make up such a story, so there is no doubt in my mind that Hurrell had read, and was happy to steal from, Waudby's journal.'

'I do hope that is not a sweeping judgement on all authors of fiction,' said Campion with raised eyebrows.

'Not all,' said Mason straight-faced, 'but fiction is not my business. The voyage of the *Abigail* is what interests me, or rather the specific voyage she made in 1692 when she was hired to take a community of dissenters from Essex to a new life in the Americas.'

'Like the Pilgrim Fathers?' Rupert asked.

'They were seventy years earlier. The Massachusetts Bay colony was well established by 1692; it was even issuing its own paper money. It had a strong Puritan belief system, so it was still an attractive destination for those fleeing religious persecution in the old country. Or, it has to be said, those wishing to continue persecuting others with different religious beliefs.'

'That sound odd,' said Perdita. 'I was taught that the pilgrims went looking for a land where they could have perfect freedom, escaping from an intolerant Europe.'

'That is the accepted version in polite society, as I'm sure Mason will agree,' said Campion, 'but one of the few things, the very few things, I learned at Cambridge was that quite a few of the dissenters who emigrated to America were too radical – what's the modern expression, "far out"? – even for Oliver Cromwell, and he's the chap who cancelled Christmas and . . .' he peered over his spectacles at his son and daughter-in-law, '. . . introduced fines for anyone *attending* a theatre, and whippings for any actor appearing on stage.'

Mason Lowell nodded in agreement, clearly appreciating that he had an interested audience.

'I'm not sure what the Billericay Covenant thought about the theatre . . .'

'The Billericay what?' asked Campion, determined to show that as an audience he was no pushover.

'I should have explained. It was common practice for groups of emigrating pilgrims, though the term "pilgrim" only came into common use much later, to draw up a formal contract to hire a ship to take them to the New World. The contract, or covenant as they called it, for the Wicken party was drawn up in a lawyer's office in Billericay in Essex, when they hired Captain Waudby and the *Abigail*. It was a common enough arrangement. Remember, there were around six hundred ships a year crossing the Atlantic, so it was only natural for the lawyers to get involved.

'The *Abigail* herself was an interesting vessel. She was a Dutch *fluyt* which had either been traded or captured in one of the Anglo-Dutch wars of the late seventeenth century, a cargo ship which could be sailed with a small crew of twenty.'

'Did you say Anglo-*Dutch* war?' asked Perdita.

Mr Campion answered her with gusto. 'Wars, plural, my dear, loads of them – well, two or three anyway. Big rivals, the Dutch, when it came to who actually ruled the waves. There was even a sea battle in sixteen-seventy-something in Sole Bay off Southwold. Amanda's family and half the population of Suffolk still haven't forgiven them for that.'

Mason Lowell gritted his teeth and pressed on. 'That contract for the hire of the *Abigail* is quoted in Hurrell's book and gives the main signatories, who would be the leaders of the community, and a passenger list with names such as Poynter, Whybrow, Munson, Bugg and – two of my all-time favourites – Livewell Polley and Abendigo Lux. One of my tasks here in England is to see if I can run down an original copy of that covenant and another is to see if any of those names still exist in Wicken today.'

'Did Livewell Polley eventually live well?' asked Amanda.

'According to Hurrell's book, he made it to Massachusetts, though it seems his brother, aged five, did not; children under the age of seven rarely survived the crossing. Livewell Polley and his father John also feature on the list of those on the voyage from Massachusetts to North Carolina, but exactly who came back to England from Harkers is still unclear.'

'Were *all* the passengers on the *Abigail* from Wicken,' Campion asked, 'and did they all move on to this Harkers Island?'

'The *Abigail* carried sixty passengers, as far as we can tell, and fifty-two of them were listed on the Billericay Covenant, who we can assume came from Wicken or very nearby. The others would have paid for their passage themselves, and Hurrell's book, if it can be trusted, lists them as "among the quality and fair-minded", which probably means they were not Puritans. There was a barrel-maker called Cooper—'

'Obviously.'

'With his wife and son, a former soldier, Giles O'Hara, and a printer and bookbinder called Lionel Astley, listed as "a gentleman of Norfolk", who travelled with three indentured servant girls. Now all their names, except Astley's, show up in subsequent records of the Massachusetts colony. But none of those who signed the Billericay Covenant does. After deciding *en masse* against Massachusetts, they persuaded – somehow – Captain Waudby to delay his return crossing and divert down to North Carolina, and Astley's three servant girls went with them. They were the women who jumped ship at the Swedish colony down the coast, Lionel Astley having died on the voyage across the Atlantic.'

'In mysterious circumstances I hope,' said Campion gleefully.

'Hurrell doesn't say, so we presume Captain Waudby's log did not note anything untoward, and I doubt Hurrell had the imagination to speculate on anything sinister. He is also irritatingly vague about how many of those who reached Harkers Island opted to return to England. He does say that among their leaders was John Whybrow who, with his wife Modesty, definitely decided to stay on the island and their family name lives on to this day. In fact, Rupert has met one of John and Modesty's descendants.'

'Natty Whybrow, the "Hoi-Tider" Kathryn Luger introduced me to, hoping I could not understand his Essex accent,' confirmed Rupert.

'He's quite a character, ain't he?' Mason smiled. 'As well as being living proof of the Wicken connection. There are other names from the Covenant which survive on the island, such as Firmin and Gladwell. Indeed, Degory and Eliza Gladwell had four daughters of child-bearing age when they landed on Harkers, which was a useful asset in a new country short on females. So we know those who stayed, but we are less sure of who returned to Wicken.'

'And you are sure they returned to Wicken?' asked Campion.

'According to Hurrell, they pleaded with Captain Waudby to take them "not only back to England, but to the actual place whence they came," even if it meant another hazardous sea-crossing. They cannot have been in the best of health after their experiences over the previous months, either.'

'Interesting. It sounds as if they were a close-knit community.'

'Yes, indeed, I can't wait to see the place for myself. I understand from Rupert that you were there recently.'

'Briefly. In fact, so briefly I more or less missed it and certainly did not interact with any of the inhabitants. I was there on a mission, to retrieve a lost dog, believe it or not, which Rupert then returned to its owner.'

'Now that is a story I want to hear,' said Amanda. 'Not that yours isn't interesting, Mason, but this could be solid-gold gossip. Let me serve the pie before you give us all the juicy details, Rupert,' she added.

Mr Campion busied himself refilling glasses while Amanda cut slices of apple pie and fetched a jug of whipped cream from the kitchen, pouring wine for the family and lemonade for Mason, having expressed (yet again) his deepest and most profound sorrow that his household did not stock Coca-Cola.

Mason accepted the lemonade gratefully, and expressed something akin to wonderment at the cream, demanding to know how Amanda had made it. After his first spoonful, however, he declared himself a convert, and Mr Campion told him he should prepare to have his taste horizons widened once he began to sample English cheese. The American guest, however, remained unconvinced that a strong, mature cheddar went well with cold apple pie and put it down to 'hazing' by his British hosts.

'I did indeed take Robespierre – that's the dog in question, a large French poodle – back to Dame Jocasta's as per my orders. That's Jocasta Upcott, the famous actress, by the way.'

'She made some old black-and-white films, didn't she?'

'All our best actors look better in black-and-white, Mason,' said Campion, 'unlike American film stars who were born to Technicolour. Was the great dame pleased to see you?'

'Overwhelmed,' said Rupert, 'positively effusive. She couldn't have gushed more if I had turned up with the Oscar she never won back in the 1940s, although most of the gushing was over the dog, not me.'

'But she did thank you?'

'Of course. In fact, she was very, very grateful.'

'How exactly?'

Mr Campion thought he detected, or at least hoped he did, a slight pinkish glow in his son's cheeks.

'She offered to advance my career, as she put it,' said Rupert, his eyes firmly downwards, concentrating on his plate.

Mason Lowell halted the progress of a forkful of cream and pie halfway to his mouth and spoke in a nervous whisper. 'Is this going to be a casting-couch story? I've heard such things go on in Hollywood . . .'

'Oh, nothing so salacious,' said Mr Campion.

'I certainly hope not,' added Amanda.

'No, no, nothing like that,' insisted Rupert. 'Dame Jocasta insisted that I talk to her agent, with a view to him taking me on, but I explained that I would be reluctant to leave Maxim Berlins, who looks after both myself and Perdita.'

'Very noble, my boy, but I expect the great dame insisted.'

'She did indeed. Said that Timothy Timms was one of the leading theatrical agents and could open a lot more doors than Maxim Berlins. She insisted that I meet him.'

'When?' asked Campion, watching the expression on Perdita's face, which happily did not seem to be one of surprise.

'Right there and then. Well, as soon as she'd telephoned him and told him that Robespierre had come home, he shot round like a scalded rabbit. Said he hadn't slept for days worrying about the poor animal and got almost hysterical. Queer fellow. Turned up wearing a deerstalker hat but whipped it off like it was a magic trick to reveal a completely bald pate, not a hair on his head, smooth as a billiard ball. Got down on his knees so the dog could lick it. Seemed to amuse Jocasta if not the dog.'

'And did he ask you to be his clients?'

'He said he could do great things for us, open doors – stage doors, I suppose – and arrange lunches with television and film producers and so on, though he made it clear he was doing it at Dame Jocasta's behest, not because he had spotted our natural talent, as he'd never seen either of us in anything.'

'So, naturally, you took the moral high ground and said you preferred to succeed through your own abilities?'

'I said we'd think about it, but I doubt he was serious. I mean, all he could talk about was the damned dog. Where had he been found? Had he run off with another dog? What had happened to the yacht he had been on and where was it now? Had the police told me anything? Of course I couldn't tell him anything as I wasn't there.'

'Was a man name Francis Jarrold mentioned?'

'No. Who is he?'

'He was the skipper of the *Jocasta* but he drowned when the yacht ran aground. Robespierre was an old sea dog, literally, who travelled with him apparently.'

'And what?' asked Mason Lowell. 'The dog swam ashore but the skipper didn't make it?'

'A possibility,' said Campion, 'though "swim" might be the wrong word, for there's more mud than water out there and poor Francis ended up face down in it. Robespierre found the body half buried in the ooze and, from the state of him, it looked as if he'd been rolling in the stuff. Luckily, a kindly farmer's wife took him in and gave him a bath. Which reminds me . . .'

Mr Campion stood and walked into the kitchen and the diners around the table heard the back door of the house open and then close. When he returned he was holding what appeared to be a small, featureless rag doll made from a burlap material and stuffed with straw.

'This was Robespierre's toy or comforter and he was found with it. It was extremely filthy and I threw it on the floor of the car and forgot about it. I found it yesterday when I was removing dog hairs from the back seat and I sluiced it under the garden hose.'

He tossed the doll to Rupert, who caught it reluctantly with one hand. 'You could return it to Robespierre, should you need an excuse to visit Dame Jocasta again.'

Before Rupert could reply, a chair crashed over, startling them all, as Mason Lowell sprang to his feet.

'That's not a toy, or a comforter,' he said, his eyes wide. 'That's a reflection.'

'Steady on, old chap,' said Campion, 'a reflection of what?'

'No, that thing is called a reflection. It's a sort of voodoo doll.'

'Now, that *is* interesting,' said Mr Campion.

SEVEN

Captain Jarrold's Log

Rupert, Perdita and Mason Lowell took their leave early the next morning, a Monday, and Campion, one arm around his wife's waist, waved the fiery red Mini Cooper down the drive with the other. Once back inside the house, Mr Campion rescued the newspaper carrying the story of the *Jocasta*'s collision with the Dengie Peninsula from the log basket next to the inglenook fireplace, read the relevant article twice and then settled himself at his desk in the small withdrawing room which served as part office, part library, and began to make telephone calls.

During his third trunk call, Amanda entered stealthily and placed a cup of coffee on the desk at his elbow, along with a sheet of notepaper on which she had written in a large flowing script: *You are retired!* Then she had turned on a dainty heel and left without a word.

Mr Campion finished his call and went in search of his wife, and forgiveness.

'I might have known you wouldn't be able to resist,' said Amanda, but in a tone of world-weariness rather than scolding. 'As soon as Mason said the words "voodoo" and "doll", I knew you were hooked. You're going down to Wicken, aren't you?'

'You have me, my darling, bang to rights, as Lugg would say, but if there is something spooky down on the Dengie Peninsula, I'd feel happier if I could do a bit of reconnaissance before Rupert takes Mason there. After all, a man did die down there.'

'And yet the dog survived, so it must be a case of witchcraft or mumbo-jumbo or voodoo, and you simply *have* to poke your nose in, almost certainly where it is not wanted.'

Campion put his arms around his wife and drew her close. 'But there would be absolutely no fun poking the old hooter somewhere it *was* wanted, would there?'

'No, that would be far too adult and responsible.'

'I have never claimed to be adult, or responsible, or able to act my age. In fact, I insist I am not my age. It's why you fell in love with me.'

'That's probably true,' said Amanda, her fist curled under her chin in a pose of contemplation, 'but it sounds rather arrogant, so you're still in my bad books and the new Divorce Reform Act allows for a "quickie" divorce in two years, so you'd better be careful. What exactly do you intend doing?'

'First of all, I want to take a look at Dame Jocasta's yacht, which my sources tell me has been pulled from the mud and towed round to its home port of Brightlingsea. Then I will try and establish a base on the Dengie Peninsula and do a bit of groundwork before Rupert and Mason turn up to interrogate the locals.'

'Will you take the Beast or Junior?'

The Campions' garage boasted two cars: the Jaguar, known as the Beast, and an Alfa Romeo Spider Junior, known, logically enough, as Junior.

'Oh, the Beast, definitely. It gives me a sedate authority whereas in Junior I feel like I am driving a jet-propelled dodgem car.'

'Now that does mean you are showing your age.'

'Perhaps, but you are the best curator a museum piece like me could wish for.'

Mr Campion had been to Brightlingsea once before in the days when a branch line connected the little river port to Wivenhoe and then Colchester further up the River Colne. He vaguely remembered that the railway line had been temporarily closed during the great East Anglian floods of 1953; what nature had attempted, Dr Beeching's swinging axe had finally achieved ten years later, and now the town was only approachable by road. And, of course, water, as it was, after all, a port. In fact, Campion recalled from half-forgotten history books, it was one of the Cinque Ports, the confederation of coastal towns lining the English Channel dating back to Anglo-Saxon times, Brightlingsea being notable for being the only Cinque Port north of the Thames. It was still, as it had been for a hundred years, a place where yachts, both sail- and steam-powered, were built, over-wintered or laid up for repair.

Campion parked the Jaguar in a small street near the town's library and stretched his long legs down towards the waterside and the local sailing club, where a rank of sailing vessels lined the quayside or 'hard', their bows secured by sturdy rope lines tied to metal rings set in the concrete. It was a tranquil scene set against a soundtrack of tinkling metal and creaking wood, occasionally underscored by the incongruous rapid thumps of rifle fire coming from the army firing range across the Colne at Fingringhoe Wick.

Several boats had gangplanks or ladders against them and, as Campion strolled the length of the hard, he caught the sounds of hammering or scraping from their interiors and the occasional whiff of paint or varnish. The *Jocasta* was easy to find, partly because of the name board on the prow identifying it, and partly because there was a uniformed police sergeant standing on deck as if ready to repel borders.

'Mr Campion, fancy seeing you here.'

'Good morning, Sergeant . . . Trybull, isn't it? I almost didn't recognize you with your uniform on. Oh dear, that sounded bad and it wasn't meant to.'

'I've heard worse, sir. I suppose you'll be wanting to come aboard.'

Campion put his head on one side and looked up at Trybull, who towered some six feet above him.

'I would love to, but I have absolutely no legitimate excuse or authority to do so. My motive for being here is pure nosiness; you see, I suffer from terminal inquisitiveness.'

'So do I, sir,' said Trybull, crouching down to steady the weathered plank leaning from boat to dock. 'I'm not on duty until two this afternoon, yet here I am messing about in another man's boat. Can I give you a hand?'

Campion placed a tentative foot on the sloping gangplank. The angle was not more than thirty degrees, the distance to the deck of the *Jocasta* only a few feet and, the tide being out, it spanned only soft, sucking mud rather than swirling water. Even so, Campion was not as young, or spry, as he had once been.

'As always, Sergeant, I would appreciate the long arm of the law. I'm sure it would be very inconvenient for you to have to explain another body face down in the mud.'

'I try to limit myself to one a month,' said Trybull, as his proffered hand closed on Campion's. 'Up you come.'

Campion planted his feet on the deck of the *Jocasta* and bent his legs, adjusting his gait to the angle the yacht rested at on its muddy bed. He made a mental note that as the tide came in, the boat would rise and the angle of the gangplank would become more acute, making disembarkation a more risky business, at least for him. There had been a time, he mused, when he would have thought nothing of leaping ashore Errol Flynn-like, but those days were long gone and he dreaded the prospect of having to make an undignified exit on all fours – a penitent pirate crawling, rather than walking, the plank.

'I take it you want to see inside the cabin,' said Trybull.

'If it is permitted.'

'I don't see why not. The *Jocasta* is not designated as a crime scene; in fact, it has not been determined that any crime has been committed – yet.'

'But you think that may happen?'

'That depends on the autopsy report on her skipper, which we should get tomorrow.'

Campion put on his 'innocence surprised' look, an expression which Amanda claimed did not fool anyone these days.

'Could that show evidence of foul play?'

'That's for the doctor to say, but we all knew Francis Jarrold round here and plenty would be surprised if the doc finds any blood in his alcohol system.'

'That would include his employer,' said Campion, 'who told me he was fond of a drink. Could that explain what happened? What did happen exactly?'

Trybull pushed up the brim of his peaked cap with a forefinger. 'My guess is that Francis was aiming for Worm Creek, which at full tide would have just enough water for the *Jocasta*, though it was a tricky thing to do in the dark and not at all advisable if drunk. Either he misjudged the tide, his speed, or steered badly, or all three, but the yacht grounded herself in the mud and when the tide turned she tilted over. He would have known he wasn't going to get off without a tow, so he abandoned ship – in the dark on one of the most dangerous, desolate bits of coastline not guarded by a minefield.'

'And the story of his sea boots?'

'They were sticking out of the mud where he'd jumped off the boat. The Worm is like a ditch cut through the mud, and he must have been trying to get near the lip and pull himself up on to the flats. He planted himself so deep he couldn't move unless he abandoned his boots, and then probably crawled on his belly until exhausted. Once he stopped moving, the mud sucked him in, or maybe he sucked in enough mud to kill him.'

'Whereas a sober man would have waited for daylight?'

'A sober sailor would have been nowhere near The Worm after dark. There's no landing there and no lights or buoys to mark the channel.'

'Should there be?'

'Why? It doesn't go anywhere.'

'Except Wicken.'

'Wicken? There's nothing there. You wouldn't take a valuable motor yacht like this to a place like Wicken, even if there was a hard landing there, when you have Maldon and Burnham at either end of the Dengie Peninsula – places which cater for the yachting trade.'

'Which suggests to you that Francis Jarrold was drunk at the wheel – or should that be helm?'

'Stinking drunk, I reckon, and I say that not because he had form in such matters, but come and look below – and mind your head.'

Campion followed the sergeant to the stern of the yacht and the small, exposed wheelhouse, then crouched, as ordered, when Trybull held open the swing doors of the cabin. Immediately beyond were three wooden steps leading down into the long, low accommodation quarters, with a bunk bed lining each side, the starboard bunk occupied by large square objects, which could be boxes but were hidden by blankets draped over them. There was clearly a kitchen area, or at least a gas stove on which a battered kettle stood proud, but the most noticeable thing about the cabin by far was the quantity of empty or part-empty bottles which stood, lay or rolled around every conceivable surface. It showed a Catholic taste in alcoholic drinks, ranging from pint bottles of pale ale, to both brown and clear wine bottles and then numerous examples of the art of the French cognac maker and both Scottish and Irish distillers.

'My God,' said Campion, remembering at the last moment not to straighten to his full height, 'if Jarrold consumed all this he could have breathed fumes into the engine and become jet-propelled.'

'I'm not saying he drank all this lot, at least not at one go. When the boat tilted over in the mud, his empties would have rolled out from their hiding places or fallen off the shelving, but my guess is that Francis had made inroads into a few.'

Mr Campion, still crouching in the low cabin, flicked his eyes along the narrow shelf which ran around the cabin, designed as a safe haven for small items which could be reached from someone sitting on the bunk without too much effort. The shelf had a thin dowelling rail about an inch above it, to keep items in place during rough seas, although it had snapped in several places. Where it was still intact, it restrained a variety of items including three paperback thrillers, a French–English dictionary, a tub of Saxa table salt, a small Japanese transistor radio and, at the end of the shelf by the cabin doors, a green glass medicine bottle.

'Of course, things got shaken about a bit when the coastguard got a rope on her and pulled her off the mud yesterday,' said Trybull, carefully placing his feet to avoid empty bottles, 'but otherwise things are just as Francis Jarrold left them, we think.'

'Did he leave a log or charts? Any clue why he was heading for Worm Creek?'

'There was a log of sorts, more a schoolboy's exercise book really, which has been sent to the Coroner's Office, and there were standard charts of the Channel, all in the wheelhouse. There was nothing to indicate why he should be near Worm Creek; he should have been heading back here. This is his berth, and he rents a flat in the town, above a greengrocer's shop. We found the keys on him and I had a look round there first thing this morning. Nothing untoward there and his landlord expected him back today or tomorrow, depending on how much *vin rouge* he'd enjoyed in France.'

'France?'

'He often took the *Jocasta* across to Honfleur. There's quite an English colony building up there. Jarrold could do the run with his eyes closed and he always came back with more cigarettes and booze than he was supposed to.'

Mr Campion indicated the square shapes under the blankets on the starboard bunk.

'Are those cases of wine?'

Trybull snorted and pulled the blanket away.

'Not this time. I reckon that was his passenger's bedroom.'

The objects revealed were rectangular cages with a hinged door at one end, too big to be a cat- or puppy-carrying basket but big enough to house a dog or even a pig or a small wolf. There appeared to be no mechanism for securing the doors other than a crude 'hook and eye' system.

'He would want somewhere secure to put the dog,' said Trybull, 'in bad weather or when he was sleeping one off. Think what Dame Jocasta would have said if her precious poodle had gone overboard.'

'You knew about the dog?'

'Everybody in Brightlingsea did. It's a small town and the dog was quite a character. It would stand guard on the boat when Francis was down the pub of an evening.'

'So Dame Jocasta was a regular visitor to the town?'

'Not really, in fact never these days. She would have the dog driven down here from London, like he was going on his holidays, and Francis would take him over to Honfleur where Lady Upcott has a house in the old quarter for entertaining all her French fans, or so they say. It's not as if the likes of me would move in those circles.'

'So when Jocasta had had enough of La Belle France, Jarrold would bring the dog back?'

'Three or four times year.'

'It seems a bit extreme to have a yacht just to keep a poodle happy,' said Campion. 'Even for an actress that is somewhat overdramatic.'

'As I understand it, she used to enjoy sailing in the early days, but the *Jocasta* soon became just a way of impressing her friends. She would host cocktail parties on board when in France, the sort of thing I'm sure you are familiar with, sir, but she preferred to travel to Honfleur by more comfortable means such as planes and trains.'

'And she liked to show off her doggy when she was there?'

'My wife tells me that posh . . . upper-class . . . French ladies never go anywhere without a toy dog on a lead; some of them even try walking a cat on a lead.' Trybull cleared his throat. 'My wife reads a lot of magazines,' he said limply.

'Ah, how the jet set live,' Campion said airily. 'Was Jarrold happy to be a sort of taxi driver for pets?'

'Why not? He had use of a yacht he couldn't have afforded himself, and a fairly cushy life with all the duty-free he could drink, all for the discomfort of a couple of all-nighters navigating the English Channel.'

'Isn't it rather dangerous to try and cross the Channel single-handed?'

Trybull gave the question serious thought. 'It's tricky, that's for sure. You'd be going through four tides – two in your favour, two against – and you'd have to be familiar with the Swatchways across the Thames Estuary, which Francis certainly was.'

'The Swatchways?'

'That's the general term for the gaps in the sandbanks, usually marked by buoys with lights and bells. Specific channels are marked as Spitways. Every Spitway is a Swatchway, but not all Swatchways are a Spitway. You've got to know the channels where you'll have sufficient water, and once off the Essex coast you'd be looking for what's known as the Swin Spitway. I can show you all this on the charts if you like.' Mr Campion flapped a hand in polite refusal of the offer. 'Well, the Swin Spitway will take you past Maplin Sands and then the East Swin should lead you to a gap between the Buxey and Gunfleet sandbars. That's if he was going for Brightlingsea. To end up where he did, he must have taken the Whitaker Channel which leads to the River Crouch and Burnham, and then turned up towards Worm Creek and Dengie.'

'Or Wicken.'

'I told you, there's no landing at Wicken.'

'You have indeed, but both the *Jocasta* and Jarrold ended up near there. Bad seamanship? You indicated that he had done that voyage before.'

'Several times,' Trybull nodded.

'How long would the journey be?'

'Francis would have been at sea for a day and a night before he drove her on to the mud, perhaps two nights depending on the winds and how much he relied on his engine. His log isn't very clear on that. In fact, it wasn't very clear about anything.'

'You read it?'

'I had a quick look before it was packed off to the coroner. Goodness knows what he'll make of it because after an entry saying simply, "Leaving Honfleur", the rest is mostly gibberish.'

'Gibberish?'

'Ravings. The entries were scribbles, sometimes just single words. Nothing was dated or timed, no notes of speed or weather, just angry words. He wrote "thirsty" about six times and once he put "problem swallowing" which may have been a sick joke, given the number of empty bottles here. Then there was stuff about the stars flashing signals to him, but their Morse code was too fast for him to follow. I reckon the medics will find, and the ship's log will confirm, that poor old Francis was as drunk as a lord on that voyage.' Trybull's eyes widened as if he had suddenly given away a state secret. 'I'm sorry, sir, I didn't mean anything specific about lords . . .'

Campion laughed. 'Do not concern yourself, Sergeant, I know several; few of them abstemious, most are worshippers of Bacchus, just as, from the evidence around our feet, was Captain Jarrold.'

'Shouldn't speak ill of the dead, but everyone round here knows Francis was fond of the bottle.'

Campion made to leave, his feet nudging empty bottles so that they rolled and clinked together. He indicated that the sergeant should lead the way back on deck as conditions were too cramped to allow for a polite 'After you', but he paused on the first step and turned his head to examine the last item on the shelf which ran around the cabin.

It was an old medicine bottle, about eight inches high, made of light green glass with no label but the words NOT TO BE TAKEN embossed down one side from neck to base. It could be a century old, thought Campion, and they had usually come with a green glass stopper but, in this particular example, the bottle was sealed with a firmly inserted wine cork.

The bottle's contents enforced the warning that they should not be taken, as ingestion would certainly be painful. As far as Mr Campion could determine, the bottle contained three long iron nails and several thin twigs in a liquid suspension which might, or might not, have been water.

Curiosity getting the better of him, as it usually did, Campion took the bottle and once on deck showed the bottle to Trybull. 'Any idea what this is?'

The sergeant shook his head. 'Not a clue, have you?'

'I have a feeling I ought to,' said Campion. 'Initially I thought it might be some sort of acid and an attempt to clean up some rusty nails, but there are no bubbles and the nails are still rusty. Bit of a mystery unless it was Jarrold's attempt at making a ship in a bottle while under the influence.'

'He wasn't short of a large bottle to choose from,' observed Trybull.

'That's very true, which makes this very odd. Would you mind if I took it with me? I'd like to show it to somebody. Unless it's considered important, of course.'

'I can't see it being relevant to anything and it's not evidence, so you might as well. We can always get the other one analysed if we have to.'

'The other one?'

'In Jarrold's flat in the town. There are just as many empty bottles there as there are on board, but there's also another medicine bottle – just like that one – with a couple of nails in it, hanging from a string on the door frame. Almost smacked me in the face when I went inside.'

Rupert and Perdita dropped Mason Lowell at the Bottle Street flat, transferring hosting responsibilities to Lugg who had promised an 'orientation tour' for their American visitor, which would include the British Museum Library, the London Library, and St Catherine's House at the Aldwych, where the registry of births, marriages and deaths had recently been relocated from Somerset House.

Perdita had felt it necessary to warn Lugg against including any public houses with quaint historical names on his tour, no matter how interesting they might sound to an American researcher, stressing that Mason was of the temperance persuasion. Lugg had grumpily agreed to keep the tour professional rather than pleasurable and said that Mason had told him he was a non-drinker within two minutes of being introduced which, in

Lugg's not so humble opinion, was a bit forward and he had not yet recovered from the shock.

As soon as they were back in their tiny Islington flat, Rupert announced that he had to telephone their agent to see if he had anything 'lined up' for the coming week.

'Try not to sound desperate,' said Perdita.

'I'm rather hoping Maxim has nothing for me,' Rupert said haughtily. 'I know you've got auditions booked but I was hoping for a free week to help Mason with his research.'

'He won't believe that for a minute. No actor rings an agent demanding that they haven't got anything for him.'

But Rupert was able to surprise his wife, as well as astonishing himself, by discovering that Maxim Berlins did have something for him, an invitation to dinner at The Savoy that evening, with Jocasta Upcott, no less, where he might hear, in the best traditions of nineteenth-century literature, 'something to his advantage'.

When he transmitted the news to his wife, Perdita's response was eminently practical, raising the vital question of what on Earth she was going to wear.

At which point, Rupert had to curb his enthusiasm and admit, somewhat shamefaced, 'I'm sorry, darling, the invitation wasn't for *us*, only little old me.'

'Well, I hope "little old you" has an absolutely spiffing time,' said Perdita, in a tone which suggested that discussion was at an end and the topic would never be referred to again.

In Maldon, Mr Campion called at a post office where he borrowed a copy of the area's Yellow Pages and located the number of The Oyster Shack bed-and-breakfast establishment at Tillingham, which seemed to be the nearest, if not only, place offering accommodation in the vicinity of Wicken. From the telephone box outside he made contact with a Mrs Young and established that she did indeed have a room available, though only if it was clearly understood that she did not do teas, dinners or suppers. When Campion insisted that he was sure he could find a local restaurant or a friendly pub to take care of the inner man, she wished him 'good luck with that' but looked forward to seeing him later that afternoon.

Pleased with himself that he did not have to stop and ask

directions until he was in Tillingham itself, Campion found The Oyster Shack was a place where oysters were neither stored nor 'shucked', but merely the colourful identity adopted by a 1930s' detached brick house determined to attract any passing tourist trade. Without such a commercial imperative, the house would most likely be called The Pines or The Oaks, or, at a pinch, The Vicarage.

Mrs Young, his hostess, was a slender woman with the facial expressions and general twitchiness of a rabbit having just heard the click of a closing shotgun. She showed Campion to his room upstairs, then the bathroom, and then the communal dining room downstairs, indicating that both the kitchen and the living room were not open to guests although, as there were no other guests at the moment, it would be acceptable for Campion to join herself and Mr Young for their evening's television viewing.

Campion demurred as politely as possible, expressing surprise that there were no other guests at The Oyster Shack, at which Mrs Young informed him that it was not a natural tourist area and most of her visitors came in connection with the nuclear power station at Bradwell, though she did have a few regular birdwatchers who stayed at various times through the year, the latest having been there only last week. As she offered a visitors' book for Campion to sign, he asked casually if that might have been a young chap called Graham Roberts, who was known to cycle round the peninsula spotting birds.

Mrs Young assured him that her birdwatcher travelled in a big black car and was always smartly dressed for the outdoors. She pointed to the last entry in her visitors' book and said that was him there, a proper London gentleman with a proper London address.

Mr Campion read the name 'Charles Wyndham' written in ink in a flamboyant, flowing script, followed by 58, Charing Cross Rd, WC2, which he was pretty sure was the address of a second-hand bookshop where he had spent many happy hours browsing.

Intent on doing his initial reconnaissance while there was still daylight, Mr Campion drove the short distance to Dengie where he parked the Jaguar near St James's Church and, having changed his shoes for the Wellingtons he kept in the boot for countryside emergencies, he set off down the road until he came to the unmarked track which led to Wicken.

He was reminded of wartime campaigns to remove all signposts which might help enemy parachutists. Perhaps the fingerposts to Wicken had been removed to confuse invaders, whether there was a war on or not.

As he was dressed in what Amanda called his 'country casuals' – brown corduroy trousers, a cable-knit fisherman's sweater and a Harris tweed jacket – he was confident that, even if he did not blend in, he did not stand out, but just in case, as he walked, he concocted reasonable reasons for his presence should it be challenged. He could not pose as yet another ornithologist, as they seemed to be fairly thick on the ground, and he immediately discounted any official occupation, as this was clearly an area where tax inspectors, census takers and local government ratings officers were likely to be seen as open targets.

Perhaps he should be something obscure, like a mud geologist or a botanist specializing in salt-marsh plants. There again, it was perhaps safer to play to his strength, his age. He could pose quite convincingly as a retired gentleman of modest means but varied interests because that, basically, was what he was. He had every right to wander aimlessly across the marshes and mudflats of the Dengie Peninsula, because it was still a free country. Should anyone demand to know what he was doing in Wicken, he could simply say he did not realize he was anywhere in particular, there being no welcome signs.

As he strolled into Wicken, the thought occurred that a 'Visitors *Not* Welcome' sign would be far more appropriate.

EIGHT
Graveyard

There was little more to be discovered about Wicken on foot than there had been from behind the wheel of a moving car. Just as when he had driven down the track following the ambulance in the previous week, Mr Campion encountered no human life as he walked the length of what certainly could not be described as a village and to call it a hamlet would be being generous. Neither did he spot any animals, and while cats would sensibly hide themselves when a stranger appeared, surely such a bleak and lonely place would have benefited from a guard dog or two. Perhaps he imagined it, but he thought he heard a single faint howl on the wind, though had not someone mentioned that there 'were no dogs in Wicken'?

There were dwellings, no more than six of them spaced out along the south side of the track. To step off the northern side would have put him directly on to flat salt marsh which, from the state of the track, was clearly prone to flooding with a high tide. In winter, it would have offered a bleak panorama from which the primary colours had been leached; not that the residents appeared to value the view from their front doors, as almost all had constructed outbuildings of black weatherboarding between their houses and the track. These buffers against the wind or any passing traffic had been thrown up with gay abandon, and could have served as barns, winter quarters for cattle or sheep, chicken hutches or simply garden sheds. They differed wildly in size, shape and sturdiness and none seemed suitable for use as a garage, but then Campion could not see any vehicle other than a tractor resting in a field behind one house, although he remembered an old black saloon parked in a front garden when he had driven in pursuit of the ambulance.

Only one building had an uncluttered frontage on to the track, a low, pillbox-grey stone chapel which had clearly seen better days, though it would be hard to imagine exactly how such a stern exterior could be softened.

A hundred yards beyond the last building, Campion reached the end of the track from where he had witnessed Francis Jarrold's body being reclaimed from the mud, though now not even a boot print remained to mark the spot and there was nothing to tempt him to venture out on to that treacherous morass. Turning on his heel he retraced his steps slowly, making a mental note of the houses, as if he was an estate agent sizing up their potential.

There were six domestic dwellings in Wicken, all of brick and tile construction, though without any uniformity of size or style. One was a bungalow, four were detached two-storey properties, and one a pair of semi-detached houses of the 1930s' era, which reminded Campion of the standard design used for civilian housing on military bases. That made seven households in theory. And there was the single-storey Methodist chapel, cold and austere in the wind coming off the mudflats.

Could such a small population provide a congregation big enough to support a chapel? There was a church in Dengie for the more conformist worshipper, but did that mean Wicken was a rebel outpost for nonconformists? There was one way to find out and, while the military commander might insist that no time was ever wasted in reconnaissance, Mr Campion always maintained that time spent rooting around in graveyards was always fascinating if not necessarily productive.

He retraced his steps to the chapel and followed a cracked and weed-infested flagstone path up to the firmly locked, very weathered, brown door. There was no external board or signage advertising the times of services or who the minister or visiting preachers were.

Mr Campion pushed his way through brambles and knee-high marram grass between the left wall of the chapel and a high wooden fence to an unkempt square of land dotted with graves and free-standing gravestones which suggested that the original owners had abandoned or sub-let their plots. A few graves were decorated with jam jars full of dried and withered flowers, but nothing he could see persuaded Mr Campion that he was anything but the first visitor in a long time.

He began to read the gravestones, at least those that were

readable through dark green moss stains, reflecting on the many gentle epitaphs which a loved one had used to soften their loss.

There lay Bert and Nellie Bloomfield, a father and daughter, 'Sever'd only till HE comes', in 1899, and near them George Hankin, 'who fell asleep' in 1903. There was a Mary Louisa Diss and, almost as an afterthought, her husband Alfred, who was assured in 1908 that her children 'would rise up and call her blessed', and Ann, wife of the rather anonymous C.W. Doe, 'who entered the homeland' in 1909. Then there were plain, uninscribed markers for an Octavia Bugg (1919) and a Barbara Jarrold (1932) but a joint endorsement for Jeremy (1927) and Ada (1930) Worskitt who had 'arrived in the lasting city'. The most recent inhabitant of the cemetery as far as Campion could deduce was one Theodora Jones (1900–1936), daughter of John and Eunice Jones 'and beloved sister'.

Mr Campion looked around the graveyard, willing the stones to tell him more, for he was sure they had more to tell, just as on the war memorial in any decent-sized village in East Anglia, a list of names, often of the same surname, could give an instant picture of the devastating effect of a war on a close-knit community. But here there was only the silence of names forgotten, not even whispered on the wind.

'Can I help you?' said a voice.

'Say "opportune".'

'Wot?'

'Say "opportune" as in "the opportune moment".'

'Wot if I don't fink this is the opportune moment?'

'Thank you,' said Mason Lowell, 'that was most helpful.'

'It was?' said Lugg.

'It means you're not originally from Essex. If you were you'd have said *opportoon*.'

Lugg drew in his stomach, a sure sign that his dignity was in jeopardy. 'I knew that for a fact, always have known it, and could've told you had you but asked in a straightforward way like wot the perlice do.'

'Ah-ha, *perlice* – that's London Cockney, isn't it?'

'Are you that Henry Higgins fellow from the film?' asked Lugg, remembering not to drop his aitches.

'Only if you're Eliza Doolittle,' Mason Lowell laughed until he saw the expression on Lugg's face. 'I wasn't showing off, just trying to answer your question as to why I was interested in Wicken and the Dengie Peninsula.'

'You reckon some of the yokels went to America across the ocean blue in 1492 . . .'

'In 1692 actually, not with Columbus.'

'Whenever they did, they took their Essex accents with them and they still speak like that today; that's the nub of your argument, ain't it?'

'Part of it. I can't wait to visit with the locals to see if I can understand them, maybe even find some family connections.'

'You probably will,' conceded Lugg. 'Things don't ever change much out there.'

'You've been to Wicken?'

'Not exactly.' Lugg pursed his thick lips as though savouring the moment. 'Can't say I'd ever heard of Wicken till you tiptoed into my life, but I 'ave been out on the Dengie. During the war it was.'

'Was that with what you guys called the Home Guard?'

'Certainly not!' snapped Lugg. 'I was in Heavy Rescue coping with the air raids, but between Blitzes they'd bus us out there to salvage or clear aircraft that'd crashed in the marshes or the mudflats. The place was littered with 'em, Germans and ours, plenty with their bomb loads still intact.'

'Dangerous work for you, and I guess pretty terrifying for the local population.'

'Population? There wasn't much of one. Hardly saw a soul, can't remember exchanging the time o'day with anyone. Picked some nice apples one time, though. D'Arcy Spice they were called, a local variety, brown and gnarled as a farmer's hands but juicy and very tasty. One year so many dropped we were ankle deep. Used them as cricket balls for practice.'

Lugg made an overarm bowling motion and the American noticed how lightly the big man moved on his toes.

'You English – even had time for tea and cricket in the middle of a war.'

'Tea was rationed, cricket wasn't,' said Lugg as if that explained everything. 'You Yanks never appreciated cricket and your idea of football's simply not natural. I'll have to take you to watch West Ham while you're over here.'

'West Ham? Are they the champions of Britain?'

'Not really,' said Lugg quietly. 'Nobody lets 'em win enough.'

'Well, if I get the time, I'll take you up on your offer, though I'm not big on team sports.'

'Bit of a bookworm, are you? Prefer the library to getting fresh air and exercise?'

Mason Lowell's eyes betrayed the thought that Lugg's physique was the worst possible advertisement for fresh air and exercise he could imagine. 'Single sculling is my sport,' he said, 'as in rowing, and in my university I'm considered pretty good. If I was at your Cambridge, I'd probably get a blue.'

Lugg's face contorted in a mixture of surprise and distaste. 'You mean you go out on the water in a rowing boat *for fun*?' He shook his globe of a head. 'Well, each to 'is own.'

'Looking for anyone particular?'

'No, just snooping. It's a bad habit of mine, but I can't resist a good graveyard. So many stories here, but all of them tantalisingly out of reach.'

Mr Campion had little experience of neighbourly chats over the garden fence, but felt the need to engage with the man who lived next door to the chapel, as he had every right to be there while Campion was the intruder – and intruders, he suspected, were rare beasts in Wicken.

'You're not chapel yourself?'

'No, I am not, and to be honest, I was quite surprised to find a chapel here.'

'It's not used much these days,' admitted the voice from the other side of the six-foot-high wicker fence, 'and there's only been one interment since my mother was laid to rest nearly forty years ago. Just a minute.'

Campion scanned the fence to try and locate the source of the voice. He heard a scraping sound and a thump and then a head, shoulders and two arms appeared over the top.

'My name's Worskitt,' said the grey-haired, sallow-faced head.

'Son of Jeremy and Ada, who made the journey to the everlasting city. Mine's Campion. I'm just passing through; Wicken that is, not the everlasting city.'

'You've been reading the inscriptions,' said Mr Worskitt, folding his arms on the top of the fence and looking down on Campion.

'I find them fascinating; I simply couldn't resist taking a peek. There was another which says someone has "entered the homeland", which I presume is the same as the everlasting city.'

'So?' asked the fence ornament suspiciously.

'It reminded me that they that say such things declare plainly that they seek a country of their own.'

'Hebrews,' said the face on the fence. 'You know your scripture.'

'Enough to appreciate the language and the sentiment, but not enough to follow their instruction.' Campion looked up into the face of the older man. 'And I'm sure there must be something in Hebrews about not being rude to one's neighbours, but I simply have to ask: are you really seven feet tall?'

Mr Worskitt looked confused, then surprised, at the question. 'I'm standing in a wheelbarrow,' he said, without a trace of humour or embarrassment. 'Ethel – that's the wife – says I shouldn't go clambering about at my age.'

'I receive similar instructions from my better half and I tend to pay more attention to them than to any scripture, I'm afraid. Tell me, Mr Worskitt, have you lived here long?'

Mr Worskitt rested his chin on his forearms and Campion sensed that he was a man grateful to have a two-way conversation with someone in a graveyard for a change.

'All my life, though the wife's an incomer. She's from Shoeburyness.'

Mr Campion was unsure how to respond to that and so blithely changed the subject.

'So you would know all the residents of Wicken? I suppose the names on these stones represent the main families, or at least the chapel-going ones.'

'I dunno about that,' said Mr Worskitt, 'there's not much chapel-going these days, but there's still a few who have relatives sleeping here. I tries to keep it tidy, but it's getting a bit much for me at my age and Ethel, that's the wife, says I should concentrate on the vegetable patch as we still need to eat and they don't.'

'Mrs Worskitt sounds to be an eminently sensible woman,' said Campion, already formulating excuses should he be invited to meet her. 'Wicken seems such a small place, you must know everybody.'

'There's not many to know, never was, but some have been here longer than me and Ethel. Going that way' – he pointed a finger across the graveyard – 'there's Sylvia Jones at Abigail Cottage, then after the bungalow in the two cottages there's Bob Barly and his missus, and next door to them is George Bugg. The last two houses on the lane are the Jarmins and then Richard Polley and his sister Octavia. Their families were all here before mine. Only Mary Ann Allen at the bungalow has come in since the war, when she bought it off the Jarrolds.'

'Jarrold?' said Campion sharply, hoping that his ears had not pricked up too obviously.

'Barbara Jarrold as was, mother of Francis and now he's gone too.'

'So I understand. It must have been quite a shock for Wicken to find one of their own out there on the mud.'

Mr Worskitt sniffed noisily. 'Sounds bad to say it, but though Francis may have been born here, he was no more than a visitor, turning up like a bad penny. His father took off when he was a nipper and Barbara did her best, but on her own it was difficult, especially in them days. The last thing she did before she passed was to get young Francis into HMS *Ganges* at Shotley, the navy training place, and then there was the war. When he came back after VE day, first thing he did was sell the bungalow and put the money behind the nearest bar.'

'I hear he was fond of the demon drink,' Campion said carefully, aware that he had a Methodist looming over him.

'Far too fond, and in the end the demon got the better of him. I never thought he'd see his end out there, though.' Mr Worskitt jerked his head towards the mudflats. 'Dead in a pub doorway maybe, but not falling overboard and drowning in mud.'

The head on the fence blinked rapidly, as if rewinding the brain back to the matter in hand.

'The Jarrolds' bungalow was the last house in Wicken to come on the open market and, if memory serves, the only one this century. Houses in Wicken stay in the family. Me and Ethel got our place when my mum and dad went on before. Same with the Joneses' house and the Polleys', and the Jarmins and Buggs went half-and-half on the semi-detached when Bob Barly married George Bugg's sister Modesty. All of us is getting on a bit now, so mebbe some property will come up for sale soon.'

'My goodness,' said Campion with a smile, 'I'm surprised they bothered to run the census this year, they should just have asked you! But are there no children likely to inherit in Wicken?'

'No young 'uns any more. It's not a place you'd bring up kids, there's not a lot here.'

'Very true. There's no school for a start.'

'Never was. Nearest infants is Tillingham, but kids today won't walk that far, not like we had to. There were plenty born here over the years, but they leave and very few come back, not even to eternal rest. My wife Ethel says there's still room enough here for them of us that's left in Wicken, and then that'll be the end of it.'

'I noticed,' Campion turned and glanced over the nearest gravestones, 'that the most recent interment was some time ago.' He located his target. 'There, Theodora Jones, died in 1936.'

The head on the fence nodded gently as if agreeing with a memory. 'Theodora Jones . . .' Worskitt said dreamily, then barked a laugh. 'Theodora was Wicken's greatest export!'

'In what way?' asked Campion, genuinely curious.

'Because she left.'

'I hear stories about people of Wicken exporting themselves to America a long time ago, three hundred years ago.'

'Oh yes, I heard those stories when I was a lad, but Theodora Jones didn't go to America, at least not at first.' He paused dramatically, hinting at a far worse destination. 'She went up to London.'

Mr Campion politely expressed surprise, then indicated the grave of the 'Beloved Sister'.

'But she came back to Wicken.'

'Oh yes, she did,' said Mr Worskitt, his voice suddenly deeper, 'in the end.'

When Rupert Campion returned to his flat late that evening, after his dinner appointment at the Savoy, his brain was in turmoil, and not simply from the amount of alcohol he had consumed. The rich mixture of cocktails, wines and *digestifs* would, on an empty stomach, have felled him but, being a resting actor, Rupert had developed a ruthless trait whenever a free meal was on offer and so had greedily accepted everything placed in front of him. The instinctive lining of his stomach with absorbent material meant that he retained the use of his legs, and his arms and hands worked well enough to find change for his tube fare and to insert a key into the lock of his flat door. His brain, however, seemed fogged, and his memory of the rather bizarre evening fading fast. He knew he had to report to *someon*e on the evening's events because there was *something* he thought might be important, but quite what, he could not be sure, and he was worried he might not be able to remember in the morning.

He was relieved of any responsibility by the fact that his wife, although in bed, was sitting up, awake, alert and anxious to know how the evening with Jocasta Upcott had gone.

'She didn't turn up,' said Rupert, weaving gently towards the wardrobe to hang up his dinner jacket, a jacket which formed part of a dinner suit which he told fellow actors he had 'borrowed' from the props department of the Theatre Royal, Norwich, but had in fact been a present, via Jermyn Street, from his father on his twenty-first birthday.

'She stood you up?' Perdita, ever loyal, was outraged. 'How rude!'

'Not exactly,' said Rupert, struggling with his bow tie.

'How not exactly?'

'She never intended to come. It was her agent, Timmy Timms, who fed me dinner. He couldn't ring Maxim Berlins himself, could he? So, he got Jocasta to issue the invitation. It's just not done for one agent to poach a client from another.'

'Yes, it is,' said Perdita, 'I can think of lots of people who have changed agents.'

'But the client must make the move, the agent can't be seen to poach.'

'And you were being poached?'

'I think the offer was for both of us – well, I would have insisted on it – but the whole thing was rather bizarre. Oh, bugger!'

In trying to remove his shirt, a button had flown off across the bedroom. Perdita sighed loudly, reached under the pillow next to her and threw Rupert's pyjamas down to the end of the bed. 'How bizarre?'

'Well, for a start, Timmy Timms, who is as bald as a coot, turns up wearing a red-haired wig, so obviously a toupee it might as well have had a sign pointing to it.' Rupert exhaled with relief as he loosened the belt of his trousers. 'I thought it was him being in disguise, but all the waiters recognized him and he kept waving to people he knew across the restaurant.'

'So he wasn't ashamed to be seen with you, but what did he want?'

'He said he wanted to represent me – us – and could open doors, arrange meetings: theatres, films, telly drama, commercials, voice-overs. He would be delighted to handle me . . . I mean, handle our careers.'

'And what did you say?'

'Naturally, I said I would have to think it over carefully and, of course, I had to talk to you first.'

'Naturally, but did that take you three hours and, clearly, a lot of wine?'

Rupert staggered a pace backwards as he tried to kick off his shoes while reaching for his pyjama jacket. 'No, it didn't – take three hours, that is – but there did seem to be a lot of wine. Timmy – he insisted I call him that – wanted to know what my father was doing down in Wicken last week. Apparently he saw him talking to some policeman there and then I turn up in Chelsea with his most famous client's lost dog. He wanted to know what was going on and I'm not sure he believed me when I said I'd never been to Wicken and, as far as I knew, Pop had never been there before either; he was just doing Dame Jocasta a favour.'

'What's his obsession with Wicken?'

'I don't know. I told him about Mason Lowell and how I'd be taking him there to do his research and he seemed quite interested in that, but perhaps he was just being polite because he kept coming back to the same damned thing, which didn't make any sense.'

'What thing? And, darling, do be civilized and put those trousers on a hanger.'

'Timmy kept on and on about Pop rescuing that bloody dog Robespierre from the Dengie marshes. He made it sound like a scene from *Great Expectations*. Where had the dog come from? Where had it been?'

'As the dog belonged to his main client and she was decidedly upset when he got lost, it's no wonder Timmy Timms was worried about the beast,' said Perdita, trying to be rational and logical and not strangle her husband with his pyjama trousers, although he seemed likely to do a good job of that himself.

'But he kept asking about the other one,' said Rupert with an anguished wail.

'What other one?'

'I don't know! But he kept asking what Pop had done with the other dog. I just don't know what he was talking about.'

'Neither do I, darling, but I do know one thing. If you don't sit down to take your socks off, you're going to do a pratfall and probably knock yourself out on the skirting board, and I have absolutely no intention of picking you off the floor.'

NINE
Field Trip

'This can't be it, there's nothing here.'

'All the maps say this is Wicken,' said Mason Lowell, shaking the three open maps draped over his cramped knees as if reprimanding them.

'Perhaps you took a wrong turn,' croaked Rupert, lying scrunched up in the back seat.

'I did not take a wrong turning. Mason was navigating and I followed his directions immaculately,' said Perdita through gritted teeth.

'You sure did,' said Mason, who knew better than to disagree with his driver, especially when the driving was done on the wrong side of the road.

Mason's back hurt and his legs were cramped because he had folded his American height into the front passenger seat of Perdita's Mini Cooper. Rupert was uncomfortable in the back because he too was contorted, having foolishly told Mason to 'put his seat back' and then tried to lie at a diagonal so as not to hinder the view in Perdita's rear-view mirror, though if truth were known, most of his discomfort was down to his hangover.

'Well, that settles it,' said Perdita, applying the brake and bringing the little red car to a halt.

'What does?' asked Rupert from behind her seat.

'It's a dead end. There really is nothing here, we've run out of road, or rather the road has run out of dry land. It wasn't much of a road anyway; I don't think its heart was ever really in it.'

Rupert struggled to sit upright so that he could see the same view as Perdita and Mason through the windscreen. It was a view of damp grey-brown mud stretching as far as the eye could see until it merged with a milky sky. There was vegetation of a sort – thin grasses bending in the breeze off the sea – and overhead a few predatory gulls, but otherwise no sign of life.

'It must be that line of houses we've just driven by,' said Mason hopefully.

'One of them looked like a Methodist chapel,' said Perdita, 'and that's usually a sign of civilization of a sort.'

'We could always knock on a door and ask,' said Rupert into the rear-view mirror.

Perdita and Mason exchanged looks.

'That's not a bad idea,' said the American. 'We're lost and looking for directions.'

Perdita shook her head. 'Only a complete idiot would turn down an unmarked track heading straight for the sea. They would think that highly suspicious and probably tell us to sod off. We need to take a leaf out of Albert's book if we want to get any information out of the inhabitants. He always has a cover story; we need one.'

'We could pretend to be selling encyclopaedias,' said Rupert enthusiastically.

'Except we don't have any samples and are we sure the locals can read?'

'Oh, they'll read the Bible,' said Mason, 'you can be sure of that. If they're anything like the Harkers Island colony, there'll be a Bible in every house. How's about we become ratings people, asking what their favourite TV shows are? Everybody has a favourite show.'

'Don't be too sure round here,' said Perdita. 'I didn't notice a single television aerial on the houses in this lane.'

'We could be market researchers trying to establish who likes Corn Flakes and who prefers Sugar Puffs.' Rupert was undeterred by his wife's prominently raised eyebrow. 'Or . . . we could say we were tracing the family histories for our American friend here.'

'You mean, sort of, tell the truth?'

Perdita patted Mason's knee, which in his hunched position was conveniently at dashboard height.

'Don't look so worried, Mason. Rupert and I are actors; we get paid to fake the truth.'

Before they decanted themselves from the car, Perdita did a nifty three-point turn so that the Mini was pointed in the right direction for a quick escape should an exceptional high tide suddenly sweep in and swamp the track. It had been Rupert's suggestion, and though Perdita thought such an event unlikely, she had seen tides sweep with frightening speed into flat, sandy bays in Normandy and Brittany, and she was not prepared to risk her precious car.

It was decided that Perdita would accompany Mason while Rupert operated alone. The logic behind this was that Perdita's presence might soften the effect of Mason's American accent on the inhabitants, which they agreed was rather ironic as Mason was interested in *their* accents.

Rupert begrudgingly agreed to the arrangement, accepting that the three of them appearing together on a doorstep might be too intimidating, and that by launching a twin-pronged attack they could be finished in half the time. On the other hand, as Wicken consisted of only half a dozen houses, time pressures did not seem, well, particularly pressing.

'I'll start at this end,' Rupert volunteered, stretching his cramped legs and arching his back.

'Take this,' said Mason, handing him a small notebook from his airline shoulder bag, 'and make a note of the names of the families who live here, plus any other details they offer. Don't press them, but ask if they would be willing to talk to me at a later stage.'

'Can I tell them you're a rich American tracing his family history?' Rupert caught his wife's look of disapproval. 'I need a back story to get into character,' he offered in mitigation.

'Do I have to be rich?' asked Mason Lowell.

'It's expected.'

'Then call me Jean Paul Getty, but next time we'd better bring a bigger car.'

'Just for that, you're buying dinner tonight,' said Perdita. 'Come on, let's go to the end of the lane and work backwards. Hopefully, we'll meet in the middle.'

They set off down the lane, buttoning and zipping up their jackets against the salty breeze which only rustled the tops of the marram grass dotting the mudscape but seemed to penetrate every layer of clothing, with Rupert peeling off towards a rickety gate in the knee-high garden fence of the first house while Mason and Perdita strode on past the chapel.

The house Rupert approached up a rough brick path had no name or number, and its green door was adorned with a home-made door knocker which had started life as a horseshoe. It had been crudely soldered on to a rusty metal plate and would have been what the antique dealers would have called 'shed work', had they ever had to sell one.

The horseshoe did serve its purpose, though, and two swift raps on it produced the required result as the door was opened by an elderly bespectacled woman, encased in a cardigan the proportions of which suggested it was a hand-me-down from a giantess.

'No hawkers, no circulars, no ragmen,' she said automatically, rapping the walking stick she used to punctuate and emphasize her speech.

'I am none of those things . . .' Rupert stuttered uncertainly. 'I'm researching a family history.'

He was about to add 'for a rich American', but that particular piece of icing on the cake was not required.

'Then you'll be wanting my husband Frank,' said the woman. 'He deals with the dead. You'd better come in.'

Perdita and Mason Lowell had set of with every intention of starting their enquiries at the end of the track, as that seemed to be the limit of the parish of Wicken, if it did indeed constitute a parish, but as they passed the first house beyond the chapel, Mason came to an abrupt halt.

'Bingo!'

'What's bingo?'

'I think we may hit the jackpot with our first cold-call,' said Mason with a boyish grin. 'Look at the name of this place.'

Perdita read the wooden sign above the front door, a piece of driftwood into which the words Abigail Cottage had been roughly burned with a hot poker.

'Captain Waudby's ship was the *Abigail*,' she said, thinking aloud. 'It could be just a coincidence.'

'Let's find out,' said Mason, stretching his long legs into a gait which Perdita found impossible to match except by actually running to keep up, until the tall American loomed over the door of the cottage and, with an unexpected delicacy, knocked politely on it.

As with Rupert's experience forty yards away and two minutes earlier, a Wicken door was opened by a Wicken female, a slender, white-haired woman tall enough not to suffer from neck strain as she examined Mason's eager face.

'I'm sorry to bother you, but I'm here in Wicken to trace some old family names and I – we – hoped you might help.'

'I will do my best,' said the woman. 'Do come in, I've been expecting you.'

As two front doors closed behind the three visitors to Wicken, three others opened to allow three men to leave their dwellings and make their way furtively to a fourth door which opened to welcome them in.

'My name's Mason Lowell Clay and this is Perdita Campion, and you cannot possibly have been expecting me.'

'Well, perhaps not you specifically, Mr Clay, but I certainly saw someone coming from America. My name is Jones, by the way, please do come in and have some tea.'

Mason stood aside to give way to Perdita and, as she squeezed by him into the cottage, he lowered his head to ear height and whispered, 'Double bingo!'

'We don't want to put you to any trouble, Mrs Jones,' said Perdita as the woman ushered them into a very snug, well-appointed living room.

'No trouble at all, and it's Miss Jones, by the way, Sylvia Jones.'

'Eureka!' said Mason.

'Eureka? Please take a seat and explain. Anywhere, but not there.'

The room, warmed by a glowing coal fire, was comfortably furnished with a small sofa and two armchairs in floral pattern chintz, a low coffee table and a small bookcase. The only incongruous item was a four-legged stool made by cutting the back off a sturdy dining room chair, which stood on its own square of white rug laid over the red carpet. It was this seat which Miss Jones had advised her guests from taking; neither objected and both settled for the sofa.

'Can I offer you tea?'

'No, thank you,' said Perdita, 'we have no wish to disrupt your life any more than we have already.'

'Visitors in Wicken are rare, but hardly disruptive,' said Miss Jones with a smile. 'We are somewhat off the beaten track.'

'You can say that again. Tracks don't come much more unbeaten than the one outside. We weren't sure we'd found you – there don't seem to be any signs to Wicken.'

'Who would want to come here? Apart from Americans tracing their history? I take it the name Abigail Cottage was what drew you to my door. Was that your Eureka moment?'

Mason began to fumble in his shoulder bag, eventually producing a leather-bound notebook and pen. While he was distracted, Perdita tried to assess their hostess.

Miss Jones was, she estimated, in her mid-sixties, and her clothes were clearly of the highest quality. She wore the minimum of make-up to mask the weathering which naturally occurred when living near a windswept coast; her nails were unpolished but manicured and she wore a string of white pearls around her neck. The plaid skirt, pink shirt, white cashmere cardigan and dark tan stockings with sensible low-heeled court shoes could have been the uniform of any middle-class Englishwoman of that 'certain age' officiating at a garden party or church fete, but instead of the blue-rinse perm which would have completed the picture, Miss Jones's white hair had been cut short, almost brutally, in masculine style but with a right-hand parting. It was the one aspect of unconventionality about her demeanour and would have knocked years off her age to the untrained eye, but Perdita, who had often played the dowager older woman (not to mention scullery maids, waitresses and, once, a corpse) on stage, regarded her eye as well-trained in such matters.

Mason opened his notebook on his knees and delved into his inside jacket pocket for a pen. Perdita could not help but notice that his hands were shaking with excitement and, from the smile on her face, Miss Jones had also.

'I cannot deny that it was the name of your cottage which caught my eye,' Mason began, 'because I have spent two years researching a ship of that name.'

'That would be the famous *Abigail* which carried the Billericay Covenanters to the New World. You look surprised, Mr Clay. Americans are very keen on tracing their family origins and their English roots, although most seem to prefer to find Scottish or

Irish roots. They seem much more interested in our history than we are sometimes, and you are certainly not the first researcher to struggle as far as Wicken to ask about the Billericay Covenant; in fact hardly a summer goes by without someone knocking on the front door and asking me about the *Abigail*'s passengers.'

'Why do they pick on you?'

'The fact that this house is called what it is draws them like moths to a flame and they are invariably disappointed when I tell them that this cottage was built a hundred and fifty years *after* the *Abigail* sailed and the connection is probably no more than coincidence. Although quite a few Americans do turn up here because they've read about my sister.'

'Your sister?'

'My late sister, Theodora. She died before the war, far too young; about your age, Miss . . .?'

'Campion,' said Perdita, 'and it's Mrs not Miss.'

Miss Jones conceded the point with a slight nod, then clasped her hands in her lap.

'What did they read about your sister?' Mason pressed her.

'Theodora was what you might call a late-flowering suffragette. She was too young for the really militant wave of the Votes for Women campaign and really only took up the cause after 1918—'

'When women actually got the vote?' Perdita interrupted.

'*Some* women, and only if they were over thirty and owned property or had a university degree, at a time when few universities gave degrees to women. It wasn't until 1928 that women could vote at the same age as men, twenty-one, and without a property qualification, but the anomaly was that although women between twenty-one and thirty could not vote, they could stand for election as an MP.'

'That's insane,' breathed Perdita.

Mason, being neither British nor female, wisely remained quiet.

'Of course it was, and my sister the young firebrand complained loudly about it and tried several times to stand in by-elections. She was inspired by a woman called Ellen Wilkinson, who was elected for Labour somewhere up north. She was elected as an MP but could not herself vote in an election because, as she so succinctly put it, she had "neither husband nor furniture".

Theodora wanted to emulate her. Not her political stance, of course, Theodora was far more sensible, but she became quite a campaigner for the rights of women. She would have been in the vanguard of that demonstration in London this March, the one that called for the liberation of women.'

'And she wrote a book about it all?' asked Mason.

'No, she never wrote a book,' answered a puzzled Miss Jones.

'But you said Americans had read about her.'

'Theodora was young, intelligent and very attractive, something of a darling with the newspapers and magazines, especially in America, where she went on a lecture tour at the invitation of some women's groups in Boston round about 1926. One newspaper even suggested she might have a career in the movies, but I suspect they said that about any young woman who could attract publicity. Every speech she made was quoted widely as the voice of the thinking woman, but what really boosted her popularity in New England, if not old England, was that some of her – our – ancestors had emigrated to Massachusetts on the *Abigail*.'

'Henry and Silence Jones,' said Mason, without the need to consult his notebook.

'So I believe. Their story was part of our family history, or rather I should say folklore, as is the name of this house. It was very naughty of Theodora to play on it because Jones is a very common name, and I doubt she could *prove* the Joneses on the *Abigail* were distant relatives; I certainly could not. The good people of Massachusetts, however, were delighted that this fierce young radical might be a true daughter of the American colonies, and they treated her most royally.'

'I'm surprised I've not come across her,' said Mason, 'but then I'm more of a seventeenth-century man.'

'Most men are,' said Miss Jones, which drew a smile from Perdita.

'What I mean is that my research is focused on identifying the passengers on the *Abigail* who came from Wicken.'

'The Billericay Covenanters.'

'Exactly.'

'Well, as you rightly say, there was a Henry Jones and his wife on board, but whether they were definitely ancestors of my family, I couldn't say.'

'But you live in Wicken.'

'Obviously, but clearly this house does not date back to sixteen-whatever-it-was. Jones is a very common name in England, Mr Clay, and I cannot honestly claim any relationship with the Joneses who settled in Massachusetts – unless of course there is a long-lost spinster cousin on a deathbed in Boston who has a fortune to leave.'

'Salem,' said Mason.

'Pardon?'

'The *Abigail* landed at Salem, not Boston.'

'Where the witch trials were? How interesting.'

'I thought so,' said Mason, 'which is one reason why I'm interested in tracing the passengers on the ship. Several of them turn up in the records of the Massachusetts colony, but those families who had signed up to the Billericay contract, and there were thirteen of them, seem more difficult to trace.'

'I'm not sure how I can help.'

Mason consulted his notebook. 'Do any of these names mean anything to you? Whybrow, Stow, Poynter?'

'Not a thing,' said Miss Jones.

'Gladwell? Astley? Jones?'

'Obviously, but as I say, it's a very common name.'

'Lux?'

'Lux? As in the soap powder?'

'I don't know what that is,' said Mason, 'but the name is L-U-X.'

Miss Jones shook her head. 'Munson? Barly? Gurnham? Firmin? Waudby?'

'I'm sorry, Mr Clay, but I thought I had made it clear that my knowledge of the *Abigail* is based on romantic stories passed down through the family, not on any sort of historical research. I don't think anyone in the family took them at all seriously before Theodora went to America and some journalist there mentioned the connection when she said she came from Wicken. Not that she spent much time here; Theodora couldn't wait to get out of the place.'

'She was your older sister?' Perdita asked.

'Four years older.'

'And she died young, you said.'

'She was thirty-six. She never got to be a radical Member of Parliament, but at least she got to vote in two or three elections.'

'She sounds a fascinating person,' said Mason, anxious to get back to his subject matter, 'and I'm sure there's a research paper in her story, but I'm afraid my work is limited to colonial history. My job is to trace those families who signed the Billericay Covenant.'

'Surely the best place to do that is America, isn't it? Going there was the whole point of the Covenant.'

'I am interested in their origins, who they were, where they came from, so I'm over here to look up any records which still exist.'

'You won't find any in Wicken.'

'Not even the church?'

'We have a chapel, not a church, and it dates from the nineteenth century, long after the *Abigail* sailed. There is the County Records Office in Chelmsford, I suppose, but I have no idea if there's anything there. I'm sorry not to be of more help, Mr Clay, as I really like the idea of some of my ancestors crossing the ocean to find a new life in America. It was actually a common thing to do for religious dissenters in East Anglia, so it is possible that the Joneses on the *Abigail* really were distant relatives of mine – the romantic in me would like to think so – but I couldn't prove it.'

'Perhaps we should start with the official record,' said Perdita, locking eyes with Mason.

'Once again, I'm sorry not to have been more help.'

'No, thank you for your time, Miss Jones. It was fascinating talking with you and you must excuse us for dropping in on you out of the blue like we did.'

'What a charming accent,' said Miss Jones. 'You are from the South?'

'I most surely am, ma'am.'

Perdita hoped he was not laying it on too thick.

'From the great state of Georgia, though my work takes me to North Carolina and Massachusetts.'

'And now Wicken. That's quite a journey, just like the one those pilgrims from Billericay made all those years ago.'

'Wicken,' said Mason automatically. 'The Covenanters all came from Wicken.'

'Of course. It was probably a much larger place in the seventeenth century, though there would have been even less to induce young people to stay than there is today. We are rather isolated and not big on community activities. People keep themselves to themselves out here on the peninsula.'

'I suppose you must have to make your own entertainment,' said Perdita sweetly. 'For instance, there is no village pub, is there?'

'Methodists don't drink, as a rule,' said Miss Jones rather primly.

'Is everyone in Wicken a Methodist?'

'Not any more; neither the chapel nor the graveyard has been in regular use for several years.'

Miss Jones noted both the sudden glint in Mason's eyes at the word 'graveyard' and the rapid scribble he made in his notebook.

'If you want to know more about the chapel, call in on Frank Worskitt in the house on the other side. He looks after the graveyard when it needs looking after, and his family have been in Wicken for ever. You might find some useful names on the gravestones, Mr Clay. You'll certainly find Jones. My parents were buried there, and my sister subsequently joined them.'

'We may well do just that,' said Perdita as she stood up, 'but for now we'll leave you in peace.'

'May we come back if I have any more questions, please?' asked Mason, shaking her hand.

'By all means,' said Miss Jones, 'I'm usually here or, if not, I'm out walking on the marsh.'

'Isn't that dangerous?' asked Perdita as she allowed herself to be shown to the door.

'Not if you watch for the tides and know where to put your feet.'

'I understand there was a fatal accident around here last week.'

'Yes, most unfortunate. Some poor chap from a yacht that had run aground. Foolish man tried to walk to land in the dark. I don't know what business he had sailing so close to the coast in the first place. Tragic, really quite tragic.'

Outside on the track, Mason turned and waved to Miss Jones as she closed the door of the cottage on them.

'What a nice lady,' he said as they walked to the Mini Cooper.

'She's a liar,' said Perdita.

'*What?*'

'When you read out the names of the passengers on the *Abigail*, she said she'd never heard of any them, but she reacted as if she'd been stung when you said Barly.'

Mason looked down at her in disbelief. 'But she didn't move a muscle!'

'Oh yes she did, you weren't watching her fingers. She was cool, calm and collected throughout, except when you said Barly, and then her hands clenched like she'd had an electric shock. She twitched again exactly when you said your work took you to North Carolina.'

'And you noticed these twitches?'

'Of course I did. I'm an actress; I have to observe people and learn their little foibles and traits, so I can use them.'

'Wow! Remind me never to play poker with an actress.'

'I surely will,' said Perdita, copying Mason's Southern drawl, 'but I wasn't the only actress in there.'

'You're gonna have to explain that one, slowly and with small words, please.'

'As we were leaving, all that "Tragic, really tragic" stuff about the dead man from the yacht, that was completely fake.'

'It sounded sincere to me,' said Mason, his lower lip jutting out.

Perdita poked him in the chest with a forefinger. 'My point exactly. If you can fake sincerity, you're an actress. And here's Rupert, the light of my life, the very soul of my being.' Perdita turned and gave Mason a full-face grin. 'See, it's easy if you know how.'

'Good timing,' said Rupert, striding across from the chapel. 'How did it go?'

'It was interesting,' said Mason, 'but not conclusive. You?'

'Well, at first I thought I'd found gold as the old man there looks after the graveyard at the back of the chapel. He seemed to know everybody and everything in Wicken, but his wife, a wizened little crone who threatened him with her walking stick every five minutes, told him not to be a tittle-tattler, so he hardly got a word in edgewise.'

'Did you get any names?'

'Well, I got theirs – Frank and Ethel Worskitt – and a bit of family history.'

'There was no Worskitt on the *Abigail*,' said Mason.

Rupert waved his notebook proudly under the American's nose. 'And the house you went to belongs to a Miss Jones, Sylvia Jones.'

'We've been chatting to her for the last half-hour,' said Perdita. 'I'll tell you about it later. What now?'

'There are four more locations to try,' said Mason, 'starting with that ranch-style house next to the Jones property.'

'We call them bungalows.' Perdita laughed.

Rupert consulted his notebook. 'And that, I can tell you, is the home of Mary Ann Allen, except she's not home, she's at work. The awful Ethel Worskitt took great delight in telling me that.'

'Then we try the split house next along,' said Mason.

'And that's what we call a semi-detached, so it's two houses.'

'Then that's two birds with one stone. What are we waiting for?'

The trio had not gone more than three or four paces when another trio appeared on the lane at the far end, clearly having come out of the last house. That trio, all men dressed in dark workmen's clothing and gumboots, spread themselves across the lane and marched in unison slowly towards the three visitors, two of whom automatically slowed their pace.

'Hi there!' yelled Mason, raising an arm in salutation, only to realize that his greeting was not going to be returned, that he was now two yards ahead of Perdita and Rupert, and that Perdita was gripping her car keys tightly in a fist.

Opposite the bungalow the two groups stopped dead, some twenty feet apart, and glared at each other. The scene reminded Rupert of wet afternoons on the school rugby pitch when the six unluckiest boys were picked for scrum practice. He thought he, and certainly Mason, might acquit themselves well enough – they were both much younger, fitter and taller than the three weather-beaten figures on the other team – but there was Perdita to consider, and silently he willed her to run back to the car.

Of course, no such thought entered Perdita's head. 'Good day to you,' she declared loudly in her I-will-be-heard-in-the-upper-circle voice. 'We are conducting a survey of—'

'There's nobody home,' said the middle man of the trio, shaking his head.

'Yes, we know, so we thought we'd try the next house along.'

'There's nobody home there either,' said Middle Man, expressionless.

'Or the next 'un,' said the man to his left, deadpan. 'Can't be, we're all here.'

'Then perhaps we could talk to you,' said Mason.

'Tell the foreigner we're too busy for claptrap,' said Left-Hand to Middle Man.

'Or perhaps we could come back some other time,' said Mason, his accent suddenly thickening, 'but we sure thank y'all for your down-home hospitality of the kind I ain't seen since that shown to General Sedgwick.'

Taking their cue, Rupert and Perdita turned and strode quickly back to the Mini. Mason followed and squashed himself into the passenger seat with as much dignity as he could muster.

The three men in the lane stood silently to one side as Perdita drove by them, all three pairs of eyes watching the Mini as it turned out of the lane and on to the narrow road to Dengie.

Only when all trace of Wicken and its inhabitants had vanished from her rear-view mirror did Perdita exhale loudly, then turn on Mason. 'Just who the hell is General Sedgwick?'

'He was a Civil War general,' said Mason, 'who chastised his troops for flinching while under enemy rifle. He told his men to stand up and stop cowering because the Confederate snipers "couldn't hit an elephant from that distance". Those were his very last words.'

TEN
Doctor's Orders

The first surprise for Mr Campion that morning was breakfast. He had thought that an establishment called The Oyster Shack might offer some form of seafood, though he had not expected, on the nightly tariff charged by Mrs Young, anything as grand as Oysters Rockefeller. On that score he was not disappointed, but he was surprised when he was presented with what Mrs Young announced proudly as 'Grapefruit Maritime': half a grapefruit with a single prawn standing to attention in the centre, drizzled with a teaspoonful of a bright red sauce which, on a tentative tasting, Campion decided was salad cream coloured with cochineal.

The exotic was followed almost immediately by the literal definition of the full English breakfast, for it was very full indeed and could have been used to break several fasts. Mr Campion would certainly have settled for a single fried egg, fewer button mushrooms (tinned), two fewer rashers of bacon, and abjured the sausages, fried bread (both slices) and baked beans entirely, but did not want to offend his hostess who had clearly slaved in a hot kitchen for her one and only guest.

His second surprise of the morning was that he was saved by the bell, a telephone bell, and the call was for him. Mrs Young informed him, in hushed terms so they could not be picked up by the receiver, that she would put his plate in the oven to keep warm while he took the call. She was so reverential, though whether towards the breakfast or the telephone call was not clear, that Campion was not surprised to see her back out of the room as if leaving a royal audience.

With relief he broke from the shackles of the breakfast table and strode into the hall, where the telephone had a place of honour on a small shelf. There was no chair in sight and the hallway was draughty, presumably both factors designed to make guests keep their calls short.

'Hello, is that Campion? Albert Campion?'

'It is indeed.'

'Harry Fathoms here, hoping you might remember him.'

'*Doctor* Fathoms?'

'For my sins. I saw you out on the peninsula last week but didn't get a chance to speak to you.'

'You were otherwise engaged in a professional capacity, I believe.'

'Yes, duty called, I'm afraid. A bad business.'

'It looked it,' said Campion. 'May I ask how you found me at this number and, more to the point, why?'

'Tom Trybull, the police sergeant over at Maldon, told me you were snooping around the area and, frankly, there aren't too many places to stay, so he guessed at The Oyster Shack, which is popular with birdwatchers.'

'So I understand. Anyway, now you've found me, what can I do for you?'

'I'll be straight with you, Campion, because I know your reputation, and because I've talked with Sergeant Trybull. If you have an interest in the death of Francis Jarrold, then I think we should talk. If I am mistaken, then I apologize and will let you get back to your breakfast.'

'Oh, please don't do that,' said Campion quietly in case he was being overheard in the kitchen, through the door which had been left suspiciously ajar. 'I admit I am intrigued rather than professionally interested, you understand. I have absolutely no status other than as unofficial Nosey Parker.'

'It was ever thus from what I hear,' said Dr Fathoms, 'and I should say that I too am acting unofficially, though on the advice of Sergeant Trybull. He tells me you showed an interest in the death of Francis Jarrold. In fact, you seem to be the only person who has.'

'There's no family?'

'None has come forward and, as it seemed to be a straightforward accidental death, no one seems particularly interested in the findings of my autopsy, apart from Tom Trybull.'

'Who thought I might be too?'

'Exactly. Are you? I have no wish to burden a busy man.'

'Then you've come to the right man, doctor, for my trusty Boy Scouts' diary is blissfully blank at the moment, so you will not be a burden at all, though I get the feeling you want to *un*burden yourself.'

'You could say that. Is there any chance you could come to my surgery here in Southminster later this morning? I should be able to get away for lunch around twelve thirty.'

'I can do that,' said Campion, relieved that the doctor had not suggested meeting in a mortuary or over a dissecting table, 'but how do I find you?'

'Ask Mrs Young,' said Fathoms cheerfully. 'She knows how to get here; she's one of my patients.' There was a pregnant pause before he added: 'Has she given you one of her breakfasts?'

'Yes.'

'Then my expert medical advice is to walk here. You'll need the exercise.'

Dr Harry Fathoms, as Lugg would have said, lived above the shop, in that his practice surgery occupied the front two ground-floor rooms of his large detached house: a waiting room to the right, the doctor's examination room to the left. In the hallway in the middle, sitting behind a desk, a white-coated nurse acted as receptionist, shepherdess of patients and, as is always the case, something of a sergeant major.

Campion almost snapped to attention when he was asked if he had an appointment, and his rather flippant response that he was the last of the doctor's list that morning did not go down well. No, he had to admit, he wasn't actually registered with Dr Fathoms as an NHS patient, it was more a *private* matter, stressing the word in the hope he would be deliberately misunderstood. The receptionist sniffed loudly and told him he would have to wait his turn, and was far from impressed when Campion said that was exactly what he had intended to do.

When the last legitimate patient had left and Campion was alone in the waiting room with only an old copy of *Punch* to distract him, the receptionist announced that the doctor would see him now.

'Sorry to keep you waiting, Campion.'

Dr Fathoms stood at a small corner sink washing his hands, before proffering one in greeting. He wore a fawn three-piece suit, crisp white shirt and the bow tie, which was obligatory, in Campion's experience, for professions where a dangling tie might be an inconvenience if not a hazard: doctors, surgeons and snooker players, to name but three.

'Not a problem, Doctor. I would hate to think I had jumped a queue of genuinely sick patients.'

'I wouldn't worry about that; Mary Ann would never allow it.'

'Your receptionist? I'm sure she's not as fierce as she likes to think she is.'

'Oh, yes, she is,' said Dr Fathoms without smiling, 'all medical receptionists are. They are trained on a regime of harsh language and dragon's blood. Now make yourself comfortable, while I tell you what's on my mind.'

Campion indicated the surgical bed and folded screens against one wall. 'Not there. I'm not going to examine you. Take the chair.'

'That's a relief,' said Campion, sitting as Dr Fathoms took his more comfortable leather-padded captain's chair on the other side of his desk, after clearing away a stethoscope and a blood-pressure cuff. 'At my age, I don't pass many exams.'

'And I much prefer to give them to living patients, which is why Francis Jarrold troubled me.'

'You found something troubling?'

'I did.'

'And the police were not interested, but you thought I would be.'

Dr Fathoms cleared his throat, the doctor's standard preamble to delivering bad news.

'They were not so much uninterested as unmotivated to take any action. Jarrold had no relatives, nobody claiming his body or taking an interest in his estate, though I think there's little enough there; plus the fact that his death had all the hallmarks of accidental death. I've sent samples off for analysis, but I'm pretty sure his blood will show a considerable level of alcohol.'

'Being drunk would explain him running his boat aground and the fact that he left an almost incoherent log of his last journey,' said Campion, crossing his long legs. 'It would also explain why he thought he could walk on water, or at least liquid mud, and he came a cropper. Large quantities of alcohol can induce a sense of invincibility as well as bad decision-making – or so I'm told. He got stuck, fell flat on his face, and drowned.' Campion tried to judge the doctor's expression. 'Didn't he?'

'I am just a run-of-the-mill GP, Campion, who occasionally does work to help the police. I am no forensics expert but I try to do a thorough job with the skills at my disposal, and I noticed something I could not explain almost as soon as the body had been washed.'

The doctor placed his forearms on the desktop and his fingers began a rhythmic drumming motion, conjuring an image in Campion's mind of two large spiders on a hotplate. The right spider then jumped and landed on the back of the doctor's neck.

'There was a mark, just there, top of the spine, bottom of the skull; not a puncture wound, more a bruise.'

'Not the traditional blunt instrument by any chance?' Campion asked, hoping he did not sound too enthusiastic.

'No, I don't think so. The mark was round and about the size of the old half-crown. Remember them? Or have you gone decimal?'

'One has to move with the times, Doctor, but I admit to still thinking in old money. What made the mark?'

'I don't know. The only thing I've seen like it was the most bizarre thing I thought I'd ever see. Again, that was a police matter. Chap on a train, travelling first class of course, celebrating something or other with his wife, got hit right between the eyes with a champagne cork from a distance of about twelve inches. Died instantly and the wife was arrested for murder. She got off, though, as it was declared accidental, which was correct. It gave rise to some black humour about famous last words such as, "Let me open it, darling, you're doing it wrong". Not the sort of thing you want on your gravestone.'

'Indeed not,' said Campion. 'The epitaph I dread is, "Don't tell me how to change a fuse, woman" – but let us not get distracted. Are you telling me that Jarrold was hit by . . . by *something* which incapacitated him, apart from the booze in his system, so that he just lay down and drowned?'

'I don't think he drowned, although there was water in his lungs. I think he was somehow held face down and he suffocated in the mud. Of course, a full post-mortem by an experienced pathologist would be required to prove anything.'

'Such as murder?' Campion straightened in his chair. 'Really?'

'It may have been nothing of the sort, but it niggled me, perhaps because it wasn't the only odd thing about Jarrold's body.'

'What else did you find, Harry?'

'A bite mark, on the back of his right thigh. It had scabbed over so it wasn't fresh, but it was a recent wound. It could explain his irrational behaviour, what prompted him to jump off the ship and plough his way through the mud.'

Campion squirmed in his chair, suddenly on edge and ill at ease. 'A bite mark, you say. He'd been bitten by something?'

'By something with rabies,' said Dr Fathoms confidently. 'Almost certainly a dog.'

'Are you sure, Doctor?'

'I can't be one hundred per cent sure, but it could be an explanation for his behaviour. It can take anything from three weeks to three months for the symptoms to take hold after being bitten by a rabid animal. The disease comes from the animal's saliva, by the way.'

Mr Campion winced, but Fathoms continued with professional enthusiasm. 'Assuming Jarrold was bitten, he would have noticed a high temperature, then a fever coupled with feelings of anxiety. He would have muscle spasms and difficulty swallowing – ironically frustrating for a hardened drinker. And then he would become very confused and suffer hallucinations. A man with those symptoms, after two days of hard sailing across the Channel with little if any sleep, plus whatever alcohol he'd managed to get down his throat . . . well, that man might well do something stupid and jump overboard. Those mudflats and quicksands near Wicken are treacherous at the best of times, but at night in a delirious state, positively lethal.'

'Has anyone suggested suicide?'

'Not seriously. If Francis Jarrold wanted to end himself, then the easiest way would surely to have been to jump overboard halfway across the Channel.'

'But your theory is accidental death while his mental state was affected by rabies?' Campion asked gently.

'That is certainly one theory,' said Fathoms, hinting that it was not the only one, 'and it leaves us with one outstanding problem.'

'Robespierre,' said Mr Campion, nodding sagely.

'Are you feeling all right, Campion? You seem to be wandering off the point.'

'Apologies, Doctor. Robespierre is the dog who found Jarrold's body. I had him returned to his owner at the weekend, when he seemed in tip-top condition, shiny coat once the mud was washed off, wet nose, tail wagging madly and absolutely no foaming at the mouth. I will take it upon myself to inform the owner of our concern and make sure the dog is thoroughly checked by a vet. Is there anything we, or the police, could or should be doing in Wicken?'

'I'm afraid the police are not willing to take my suspicions seriously until more tests are completed. Jarrold didn't die of rabies – he died by inhaling mud until he couldn't breathe, and no one has reported a rabid dog roaming the Dengie marshes. They are convinced that his irrational decision to try and walk across the mudflats was brought on by alcoholic befuddlement.'

Campion supressed a grin. 'I do like that term, though I suspect it's not an approved medical condition. You are sure in your mind that it could have been the effects of rabies?'

'Hallucinations, disorientations, confusion – all symptoms which emerge after a bite from an infected animal.'

'Symptoms which develop after how long?'

'That can vary, but usually at least three weeks, often longer.'

'Then I think Robespierre is almost certainly innocent, but we will have to check his movements of late, as well as Jarrolds's. What about other animals?'

The doctor shrugged his shoulders. 'You can get rabies from any infected mammals – bat, fox, cat, goat, cow or sheep – but mostly dogs. Funnily enough, there's never been a case from being bitten by a rat in this country.'

'Forgive me if I take little comfort in knowing that. I was thinking of other animals in the Wicken-Dengie area. Somebody mentioned that there were no dogs in Wicken – the farmer's wife, that's who it was. Where our young birdwatcher friend – Graham Roberts? – took Robespierre and used the phone to call you.'

'That would be Mrs Laverick, and you have just reminded me that I should check on Graham Roberts, as he's my patient, to ask if he was bitten, just in case. I'm not too worried about the Lavericks as they're farmers and should know all the risks. But as to any livestock in Wicken, I have no idea, but we could always ask our resident expert on all things Wicken.'

Campion peered over the top of his spectacles. 'I'm sorry . . .'

'My scary receptionist, Mary Ann. She lives there. I'll ask her to join us.'

As with most medical receptionists, Mary Ann Allen appeared far less frightening in person than she did when at action stations behind her desk, a position from which she commanded all she surveyed. Under the strip lighting in Dr Fathoms's office, her features looked less sharp and her white nurse's uniform less starched on a slim, well-proportioned figure. Campion put her age at around fifty and thought he detected a natural intelligence behind her pale blue eyes, perhaps an intelligence which felt it could be better employed than behind a receptionist's desk.

'Mary Ann, this is Albert Campion, who is helping me with a few points concerning the death of Francis Jarrold. I have no intention of breaking patient confidentiality, but we can speak freely in front of him.'

Campion shook the firm, dry hand offered while taking a surreptitious glance to note the absence of a wedding ring. 'Mary Ann Allen, isn't it?'

The woman's eyes flashed towards Dr Fathoms.

'I heard your name in Wicken only yesterday,' Campion continued quickly, 'but never thought I would meet you here on doctor's orders, as it were.'

'You were in Wicken asking about me?' she said sharply, as if to a patient without an appointment, old habits dying hard.

'Not at all, Miss Allen. I was sightseeing and fell into conversation with an elderly gentleman called Worskitt, who seemed very knowledgeable about the residents of Wicken.'

Realization dawned behind those blue-grey eyes, but her face did not soften. 'Oh, yes, Frank Worskitt knows everything that goes on in Wicken, or thinks he does; and it is Mrs Allen, by the way, though I am a widow. I'm surprised Frank Worskitt didn't add that little titbit. Ethel would have, as she doesn't approve of a woman living alone.'

'I presume Ethel is Mrs Worskitt, and I didn't have the pleasure of meeting her, only her husband, and that only over the garden fence. I remembered your name because you live in a house previously owned by Francis Jarrold.'

'He didn't own it for long,' said the woman, as if teaching a class of infants. 'He inherited it when his parents passed away and couldn't sell it fast enough. My late husband was a soldier, based in Colchester, and was coming to the end of his enlistment. He knew the Dengie Peninsula and wanted to live there, but then he was sent to Malaya where he was killed by the Communist insurgents. I was left with a small pension and a bungalow at the back of beyond, so I decided to just get on with life.'

'Mary Ann is a natural-born nurse,' said Fathoms, 'and could have been a doctor. Should have been.'

'That's nice of you to say so, Doctor, but what's past is past.' She consulted the watch pinned to her uniform bib. 'I would remind you that I am officially on my lunch break, so how can I help you gentlemen?'

'You've lived in Wicken for quite some time, Mrs Allen,' said Campion.

'Since 1949, so that's twenty-two years almost.'

'And you know everybody there?'

'There are not that many people to know in Wicken itself, and we all tend to keep to ourselves. Just what is it you're asking, Mr Campion?'

'This may sound bizarre, but do any of your neighbours keep pets?'

Mary Ann Allen took a mental step backwards, shaking her head slightly before she answered. 'There are a few cats around; some keep chickens, if you can call them pets, and Joshua Jarmin has a few sheep which he raises as salt-marsh lamb. So does Robert Barly, I think.'

'Cats but no dogs? Isn't that strange?'

'Cats keep down mice and rats,' said Mary Ann automatically, 'and are happy wandering wild. They're feral rather than pets and don't require maintenance. Dogs are loyal pets and those of a certain religious persuasion abjure pets "less they be taken familiar", as they say.'

'Is Wicken strongly Methodist? I wasn't aware that Methodists were against dogs.'

'I don't think they are. I think it goes back to the Puritans; the Methodist chapel is only about a hundred years old. There were dissenters in Wicken before then and some funny habits persisted.'

'Are you yourself . . .?' Campion's question trailed off under Mary Ann's steely glare.

'I'm Church of England and a regular worshipper at St James's in Dengie.'

'And the other God-fearing members of the population?'

'I suppose they went to the chapel once, but it is not visited these days apart from Frank Worskitt, who sort of looks after it. For a long time, it's been a useful place to bury the dead – so many families will have claimed to be Methodists even if they only attended a service on high days and feast days – except Methodists don't have them, do they?'

'I am no expert on religious ritual,' conceded Campion, 'but you did say there were some "funny habits" among the residents. What did you mean by that?'

'Perhaps I should have said quirks,' said Mary Ann. 'No one has a television and I have the only radio. I don't miss the goggle-box but I couldn't live without the BBC, and I'm the only one in Wicken with a car and a telephone.'

'Then you must be very popular.'

'I am at times, especially when it comes to doing the shopping for some of the residents if they can't walk to Dengie or Tillingham to catch one of our very infrequent buses.'

'You shop for the whole village?'

'No, mostly for Frank and Ethel Worskitt and also Richard Polley and his sister Octavia. All of them are over eighty, if not ninety in Frank's case. Joshua Jarmin does have a tractor and trailer and he and his mates will drive it into Burnham to load up with supplies once a month, though I'm not sure it's taxed for driving on the highway.'

'I'm not a policeman.' Campion smiled.

'What exactly are you, Mr Campion?'

'I'm a sort of researcher, or rather the advance guard for a proper, academic researcher. He's an American, a jolly nice chap called Mason Lowell Clay and he is over here tracing the family names in Wicken. I take it you know them all?'

'There aren't many to know: Polley, Jarmin, Bugg, Barly, Jones and Worskitt. There were Jarrolds, of course, but they're all gone now.'

'There seem to be – and please forgive me – no young people in Wicken.'

'There aren't and, when we are gone, the place will probably die completely. Young families are not exactly hammering on our doors asking to buy property there. Of course, there *were* babies born in Wicken. I believe Francis Jarrold was one.'

Dr Fathoms nodded sagely in agreement. 'And then there was Wicken's most famous citizen, Theodora Jones.'

'The campaigner for equal voting rights for women?' exclaimed Campion.

'You've heard of her?'

'I once heard her speak, around the time of the General Strike. Her view was that if women had parity with men in the franchise, things would not have got into such a state, and who's to say she was wrong? She was speaking at a Cambridge college. I forget which but I do recall the audience, all male of course, treated her abysmally. I saw her grave at the chapel yesterday but didn't put two and two together. Frank Worskitt said something about her moving away from Wicken, but never mentioned it was *the* Theodora Jones.'

'He wouldn't. Theodora went out into the big bad world and that's just not done among the locals, unless they were men and called up for a war. Many didn't come back. There's a war memorial with their names on it in the chapel, but I suspect quite a few weren't missing in action; once they were out of Wicken they just kept running.'

'Her gravestone inscription said only that she was a "beloved sister", which is odd as she was buried with her parents. One would have expected "beloved daughter" perhaps.'

'It was well before my time in Wicken, but it could have been her sister who brought her home to be buried. She still lives in Wicken.'

'Sylvia Jones,' offered Dr Fathoms, adding in explanation, 'another of my patients; not that my Wicken patients need my medical expertise very often. They seem to look after themselves.'

'Yes, they do,' said Mary Ann, 'and they look after each other. Silence Jones even cuts their hair so they don't have to leave the place to go to the hairdresser or the barber.'

'Silence?' queried Mr Campion.

'Sylvia Jones. Her real name is Silence but she goes by Sylvia.'

'What a curious name.'

'It is, especially for a hairdresser. Whoever heard of a silent hairdresser? Part of their job is being chatty – too chatty sometimes.'

Campion laughed politely. 'Something I have been accused of in the past, and now I am conscious that I am eating into your lunch break. Would you mind awfully if I gave your name to the young, very dashing, American academic who is interested in researching some of the old families in Wicken?'

Mary Ann looked surprised but weighed up the suggestion for only the briefest of moments. 'If I can help at all, I will, as long as it is out of surgery hours.' She glanced at the doctor, who acknowledged her condition with a nod of approval.

'Thank you so much,' said Campion.

Mrs Allen rose to leave but stopped at the office door, her hand on the handle, when Dr Fathoms said, 'I hope your American chum has an open mind, Campion. They're an odd lot out at Wicken, you know.'

The doctor spoke with his best patient-comforting smile, but Mary Ann replied in all seriousness. 'The doctor is right, Mr Campion, we're all oddities out on the peninsula.'

'But I like oddities!' Campion gave her his most inane grin. 'In fact, I collect them. Look what I found yesterday on Francis Jarrold's yacht.'

Campion delved into his jacket pocket and produced the medicine bottle containing rusty nails and twigs which he had found on the *Jocasta*, holding it out at arm's length.

'I doubt you prescribed this for Francis, doc. There again, it might not have been his.'

'Oh, it was his,' said Mary Ann Allen solemnly. 'It's a witch's bottle, used to ward off witches or prevent them from entering a place. When I bought the Jarrold bungalow I found a dozen of them scattered about the place.'

ELEVEN
The Billericay Covenant

'Ow am I supposed to cater for the ravenin' 'ordes at five minutes' notice? After a day of 'ard graft I wuz lookin' forward to puttin' me feet up, not feedin' the bleedin' five thousand.'

'Oh, do stop grizzling, Lugg, or I won't let you sit at the grown-ups' table.'

Lugg's facial expression changed from hurt indignation to innocent expectation, a feat which a cat could manage with a twitch of a whisker but – on Lugg's red-jowled moon of a face – the transformation was more like the aftermath of a hot mud geyser eruption.

'I had not planned on coming to London tonight, but needs must,' said Mr Campion, 'and it was pure coincidence that our little gang chose to rendezvous here at Bottle Street. I have booked myself into The Dorchester and thought we might all have dinner there, my treat, of course. We can exchange notes and come up with a plan of action. Lugg can take the minutes of the meeting. No, on second thoughts, he'd better not. When we use long words it will only set him off sulking again.'

'Best bib and tucker, is it?' asked Lugg, who had suddenly cheered up.

'No, come as you are,' said Campion pointedly, looking down at the threadbare tartan slippers straining to contain Lugg's feet.

'We had a very interesting day in Wicken,' said Perdita. 'Quite exhilarating in a way.'

'And I had an interesting day there yesterday, and a *very* interesting appointment at the doctor's today, but I'll tell you all about it over dinner, along with my most important discovery in many a year.'

'There's a claim,' said Rupert, 'and I have to ask what it was.'

'My dear boy, I pass on this secret to you as my son and heir.'

Campion lowered his voice conspiratorially. 'I have discovered a little guest house which serves a breakfast Lugg couldn't finish.'

The waiters at The Dorchester were highly trained when it came to keeping eccentric diners happy. Their training came from years of dealing with a long line of eccentrics drawn from the performing arts, the armed forces, the diplomatic community and, sometimes worst of all, the clergy.

Yet they were not quite sure how to deal with Mr Campion's table, even though Campion was a known and trusted patron. There was an American in the group, so an explanation of the cutlery might have been needed, but that was only a minor concern, as was his idiosyncratic request to be served Coca-Cola rather than wine. It was the way, once dessert had been consumed, that the tall American had covered the table with books, notepads, maps and charts, which most disconcerted the waiters standing to attention on the periphery of the party, almost as much as the malevolent stare with which the rather menacing bald man skewered them, as if daring them to object.

The clean-cut American seemed to be giving a lecture, supported with enthusiastic interjections from the young couple sitting on either side of him, and the audience was clearly intended to be Mr Albert Campion. It was unclear precisely what the role of the large fat man at the end of the table was, but even though one waiter was later to refer to him as a troll in need of a bridge to guard, he did at least appreciate the dinner presented to him, taking far more interest in it than in the topic under discussion.

'I've drawn up a hit list,' said Mason Lowell, then immediately held up his hands in apology. 'I'm sorry, I did not mean that to have any gangster connotation. What I should have said was a list of targets. Oh dear, that's almost as bad, isn't it?'

'Should we call it a cast list?' Perdita suggested sweetly.

'How about passenger list?' said Campion. 'Or at least "passengers of interest"?'

'Much better,' agreed Mason. 'I have a list of the passengers and some of the crew of the *Abigail* but what we are really interested in are those who signed the Billericay Covenant, sailed from England and landed in Salem, Massachusetts in 1692.'

He flipped open a notebook and began to read: 'Abendigo Lux, who was referred to as an elder and possibly therefore the leader of the group; John and Modesty Whybrow; Christopher Stow and wife unnamed; John Polley, widower, and his son Livewell, his other son Nathan having died on the voyage; Devon and Rosennah Jarmin; Samuel Bugg and his daughter Achsah; Richard and Rhoda Poynter; Amos Gurnham; Joseph Barly and his sister Ruth; Edmund Munson; Roger Firmin; Henry and Silence Jones; and Degory and Eliza Gladwell and their four daughters.'

Mason paused and refreshed himself from his wine glass of Coca-Cola without any visible embarrassment.

'Thirteen,' said Mr Campion. When all the faces around the table turned on him, he added, 'Thirteen family names.'

'Is that significant?' asked Perdita.

'Give you the makings of a rugby team – League, not Union, mind,' said Lugg.

Campion ignored him. 'Would you enlighten the innocents, Mason, or shall I?'

'Thirteen was traditionally the number of participants in a witches' coven, although some authorities insist it was twelve, with the Devil himself as the thirteenth.'

'Acting as a sort of non-executive director, no doubt,' said Campion.

'But it would support Professor Luger's theory, wouldn't it?' Rupert offered.

'Really?' Perdita exclaimed. 'Are you really suggesting that a coven of Essex witches emigrated to America and had the bad luck to land in Salem just at the time of the witch trials?'

'It would explain why they took one look at what was going on there and decided, quickly, to find another spot to colonize.'

'Bit like "I won't take my coat off 'cos I'm not stopping"?' said Lugg, deadpan.

'I'm sure that's exactly what they said. Mason, we are so rude, please continue.'

Mason turned a page in his notes. 'As far as I have been able to discover, and both I and Professor Luger have looked hard, no member of these thirteen families stayed in Massachusetts. The few passengers who were not signatories of the Covenant did stay, and left a paper trail in the records of the colony. The assumption I am working on is that all the Billericay Covenanters decided to move on, and somehow they persuaded Captain Waudby to sail the *Abigail* south down the coast until they reached what is now North Carolina. It would not be a voyage he would have undertaken lightly, so presumably the Covenanters carried enough wealth with them to make it worth his while.'

Campion raised a questioning finger. 'Was there any indication they were a well-off bunch?'

'None. They were all from humble farming stock as far as we can tell.'

'So without money to bribe him, Captain Waudby somehow . . . how shall I put this . . . fell under their spell and sailed hundreds of extra sea miles at their bidding?'

'You're back to your witchcraft theory, Pop. You don't really believe all that hokum, do you?'

'Don't cheek your elders, young Rupert,' growled Lugg. ''Ave some respect for your dear old papa, even if 'e is goin' senile before our very eyes.'

'Don't dismiss things you don't understand, my boy. Take income tax, for example; I don't understand it, but I have to accept that it exists.'

Mason Lowell took a deep breath and pressed on. 'The evidence points to all the Covenanters moving on down to Harkers Island and some of them certainly settled there. There are few written records from the period, but certain family names pop up in the nineteenth century and some even survive on the island today. I have interviewed a large proportion of the islanders who claim an English heritage and have identified the following family names that indicate existing descendants of those who arrived on the *Abigail*: Whybrow, Stow, Poynter, Gurnham and Munson.'

'That's five of your thirteen,' said Mr Campion, 'so, according to your theory and doing the arithmetic – I refuse to "do the math" as you say in the colonies – that leaves eight families, or at least names, unaccounted for.'

'Not quite. I have traced the last descendant of the Covenanter Roger Firmin, a man called Willard Firmin, who joined the Confederate States navy in 1861 and was killed at the battle of Elizabeth City in 1862. In addition, I have discovered two families on Harkers who claim one of Degory Gladwell's four daughters in their family trees.'

'Which means seven families of settlers. Do any of the islanders owe any allegiance to their Essex heritage?'

'Not really. The "Hoi-Tiders" in general are either uninterested in their English roots or totally ignorant of them.'

'But you are convinced they have a connection to Wicken.' Campion did not pose it as a question.

'If we can believe *Captain Waudby's Log*, the *Abigail* returned to England with' – Mason consulted a notebook – '*with many families who had abandoned hope of a better life in the newest world and begged to be returned to their homes in the oldest.* But what we didn't know for sure, until yesterday, was that the Covenanters had definitely returned to Wicken.'

'We're still not absolutely sure about that,' said Perdita. 'Jones is a common enough name and Sylvia Jones herself said that the *Abigail* story was something of a family myth and she couldn't prove it one way or another.'

Before Mason could form a reply, Mr Campion rapped the table with his knuckles. 'Lugg, make yourself useful and tell the staff we're ready for the port, and something non-alcoholic for Mason. It's time for my party piece.'

'Oh, Pop,' groaned Rupert, 'not your card tricks again.'

'No, Rupert, this is my famous Mr Memory act, which I used to do twice nightly at The Windmill, matinees Tuesdays and Saturdays.'

'The Windmill?' Mason whispered at Lugg. 'Wasn't that the theatre where the girls took all their clothes off?'

'Yes,' Lugg replied, his bloodhound face drooping with disappointment, 'but they weren't allowed to move.'

'These days,' Campion continued, 'it's not so much a speciality act as reassurance that this old brain has not withered on the vine, so Mr Memory asks you, Mason, to consult your list of the Billericay Covenanters and tell me which, if any, of these names signed up for passage to America.'

Mason shuffled papers and turned pages, nodding when he was ready.

'Bugg, Barly, Jarmin, Polley and, of course, Jones,' said Campion with his eyes closed.

'Five bullseyes!' laughed Mason. 'There's nothing wrong with your memory, sir.'

'But you read them out loud not five minutes ago!' wailed Rupert.

'I am not repeating them parrot-fashion, dear boy,' said his father. 'Look at your list, Mason, and tell me how many of those names you have traced in Massachusetts or on Harkers Island.'

'None,' said the American without the need to consult his notes.

'Yet those names survive in Wicken today, which would indicate . . .'

'They are the Covenanters who returned! You found them?'

'Well, not *them*, merely Wicken residents who share the same surname, and I do not claim to have found them all. Go on, do the . . .' Campion corrected himself, '. . . arithmetic.'

'Seven descendants traced on Harkers plus your five surnames in Wicken, that makes twelve.'

'So no longer a coven,' said Perdita.

'If thirteen really was the required quorum, it does seem that the coven split when they reached Harkers. Remind us who is missing, Mason.'

'Abendigo Lux.'

'What a splendid name,' said Campion, 'I'd love to meet an Abendigo.'

'The Three Stooges,' said Lugg, shuffling a decanter of port to his left, indicating to a bemused Mason that he should help it on its journey.

'Lugg is referring, rather disrespectfully, to the biblical story of the three Hebrews thrown into a fiery furnace: Shadrack, Meschach and, to be accurate, Abednego, though everyone says Abendigo. Come to think of it, I did once meet a Shadrack, but that's beside the point. Do you have any idea what might have happened to dear old Abendigo?'

'I was hoping we'd find a trace of him in Wicken,' said Mason. 'It's my belief that he was the group leader and he would have taken the decision to leave Salem after seeing what was going on there. He would, I guess, have been in charge of things at Harkers, but there's no lasting trace of him there.'

'And if he was their leader, he would have been central to the decision to up sticks and return to England, wouldn't he?'

'He surely would, but lots of things could have happened. He could have died on Harkers, soon after the *Abigail* arrived, and that might have sparked the move to give up on America and come back home. Or he could have died on the voyage home, or got home and slunk away somewhere because the whole venture had been a failure.'

'There's nothing in Hurrell's book about him?'

'*Captain Waudby's Log* is frustratingly vague on many things. Florid descriptions of American flora and fauna and gruesome encounters with the natives were more Hurrell's *forte*. The voyage home was hardly mentioned; it was just not exciting enough. No storms, shipwrecks, pirates or attacks by great white whales, and of course they came back having failed to find paradise on Earth so it didn't make for a happy ending. A great shame, old Abendigo. Finding a Lux somewhere in Wicken would have clinched the deal. That cannot be a very common name.'

'Well, I can't offer you an Abendigo Lux, but I might have another interesting name for you.'

Mason, Rupert and Perdita looked at him expectantly. Lugg crooked a finger, summoning the port back down the table.

Mr Campion paused before speaking, as if the thought had just occurred. 'You spoke with a Miss Jones out at Wicken today.'

'She was very polite,' said Mason, 'but she didn't seem to take her ancestry very seriously, kept saying Jones was a very common name.'

'It is,' said Mr Campion, 'but Silence Jones is quite unusual, wouldn't you say?'

'That was the name of Henry Jones's wife on the *Abigail*.'

'And it's the name of your Miss Jones of Wicken. Coincidence?'

After a far less daunting breakfast at The Dorchester, Mr Campion embarked on the two errands he was determined to complete before leaving London. The first had to be rescheduled following a telephone call where a strict female voice with a hint of Austria or Switzerland about the accent informed him that 'Lady Jocasta' never rose before noon, but Mr Campion could be assured that he was on the list of approved callers, should he wish to telephone later for an appointment.

Consequently, his second errand was run first, for no one in the specialist department of the British Museum he wished to consult was ever allowed to sleep in.

In truth, Mr Campion was not sure that Dr Glendenning slept at all, at least not at night, his pallor suggesting that his exposure to sunlight was limited. His eyes were sunk far back into his skull as if prepared to retreat from any advancing rays. If he had an official title, Campion did not know it, and he had always referred to him as his personal expert in 'the esoteric, the strange and the probably ridiculous'.

Directions to Dr Glendenning's office were not advertised to museum visitors, nor indeed members of staff and, had Mr Campion been asked for them, he would have replied in an appropriately vague manner. He would have advised walking through the Persian department then into the Egyptian display, turning sharply left at the third large Pharaoh head and then taking the door marked Staff Members Only, which was guarded by a stone scarab beetle the size of a small pony, and two flights down a dimly lit staircase would be found a door bearing the legend 'Temporarily Withdrawn from Exhibit'. Whether this was any sort of comment on Dr Glendenning's value to the institution – or his personality – was not clear, but that was where he was to be found at any hour of the day and, it was rumoured, most of those at night.

The office which Glendenning occupied, or nested in, was a cornucopia of forgotten items donated to the museum by well-meaning members of the public who were happy not to have to dust them any more. Every flat surface and most of the walls were covered with paintings, photograph albums, books, stuffed animals, encased collections of birds' eggs, curios of every kind, even some genuine antiquities, and it had been referred to in the past as the Harrods of white elephant stalls. Dr Glendenning might have had a desk in there at one time, but it had long disappeared and he did whatever work he did sitting on a high stool, legs akimbo, reminding Campion of an East End tailor from a bygone era, surrounded by bygones.

'Good morning, Hamish. How are things in the Not Wanted on Voyage department?'

'You are as amusing as ever, Albert,' said Glendenning in a thin, reedy voice, 'but I cannot spare you too much time, I'm afraid. I really have to get these things catalogued by the end of the year.' He waved the fountain pen he held in one hand and the wedge of Rolodex cards he held in the other.

'Which year?' Campion asked.

'Nineteen sixty-five,' he said without missing a beat.

'Then I will certainly not detain you long, Hamish. I just need your expert assessment of a couple of items.'

Campion opened the briefcase he was carrying, clutching it to his chest as there was no room to put it down, and produced the small medicine bottle he had taken from the *Jocasta*. 'Have you ever seen anything like this?'

Dr Glendenning put the fountain pen he had been holding behind his right ear, where it balanced precariously. Campion noticed that there were already bluish stains in that region, almost as if he had tried to ink in sideboards, something naturally missing from his distinctive coiffure, for the front half of his head was completely bald, yet the back half of the dome sprouted long straggles of white hair dangling down to and over his shirt collar. He reached out a pale, cadaverous hand, thought the better of it, and leaned back on his stool.

'Of course I have,' he said with a casual wave of his empty hand, 'it's a witch bottle. It contains iron nails and thorn cuttings in holy water and would usually be found at a doorway or near a fireplace, to deter witches from entering a place. I have at least four of them somewhere in this room.'

'Do they work?'

'If you believe in witchcraft, they might, but if I believed in half the rituals and religions represented in this room, people would think me odd to say the least.'

Mr Campion studied the figure curled and hunched on that high stool, surrounded by dust motes, his dark jacket, clearly a stranger to dry cleaning, shiny with age, surrounded by medieval Italian towers of books which might collapse and bury him at any time.

'Oh, I doubt that very much,' he said eventually, 'but I gather this is not an exceptional item.'

'You can find them all over Essex and Suffolk, which is not surprising as those were, historically, the happy hunting grounds of the self-appointed witchfinder generals of the seventeenth century, when witches were treated as a real threat.'

'But hardly in common use these days?'

'Who knows? Old habits die hard – very hard in places like East Anglia. And remember, these were defences against witches. Having one didn't mean you were a witch, just that you believed in them. Where did you find it?'

'On a boat, actually.'

'That's unusual.' Dr Glendenning was, thought Campion, in danger of becoming interested.

'It is?'

'A boat suggests water and witches never do well over water. Putting to sea on a boat was a good way of getting away from them.'

'Interesting,' said Campion, replacing the bottle in his brief-case and producing another item. 'Now, what about this?'

Dr Glendenning had no hesitation in reaching out and taking the small stuffed toy doll from Mr Campion's hand. He examined it closely, his nostrils flaring and his top lip curling, then held it away from his face. 'Has a child been playing with this? There appear to be teeth marks.'

'I fear a dog may have worried it somewhat. He seemed rather fond of it, but it has been thoroughly washed.'

A pale, almost bloodless hand, with thin fingers and suspiciously long fingernails, squeezed the plump body of the doll, its most substantial part. The effigy, if that was what it was, was no more than five inches in length and made up essentially of two stuffed orbs of hessian for the trunk and the head, the arms and legs being represented by simple strips of coloured material; all the elements held together by small neat stitching in red thread. There was no identifiable front or back to the doll, no face to give it a personality or a sex.

'Do you know what this is?' asked Glendenning.

'I was told it was called a reflection.'

'You were told correctly. Many would have guessed at a voodoo doll and tried to stick pins it.'

'And that wouldn't work at all, would it?'

The museum man looked at Campion from under the hooded lids of his faraway eyes.

'The effectiveness of a voodoo effigy is that it terrifies the person represented by the doll, because the doll is *recognizably* him or her. This little idol has no face, which is why it is a reflection. Whoever receives it is supposed to see their own personality in its reflection, though obviously it has no reflective surfaces.'

'So whoever receives one of these has to know what it is; otherwise they might dismiss it as a crudely made child's toy, and therefore the curse wouldn't work.'

'Curse? What curse? Reflections are not curses, they are warnings. Whoever is given one is being told that something is coming and they'd better watch out.'

'So it's not witchcraft?'

Dr Glendenning adopted a pained expression which Campion could only assume was one of pity. 'No, no, no. The witch bottle, that's to ward off witchcraft. The reflection, that's not strictly witchcraft, it's more wicken.'

'*What did you just say?*'

'Please do not shoot the messenger, Albert. You asked me if it was witchcraft and I answered honestly that I think this is more wicken.'

'And what,' said Campion, controlling his impatience, 'do you mean by wicken?'

'Let me put it this way,' said Dr Glendenning, leaning back at a precarious angle on his high stool, 'witchcraft relies on spells, magic, potions and rituals to make things happen. Wicken relies on the power of a "third eye", the ability to not so much foresee the future as *sense* what is about to happen.'

'So in olden days, somebody who might have been thought of as a seer or a soothsayer or even a prophet, they might have been a follower of wicken rather than a witch or a warlock?'

'Absolutely.' Dr Glendenning bared his teeth in a grimace which on a normal face might have been a smile. 'Of course, in the good old days, they would have been treated like witches and burned at the stake. Or was it hanged? I forget. Which was more popular?'

Mr Campion's second errand took less time but was, in a different way, equally disconcerting.

He was confronted rather than greeted at the door of Jocasta Upcott's Chelsea home by a tall, blonde woman wearing a pinstripe three-piece trouser suit; her hair scraped back into a severe bun, her accent Germanic, her attitude uncompromising.

Mr Campion admitted that he had not made a specific appointment, but he had waited, as instructed, until after noon before calling on Dame Jocasta, who he knew would want to see him. The modern day Valkyrie remained unimpressed and the doorway remained firmly blocked with her pinstripe suit until a distant barking from inside the house broke the impasse and Robespierre, recognizing a friendly voice, snuffled up behind the gatekeeper in order to vouch for the visitor.

Which was almost more than his mistress did, for as Campion was shown into her drawing room, he distinctly heard her say in a faux stage whisper, 'I was hoping for the younger one.' Dame Jocasta had clearly been up and awake for some time, Campion thought unkindly, for that much make-up could not be applied so well in haste. She had not gone as far as getting fully dressed, however, and was wearing a green lace peignoir and high-heeled backless slippers decorated with large furry green pom-poms. She reminded Campion of the hand-tinted pin-up photographs of sweethearts carried by soldiers of the war before last.

Having thanked Mr Campion for the safe return of Robespierre, and finally recalling where she had met him before (she had not, rather she had met his late mother, but it did not seem polite to remind her), she listened carefully to his concerns about her poodle's health and assured him that Robespierre had been thoroughly examined by his consultant vet on his return from his adventures on the Dengie Peninsula.

'I have to ask,' said Campion, summoning every sinew, 'has he bitten anyone?'

'Never!' Dame Jocasta delivered the line thunderously in a manner which would have brought down the curtain on any operatic climax. 'He's a sweet and gentle dog. I don't know how you could suggest such a thing!'

'I have my reasons, dear lady, trust me. Is there any chance Robespierre might have bitten Francis Jarrold?'

Outrage turned to indignation. 'I find that impossible to believe.

They got on very well together, have done since he was a pup. That wasn't a sly suggestion that I should attend Francis's funeral, was it?'

'Not at all,' said Campion, surprised. 'That was the farthest thing from my mind. Actually, I have no idea what the funeral arrangements might be.'

'Well, I'm far too busy, though I will send flowers of course, and probably my agent. Then I suppose I will have to do something about the boat, though it is such a busy period for me at the moment and, in my world, one should not complain about that.'

'So I believe,' Campion observed dryly, 'and I will not impinge on your busy schedule much longer, though there is something I must ask. When did you last see' – he was about to say Jarrold but opted for a softer target – 'Robespierre before my son brought him back at the weekend?'

'I left him in Honfleur about two weeks before when I was called back to Pinewood to record some more dialogue. It was only for television, not a proper film. It meant cutting my short holiday even shorter, which was a pity. There is a nice little colony of English people out there and one of my neighbours is Geoffrey Clegg, the most dynamic young director in the West End at the moment. We gave house parties together and took the dogs for walks along the beach. A charming man.' Dame Jocasta's eyes took on a dreamlike quality. 'If only I were ten years younger.' She sighed.

Or Geoffrey Clegg was thirty years older, Campion thought.

'I was hoping to pop back over there, but once word got out that I was back in town . . . well, darling, I was in demand, and my feet have hardly touched the floor since, so I contacted Francis and told him to bring the boat, and Robespierre, home.'

'When you recalled Jarrold, did he sound *compos mentis*?'

The actress burst into giggles. 'Do you know, that's the title of a play I've been asked to read. Frightful modern stuff, all psychology and wordplay rather than drama. I doubt I will do it, but one has to show interest. As for Francis, I'm not sure he was ever *compos mentis*, or not after his first drink of the day, which was usually taken shortly after, or instead of, breakfast. He would have sounded drunk, because he usually was, but then we all have our weaknesses, don't we?'

Campion wondered what possible weakness Dame Jocasta would admit to but said nothing apart from a polite goodbye and an apology for disturbing her.

'I'll get Verbena to show you out,' she announced loudly, and the blonde woman in the trouser suit appeared so quickly and stealthily that Mr Campion thought he had misheard the instruction as 'throw you out'.

When she heard the front door close behind him, Dame Jocasta summoned her assistant in a voice which brooked no dissent. 'Verbena! Get my bloody agent on the phone. Now!'

TWELVE
Conjuration

In Tillingham at The Oyster Shack, Mrs Young took the sort of telephone call she lived for.

'Of course we can fit you in, Mr Wyndham. Just the one night, is it? No, it doesn't matter what time you arrive; we have no plans for this evening and I've got time to nip to the shops to get things in for your breakfast . . . What's that? You want to be out on the marshes at dawn? Goodness me, that's keen . . . I could leave some sandwiches out for you. It is the most important meal of the day, they say . . . Well, if you're sure. The early bird catches the worm; and who knows that better than a birdwatcher?'

In London, Mason Lowell spent the morning organizing his notes and making contact with 'trusted sources' recommended by Professor Luger at King's College and the London Library. He was persuaded to join Lugg for a pub lunch at The Guinea in Bruton Place, where he looked at one of the hostelry's famed steak pies, despite assurance that it did not contain kidney or other 'organ meats', with the same suspicion with which Lugg regarded his glass of fizzy cola, something not improved, in Lugg's opinion, by the addition of a slice of lemon and an ice cube.

Mistaking Lugg's beatific expression produced by his appreciation of Young's Special Bitter for one of interest in his pet subject, Mason, using the notebook he now seemed to carry everywhere, sketched out a plan of Wicken drawn from his visit and information supplied by Mr Campion, each property represented by an annotated rectangle.

From top to bottom it read:

??
??
?
??
Mary Ann Allen
Abigail Cottage: Silence Jones
CHAPEL
Mr & Mrs Worskitt

'You've got a lot of question marks there,' said Lugg, sipping his pint contemplatively.

'I need to get a better handle on the location of the Wicken population to fill in the gaps.'

'Why?'

'So I know who might be approachable and who to avoid.'

Lugg's eyes narrowed. 'There are some there who need avoiding?'

'I got that impression yesterday,' said Mason hesitantly.

'Oh, you did, did yer? And what gave you that idea?'

Reluctantly Mason told of their disconcerting experience with the three Wicken men who had made it clear they were no longer welcome, describing the event as a stand-off rather than a showdown.

'They don't sound a friendly bunch, but that's not unusual for the badlands of Essex. You might have your wild west but we've got our wild east.'

Mason cracked a smile. 'Yeah, it did feel like we were being run out of town.'

'You're not going to stand for that, are you? You bein' a rootin'-tootin' cowboy, are you?'

'If you mean am I going back there, you bet I am. But not with Perdita.'

Lugg looked at the young American with something akin to approval. 'Good lad.'

Mary Ann Allen drove home from work in the dark, having stayed to assist with Dr Fathoms's evening surgery. She was used to driving the narrow, unlit roads and darker, narrower lanes on the peninsula; even in deepest winter, when the tides were high and the rain and mist came in off the sea, she was confident that her little car, her much-loved Ford Anglia, could find its way safely home by itself.

Both driver and car were familiar with the way the lanes suddenly turned at right angles for no good reason, when the landscape ahead appeared flat and clear, and both appreciated that this was to avoid plunging off a raised dyke and into a flooded drainage ditch. Both were aware that it was essential to remain glued to the hard surface of the roadways, for the land to either side, seemingly flat and free of obstacles, was not solid ground but soft, yielding mud which, if the wartime stories of the Dengie marshes were to be believed, could swallow an aircraft whole, let alone a wayward Ford Anglia.

Still, it was always a relief when the car turned on to the track which led to the line of dwellings which was Wicken, for at least there would be lights there. Not more than one per dwelling and often hidden behind thick curtains or masked by dark wooden outbuildings, but better than nothing if there was no moon.

On this particular evening there were lights Mary Ann had not expected, red lights low down in the roadway, glowing like some demonic animal. Her own headlights revealed they were the rear parking lights of a large dark saloon car parked outside the house shared by Richard Polley and his sister Octavia. Mrs Allen would never have described herself as a nosey neighbour, but it was rare for the Polleys to have visitors. Indeed, it was rare to see another car on the track which served as Wicken's high street and thoroughfare, though both were highly misleading descriptions, as high streets usually had shops and places of business and thoroughfares usually took travellers somewhere other than just to a watery end in the North Sea.

There was enough room, just, for the Ford Anglia to manoeuvre around the parked car without slipping off the track. It was an old-fashioned saloon, with running boards down the side and a bonnet which seemed to go on forever, but the make and model would mean nothing to Mary Ann. She was simply relieved that the Anglia passed it without making contact.

Turning on to the gravel rectangle which served as a driveway and parking space in front of her bungalow, she caught sight of two figures, almost certainly male, emerging simultaneously from the front doors of the semi-detached house next door, almost like mechanical figures on a Black Forest cuckoo clock.

By the time she had reached her own front door, there was no sign of them, and she wondered, briefly, what George Bugg and his brother-in-law Robert Barly were doing wandering about in the dark. Then she reminded herself that she was not a nosey neighbour.

Mr Campion arrived home at almost exactly the same time as his wife. After a makeshift dinner of whatever Amanda 'could scavenge from the larder', they settled themselves with freshly brewed coffee and engaged in the ritual of asking if each had had a productive couple of days away from each other.

Amanda's report had been brief, seemingly having spent her time visiting the sick, reorganizing several charities of which she was a patron, and a shopping trip to Cambridge. She failed to supply any details of how 'the sick' she visited was a thoroughbred racehorse stabled at Newmarket, on whose health she had been asked to report to its owner – and fellow charitable patron – who happened to live not far away at Sandringham. Amanda had indeed done some shopping in Cambridge, but only after she had shared a high tea with an old schoolgirl chum who now worked at the Fitzwilliam Museum.

Mr Campion, with due modesty, claimed he had little of interest to report. He had been on board a famous actress's yacht, though it had been tied up to the harbour at the time and the tide was out. He had met a man standing in a wheelbarrow and talked about graveyards with him. Then he had consulted a doctor, though there was absolutely nothing wrong with him, and had then had a jolly nice dinner with Rupert and Perdita and their American chum Mason. Oh, and Lugg had invited himself along. And while he was in London, he had run into an old acquaintance, the odd but perfectly harmless Hamish Glendenning.

'Of the British Museum?' Amanda had asked casually.

'Yes, he's still there. Something of a fixture; I think they just dust round him these days,' Campion said lightly.

'I popped into a museum when I was in Cambridge,' said his wife equally casually.

'Was it raining?'

'Of course not. I went to see one of the curators, just as you went to see Horrible Hamish. And don't give me that look, you know he resembles something out of an Expressionist German film. We should compare notes on what we learned.'

Mr Campion's vacuous face glowed with innocence. 'Notes about what, darling?'

'About witchcraft, of course.'

Mason Lowell Clay decided, for the sake of speed as well as international relations, to refer to himself simply as Mason Clay when it came to completing the paperwork required to hire a car in England. The prospect of driving on the wrong side of the road, as he saw it, and on controlling a manual gearbox, which seemed to require a stirring motion rather than the simple pushing of a lever he was used to, were daunting enough. The hire agreement, insurance and instructions about which petrol to use were all added complications not eased by the fact that the girl dealing with him had never seen an American passport or a State of Georgia driving licence before, though she was impressed by his American Express card.

Eventually, she was able to hand over the keys to one of their new, large saloon cars, along with a copy of the Highway Code, which she assured him had been read and memorized by every driver in the United Kingdom.

Within half an hour of negotiating the North Circular Road and those baffling whirlpools of traffic which the British called roundabouts, Mason was beginning to doubt that statement. He also took umbrage at the hire firm's description of the car being a 'large' model. True, he had more headroom than he had enjoyed in Perdita's Mini, but his knees were still situated dangerously close to his chin as he drove.

As Mason was attempting to navigate the highways, but mostly byways, of northeast London, Rupert Campion was driving his wife's Mini Cooper in entirely the opposite direction, getting lost twice in Wimbledon before lighting on the address he had been given: an imposing detached house on the edge of Putney Heath within, as Lugg would have said, 'staggering distance' of the famous Green Man Inn.

He was responding to a summons received late the previous evening. The summoner had surprised him, the address astonished him, for he had never met anyone who had been invited to the home of theatrical agent and impresario Timothy Timms rather than to the rather shabby office he rented above a bookshop in the Charing Cross Road.

If his cramped and dingy office was designed to give the impression of a man solely dedicated to the careers of his clients at the expense of any personal creature comforts or luxuries, then a first glimpse of his home would suggest that every penny saved on rent, heating and lighting in his office was to ensure the maximum of domestic gratification.

No one, but no one, Perdita had lectured him, got invited to Timmy Timms's home, especially not at nine o'clock in the morning, but Rupert had assured her that had been the gist of the telephone call.

'I bet Dame Jocasta's never been invited there, and he's been her agent for years,' Perdita had said with a hint of malice. 'But then, he probably doesn't fancy *her*.'

Rupert had not dignified that with a response but had set out after a nervous breakfast with some trepidation.

At the door of the address he had been given in the strictest confidence, Rupert pressed the doorbell, and from inside the house heard the muted tones of a melody he was sure was the title song from the musical *Oklahoma!*. Above him he heard a sash window slide up and a disembodied voice.

'It's open, come on in, but stay downstairs because I'm not decent. Won't keep you long!'

Rupert entered and found to his relief that Timmy Timms was as good as his word both when it came to keeping him waiting and when it came to being 'decent', though it took him a few moments to realize that by 'decent', Mr Timms meant he had wanted to ensure his fiery orange-red toupee was firmly in place.

He followed Timms into a chintzy drawing room and the two of them sank into soft, yielding armchairs facing each other.

'Firstly,' said Timms, 'thank you for coming all the way out here at such an unsociable hour, but my diary is a nightmare from luncheon onwards.' He consulted a wristwatch which sparkled with gemstones. 'Let me get straight to the point, young Rupert. Do you know Geoffrey Clegg?'

'The stage director?' Even as he said it, Rupert felt foolish, as what other Geoffrey Clegg would someone like Timmy Timms refer to? Geoffrey Clegg, greengrocer of Wandsworth? The Reverend Geoffrey Clegg of some windswept parish in Lincolnshire? 'Of course I know his reputation, but I cannot say I know him.'

Timms made a prayer temple of his fingers. 'He's a client of mine,' he said dreamily, without elaboration. 'Do you have a classical piece?'

'You mean an audition piece?'

'I wasn't talking about furniture. Something respectable but not too well known. Perhaps not Shakespeare; how about Marlowe, or Webster? Geoffrey does have a tiny sadistic streak.'

'As a student I was in *The White Devil* and played Flamineo; he was a pretty nasty piece of work. I'd have to brush up on it, though.'

'Good. I take it you'll have no problem reading for Geoffrey? He's planning a series of television programmes on staging Elizabethan and Jacobean drama and he will be putting together a little company of actors who can do multiple roles to illustrate various points.'

'Sounds exciting,' said Rupert, leaning forward in his chair.

'It could be a . . . a . . . springboard for an aspiring young actor, not only working with Geoffrey but *being seen* working with Geoffrey, even if it's only bits and pieces and even if it's only television.'

'It would be a wonderful opportunity . . .' He let his voice trail away, quite dramatically, he thought.

'Were you a client of mine, I would have no hesitation in putting you forward, but I get the impression you wish to stay loyal to dear old Maxim Berlins, which is commendable. But I cannot deny I have some influence over Geoffrey and I could put in a good word for you.'

'Would you do that?'

'Normally I would do that in a heartbeat, dear boy, but I'm afraid Geoffrey is in a bit of a mood just at the moment, very distraught. You see, he's lost his pet dog, and he was very attached to that pooch. Poor chap can't think of anything else at the moment.'

Rupert was unsure how to react, his brain in something of a whirlpool of despair as he saw a golden career opportunity disappearing almost as soon as it had materialized. What Timmy Timms said next brought him back down to earth with a bump.

'But you found Jocasta's dog out at Wicken, didn't you? Are you sure you couldn't find Geoffrey's?'

Driving slowly and *very* cautiously, Mason Lowell arrived in Wicken early in the afternoon of a grey, overcast day. It was obviously not a day for casual visitors or birdwatchers, as the place was as empty of life as on his first visit, but then Wicken was unlikely to be on any tourist trail.

He drove his hire car, something called a Morris Marina, which he had been assured was the absolute latest in British motor manufacturing, to the tip of the dead-end track, and parked so that he could admire the bleak expanse of coastal mud through the windscreen while he ate his lunch. It was a picnic, prepared by Lugg, of two hardboiled eggs, a thick white bread sandwich of sliced beef tomato and a sort of liver sausage the British called polony, and a Thermos flask of strong, sweet tea.

The nervous energy required to keep the rented car on the correct – he had conditioned himself not to say 'right' – side of the English road network had given him an appetite, and he wolfed down everything Lugg had packed, even the Mars Bar he had added as an extra treat, with the confusing recommendation that it would help him work, rest and play.

He turned the car around carefully and parked in front of the bungalow beyond Abigail Cottage. On his schematic plan of Wicken, the bungalow was the home of the doctor's receptionist with whom Albert had talked, and who would be at work now. Sylvia Jones – more interestingly Silence Jones – at Abigail Cottage, he had interviewed with Perdita. The house before the chapel belonged to the Worskitts and the name Worskitt did not figure on the Billericay Covenant. That left him with four homes, four front doors and four names to put to them: Bugg, Barly, Jarmin and Polley, and he was conscious that the three sullen men who had appeared on his last visit could very well live behind those front doors.

He hoped that wearing his Brooks Brothers suit and a tie, and clutching the clipboard he had purchased, gave him an air of respectability if not officialdom. For the rest he relied on Southern manners and an accent he hoped the natives found charming.

The first house, the semi-detached, seemed deserted in both halves; not that Mason was too sure what an inhabited, un-deserted house in Wicken should look like. He approached one front door, knocked, and then moved two or three paces on to the next to achieve the same negative result.

He returned to the track, irrationally comforted to find the Morris Marina still parked there, and moved on to the next property with the distinct feeling that his movements were being followed by an unseen observer.

To approach the front door of the next house, Mason wove his way between three wooden outbuildings painted with black pitch. None was big enough to act as a garage or barn, and they did not smell of animals, but seemed too big to be mere tool sheds or – surely not? – outside toilets.

Mason's fist rapped on the door and, to his surprise, it was opened almost immediately by a woman certainly old enough to be his mother, but there any resemblance ended abruptly. Where Mason thought his mother's most endearing attributes were a soft and generous humanity displayed equally to all and sundry, here was a woman he instantly thought of as sharp, hard, flint-edged.

'No hawkers!'

'I'm sorry?' Mason took a step back.

'There's a sign saying "No Hawkers, No Circulars, No Ragmen", down there by the gate.'

Mason did not think it polite to mention that there was no front gate. 'I'm sorry if I missed it, but I assure you it does not apply to me.'

'You's a foreigner.'

'I am indeed,' said Mason delighted to detect a hint of Harkers Island in the woman's accent. 'Would you be Mrs Barly?'

It had been a shot in the dark and he felt unreasonably smug that he was proved half right.

'I ain't a Barly no more, not since I was married,' said the woman with a shrew-like wrinkle of her pointed nose.

'Then you must be Mrs Polley.'

Another blind stab, which this time produced a snort of derision.

'There ain't no Mrs Polley. There's Octavia Polley, sister to Richard, but they live in the end house.' She jabbed a stiletto forefinger to Mason's right. 'Best you try and sell them your wares.'

'But I'm not . . .' was as far as Mason got before the door closed in his face.

Even as Mason prepared to knock on the door of the next house, back down the lane Sylvia Jones was answering a discreet knock on her front door. She had heard a car drive down the lane and then back again and – thanks to a twitching curtain – she had seen, and recognized, Mason as he parked and approached the semi-detached homes of Robert Barly and George Bugg.

The gentle rap on her door took her slightly by surprise as the tall American could not possibly have retraced his steps so quickly; not that she minded seeing him again as he seemed intelligent and well-mannered, though possibly not as sharp as the young woman who had accompanied him.

She opened her door to find her neighbour from the other side of the chapel, Ethel Worskitt, leaning at an angle on a sturdy walking stick, looking up at her with steely, accusing eyes.

'Ethel, what a surprise.'

'You know anything about all these visitors?'

'I take it you mean Mr Clay and Mrs Campion.'

'Aye, Campion. That was the name.'

'Mr Clay is an American and I believe he is tracing some family histories.'

'American? So he's a foreigner?'

'I don't think he makes any attempt to deny that,' said Miss Jones, 'and the Americans were always interested in my sister Theodora.'

'What's past is past and should be left alone,' said the smaller woman, her hand quivering on the crook of her stick.

'Oh, I didn't mind talking to him. Why don't I put the kettle on and we can have a chat?' She held the door ajar and locked eyes with Mrs Worskitt. 'Won't you come in? No, of course you won't.'

In Tillingham at The Oyster Shack, Mrs Young heard the deep-throated roar of a tractor engine, which was not an uncommon sound in the village, but one which usually disappeared into the distance. Rarely did a tractor stop right outside her establishment, and her guests *never* arrived by tractor.

But the tractor had stopped outside and somebody, certainly not a booked-in guest, was ringing her doorbell.

''Scuse I for disturbin', missus,' said the tractor driver, a weather-beaten, middle-aged man dressed in blue coveralls, Wellington boots and a flat cap, which he had removed and was twisting between gnarled hands. In another era he would have bowed and tugged a forelock, and Mrs Young instinctively thought such a gesture would not be out of place.

'It's Joshua Jarmin, isn't it? From Wicken.'

'That's roight.'

'I know your wife, Leonora – well, when we were girls and she was Leonora Barly I knew her.'

'She sent me round, said you'd 'elp.'

'If I can,' said Mrs Young uncertainly.

'You 'ad a gentleman stayin' here recent. He must have come to Wicken to bird-spot on the flats. Well, he left a pair of very fancy binoculars on a fence post. They look expensive.'

'Oh dear. I'm sure Mr Campion would have telephoned if he'd noticed he'd lost them.'

'That weren't his name,' said Joshua Jarmin with a face of stone. 'Doctor Fathoms knows him.'

'You're right, he does. He rang Mr Campion when he was staying here and I'm sure I don't know what he said, but it put the poor man right off his breakfast. When he left here he went to the surgery in Southminster. I had to provide directions.'

'Must have been the other fella who visits.'

'The only other resident in the last week or so was Mr Wyndham, the gentleman with the colourful hairpiece.'

'That'd be him. You got an address for him? My Leonora wants to write him, tell him we've got his fancy opera glasses.'

'Well, I suppose he wrote it in my guest book. Let me have a look. It would be a London address if he did.'

'London, eh? You reckon you could write it out for me?'

Joshua Jarmin may have the look and manners of a rough peasant, but when his voice softened and betrayed an almost childlike pleading, Mrs Young's heart melted.

If a grown man had trouble reading and writing, she would naturally help.

What possible harm could it do?

'Where is it you're going?' Mr Campion asked his wife as she closed a suitcase.

'Lossiemouth,' said Amanda, snapping catches. 'It's in Scotland.'

'Of course it is. Right at the top end near Inverness, if memory serves. That's quite a trek; you're not driving all that way, are you?'

'I've told you several times but you've been too busy thinking about other things. I am driving over to Peterborough and taking the train to Edinburgh, where a car and driver will meet me. The engine tests take place tomorrow and I'll be back the day after. I'll bring you a kilt or some kippers back as a souvenir.'

'So the RAF are looking after you?'

'Technically Lossiemouth is still a naval base, but the Fleet Air Arm has been chopped so much, they're giving it back to the RAF next year.'

'Then don't forget to say "Hello, sailor" when your chauffeur picks you up.'

'Oh, Albert, *please* . . . Now take that case downstairs for me while I find my winter coat. I know I'll probably get eaten alive by midges, but you really do need a third eye to predict the weather in Scotland.'

'So you were listening when I told you what Hamish Glendenning had told me.'

'I always listen to you, darling. It's just that I have become rather selective in the bits I choose to hear.'

Mr Campion hefted the suitcase off the bed and held the bedroom door open for Amanda as she draped a long camel-coloured cashmere coat over her shoulders.

'Whereas I,' said Campion with genuine affection, 'hang on your every word.'

'Good, then you'll remember what my chap at the Fitzwilliam told me if you intend to go on meddling in witchcraft, and don't go for a haircut while I'm away.'

Campion automatically raised his spare hand to the side of his head and ran his fingers through his hair. It was now white but, on a good day, he was sure he could detect, in a mirror, strands of the straw colour of his youth. 'A haircut? I didn't think I was due for a trim just yet.'

'Good, because those little dolls, those *reflections*, are stuffed with human hair.'

THIRTEEN
Census

'Good afternoon, sir, I'm . . .'

'An American unless my ears deceive me. What can we do for you?'

Mason Lowell rocked back on his heels. A friendly welcome – in Wicken? 'I'm tracing some family names.'

'Of course you are – that's what Americans do. You'd better come in.'

It was with a sense of unease that Mason stepped over the threshold. Not unease in the sense of entering a lion's den, but a slight discomfort because he did not have Perdita at his side to make sure he did not commit any crimes against English hospitality or good manners. This was, after all, the first time he had been invited alone into an Englishman's home, and he was unsure of the etiquette of storming that particular castle. He drew on the strongest weapon in his arsenal, his genuine Southern charm.

'I guess you must be Mr Polley.'

'A good guess, though I suspect Leonora next door tipped you off. Nothing much goes unnoticed in Wicken – not that much ever happens here.'

The man speaking was small and wiry, with thinning white hair and incredibly bushy, positively spiky white eyebrows. He was, Mason guessed, in the autumn of his seventies if not the spring of his eighties and, dressed as he was in a light blue shirt and tie and a moleskin waistcoat, he had something of the air of a retired schoolteacher, especially when he peered over the rims of those ugly spectacles that the famous National Health Service provided.

'My name is Mason Lowell Clay,' said the younger man, offering his hand.

'That is a very impressive name, possibly a famous one, but not one I'm familiar with.'

'Only my mother would agree with that, and it is nowhere near as interesting a name as Polley.'

'Really?' Mr Polley seemed genuinely surprised, his eyebrows jumping like caterpillars on a trampoline. 'I cannot think why. I assumed you were here to research some arcane piece of your family history. That's what brings Americans to Wicken, that and servicemen who were hereabouts during the war, though we were never a big draw even then as we had no dance hall or pub.'

'I'm not interested in Americans who came to Wicken,' said Mason, 'rather people from Wicken who went to America in the seventeenth century and then came straight back again.'

'Ah, you mean the Billericay Covenanters,' said Mr Polley.

Mason followed his host inside, thinking it could not be this easy. Miss Jones had been polite and welcoming but not terribly forthcoming, though the politeness might have been out of respect for Perdita and the Campion name, which he was learning carried weight in the oddest corners of this sceptred isle. But now he was being politely taken on his own merit as a wandering, inquisitive American, and had come across a person who not only knew of the Billericay Covenanters but seemed willing to talk about them. Correction: two people.

'Please call me Richard,' said Mr Polley, 'and this is my sister, Octavia.'

'Thank you for allowing me into your home,' said Mason with a low bow, not only out of reverence, but because the woman whose hand he was gently shaking was looking up at him from a wheelchair.

'I am surely pleased to make your acquaintance, ma'am.'

Octavia Polley had a round, slightly simian face, but twinkling blue eyes made it a kindly one. Her long white hair, corralled in a single rough plait, snaked down over her left breast and coiled on the tartan travel rug which covered her knees.

'A Southern gentleman, I believe,' she said, and Mason was sure he saw an eyelash flutter.

'Well, Southern certainly; the jury's still out on the gentleman bit. You've been to America?'

'Bless my soul, no!' Yes, those eyelashes definitely did flutter. 'During the war I saw *Gone with the Wind* eleven times. Not here, of course, we don't run to a cinema here in Wicken. I was in the Wrens in Portsmouth. I met lots of Americans there.'

'Now, now, Octavia, Mr Clay doesn't want to hear about your ancient history, however salaciously you remember it,' said her brother.

'Oh, but I do,' said Mason. 'Well, not the salacious bits perhaps, more the very ancient bits of your family history, your ancestors.'

'The Covenanters, Octavia. The gentleman isn't interested in us, merely our family tree, though why an American should be interested in a family which so conspicuously failed to emigrate there two centuries ago is a mystery. Perhaps he will tell you while I put the kettle on.'

As Richard Polley left the room, his sister waved Mason to be seated and manoeuvred her chair so that she was directly in front of him, if still not at eye level.

'I am researching the links between Wicken and Harkers Island,' he began, to be quickly halted by Octavia's thin and mottled upraised hand.

'What is a harker's island, may one ask?'

'It's a place, an island near the coast of North Carolina, in what we call the Outer Banks. Geographically, the coast is sort of similar to the one here. Is the name not familiar to you?'

'I've never heard it before. Richard!' she shouted towards the doorway her brother had disappeared through. 'Have you ever heard of a Harkers Island? It's in America somewhere.'

'Can't say I have, dear,' came the disembodied voice, 'but we've got an old school atlas somewhere.'

Octavia Polley leaned forward towards Mason and whispered, 'It's pre-war and has Germany marked with a swastika for its national flag.'

Mason raised his voice so that it would carry to the kitchen. 'Harkers Island is the place where the Billericay Covenanters ended up when they crossed the Atlantic in 1692, or at least some of them did. Almost half, as far as I can judge, didn't like it and came back.'

'*I'm not taking my coat off, I'm not stopping*,' came from the kitchen amidst a crash of crockery. 'Isn't that what they say up north?'

Again, the old woman in the wheelchair leaned in. 'Ignore him, he's never been north of Birmingham in his life.'

'I'm interested in those families who left from Wicken and who came back to Wicken. They seemed like a tight-knit group.'

'And Polley is on your list, I suppose,' said Richard, advancing with a tea tray.

'There was a John Polley on board the ship, the *Abigail*, which took the Covenanters to America and then brought some of them back,' said Mason, pulling a notebook from his jacket pocket.

'And we have an Abigail Cottage here in Wicken,' offered Octavia.

'I know, I have talked with Miss Jones there.'

'I bet she told you all about her sister, Theodora,' said the old woman almost conspiratorially, 'who went to America and was treated like a film star. She certainly put Wicken on the map.'

'Not quite every map, thank goodness,' said Richard, pouring tea. 'Was Sylvia Jones of any help in your research? . . . Sugar? We've no biscuits, I'm afraid, Octavia has to watch her girlish figure.'

'Two please, and don't worry about biscuits on my account.' Mason patted his tight-as-a-drum stomach. 'Miss Jones did tell us about Theodora, who sounds as if she was an interesting woman, but she was unable to help much with anything more . . . historical.'

'For Sylvia, history begins and ends with Theodora,' said Polley. 'I'm afraid she has lived her life very much in her shadow. I take it she wasn't very forthcoming about her antecedents, even though the name of her cottage is a bit of a giveaway.'

'Miss Jones said she had no proof that the Jones listed in the Billericay Covenant—'

'Henry and Silence Jones, I seem to recall,' said Polley, his eyes rolling.

'—that she had no documented proof that she was connected to them. It is, after all, a fairly common name.'

'Polley is less common, and unlike Sylvia, we are proud of our family history.' Richard raised a teacup towards his sister in salute. 'For we are the last surviving descendants of Livewell Polley, and we know this for a fact. Please do not ask us to prove it with documents, though. I believe the current expression is "oral history", but that doesn't mean it is not valid. My grandmother told me that she had a Bible in which Livewell Polley had written his name, though I never saw it and where it is now I simply do not know. But since we were children, we have known the story of our emigrating ancestor, Livewell Polley.'

'It was John Polley who signed the Billericay Covenant,' said Mason, 'and he is listed as a passenger on the *Abigail* as a widower, accompanied by two sons, Nathan and Livewell. There is one source' – Mason did not specify – 'which states that Nathan died on the crossing to Massachusetts.'

'Of Nathan Polley we know nothing, do we, Octavia?'

'Not a thing,' said his sister, all innocence. 'So they went to Massachusetts, did they? I have heard of that.'

'Only briefly. They landed near a place called Salem, but very quickly the *Abigail* left there and took the Covenanters down the eastern seaboard to North Carolina.'

'This Harker place you mentioned?'

'Yes, but they didn't stay there long either, or about half of them did. The other half returned to England. I would like to know who broke the Covenant and why.'

'Well one part of your mystery is solved,' said Richard carefully settling his cup back on its saucer. 'Livewell Polley did return to England, and we are living proof of that. There are others in Wicken who share a name with the original Covenanters as well. Our neighbour, Joshua Jarmin, for one.'

Mason consulted his notebook, though he did not really need to as he knew its contents by heart. 'He would be a descendant of Devon and Rosennah Jarmin.'

'And his wife Leonora, she's a Barly,' said Octavia.

Now it was the turn of Mason's eyebrows to dance upward. 'As in Joseph Barly, who was a Covenanter and who travelled with his sister Ruth?'

'If you say so,' said the woman demurely.

'And her brother Robert Barly,' said Polley, 'is not only married to a Bugg, but lives next door to one.'

Mason produced a pen and opened his notebook to a fresh page. 'If you don't mind, sir, I'd like to make notes. You see I'm taking a sort of census, a small one, just of this street in Wicken.'

'The *only* street in Wicken.' Richard Polley smiled. 'If it helps in your research, please go ahead.'

Mason scratched furiously with his pen as he spoke. 'So if I've got this right, moving due east, we have Polleys, Jarmins, Buggs . . .'

'Just one,' said Octavia. 'George Bugg never married but his sister Modesty married Robert Barly, and they live next door in the other half of that semi-detached house, so she can look after George quite easily.'

'So then that's Barly and Jones, all names which feature on either the Billericay Covenant or among the passengers on the *Abigail*, and none of those names feature on Harkers Island. That's a remarkable hit rate.'

'I'm sorry, but hit rate sounds ominous. What exactly do you mean?' Polley asked him.

'Forgive me for a crude Americanism.' Mason thought that Mr Campion would approve of that term, though Lugg would have used a more colourful description. 'What I meant was that all those Covenanter names can be traced back to the same street in Wicken after nearly three hundred years.'

'All of them?'

'Well, not quite all. I was hoping to find the name Lux here in Wicken. It's very unusual and hasn't shown up in our research in either Massachusetts or North Carolina, so the assumption was that he returned to England and to Wicken.'

'That would be Abendigo Lux,' said Polley.

'Correct.'

'But you don't *know* that he came back to Wicken or, if he did, that his descendants would leave a trace here at this distance in time. They may have moved away. I have no idea whether Livewell Polley settled back in Wicken or where he found a wife or started a family, but at some point the Polleys lived in London and it was our parents who moved out to Wicken so we could be brought up in the country. That would be around 1890 and, of course, this house would have been brand new then; it certainly wasn't the ancestral home that Livewell Polley came back to. Wicken was probably a collection of mud huts back in 1692; if the Covenanters really did come back *to Wicken*, they did not necessarily stay here. After all, people move away, get married, go off to fight in foreign wars, or just die without issue.'

'As we will,' said Octavia, catching Mason's look of surprise. 'Please don't be shocked, Mr Clay, I suspect you thought it as soon as you met us. My brother is almost eighty and I am his older sister and confined to this chair. Neither of us have had or will have children, so the Polley name will soon disappear from Wicken. Perhaps you have traced us just in time.'

'But you must admit,' said Mason, exuding boyish charm, 'that it is curious that so many of the names of those who returned from America are present in Wicken *today*, even if they haven't been a permanent presence.'

'I doubt any resident can really claim a permanent presence,' said Polley. 'The Wicken that the Covenanters left all those years ago is long gone, somewhere under the mud out there on the flats. This Wicken, such as it is, dates from the nineteenth century.'

'The Methodist chapel should have been the clue,' smiled Octavia.

Mason's eyes widened. 'Somebody has mentioned that there was a war memorial in the chapel. It might be worth checking the names listed on that.'

'It's quite a short list, as I recall,' said Richard, 'and it doesn't go back before the First World War.'

'Still, it would be interesting to see who's on it. I may go take a look.'

'The chapel's locked up these days unless there's a meeting taking place,' said Octavia rather sharply, 'though I'm sure Richard could get a key for you if you plan on coming back here.'

'Oh, I do, I will surely have lots of other questions, but you've already been most helpful filling in some gaps on my census form for Wicken. I've met Miss Jones and, briefly, Mrs Jarmin. Do you think her husband – or Mr Bugg or Mr Barly – would be willing to talk to me?'

'None of those gentlemen are very good conversationalists, especially not where strangers are concerned,' said Polley apologetically.

'Josh Jarmin and Bob Barly don't talk to their wives if they can help it,' giggled Octavia, 'and for them foreigners start at Dengie. They would not be forthcoming.'

'I think I've witnessed their hospitality, or lack of it,' said Mason, remembering the grim faces of the three men who had stared them out of Wicken, 'but I would like to talk to them at some point, as well as the two of you.'

'I'm not sure how we can help any more, though we are more than willing to,' said Mr Polley.

'If you can dig out any old family records – births, marriages, deaths – those would help.'

'Of course we will, but they won't go back more than two generations, Mr Clay, certainly not as far as Livewell Polley.'

'Anything at all would help. There are also several sources in London I can consult.'

'There are?'

'Land titles, property records, wills, legal contracts, things like that.'

'That sounds like a Herculean task.'

'There are some first-rate archivists in London and, I understand, in Chelmsford at your County Records Office. I'm sure I'll turn up something, but I'd still like a look at that memorial inside your chapel.'

'Hardly ours,' said Octavia with a slight flutter in her voice. 'We are not of that congregation – hardly anyone is these days.'

'Well, I would be grateful if you could get me that key. Can I phone ahead when I plan to return here?'

'We do not have a telephone I'm afraid, but don't worry, Mr Clay,' said the woman with a broad smile, 'we'll see you coming.'

Mary Ann Allen had finished her day's work at Dr Fathoms's surgery and prepared as best she could for the next morning's influx of patients. Having given serious thought to what she needed to purchase at the shops before they closed, she put on her coat and said goodnight to her employer.

By chance, Dr Harry Fathoms was looking out of his office window as Mary Ann reversed her car away from the front of the house.

Looking at the front bumper and grille of the Ford Anglia as it pulled away, he screwed up his eyes and then automatically opened his mouth to shout something to Mary Ann before realizing she could not possibly hear him.

Best not to worry her, he thought; at least not before he had made a phone call.

Dusk was falling as Mary Ann Allen approached Asheldham and the turn-off to Dengie and Wicken, and she had made sure the Anglia's headlights were on and safely dipped. They gave her enough warning to allow her to touch the brake pedal and steer close enough into the hedgerow to avoid the three shadowy figures riding abreast on bicycles without lamps.

She heard the metallic scraping as the hedgerow attempted to scratch the Anglia's paintwork from stem to stern, cursed the county council for not providing street lights, or pavements and kerbs, or even wider roads, and then cursed a world where young men – for the shadowy figures were undoubtedly male – were stupid enough to ride around narrow country lanes without any lights on.

Her lights were on, as required by the law and all sane practice, so they must have seen the Anglia approaching, yet they had seemed almost oblivious to its presence. They had not even paused in their furious pedalling and had disappeared towards Southminster at high speed.

For the rest of the journey, Mary Ann drove with headlights on full beam, prepared to dip them only if she met an oncoming vehicle, which she did not. In fact, she saw no other sign of life until she turned into the single street of Wicken and the beams picked up the outline of something even more unexpected than a trio of wayward cyclists.

Pedestrians on the sole road through Wicken were rare enough on balmy summer days good for birdwatching, but of an evening, such traffic was unusual.

It took her several seconds, and a dipping of the Anglia's lights, before she could make out the silhouetted figures who were walking away from her advancing vehicle and were level with Abigail Cottage.

Well, one of them was walking, the other was being pushed in a wheelchair.

Mary Ann pulled into the gravelled space in front of her bungalow and turned off the Anglia's engine and lights. She got out of her car and began to unload her shopping from the boot, while peering out into the darkness, but saw no sign of the late evening strollers.

In a way, though, it was good to see the Polleys getting out of the house.

'Campion? It's Harry Fathoms.'

'Dr Fathoms? What a surprise, although it's rarely a good surprise when a doctor telephones out of hours.'

'I am not your doctor, Campion, and to be honest, slightly relieved that I am not and I'm not ringing on medical matters.'

'Then how can I help, Harry?'

'You remember that thing you showed me, that little bottle with the rusty nails and the thorn twigs?'

'The witch bottle? Yes, of course. Your receptionist, Mrs Allen, she knew what it was. Said they were as common as horse brasses in a Wicken pub, if there were any pubs in Wicken, that is.'

'It's about Mary Ann that I'm calling you. I hope I'm not disturbing anything by the way.'

'Not at all. My wife is away on business for a few days, so I have the run of the place. I'm rarely out of my pyjamas, can watch what I like on the telly and am living off cold cuts and cheese on toast, so please, disturb away, my wife will thank you in the long run.'

Down the line, Campion heard Dr Fathoms take a deep breath.

'Well that rather bizarre conversation in my surgery got me thinking today.'

'Are we talking delayed-reaction here, Harry? The penny just starting to drop? It's a sign of getting old, you know. Perhaps you should see a doctor.'

'Oh stop waffling, Campion, and listen. Something I saw this evening got me thinking about your witch's bottle and all things witchcrafty, if that's a word.'

'If it isn't, it should be, it's a jolly good word. What prompted it?'

'I saw what I am sure could only be described as a voodoo doll, a small home-made thing, a straw doll, the thing people stick pins into in the horror films.'

'I know what you mean,' said Mr Campion, suddenly serious, 'and I think it's called a "reflection", which is more of a warning than a curse, if you believe in that sort of thing. Where did you see it?'

'It was tied to the front bumper of Mary Ann Allen's car, but I don't think she has any idea it's there.'

FOURTEEN
In the Wild West End

It was Brian Heard's favourite time of day because it was so unexciting. As the senior, often only, official at Southminster station, he did not like excitement, which was why he preferred the late afternoon/early evening shift. Morning trains to London Liverpool Street were hectic, with commuters jostling for places on the platform and then scrumming for favourite seats on the short diesel trains which would transport them to Wickford, there to connect with the Southend trains running in to London. There was a time when he would have been on nodding terms of recognition with almost all the morning travellers; the patient, regimented way they used to line up on the platform, bowler-hatted and pinstriped, had always pleased his eye. Standards had, however, slipped, and just anyone dressed in the most cavalier fashion seemed to have a job up in London now. In the mornings, everyone was frantic to claim their personal seat on a train at the expense of courtesy and good manners.

In the evenings, after a hard day's work, the passengers detraining at Southminster were a far less boisterous crowd; they would slink away into the evening, causing Brian Heard and his station few problems. Which was exactly how Brian preferred it, for he deserved a quiet life, given the awesome responsibility which was his lot every Wednesday when, late in the evening, he supervised the loading and departure of a short goods train carrying a 'nuclear flask', which transported nuclear waste from the Bradwell power station at the far tip of the Dengie Peninsula. Quite where it went once the train left the Southminster platform was of little concern to Brian Heard; he was always just relieved that the operation had gone, once again, without a hitch.

Apart from Wednesdays, the evenings tended to be uneventful once the 'London crowd' had returned from their daily grind. It was not unknown, but rare, to find passengers wanting to travel back up to London, other than on high days and holidays, and so Brian was mildly annoyed that the restful evening he had planned around the small television he had installed in the station-master's office was disturbed by would-be travellers demanding tickets.

Brian had certainly no intention of shirking his duty, so he sold three day-return tickets 'to Lunnon' to the men who had, blatantly disregarding the advertised by-laws, chained their bicycles to the iron railings outside the entrance hall. It irked him that their spokesman said neither please nor thank you, and merely grunted when Brian freely offered the advice that they should change trains at Wickford and that the last train back from Liverpool Street would be the 10.13; miss that and it meant waiting for the milk train the next morning.

For his pains and all his good intentions, he received only a non-committal grunt from the man he assumed was the leader of the trio, or at least the holder of the purse strings, quite literally, as he paid for the tickets with crumpled notes pulled carefully from a small leather purse, accepting his change with another grunt.

He was almost tempted to point out that good manners cost little, but thought the better of it, given the general roughness of the men's appearance. Most of their faces were covered with scarves or caps pulled low and they all wore thick leather gloves. Their clothes were those of workmen, possibly fishermen, and even through the window of the ticket booth, they gave off a distinct whiff of sweat and oil.

Brian Heard could not imagine what sort of a night out in London town those three were planning, dressed like that.

'Will we see the Protein Man?' asked one of the men as their train pulled into Liverpool Street.

'I doubt it,' said their leader. 'He'll have knocked off for the day.'

'Pity. He was a laugh, he was.'

On his one previous trip to London, the man who had spoken had come face-to-face with the famous Protein Man while walking along Oxford Street. He'd been much taken with the 'walking billboard' as he was known – a man dedicated to promulgating the message of 'less passion from less protein' as displayed on the billboards strapped to his person. Of all the sights the man had seen, from double-decker buses painted yellow to promote something called *Yellow Pages*, the extreme miniskirts worn by the girls, the lurid posters for *No Sex Please, We're British* or, proving the alternative, the window display of the Lovecraft sex shop in the Tottenham Court Road, the one encounter that had stuck with him had been the Protein Man, walking down the street quietly and politely handing out leaflets advising on how to avoid lust.

On this occasion, the three men were not on a sightseeing trip but had a distinct purpose in mind.

They took a Central Line tube train, choosing the smoking carriage, the second from the front, where they thought they would stand out least amongst the other passengers who invariably travelled with their eyes down or focused on the evening newspaper.

Once they disembarked at Tottenham Court Road station and turned down the Charing Cross Road, however, their eyes were everywhere but pointed down as the brightly lit shop fronts, the pub doorways exhaling a tobacco and warm beer breath, the garish illuminations of a cinema here and a theatre there, magnetically drew their attention, none more so than the bright shiny emporium which claimed to be a Chef & Brewer Steak House, even though the locals still referred to it as The Crown.

The trio moved in silence, avoiding contact with a torrent of fellow pedestrians and wary of the constant stream of traffic in the road, never having experienced either in such volumes before.

Only the leader seemed alert and attentive to their progress, actively counting off the street numbers on the awnings of the shops. Despite the profusion of lights of every colour and brightness, it was as if the trio moved as one composite shadow.

The leader signalled a halt outside the window of a bookshop, the display of old, leather-bound books illuminated from below by a single yellow bulb in a small spotlight. The leader consulted the name and street number above the window and moved to his right and the door at the side of the shop, then he took a step backwards into the road and looked up, nodding to the others in satisfaction when he saw that the lights were on in the window above the shop. He drew his companions closer and, with an erect forefinger, made an upward jabbing motion, then pointed towards the black street door which bore a small brass plate bearing the legend Timms's Theatricals.

One of the men – it would have been unclear which, had any pedestrian noticed anything unusual about three men lurking in a doorway on the Charing Cross Road of an evening – produced from the depths of his overcoat a knife with a long and very thin blade. The knifeman inserted the flexible blade into the door jamb near the circular plate of the Yale lock which secured it, probing for the latch and giving a snort of satisfaction when the door swung silently inwards.

The three men found themselves at the foot of a staircase lit only by the glow of light coming from an upstairs room. There was music coming down the stairs along with the light, a classical piano piece which meant nothing to the three intruders, other than indicating that the upstairs room was inhabited and their target was in place.

It was well known in London's Theatreland that Timothy 'Timmy' Timms, theatrical agent to the stars, worked odd office hours. Indeed, some said the fact that he had an office at all was odd, for he was rarely present except in the early evening. During the normal 'office hours' of daylight, his secretary, an ambitious young lady named Paula Whittle, held the fort and dealt with the suggestions, complaints and whines – mostly whining complaints – of Timms's many thespian clients. After a day spent in meetings or lunches with producers, directors, television companies and advertising agencies (a growing part of his business), Timmy Timms would check into his office, be briefed by Miss Whittle on the day's telephone calls and any mail he had to answer, and after dismissing her, would settle down to sign the letters and contracts she had prepared for him.

That he chose to spend his evenings in his slightly sordid West End office rather than his more comfortable home out in Putney was a deliberate choice on his part and responsible for his unrivalled grasp of theatrical gossip and rumour. As he knew the running times of every show in the West End, he would visit certain pubs, the pubs to which backstage theatre staff, musicians and occasional actors would pay a furtive visit, at certain times, and there receive the latest gossip about who had done what well, or – more often – failed at. Thus, he was ahead of the game when it came to predicting which shows were succeeding and which had outlived their welcome; which actors were doing well and whose careers were faltering.

He had even featured in the more scurrilous press when an incident was widely reported of how he had been deep in conversation with a well-known actor during the interval of a play staged in a Shaftesbury Avenue theatre. It was only after Timmy had bought a third round of drinks – for he was a generous host – that the actor remembered suddenly, and with an expletive, that he had been due on stage next door several minutes ago.

Whatever his plans for that particular evening, Timmy Timms was certainly not expecting visitors, though some were to say later that perhaps he should have been.

They were not welcome visitors.

Rupert Campion had had a frustrating day. It was about to get worse.

He had spent an uncomfortable afternoon attempting to pull the wool over his agent's eyes. Whenever agents sensed that their commission might be at risk, that was never a sound tactic.

Rupert, intrigued and not a little flattered by Timmy Timms's blatant hints of employment with the director Geoffrey Clegg, had determined to discover as much as he could about the proposed project involving Jacobean theatricals and, most importantly, television. He could not, of course, come out and ask his agent, the jovial Maxim Berlins, in any straightforward way, as he could not leave a trail of clues which might lead back to Timmy Timms; a rival agent and therefore a deadly enemy.

Their conversation, over lunch and beyond, had therefore been rather elliptical, with Rupert claiming to have 'overheard some tittle-tattle' down in Gerry's, the actors' club in Dean Street, about a possible television extravaganza written, or produced, or something-ed by Geoffrey Clegg, the inevitable question being: was there a part in it for him? Maxim had denied knowing that any such programme was planned or in development, adding that if he believed everything he heard in Gerry's, then he would be either a very rich man and no longer an agent, or he would be on the dole in the company of half the actors in London. But Maxim was a considerate agent when it came to his younger clients, and never liked to admit that he had not himself heard a juicy rumour of potential employment, so he made a series of long telephone calls to his various contacts 'in the business'. He began, naturally, with several 'dear friends' at the BBC, for surely the project Rupert described would not be meat and drink to any independent television company, but no one in Maxim's thick and dog-eared contacts' book knew anything of value, let alone substance.

Finally, Rupert had admitted that perhaps he had got the wrong end of a very vague stick, or possibly had enjoyed himself too much down in Gerry's – a far from rare occurrence given the sociable nature of that establishment – and had thanked Maxim for all his efforts.

In the evening, he had haunted the theatre bars and pubs known to be frequented by actors, in the faint hope of picking up a morsel of useful gossip. He was careful in pacing his alcohol intake and only buying small drinks, as actors usually do, from the Haymarket up to the Lyric and then the Apollo, the Globe, the Queen's and the Palace until he reached the Charing Cross Road.

By that time he was tired, hungry, disenchanted and a little bit confused. He could not face standing at another bar nursing a half-pint of cold, thin bitter, and decided to take the bull by the horns, confront Timmy Timms in his office and demand to know if the prospect of television work he had dangled in front of him was a reality, or yet another example of the aspiring actor's determination to clutch at any straw, no matter how thin, mouldy or out of reach it might be.

He was surprised to find the door to Timms's Theatricals open to the elements and, had he been thinking more clearly, a faint warning bell might have sounded as he started up the staircase towards the light and the tinkling of piano music. On the fourth or fifth step he became aware of other sounds, and the fact that the light from the office seemed to flicker as if figures were moving across the lamp. He froze, mid-step.

He heard a thumping sound and the scrape of furniture being moved, then more thumps and bumps and, perhaps, a gasp and a grunt and a curse; and then, quite definitely, a cry of pain, all incongruously in time to the music.

Rupert took the last few steps at the charge until he was level with the open door of Timmy Timms's office, where once again he froze.

He caught a glimpse of Timmy Timms's body sprawled supine and inert over a desktop, but it was only a glimpse, for his view was obscured by the two dark figures hurtling, heads down, towards him.

The last thing he remembered was being bowled over and propelled painfully down the staircase with several pairs of feet clumping after and over him.

'Now don't get in a twist,' said Lugg with a dry mouth and a quivering bottom lip.

'When the telephone disturbs my beauty sleep in the dead of night,' said Mr Campion, 'I have every right to get in a twist. When I hear your dulcet tones and mangled vowels, I positively corkscrew.'

'Is Lady A there?'

'No, she's up in Scotland flirting with the Fleet Air Arm.'

'Good.' Lugg's exhale of relief thundered down the line. 'Perdita told me to tell her not to panic, but I'd rather tell you.'

'Tell me what? And tell me quick because I am certainly starting to panic. Is Perdita all right?'

'She's fine and so's Rupert, all things considering . . .'

'Lugg . . .' Campion's warning tone was unmissable.

''E 'ad a bit of a mishap down the Charing Cross Road.'

'What sort of mishap?'

'Well 'is head connected with a solid lump of it, but that was after he fell down the stairs.'

'What stairs?'

'The stairs from the office where the body was.'

'*Body?*'

'That's why the police are keeping tabs on 'im. At best he could be a witness, at worst he could be their number one suspect.'

'Lugg, I'm not following this and, worryingly, I don't think you are either. If this is really serious, we must pull in a few favours and get Charles Luke on the case.'

'Already done that, thank you very much. Charlie wasn't pleased at being dragged out of bed either, but was grateful for the news, unlike some people . . . Said he'd look into things, get his best men on it. Always 'ad a soft spot for young Rupert, Charlie did.'

'And where exactly is Rupert?'

'Back 'ome now with the little woman. He took a mighty whack to the back of his head by all accounts, but came round in the ambulance. They checked him out at St Mary's in Paddington for concussion and such, but they let him go home.'

'So his memory was intact, he could remember where he lived?'

'Seems like it, not like some I could mention. No fear of like father, like son there.' Lugg could not resist referring to the famous case of amnesia which had struck Mr Campion before Rupert was born. 'I told Perdita that if he suddenly went blank and asked, "Who am I?" she was to tell him he was Steve McQueen.'

'What a comfort you are in times of trouble, a real Uncle Job among the agony aunts. Look, I was planning on heading down to Essex in the morning anyway, but as it is almost morning . . . What time is it anyway?'

'Quarter-past two by the fob watch I just 'appen to have in my pyjamas. You're not the only one losing beauty sleep, you know.'

'You do need it more,' conceded Mr Campion. 'Are you at Bottle Street?'

'I am. Me and Mason are getting on famously.'

'Oh dear, that's a pity. Just when Anglo-American relations were going so well. Listen, I'll be with you for breakfast, after I've looked in on Rupert. If Luke gets in touch, tell him I'm on my way.'

'Perdita told me to let his mother know the score, not you. Said Lady A would react calmly and for the best.'

'And as usual, given one simple task, you bungled it. But fear not, old fruit, I've another job lined up for you, a nice trip out to the country.'

'Doing what?'

'We're going witch-finding.'

'He's sleeping. The doctors gave him something for the pain, and now it's kicked in he's likely to be out of it for most of the day.'

Mr Campion put an arm around his daughter-in-law's

shoulders. 'Sleep is probably the best healer. Lugg says there was no concussion.'

'No, but there could be delayed shock and the painkillers are for his ribs – he may have cracked a couple. Or rather, whoever gave him a good kicking cracked them. Luckily, whoever did it was wearing rubber boots, like Wellingtons.'

'Really? How odd. Not the normal dress code for a night out in the West End. Perhaps it's a fashion thing.'

'It's not,' said Perdita, 'but Rupert remembers that quite distinctly.'

'Was he able to tell you what happened?'

'Some of it, though he nearly died of embarrassment doing so.'

'How is that possible? It wasn't his fault he was beaten up, was it?'

'Oh no, it was why he was lurking around Timmy Timms's office in the first place. That odious little man with his terrible wigs had been dripping poison into Rupert's ear, promising him a great career boost with the sainted Geoffrey Clegg. He's a big-time director, by the way.'

'And a friend of Jocasta Upcott, I believe.'

'That doesn't surprise me,' said Perdita wearily. 'They regard themselves as theatrical royalty and, to be fair, getting in with that crowd could help Rupert's career. It's always who you know, not how good you are . . .'

Mr Campion gave her shoulder a comforting squeeze as he shook his head slowly. 'So cynical, so young. You think Rupert should let his talent do his talking for him?'

'If the alternative is becoming some sort of lapdog or errand boy, yes. Timms dangled the prospect of working with Geoffrey Clegg on a television special, serious dramatic stuff, not a knock-about sit-com with canned laughter. All Rupert had to do was find some damn dog Clegg had lost, just like you'd found Jocasta's pooch. Timms said he should go and look for it in Wicken. What is it about Wicken? Is it where dogs are supposed to go to when they're lost?'

'I'm beginning to think so,' said Mr Campion.

Campion was mindful of Perdita's complaint that in her profession it might very well be who you knew that advanced your career, but he had no qualms about consulting one of London's most senior policemen on a personal problem in the same spirit.

Mr Campion knew Commander Charles Luke well. He had in fact known him for more than twenty years, from his days as a lowly divisional detective inspector – if such a rank could ever really be described as lowly – to his present, far more exalted position. The two had worked together, shared dangers and confidences, and they trusted each other implicitly. Campion had always said that Luke's oak-like presence alone gave solidity and security to any perilous situation, though he did flippantly admit that in the Bottle Street flat, Luke did take up a lot of room.

'I'm sorry to drag you into this, Charles, but I thought you might be interested, and you know my philosophy has always been that a trouble shared is two people worrying unnecessarily.'

Luke flexed his shoulders as he unbuttoned his uniform jacket and took the cup of tea Lugg had proffered. Mason Lowell, once he had been introduced and experienced the awesome power of a Luke handshake, adopted the role of silent observer. He was fascinated by the fact that his mild-mannered, white-haired, owlish host, who didn't look tough enough to tree a frightened squirrel, could snap his fingers and summon one of the top cops in the city to make a house call. What's more, this policeman friend, in a uniform so smart it would not have looked out of place at the Trooping the Colour, seemed to be on more than nodding terms – perhaps even drinking terms? – with the lugubrious Mr Lugg, and while he was unclear as to what Lugg's actual role in the Campion household was, he struck Mason as a character who had not, in the past, always seen eye to eye with the police.

'Have you any thoughts on what happened down the Charing Cross Road, Charles? Official ones, that is.'

Luke blew on his tea then sipped with such delicacy that Mason half expected to see the 'extended pinkie' the British were famous for.

'Officially,' Luke began, puffing out his chest, 'a beat bobby was called following a report of a person drunk and disorderly lying in a bookshop doorway. Said person was found to be Number One Son Rupert, who, when he came round, did admit that drink had been taken. When the uniforms on the scene went upstairs to the office above the shop, they found a body spread-eagled over a desk and very dead, so they did the obvious thing and arrested Rupert.'

'They felt the nearest collar,' muttered Lugg, 'not the right one.'

Luke ignored him. 'The deceased was a gentleman named Timothy Timms, a theatrical agent and impresario who was known to occupy his office in the evenings when there were shows on in the West End, which is almost always.'

'He also used the name Charles Wyndham,' said Campion, 'but only when he went birdwatching.'

Luke furrowed his brow, creating an expression which had terrified many of the criminal classes. 'If you say so, Albert. Is it relevant?'

'Perhaps not. Possibly, though not directly, to what happened to Rupert.'

'What the hell *did* happen to Rupert?' wailed Mason. 'You guys may be on some sort of mind-reading wavelength, but I'm feeling left out of the loop.'

'Young Mr Campion's version of events,' Luke began in official mode, 'is that he stumbled, quite by accident, into the middle of an assault on this Mr Timms. A fatal assault, as it turned out, by two or perhaps three assailants. As he was, in effect, blocking the escape route of the assailants, and his sudden appearance on the scene clearly surprised them, they simply ran him over, pushing him down a flight of stairs and giving him a good kicking on the way. Considering what they did to Timmy Timms, Rupert got off quite lightly. Must have flexible bones and a thick skull.'

'Runs in the family,' growled Lugg, and was again ignored.

'What *did* they do to Timms?' asked Campion quietly.

'Best guess: it was a robbery which got out of hand. There was a cash box which had been forced open and Timms's wallet had been emptied. The girl who works as his secretary says there was probably fifty quid in the petty-cash box and Timms used always to carry fifty or so in cash on his person.'

'Opportunist, then?'

'Could be, but maybe they expected more – thought there was more hidden about the place and set about poor Timmy to tell them. There was a lot of fist work involved, but then either Timms started to fight back or one of the thugs saw the red mists and pulled a knife. We'll have to wait for the medical report, but I'm told he was stabbed at least twice and whoever did it would have blood on them.'

'And did any concerned citizen out and about their lawful business see a bloodstained assassin running down the Charing Cross Road?'

'We're checking the new closed-circuit television cameras at Tottenham Court Road station, but that'll take a while. In the meantime, we do have a witness, but not what you might call a reliable one, at least not one that I'd put up in court, but useful to your lad's side of things though. He saw Rupert being chucked downstairs and jumped on by three men, maybe five.'

'You did say he was an unreliable witness.'

'One of our homeless brethren in a shop doorway across the street with only a bottle of Wincarnis for company.'

'A bottle of what?' Mason interrupted.

'You don't want to know, lad,' said Lugg, then to Luke in explanation, 'Mason's a teetotaller, but don't you hold it against him; that's my job.'

'Our witness had no reason to tell lies; in fact he was keen to come forward and was angling for a night's bed-and-breakfast in a nice warm cell, which we provided, but from what he told my detectives, Rupert's status changed from prime suspect to secondary victim.'

'Did you get any sort of description from our witness?' Campion asked.

'A very vague one,' said Luke. 'He said they looked like sailors.'

'Sailors? As in Royal Navy ratings?'

'That's what my lads asked him and he said no, not sailors, trawlermen – like he used to see at the seaside when he was a kid. Mean anything?'

'It might, as it ties in with what Rupert told Perdita, about being kicked by rubber boots. I'm not aware of any fishing boats unloading boxes of kippers on the Victoria Embankment, not recently anyway, so I think we must turn a suspicious eye towards the eastern marches.'

Campion's expression became suddenly serious and Mason

Lowell witnessed what Lugg and Luke knew very well was a Campion 'thinking moment', indicated by him removing his spectacles and polishing the large round lenses with a blazing white handkerchief.

'As this is now a murder investigation, Charles, can I persuade you to use your influence on a neighbouring police force?'

'Would this help us in our inquiries, or is it as a personal favour to you?'

'Both, of course, but if you help me follow a hunch, I am sure it will help with your inquiries.'

'It's a good job we go way back, Albert. I'm getting that old familiar feeling that you are a hop and a step – if not a jump – ahead of me in all this. Let me hazard a guess – you want me to contact Essex County.'

'Yes, please, Charles, if you would. If you can pull a few strings I would be very grateful. You see, I need the help of one of their sergeants, a first-rate chap called Tom Trybull, stationed at Maldon. I want him to take me sailing on a boat called the *Jocasta*.'

'This is to do with you snooping around the Dengie Peninsula, isn't it?' The policeman flashed a look towards Lugg, clearly identifying the source of his information. 'What's going on out there?'

'I'm not exactly sure,' said Campion, replacing his spectacles on his face and putting his handkerchief in his pocket. 'Something bizarre, something off-kilter as far as the modern world goes. There's a place called Wicken, a forgotten place that wants to stay forgotten, but something has disturbed it and brought it to people's attention, and it doesn't like that. I think it's fighting back.'

'Can you hear yourself, Albert? You're not telling spooky stories round the camp fire now.'

'I know it sounds ridiculous, Charles. I'm still trying to get things straight in my head. Tell me, was there anything unusual about Timmy Timms's body?'

'Unusual? In what way? He was dead; that's fairly unusual, even in the Charing Cross Road.'

'I mean was the body displayed or laid out in any sort of ritual way?'

'I don't think so. From what I know he collapsed dead across his desk, though of course Rupert might have disturbed the killers before they could . . . arrange anything. Hang on, what sort of ritual are we talking about here? Black Magic? Religious cult or somebody playing at witchcraft?'

'I do think there's a hint of witchcraft in this business, but I can't see it clearly.'

'You don't believe in all that stuff, though, do you?' Luke was genuinely concerned when he asked his old friend the question.

'It doesn't matter whether I do,' said Mr Campion, 'it's whether the men who killed Timms, and perhaps a chap called Francis Jarrold as well, believe it.'

Luke narrowed his eyes, sighed and stretched his neck, as though his collar was too tight, then reached into the right-hand flapped pocket of his uniform jacket. His hand came out holding a plastic bag in which was a small doll-like figure made of what seemed to be padded hessian material.

'I was going to hand this over to the senior investigating officer,' said Luke, offering it to Campion. 'We didn't think it important, though we've no idea what it is, but when we found Timms's car – a big old Austin 10 saloon parked round on Denmark Street – this was tied to the radiator grille. One of the lads thought it might be a mascot or a good luck charm.'

'It didn't bring Timms much luck, did it?' said Mr Campion.

FIFTEEN
Sea Dogs

Having made several telephone calls and then shared his plans – or given his Action This Day orders, as Lugg put it – Mr Campion left Bottle Street and London, driving northeast towards Essex. It was only fair, Lugg announced, to give him a good head start, so that left time for a second breakfast. He had, after all, had a disturbed night, and felt the need to have a settled stomach or he might prove to be a nervous passenger in Mason's hire car, him being a foreigner who had probably never read the Highway Code.

To his surprise, Mason negotiated the North Circular with ease, despite being cut up twice by black cabs honking their horns, though they, Lugg argued, did not count, as in London, black cabs owned the road and all other traffic was duty bound to get out of their way.

Beyond Romford, Lugg pointed out the road signs to Basildon and then Wickford, and after that he announced solemnly that they were 'in bandit country', where there was 'hardly a friendly face or a pub between here and the horizon'.

In Southminster, Lugg insisted on an unscheduled stop at the railway station, where he asked several questions, in a tone which suggested they had better be answered, of a stationmaster all too easily bludgeoned by Lugg's domineering personality. The fat man rejoined Mason in the rented Marina, satisfied with the answers he had extracted, which included directions to the surgery of Dr Harry Fathoms.

Few of those who knew Mr Lugg well were aware of his almost pathological unease when it came to entering a doctor's surgery. Even though, on this occasion, he had no minor ailment or unsightly bodily blemish to report, he was convinced that medics of all grades, but especially receptionists, could smell fear.

'Yes?'

The single word uttered by the woman who did not look up from her note-taking was as starchy as her uniform blouse. It caused Lugg to stop in his tracks a yard from her desk and ponderously shift his considerable weight from one foot to the other. Mason, who had followed close behind into the doctor's house, almost collided with the quivering statue.

'Mary Ann Allen?' asked the colossus after much clearing of the throat when she finally turned her face up to him, a face which contorted into utter confusion when the big man said meekly: 'My friend here's got three names as well.'

Mason stepped from behind the bulk which had eclipsed him. 'Mason Lowell Clay,' he announced cheerfully, 'pleased to meet you.'

'And who is your friend?' Miss Allen levelled a ballpoint pen like a gun.

'He uses just the one name, Lugg,' said Mason, as if that explained everything.

'Are either of you here to see the doctor?'

'No, love,' said Lugg, stiffening his spine and finding his voice. 'We're your bodyguards.'

'Ahoy there, Cap'n, may I come aboard?'

The head, shoulders and top half of the police uniform of Sergeant Trybull emerged from the cabin of the *Jocasta*, the smile on his face reminding Mr Campion of a schoolboy who had just been excused Latin homework or a cross-country run during a hailstorm.

'Come ahead, Admiral, welcome back to Brightlingsea. You made good time, Mr Campion.'

'Admiral? That sounds like quite a promotion. Last time I was here I wasn't sure I qualified as an able-bodied seaman.'

Campion stepped delicately on to the angled gangplank and, arms outstretched for balance, he quickstepped his way on to the boat's deck.

'Neatly done, sir,' said Trybull, 'and I reckon you must be an admiral because you seem to be in charge. My inspector thinks you must be, because the superintendent told him you were and the chief constable confirmed it.'

'I had no idea admirals had so much power.' Campion grinned. 'I always associated them with Gilbert and Sullivan.'

Trybull smiled and gave his visitor a mock salute. 'I don't ask where the orders come from, I just follow them. They told me to get things shipshape here on the *Jocasta* and be ready to go to sea under your command.'

'I hope you don't mind me disrupting your day.'

'Not at all, going out on the water is a day off with pay as far as I'm concerned, though I understand I will still be on duty.'

'It may be necessary, if only to get me out of trouble.'

'Are we expecting trouble?'

'I'm not quite sure what we can expect, to be honest. I'm stirring things up to see what happens. How long will it take us to sail round to Wicken, or as near as we can get to it?'

Trybull peered over the side of the yacht at the cloudy waters of the River Colne. 'With the ebb tide, which will be around five o'clock, and no headwind, we should make a steady five knots, so two hours, perhaps less. Be there at dusk.'

'And you're confident about navigating the sandbanks and the channels through the mud?'

'As long as we have enough water under us, I can get you in close. And in case of emergencies, I've checked that the radio works, as well as providing us with our own personal lifeboat.'

He crooked a finger, indicating that Campion should follow him to the stern of the boat, where he showed him the bright orange inflatable dinghy wallowing in the water, tied to the rail.

'Good thinking, Captain,' said Campion, 'but I hope we don't have to abandon ship. Did you get my other rather odd request?'

'I did,' said Trybull, turning to the saloon doors of the cabin and pulling them open.

There was a flurry of noise, a scrabbling sound from the cabin below and then a head appeared, butting against the policeman's knees.

'Meet Constable Siegfried,' he said formally, 'one of the brightest and best officers on the force.'

Dr Fathoms had patients to see, real patients with genuine ailments, before he could accept casual visitors, and so Lugg was told to take a seat in the waiting room and, well, wait. There was a wide range of reading material provided there; with something, he was told as an afterthought, suitable for all ages.

Mason Lowell watched in open-mouthed amazement as a docile Lugg padded into the waiting room, picked up a well-thumbed copy of *Horse & Hounds* from a low table and then settled his bulk carefully into one of the plastic chairs lining the wall. The chair seemed to bend under Lugg's onslaught, but it did not break.

With a finger, Mason pressed down on the edge of the magazine Lugg was perusing until the fat man's eyes swivelled up to meet his.

'What did the guy at the station tell you?' he asked in a whisper in deference to the other waiting patients, a woman with a sickly child of eight or nine and a teenager wearing a leather jacket and jeans, one leg cut short to accommodate the plaster cast encasing his foot.

'Three men, rough types but not young tearaways' – Lugg's beady eyes flicked towards the patient in the leather jacket and the cast – 'got off the last London train, got on their pushbikes and headed off into the night.'

'Heading for Wicken?'

'That general direction. Stationmaster didn't like the look of them but didn't know them. Weren't his regular customers, 'e said.'

'You'll tell Mr Campion?'

'O'course I will, soon 'as I see him. Meantime I'm following orders. His nibs told me to stick to that dragon' – he jerked his head towards Mary Ann Allen's desk – 'like a corn plaster, whether she likes it or not. He spoke to her boss, the doc, this morning, and cleared it with him. So I'll sit here until she knocks off work and then see her safely home.'

'Do you really think she might be in danger?'

'Albert does and that's good enough for me.'

Mason consulted his wristwatch. 'If you're gonna be here for a couple of hours, I'll shoot over to Wicken. There's something I want to see in the chapel there. I can check out the lie of the land, see if there are any suspicious characters lurking around her house. I know which one it is.'

Lugg dropped his eyes back to the article on modern dressage he was pretending to read. 'They're all suspicious characters out there on the marshes,' he said quietly. 'So watch yerself.'

'Will do. Back before you know it.'

Mason strode out towards the hallway and Mary Ann's desk, but turned as Lugg said loudly, 'And remember to drive on the left.'

'I'm sorry to have kept you waiting,' said Dr Fathoms after sending his last patient limping on his way clutching a prescription form. 'You must be Lugg. Albert Campion rang me about you – please come through to my office.'

Lugg levered himself to his feet and glanced nervously across the hall. 'I'm not here for a consultation, doc. Albert didn't book me in for a surprise examination of any sort, did he? He has a funny sense of humour that way.'

'Nothing of the sort. In fact, Mr Campion said you were fit as a fiddle and strong as an ox, and in remarkably good health for a man of your age, which he said was ninety-three, but I think that was a joke.'

'It is, but that sounds just like him.'

'Well, come through and we'd better get Mary Ann to join us.'

They settled in the doctor's examination room, Lugg carefully avoiding the trolley bed and the blue nylon screens and suspiciously eyeing the blood-pressure machine with cuff and bulb and the stethoscope splayed across the desk.

'I'm not terribly sure what this is all about,' started Fathoms.

'Join the club, doc, I'm only following orders.'

'Whose orders?' asked Miss Allen.

'Albert Campion's,' said Fathoms. 'We talked with him about Wicken and he rang me early this morning. Said he was sending . . . sending someone to make sure you were safe. I didn't tell you until now because I didn't want to worry you.'

Mary Ann's face displayed shock and horror, which Lugg took as a reaction to the suggestion that she was in any way vulnerable, as she-dragons rarely seek the protection of mere men.

'Keep me safe? Safe from what? You're not thinking about that stupid little effigy someone tied on to my car, are you?' She turned on Lugg. 'Your Mr Campion was getting very excited about a witch bottle he'd found on Francis Jarrold's yacht, and

I bet he thinks there's black magic going on or something equally ridiculous. Stuff and nonsense!'

'Listen, lady.' Lugg cleared his throat; it was a threatening sound. 'Mr C. has come across two of them little dolls in the past few days and both have had a connection with this Wicken place and both have had dead bodies attached to them, or relatively adjacent. Mr C. don't like things like that happening in threes, so he's taking action. So you should consider yourself in protective custody, *my* protective custody, until I see you safely home.'

'This is ridiculous!' For a moment Lugg thought she was going to stand up and storm out, breathing fire, and from the look on his face, so did Harry Fathoms.

'Who told Campion about the doll?'

'I did,' said the doctor. 'I noticed it on your car last night.'

'Well, I saw it three days ago, and I even saw who put it there as a harmless joke,' said Mary Ann defiantly.

'Who?' snapped Lugg.

'One of my neighbours, if you must know.'

'You've got funny neighbours out there on the mudflats,' said Lugg. 'I told my colleague to watch his back.'

'Colleague?' asked Fathoms.

'Well, I think of him more as my apprentice really. Chap who was with me earlier, Mason Lowell Clay. Big, strapping American, so clean-cut he's razor-sharp.'

'And where is he now?'

'He's popped out to Wicken, to take a look at a war memorial, he said.'

'I didn't know there was one in Wicken,' said the doctor. 'I know the one outside St James's Church in Dengie, but not of one in Wicken.'

'It's in the chapel,' said Mary Ann, 'but he'll need a key to get in there.'

'Said he knew somebody who'd have one.'

'Frank Worskitt. He looks after the chapel, lives next door to it.'

'No, that wasn't the name,' said Lugg, remembering. 'It was Polley, that was it. Somebody called Polley.'

'Richard Polley, lives with his sister Octavia,' said Mary Ann, exchanging looks with the doctor.

'Patients of yours?' asked the fat man.

'If they were, I couldn't talk about them to you,' said Fathoms seriously, 'but they're not, though perhaps they should be.'

'I don't follow.'

'You don't have to register with the nearest medical practice,' said Mary Ann, 'though most people do. When the Polleys moved in to Wicken, they must have stayed with whoever they were registered with before. A bit risky if you ask me, considering they don't have a phone or a car and that Richard is no spring chicken and Octavia's confined to a wheelchair.'

'But they're strong chapel-goers, right? They told Mason about the war memorial.'

Mary Ann Allen shook her head slowly. 'No, the Polleys aren't religious at all and nobody uses the chapel in Wicken on a regular basis. It's only kept going for those who are lying against the wall.'

'The who?' said a startled Lugg.

'It's a local saying, or phrase, I suppose. 'Lying against the wall' refers to someone who has died but hasn't been buried yet. They're lying by the wall outside the chapel, or the church, waiting to be buried in the graveyard when there's a spare plot.'

'That's grim, missus, very grim.'

'Not really,' said Mary Ann with a weak smile, 'because everyone in Wicken knows there's room for all of us when the time comes.'

Mr Campion was striking a pose, thinking what a glorious thing it must have been to be a pirate king, and though not a particularly experienced sailor, he was never sick at sea; well, hardly ever. He had found his sea legs and was standing with them apart on the prow of the *Jocasta*. Police Constable Siegfried, who was clearly enjoying the wind on his jowls, sat on the deck next to him, his head resting against Campion's thigh.

Tom Trybull had steered the boat smoothly out of its berth, and the passage down the Brightlingsea Reach had been remarkably gentle. Relieved that Trybull had opted for engine power, a far more steadying influence than sail, Mr Campion had been able to stalk the deck, hands clasped behind his back in what he assumed was nautical fashion. It was only when the yacht passed the Outer Bar, entering the cross-currents from the Blackwater estuary on the starboard side and the North Sea to port, that the swell became more noticeable and he had to brace himself and adopt the classic 'drunken sailor' walk to maintain his balance.

He felt certain he looked the part in the oilskin bib-and-braces trousers and waterproof jacket borrowed from Trybull, and the Wellingtons he had retrieved from the boot of the Jaguar. All he needed was a sou'wester and some sea spray in his face and he could be used to advertise fish fingers or tinned sardines.

Carefully and not too bow-legged, though he was glad Lugg was not there to pass comment, he made his way back to the stern where Trybull was at the wheel, hair blowing in the breeze, taking in deep gulps of ozone, a beatific smile on his face which confirmed Campion's suspicion that this, for the sergeant, was the ideal duty.

'When I asked if you could find a dog to bring along, I hardly expected one of Essex Constabulary's finest detectives,' said Campion, pointing to the prow where Constable Siegfried was sitting proudly, ears and snout alert but as immobile as a Siamese temple lion. 'A refugee mutt from the Battersea dogs' home, or your aunt's best Pomeranian would have sufficed, as long as it could bark.'

'When the orders come from Scotland Yard via the chief constable, only the best will do, and Siegfried is our best.'

'It's a good name for a German Shepherd,' conceded Campion. 'Have you known him long?'

'Since he was a pup in training. I did a course as a dog handler, but then got lured away with sergeant's stripes. Always kept in touch with Siggy, though. It's a strong bond between man and dog in police work, plus he always liked a trip out on the water.'

Campion scanned the horizon, hopefully in a professional manner, though he thought he would have looked more professional with a pair of binoculars around his neck. Worryingly, even without them, he could clearly make out the shape of Bradwell nuclear power station in the distance.

'Are we making good progress?'

'Steady,' said Trybull. 'I'm not pushing the engine and you said you didn't want to get there before dusk.'

'You checked that the navigation lights all work?'

'Of course. For all his faults, Francis Jarrold kept her in pretty good nick.'

Campion's eyes wandered to the stern rails and the bright orange inflatable dinghy bouncing along in *Jocasta*'s wake.

'Jarrold didn't have a dinghy, did he?'

'No, just a couple of lifebelts. You're not worried about sinking, are you?'

'Like the captain of the *Titanic*, the thought never occurred to me. I was just wondering how Jarrold got ashore at Wicken. It's awfully muddy there, and from what I hear Worm Creek is not exactly a natural harbour.'

'It certainly isn't,' said Trybull, 'it's just a deep gash in the mud and a dangerous place to land – as Jarrold found out. He must have been crazy to try it. No one in their right minds would put in there during the day, let alone at night.'

Campion smiled. 'Like we are doing?'

'I've done it before.'

'And so, I believe, had Jarrold. You've gone through his log?'

'Yes, and I've even contacted the harbourmaster in Honfleur, though I did it without my inspector knowing. The case is closed as far as he's concerned.'

'Did you get a response from Honfleur?'

'Eventually. It took a while to get them to answer the phone.'

'You must have rung at lunchtime.'

'What is the lunch hour in France?'

'*Hour?*' Campion grinned. 'You haven't been to France much, have you, Sergeant?'

'Not as often as Francis Jarrold, that's for sure. He popped over there in the *Jocasta* quite often – three times already this year not counting the last run. I can get the actual dates for you.'

'You should check them against the dates in the guest book at The Oyster Shack in Tillingham, because I'll bet his return journeys coincided with the dates a certain Charles Wyndham, better known as the late Timothy Timms, stayed there.'

'Who was with us when Jarrold's body was found? That wasn't just a coincidence? You think they were meeting at Wicken?'

Campion did not answer him directly. 'You're the sailor, you tell me. On Jarrold's journeys, he would have had to negotiate those Swatchways and Spitways you tried to explain to me, and they would have brought him to Worm Creek each time, wouldn't they?'

'*Could* have, but it would have required a detour off the logical course for Brightlingsea. But why would he? There's nothing in Wicken, why try and land there?'

Unlike the driving of a car, it did not seem important to keep one's eyes on the road, or in this case water, so Campion was unperturbed to find Trybull staring intently at his face.

'You think he landed there regularly, don't you?'

'Yes, I do,' said Mr Campion.

'What was he up to? Was it smuggling?'

'Of a sort.'

Lugg's instruction to remember to drive on the left was redundant in Mason's opinion when applied to the roads between Southminster and Wicken, as they were so narrow it was impossible to distinguish a right side from a left. Thank the Lord their cars were so small but, even so, he was unsure what evasive action he could take if he met a truck or a tractor coming towards him, as for long stretches the road was bordered by either a water-filled dyke or uninviting marshy ground.

It was with a sigh of relief that he turned onto the even narrower track that led to Wicken and nowhere else, thinking, not for the first time, that the expression 'one-horse town' would be effusive flattery applied to Wicken.

He drove on down the track until he came to the bungalow which he knew, from his personal census of the place, was the home of Mary Ann Allen. She was not at home, for she was in Southminster being shadowed by Mr Lugg, a figure who really did cast a giant shadow, which meant that the parking space in front of her property would be empty and no one could accuse him of blocking the single track; not that there was anyone about to complain.

He reversed into the space so that the car would be facing in the right direction for a quick escape, a useful maxim he had learned from Perdita, and was inordinately pleased with his skill with both a gear lever and a steering wheel on the wrong, unnatural, side and without power steering. As he climbed out of the car, he realized that while he had not seen anyone in Wicken, not even behind a twitching curtain, Wicken had certainly logged his arrival.

'It's Mason, isn't it?'

The voice came from behind him, from the next property, Abigail Cottage, and its owner was standing at the open front door wearing a bright pink nylon housecoat and holding what looked to be a hairbrush.

'It surely is, Miss Jones,' he replied, biting back the urge to call her 'Silence' and see what her reaction would be. 'How are you today?'

'Very well, thank you. What brings you to Wicken?'

'A return visit to see Mr Polley. He said he would get a key for the chapel so I could get in there and have a look at the war memorial.'

'It's not a big memorial,' said Miss Jones, 'just an inscribed stone in the wall.'

'It's the names on it I'm interested in.'

'There aren't many, but I'd hate you to think we're a cowardly lot here in Wicken, it's just that there were never very many of us.'

Mason waved his trusty notebook in the air. 'It may fill in a few gaps in my research into the passengers on the *Abigail*, like your namesake was.'

Miss Jones did not rise to that particular bait. 'Well, if you're determined to visit the chapel, don't go bothering Richard Polley. You should get the key from Frank Worskitt. He's the caretaker of the chapel and the graveyard. I'm sure he'll give you a key.'

Mason reviewed his mental schematic map of Wicken and its inhabitants. 'He lives the other side of the chapel, right?' he said, indicating the general direction with his notebook.

'Yes, he does,' said Miss Jones primly, 'but come and ask him yourself. He's here, in my living room.'

'He is?'

'Yes, I'm giving him a haircut.'

Dr Fathoms's afternoon surgery, which ran from 4 p.m. to 5 p.m., was primarily for the benefit of schoolchildren, infants and their mothers, a dozen of whom quickly filled the waiting room, arguing over the meagre supply of Ladybird books and old comics or scrabbling through a box of well-worn toys and games.

Mary Ann Allen suggested that perhaps Lugg would care to go for a walk, as his very presence was frightening the younger children. After a rapid mental assessment of the situation, involving the facts that any nearby pub would be shut and that Mason had not returned, Lugg came up with a face-saving excuse to absent himself.

'You got a car here, missus?'

'Yes,' said Mary Ann suspiciously. 'It's the Ford Anglia parked on the road near the gate.'

'Give us the keys, then, and I'll check it out for you.'

'Check it for what?'

Lugg put a finger to his lips and leaned over her desk, silently communicating that it was a subject not to be mooted in front of the children and their mothers in the waiting room, all of whom had fallen silent and were looking at him. He moved the chubby finger and tapped the side of his nose with it. 'Things,' he whispered. 'Unexpected things.'

The receptionist shook her head in disbelief but reached below the desk and took her car keys from her handbag.

'If they ask,' Lugg said quietly, jerking his head towards the waiting room, 'tell 'em I'm a bailiff.' Then he turned lightly on his heels to avoid Miss Allen's fearsome scowl.

He found the Anglia easily enough, unlocked the door, climbed in after pushing the driver's seat as far back as it would go, put the key in the ignition and began to hunt for the bonnet-release catch. He found it next to the windscreen-wiper control knob and tugged until he heard a satisfying metallic click. If anything 'unexpected', in the sense of 'explosive', had been attached to the car, he wanted to find it before starting up the engine. He thought it a remote possibility, as witchcraft rarely relied on familiarity with ordnance, but was reassured to see that the internal organs of the car had not been tampered with. While out of the car, he walked around it, scientifically testing each tyre by the kicking method used by most British males and then, with great effort, having checked that he was unobserved, he got on his hands and knees and surveyed the underside of the Anglia, which carried nothing more dangerous than a coating of dried mud and dirt.

On his feet again, he closed the bonnet lid and removed the small padded fabric doll figure which had been tied to the front bumper with a length of black cotton. In Lugg's giant paw, the faceless doll looked harmless and insignificant, and he opened the car door and threw it on to the back seat, then he climbed in behind the steering wheel and settled down for his afternoon snooze.

He was rudely awakened ten seconds – but really an hour – later, by a rapping on the driver's door window and the sight of Mary Ann Allen signalling him to follow her back into the surgery.

'Surgery's finished for the day,' she told him when he reached the house after a contorted series of stretches and strains to relieve his cramped limbs. 'The doctor and I have our notes to co-ordinate and some paperwork to do for tomorrow, but then I'll be ready to head home. There's still no sign of your American friend.'

'No, there isn't, is there?' said Lugg, scratching his bald head. ''Suppose that means you'll be giving me a lift to Wicken to find him.'

'Oh, I will, will I?'

'I was ordered to see you safely home.'

'That's really not necessary.'

'Oh, I don't know. Wicken sounds a dodgy place. That voodoo doll on your Anglia, you said it was one of your neighbours tied it on.'

'It was, but I'm sure she didn't mean anything harmful by it, it's just something she does.'

'She? You know her?'

'Of course I do, Sylvia Jones is my next-door neighbour.'

Mason Lowell decided he really must stop being surprised by the English when they invited him into their homes, after the sight which greeted him in the front room of Abigail Cottage.

In the centre of the room was a square white rug laid over the carpet on which was the four-legged stool made from a cut-down chair, which Mason had noticed on his previous visit, but dismissed as an old lady's eccentricity. On the stool sat a painfully thin old man with a bath towel around his neck, clumps of white hair on it and on the rug around his feet.

'Don't get up, Frank, you'll shed hair everywhere. This is the American gentleman I told you about. Came to see me about the history of Wicken.'

'Not here for a short back and sides, then?' cackled Frank Worskitt.

'Actually, I'm here to look at the war memorial in the chapel,' said Mason, still wondering why old men with very little hair were among a barber's best customers. 'I understand from Miss Jones that you are the custodian of the key.'

The old man chuckled and the towel heaved and shed hairs as he fumbled under it and then produced a rusty, old-style mortice lock key which he offered to Mason.

'Never been called a custodian before an' I thought the wife had used every name under the sun! You're welcome to look around but you'll have to take it as you find it. The chapel's not used much these days; in fact, I can't remember the last time anybody went in there, though there was a time everyone in Wicken had a key to the place. Not long ago there was chap snooping around the graveyard. Chap called Campion, then another chap called Campion came calling and asking questions. My Ethel don't take to strangers, so if you want to look round, help yourself. More than my life's worth to be seen showing you around, not that there's much to see. Drop the key back to Sylvia here when you've done.'

'Thank you, sir,' said Mason, taking the key.

'Right, Frank,' ordered Miss Jones, taking a pair of manual hair clippers and a comb from the pockets of her housecoat, 'let's get back to making you presentable. Can't have you going round like one of those hippies, can we?'

'I'll let myself out,' said Mason, as Sylvia Jones began to flex the handles of the clippers and advance on Frank Worskitt's scalp, her tongue protruding from clenched lips in concentration.

Feeling that he had intruded on something personal and private, Mason hurried from Abigail Cottage and round to the chapel. Even in such a short distance he felt that he was being watched, though not by Sylvia Jones, whom he could see through the cottage window was leaning over and concentrating on Frank Worskitt's tonsure.

The iron lock on the chapel door, in age and rustiness, was a match for the key he had been given, but the tumblers turned surprisingly easily, as if the lock had been oiled recently. Not that Mason gave that a second thought. As he stepped inside, he was already reaching for his notebook and a pen.

There was light enough from the high windows in the chapel's side walls for him not to need to find a light switch as he studied the bare, unadorned interior. There were rows of folding wooden chairs in lieu of pews; enough to seat a congregation of perhaps twenty, with an optimistic number of spares stacked against one wall. There was a wooden table at the far end with a lectern and, above it, a plain wooden crucifix attached to the wall above head height.

The walls were bare plaster except for a single rectangle of stone halfway down one wall, as if a gravestone had been set into the plaster, and the inscription on it began with the word 'In Memoriam'.

Wishing he had brought a camera to record his discovery, Mason threaded his way through the chairs towards the memorial tablet and took only minimal notice of the metal bowl his foot collided with. There was water in the bowl, presumably put there to catch drips from a leak in the roof, but Mason's concentration was entirely on the wall plaque.

The 'In Memoriam' inscription had a subheading: *For Those Who Did Not Return*, and underneath a single column of names. There were eight in total, listed by seniority of army rank

Mason, from his research, recognized names such as Musson and Dines, with a real Essex pedigree. Only one, however, coincided with a name already in his notebook:

Cpl. Abraham Lux (Ypres, 1916)

'There you are,' he said aloud, his hand shaking as he copied it on to a blank page.

He heard the noise as he wrote, a distinct scraping of one of the wooden chairs across the concrete floor, and he looked up from his notebook. Four rows away from him, one of the chair backs was indeed wobbling slightly, but Mason was alone in the chapel and the door and windows were closed, of that he was sure.

Then another chair rocked gently. The motion in itself was neither dramatic nor threatening; the fact that it was a chair in a different row, and a row closer to him, was.

Curious, but also annoyed to be distracted from his discovery of what he was already mentally labelling 'The Lux Connection', Mason sank down on his haunches and looked along the underside of the nearest row of chairs.

He found himself uncomfortably close to a pair of glowing eyes and a curled lip revealing white and very sharp teeth.

Mason said the first thing that came into his head. 'Nice doggy.'

The dog made no reply.

SIXTEEN
Various Parties Converging on the Coast

Mason knew instantly why the dog had remained silent at his presence. It was nothing he could take personally, for any other dog disturbed in its lair by a lumbering stranger would surely have barked and the chapel, unlikely as that may be, did seem to be the dog's residence, the metal bowl Mason had almost kicked over providing it with fresh drinking water.

The dog had not barked because it was a dog which did not bark, though it was not technically accurate to say that the Basenji was a mute. It did make, when it wanted to, a yodel-like *baroo* sound, but it was widely known as 'the barkless dog' from its origins in central Africa when it had been bred as a small, speedy and above all silent hunting dog. The breed was popular in America and, although no dog expert himself, Mason recognized that he was in a staring contest with a Red Basenji, hopefully one of an equable temperament.

'What are you doing here, boy?' Mason asked, for he was clearly addressing a dog rather than a bitch.

'What are *you* doing here?' said a voice, not the dog's.

For a few confused moments though, Mason assumed it must have been the dog talking as he could see no one else in the chapel, but it was clearly insane to think a dog, especially a famously barkless one, could talk. It was only as he straightened up to his full height that he could see, over the chairs by the door, a small, elderly woman, wearing a duffel coat several sizes too big for her and leaning on a stout walking stick.

'I'm here to look at your war memorial stone,' said Mason, pointing with his notebook. 'I'm interested in the names on it. A Mr Worskitt gave me permission – well, he gave me a key.'

'That'd be my husband Frank. I'm Mrs Worskitt,' said the woman, shuffling closer, her walking stick tapping out her paces on the flagstone floor. 'Where did you see him, to get the key?'

'Not ten minutes ago, round at Abigail Cottage. Silence Jones was giving him a haircut.'

'Silence?' The old woman almost spat the question.

'I mean Sylvia, Miss Jones. It was Miss Jones who told me about the war memorial in the first place.'

'Was it now?'

Mrs Worskitt dropped her gaze from Mason's face, as if suddenly uninterested in the stranger, and turned her attention to the rows of chairs, selecting the nearest one and scraping it out of line before sitting on it.

'Did you know there's a dog in here?' Mason said, noting that the dog had not reacted to her presence, but then he was not the sort of dog who would bark to announce visitors.

'He's harmless,' said the woman, settling herself, knees apart, the walking stick between them parting her long skirt, both her hands clasped over the handle knob which appeared to be made of some sort of grey circular-shaped stone. Before her mottled and liver-spotted hands folded over it, Mason thought he identified it as a weight, the sort attached to fishing nets or old-fashioned weaving looms.

Once comfortable, the woman returned her attention to the tall American, and Mason had the uneasy feeling that he was on trial in front of a notoriously conservative judge.

'So you're taking names, are you? Why's that?'

'For my research . . . my historical research.'

'You studying the history of Wicken, then?'

'Not exactly. I'm tracing the names of families who came from Wicken but went to America. I'm an American, as you can probably tell.'

'That doesn't bother me if it doesn't bother you.'

Mason was unsure whether the inscrutable woman was joking.

'Nobody in Wicken's been to America except that sister of Silence Jones, the one who made a right exhibition of herself. That was before the war, though.'

'My research is much further back in history. What I'm interested in happened nearly three hundred years ago.'

Mrs Worskitt looked anything but impressed. 'Did you find what you were after in here?'

'Well, I didn't expect to find a dog in here with me. Are you sure he's all right?'

'He'll let you know if he's not – dogs generally do. What about them names?' She leaned back on her creaking chair and raised her stick to point at the wall plaque. 'They the ones you were after?'

'One of them was.' Mason went immediately into excited academic mode. 'It was exactly the name I was looking for, a real and solid link in my research. I feel like I've just completed a treasure hunt and my prize is Corporal Abraham Lux who died during the First World War.'

The woman's face remained blank, giving nothing away, then she leaned forward in her seat and made to look under the row of chairs in front of her.

'The dog's getting restless,' she said, although Mason had noticed nothing. 'You'll have to help me get him out of there before he does something unspeakable. I'm of an age where I can't go chasing dogs.'

Mrs Worskitt would not have struck anyone as the archetypal maiden-in-distress, but her voice and demeanour had suddenly become pathetic, and Mason realized that there was absolutely no reason why this frail old woman should be interested in him finding Abraham Lux, but it was only natural to be concerned about a rogue dog roaming her chapel.

At least that was how he justified it to himself later. In the moment, he instinctively sank back down on his haunches so he could see under the chairs and, like any dog-lover, held out an arm and flexed his fingers in the universal 'Come here, boy' gesture.

He was even pursing his lips to whistle a command when, out of the corner of his eye, he saw that the old woman had swiftly – very swiftly – reversed her walking stick and now held it like a baseball bat.

Among his last conscious thoughts were that the handle of the stick was indeed made from a lead weight, that it was approaching his head at great speed, and what would be the reaction of Mr Lugg when he learned that Mason had been beaten up by an eighty-year-old female pensioner sitting in a chair.

Mr Campion had found Constable Siegfried an amiable enough travelling companion, and possibly the better sailor, but after complimenting the dog on having a perfectly apt name for a German Shepherd, he found himself running low on topics of conversation. The dog, disappointingly, seemed totally unimpressed when Tom Trybull announced that over to starboard they were passing St Peter's Chapel, one of the earliest Christian churches in the country let alone the county, and the site of Othona, an even older Roman fort, many of whose bricks and roof tiles had found their way into the construction of the church.

Trybull, like a good tourist guide who relied on tips, was also keen to point out things which were not visible, or hardly visible to someone who needed spectacles. Mr Campion made appreciative noises when Trybull informed him that the large sheet of calm water which separated them from the coast – a thin, brownish-green smeared line which made Campion think of a loose piece of a jigsaw made from a Turner painting – concealed the Dengie Flat. Although the tide had covered them with water, the Flats formed an impenetrable sandbank to anything floating which required a draught of more than two inches.

Mr Campion, politely, asked the traditional idiot question always asked by one member of a guided tour. Would it not be possible to walk ashore in that case?

'With divine help you might try walking on water,' Trybull grinned, 'but the mud and shifting sand under the surface would get you before you'd taken ten steps. The locals call the mud "the devil's hands" because they reach up, grab you by the ankles and won't let you go. Remember what happened to Francis Jarrold.'

'I do,' said Campion soberly, 'but I can't throw off the notion that somehow the devil had help there.'

'Like I said, they'd have to have been able to walk on water,' said Trybull, one hand on the wheel, the other gently easing forward the throttle.

'I can tell from your expression, Sergeant, that my detective skills are impressing you as little as my seamanship.'

'Not entirely. You do raise an interesting point.'

'I do?' said Campion with raised eyebrows.

'Well, if Jarrold was smuggling something into Wicken on a regular basis, according to your theory, that is, how did he land the stuff? Going into Worm Creek would get him as near as he got with the *Jocasta*, but then he's still got to unload his contraband and walk across the mud and the marsh before he gets to firm footing. How did he do that?'

'Clearly when he tried it, he couldn't, and he ended up dead. The only possibility I can think of is that he must have had some sort of reception committee waiting to help take off his cargo. Except for that last trip, of course, which may have come as a bit of a surprise to his fellow smugglers. I don't think they were expecting him and, from the state he was in, he wasn't thinking straight anyway.' Campion noticed Trybull's hand moving to the throttle again. 'Are we speeding up, Captain?'

'Just adjusting for the tide which will be against us when it comes from the Rays'n.'

'The what?'

'Sorry, a habit I picked up from the locals. "Rays'n" is what they call Ray Sand, it's the sandbank south of Worm Creek.' He stretched an arm towards the coastline. 'This is Dengie Flat and down there is Ray Sand, the same sort of thing going down to the River Crouch estuary, and it's just as unwelcoming to boats like this. It took me two years before I realized what the old lags in the sailing club were saying when they told me to steer well clear of the Rays'n.'

'So this Swatchway or Spitway, or whatever it is we're on now – sailors usually stay away from it?'

'Have you seen any other vessels since we passed the Blackwater?'

'Not a one, but then I forgot to bring my U-boat commander's binoculars. What I was thinking, though, is that we must be visible from the land; in fact, we must stand out a nautical mile given the lack of other traffic.'

'For sure. Anyone working out on Tillingham or Dengie Marsh would have a good view of us across the flats. Should

I throttle back or circle around for a bit and wait for dusk before we go in?'

'Goodness me, no,' said Campion with enthusiasm. 'I want them to see us coming.'

Hunched down, as far as his bulk was allowed, in the passenger seat of Mary Ann Allen's Ford Anglia, Lugg attempted to keep one eye on the windscreen and one on his reluctant chauffeuse. As always when he was a front-seat passenger, and especially when a female was driving, his feet automatically operated a set of phantom foot pedals, especially the brake.

If Mary Ann noticed this irritating display of lack of confidence in her motoring skills – Perdita had shouted at him to cease and desist on more than one occasion and Lady Amanda had discouraged the habit simply with a look of disdain – she did not admit to it.

In fact, Lugg thought her quite a good driver, negotiating the narrow lanes and blind corners with confidence.

'Lived in Wicken long, 'ave you?' was his way of opening diplomatic relations.

'Long enough to know I'm not going to retire there.'

Lugg attempted flattery. 'You're a long way off considerations like that, surely?'

'I should have retired last year by rights, but Dr Fathoms asked me to stay on for a bit. This'll be my last Christmas in Wicken, though, if I can get anyone to buy my bungalow.'

'There's plenty would fancy a bungalow at the seaside to retire to.'

'Where you come from, maybe. East-enders who went on a day trip to Clacton or Southend on a works' outing. Well, if they've got the cash, they'd be welcome to it.'

'Not enough going on for you youngsters, then?' said Lugg, though self-deprecation was not his forte.

'I'll have you know that I am one of the youngest residents of Wicken,' said Mary Ann, sniffing loudly. 'And no, there's not a lot going on there and I'm certainly not going to end my days there. I've been saving up for ten years and they won't find me lying by the wall in Wicken. I've got my eye on a little house up in Hebden Bridge.'

'Oh aye? Where's that then?'

'It's up in Yorkshire. Lovely place, nice people, and not a stinking mudflat or marsh in sight.'

'Bit of a change there,' Lugg observed, 'after living down here.'

'I certainly hope so,' said Mary Ann rather enigmatically.

'You won't miss the locals here? You must know 'em all.'

'For my sins, I do, and even after more than twenty years, I still find them a strange lot.'

'You said they were all rather elderly . . .' Lugg let the thought trail off.

'They are.' Mary Ann responded rather quickly, Lugg thought. 'Frank Worskitt's probably the oldest. He must be in his nineties and his wife can't be far behind him. There's Miss Jones next door to me, who must be seventy but doesn't look it, and then there's Modesty Barly, who does, as does Leonora, Joshua Jarmin's wife. It's difficult to tell with Richard Polley's sister Octavia, because she's been confined to a wheelchair for so long, but both of them must have used up their three score and ten.'

'What about the men?' asked Lugg.

'What about them?'

'Are they fit and up for it or old crocks like me?'

'I'm not sure what you mean, but they must be all in their sixties, though they could pass for younger. Joshua Jarmin and the brothers-in-law George Bugg and Bob Barly all work out on the marshes as farm labourers or stockmen from Dengie up to Bradwell. The fresh-air life suits them and keeps them fit.'

'How do they get around the peninsula?'

'On their bicycles,' said Mary Ann, not realizing she had given the answer Lugg had been expecting.

Mason regained consciousness to find himself in the middle of two heated debates. One was taking place inside his head and involved seeking answers to the pressing questions of why his head hurt so much and, as a supplementary, why he could not move his arms or legs. The other was taking place outside his head and around his strangely immobile body, where several different voices were raised in anger, though he could make no sense of what they were saying.

He opened one eye and then, with a great effort of will, the other, and the first thing he focused on was the person responsible for the searing pain in his head. His initial reaction being one of relief that his assailant was real and not imaginary, for the old woman was still seated within striking range of him and he was strangely gratified to confirm his suspicion, now it was laid across her lap, that her walking stick did indeed have a substantial doughnut-shape lead weight as its handle.

Fragments of questions were scattered through his brain like shrapnel. The woman had said her name was Worskitt. Did that mean anything? It was not a name from the Billericay Covenant of the *Abigail*, but there was a name that was important. Lux, that was it, Abraham Lux, the name on the war memorial. And yes, the war memorial was there on the wall, he had not imagined it. Was it him mentioning that name which had provoked the old woman? Just how had she managed to knock him out? Her being small and frail and old, and him being so much younger and fitter, it would clearly have been declared a No Contest. But he had been at a disadvantage, for even though she had been sitting down, he had somehow been lower than her. She had not needed a golfer's stance and swing, merely the short-range strike of a batter at baseball. Why had he been crouching or kneeling, offering the old lunatic an easy target? He had been looking for, or at, something low down around his feet. A dog! A dog had been involved – or had he imagined it?

But a dog there was, sitting on its haunches, looking at him, ears alert, with that innocent curiosity dogs can manage but with cats tends to be more sardonic.

It was the same Red Basenji – for surely there could not be a pair of them – he had spotted hiding under the folding chairs, only it now had a length of rope attached to its collar. The same sort of rope, Mason realized, that was wrapped around his chest, arms and legs, tying him firmly to one of the chairs. Perhaps the Basenji was expressing sympathy with him as they had both been constrained by makeshift leads, though the dog at least could move his limbs.

Still dazed and unable to make sense of the different voices, at least three, filling the air around him with incomprehensible chatter, he let his eyes follow the dog's lead upwards to the hands of another seated woman. This was one he had met before, Octavia Polley, and she was seated in her wheelchair, a tartan rug across her knees, the dog obediently at her side, with her brother Richard standing behind her. There was another man there, not one he knew, but one he suspected he had seen before as part of the trio of threatening figures anxious to shepherd Perdita's Mini Cooper out of Wicken.

'He's coming round,' said the unknown man, and Mason was gratified to discover his hearing was functioning, or at least filtering out the throbbing in his skull, but less happy when the man jabbed two straightened fingers into his stomach.

As he gasped at the shock and pain of the blow, he heard the man say cynically 'Bit confused, are we?' which he presumed was a rhetorical question, but as the man had pronounced it 'confoosed' he had identified himself as a local. Mentally, Mason went to his *Abigail* list, which had now merged into his Wicken Census, and deduce that his tormentor must have one of three names: Jarmin, Bugg or Barly, but now was not the time, nor this the place, for polite introductions.

Mason flexed the muscles in his arms and strained his legs as much as the rope allowed, only to confirm that he had been tied very tightly indeed. His head still throbbed and he saw no point in struggling against his bonds. He therefore decided his best strategy was silence, though he did consider objecting when the next thing he heard clearly was: 'We've got to get rid of him,' followed by, 'I agree, and the sooner the better.'

But then someone came to his defence. 'You can't do that.'

Mason's relief was short-lived.

'I won't let you get rid of Pickles.'

Pickles?

'I knew it was a mistake to let you keep that dog, Octavia.' The voice was that of the Worskitt woman, a woman who was clearly in command. 'It brought the snoopers to us. You should have known that, Richard Polley. We don't tolerate snoopers in Wicken, we stick to the Covenant.'

Now Mason was listening intently while still impersonating a man with severe concussion, or what he thought such a man would look like.

'*We whose names are underwritten.* I know the words, Ethel.'

Despite the pain in his head and the fact that he had been beaten unconscious by a woman less than half his size and more than three times his age, Mason was suddenly elated as all his theories about Wicken had crystallized. He was sure he was in the presence of the descendants of the passengers on the *Abigail* and the signatories of the Billericay Covenant.

How significant this knowledge was to them, and how dangerous it could be for him, was still in doubt. Richard and Octavia Polley knew of his interest, but did the violent old woman and the surly, brutish man? And would they hold it against him?

In truth, neither were taking much notice of him. Perhaps it was a usual event in Wicken to beat up visiting academics and tie them to chairs in the middle of their place of worship. Octavia was concerned only with the dog, holding the Basenji's rope lead taut so the dog was close to the left wheel of her chair, while leaning over and making soothing noises to assure 'Pickles' that everything was all right now. Richard Polley, smartly dressed in green corduroy trousers, tweed jacket and a suede waistcoat, remained as impassive as the dog, standing to attention behind his sister's wheelchair, gripping the handles.

'That beast has brought snoopers down about our ears, Octavia Polley.' It was the Worskitt woman leading the prosecution and Pickles was in the dock. 'We don't need snoopers, not when we are all so close to the end.'

'I think it is fair to say that it was Francis Jarrold's activities that brought in the snoopers,' said Richard Polley. 'That drunken sot always was a liability and so was his queer London friend.'

'They've bin tak'n care of,' grunted the man, whose name could be Jarmin, or Bugg or Barly.

'What do you mean by that?' said Octavia in a high-pitched squeal which made the dog's ears twitch.

'Josh don't mean nothing,' said the Worskitt woman. 'Nothing for you to worry about. All you've got to do is say goodbye to the dog.'

Mason watched as Joshua Jarmin, now identified by default, held out a rough, demanding brown hand in front of Octavia's face. It could not have been more frightening if it had been a shaking fist, and with a quivering lower lip the woman handed over the rope lead.

'What will you do with Pickles?' she sobbed, which provoked a snarl of derision from the old woman.

'We'll take him out on the flats and let him go. You should never have kept the animal in the first place. You know our beliefs – maybe you forgot 'em when you lived away, but here in Wicken we don't forget.'

'And what about our unexpected visitor, Mr Clay?' asked Richard Polley to Mason's dismay.

He had almost convinced himself he was invisible, and that this strange drama being played out in front of him would not include him. Now the one upstanding, decent English gentleman (or so he thought) had drawn attention to his presence, even identified him.

'He ain't evidence, the dog is,' announced Ethel Worskitt, whom Mason was now thinking of as a judge – hopefully not a hanging judge. 'We leave him here until we've dealt with the dog, then we let him go. What's he going to say? He was trespassing in our little community's place of worship looking for something to steal and he got clobbered by the caretaker's wife. Bested by a little old lady of eighty-one who walks with a stick. That's not a story he's going to dispute among his friends.'

'Don't talk much, do 'e?' Jarmin snarled as he pulled the reluctant Pickles from behind the shelter of Octavia's wheelchair.

'Not since he saw how we deal with snoopers in Wicken,' pronounced Judge Worskitt. 'He'll keep his mouth shut or I'll hex him, and I reckon he knows I can do it.'

Mason remained silent, though his mouth was so dry he doubted if he could have spoken even if he had wanted to. If this scenario had been a movie, surely this was the moment when the cavalry or the cops burst in and came to the rescue.

The door of the chapel burst open and two dishevelled men in mud-spattered clothing and Wellington boots rushed in. They were neither cavalry nor police.

'We got visitors!' the leading one shouted angrily.

'Aye, we know,' said Joshua Jarmin.

'No, not in here,' said the incomer, taking in the situation wide-eyed, 'out there in Worm Creek. It's come back. Jarrold's boat has come back and there's a dog on board howling its head off.'

As the *Jocasta* eased her way into Worm Creek, Mr Campion imagined it as akin to a longboat entering the Foxton Locks on the Grand Union Canal, but without the ascension which was guaranteed by that staircase of water levels. Here in Worm Creek, full on the incoming tide, the *Jocasta* floated with her deck almost level with the lip of the mud gulley which formed the inlet. Campion guessed that he could step off the starboard side of the boat and be standing in no more than two inches of water, but it would be two inches of water hiding six feet of cloying mud.

Having rounded Dengie Flat, he had insisted that Trybull turn on the mast navigation lights, though it was not quite yet dusk as they approached the creek. Now it was time for Constable Siegfried to do his duty.

'How do I get him to bark?'

'Show him your hand palm down then give the command "Sing",' said Trybull.

'How appropriately Wagnerian,' said Campion as he led the dog to the prow, from which they could both see where water and mud changed to marsh and, eventually, marsh turned to dyke-drained fields.

'Now, Siegfried, sing!'

The dog obliged and began to bark loudly, the sound bouncing off the flat landscape as if creating a false, ghostly echo. After half a minute, Siegfried – either bored or rising to the occasion – changed from rasping staccato barks to long, low howls. If there had been a moon it could hardly have added to the eerie atmosphere he was creating.

'Good boy,' said Mr Campion, 'that should bring them.'

As she turned her car into Wicken, Mary Ann Allen had to brake sharply to avoid a nasty accident. Her surprise was tempered by annoyance at the fact that Lugg, in the passenger seat, was violently pumping an imaginary brake pedal with his right foot.

The cause of the near-accident had been the unexpected sight of Richard Polley pushing his sister in her wheelchair in the middle of Wicken's single lane. With no help from Lugg's right boot, Mary Ann brought the Anglia to a prompt halt a safe ten feet before any collision but, to her amazement, neither of the Polleys seemed to register the presence of her car or the danger just avoided.

Richard Polley had his head down and was pushing the chair with grim determination, totally oblivious to the approaching car. The couple disappeared at speed through the garden gate of their house, leaving Mary Ann exhaling loudly and drumming her fingers on the steering wheel.

'Are they blind as well as deaf round here?' asked Lugg.

'That's very odd behaviour, even for Wicken,' said his driver, taking her foot off the real brake and accelerating gently down the lane. 'And look at that! Some inconsiderate yob has parked in my front garden and gone off bird-spotting.'

Lugg leaned forward until his nose was almost pressed against the windscreen. 'That's no bird-spotter and he's not a yob, only an American. That's my mate Mason's car. He won't be far away; Yanks don't like being too far from their cars.'

Mary Ann pulled up outside her bungalow and they got out and walked over to the Marina, both of them peering inside just to make sure Mason wasn't hiding in there.

'He may have left a note saying where he was going and put it through my letterbox,' said Mary Ann, inserting a key into her front door.

Lugg rotated his giant orb of a head and gazed out across the lane and over the sunken marshes.

'You get post out here in this seat of desolation?'

'Not often,' conceded the woman. Then added, 'But I'm impressed that you know your Milton.'

'Don't really,' said Lugg modestly, 'I just hobnob with people who quote chunks of *Paradise Lost* off by heart just to show they had a misspent youth due to too much education. I was lucky, I never suffered that way. All I did was learn to keep my mouth shut and my eyes open. That's how I spotted your next-door neighbour waving at you from under her front curtains. Seems het up about something.'

Miss Allen did a double take and followed Lugg's gaze over the garden fence to Abigail Cottage. Her neighbour was indeed standing at a window waving with frantic 'come here' motions.

'Sylvia doesn't get "het up" about anything. She's cool as a cucumber usually. Come on, maybe she knows where your friend is.'

As they reached the door of Abigail Cottage, it was opened by an agitated Sylvia Jones, hopping from one foot to the other, waving them in with one hand but using the other to put a finger firmly to her lips, calling for silence.

When Mary Ann and Lugg had squeezed by her and oozed into her front room, she whispered, 'He's nodded off and it's best to let him sleep.'

'Mason?' said Lugg, then saw the figure slumped, totally relaxed in an armchair, eyes closed, lips quivering in time to the rising and falling of his chest. 'That's not Mason, and seventy years from now that still won't be Mason.'

'That's Frank Worskitt,' Mary Ann explained. 'He looks after the chapel and lives the other side of it. Here for a haircut, was he, Sylvia?'

Miss Jones nodded. 'It always tires him out.'

'It can be an exhausting experience,' said Lugg sarcastically, running a hand over his bald pate.

'This is Mr Lugg,' said Mary Ann, 'and we're looking for a friend of his.'

'Mason Clay, yes, he was here earlier. He borrowed Frank's key for the chapel and went in there to look at the war memorial.'

'So where is he now?' asked Lugg.

'He never came out.' Miss Jones exchanged a worried glance with Mary Ann. 'But certain others went in.'

She gasped as the big bald man moved swiftly past her, heading at speed for her front door.

Mason was unsure how long he had been left alone in the chapel. He was tied to the chair in such a way that he could not see his wristwatch and, struggle as he might, his bonds refused to loosen. All he managed to do was bounce his chair across the floor towards the door – a door he had heard the Worskitt woman lock as she had left.

When he heard the handle of the door being rattled, his immediate reaction was to try and scoot his chair backwards, until he realized that if his tormentors had returned they had a key; the way the door was shaking indicated whoever was there did not.

'Help! In here!' he yelled.

There was a silence and then the clump of footsteps, retreating at first and then quickening.

And then the door burst inwards, splinters of wood flying through the air, and, shoulder first, Lugg entered the chapel like an elephant looking for a fight.

The cavalry had arrived.

SEVENTEEN
Merrywick

They came off the track and on to the marsh in single file, walking at a funeral march pace, their tread slow and heavy, and yet each footstep was carefully placed. Ethel Worskitt took the lead, her walking stick in one hand, the dog on its length of rope in the other. Behind her the three men followed, quite literally, in her footprints. In profile, the little column could have been mistaken for a First World War tableau of weary troops plodding back from the front-line trenches across a desolate landscape.

'Who saw the boat first?' Ethel Worskitt shouted over her shoulder, tugging sharply on the Basenji's lead, although the dog seemed happy enough to trot alongside her, sampling the various aromas on offer.

'Bob Barly spotted it,' said Joshua Jarmin behind her. 'He was working out on Tillingham Marsh, clearing a ditch, when he saw it coming down the Spitway 'tween Dengie Flat and Buxey Sands. He got on his bike and fetched George who was working two dykes over. He saw it too.'

'And those two dunces back there are sure it was Jarrold's boat?'

'Aye, they were sure. They've seen it often enough.'

'Could they make out who was handling her?'

'They saw one man on deck and they heard a dog.'

'And you say it was coming down the Spitway?'

'Aye.'

'So she was coming from Brightlingsea?'

'Or from Mersea Island or out of the Blackwater, but Francis berthed her at Brightlingsea, so that seems most likely.'

'Point is,' snapped the old woman, 'that Francis always called in coming the other way, up from the south, coming home from France.'

'But it ain't Francis sailing her, is it?'

'No,' conceded Ethel, 'that's for sure.'

'Then why we going out here?'

Ethel pulled the dog even closer to her leg. 'They might have come for this little fellow.'

'I thought Octavia wanted to keep him.'

'Octavia wanted a bit of company to see her out, but she'd forgotten the Covenant we all live by. Plus, whoever's on the *Jocasta* might be willing to pay us what's due to us.'

'And if they don't?'

'Then Pickles here goes for one last swim.'

By the time Lugg had extracted a penknife from his waistcoat pocket – a waistcoat that fitted quite snugly now he was breathing so heavily – and proceeded to saw at the ropes constricting Mason, Mary Ann Allen and Sylvia Jones had joined them in the chapel, stepping daintily over fragments of shattered wood.

Before any of them could ask Mason what had happened, Mason volunteered the information. 'They're crazy! They're all in it together and there was a dog hiding in here! The old woman, Worskitt, knocked me out, and then somebody tied me to this chair and then they took the dog and said they were going to get rid of it.'

'Steady on, son,' Lugg soothed, 'some old woman clobbered you?'

'With a walking stick. She was sitting just there.'

'Let me get this right,' said Lugg patiently, helping Mason to stand upright, 'an old lady with a walking stick bested a lad like you? Now why would a nice old granny do a thing like that?'

'Because Mrs Worskitt's maiden name was Ethelreda Lux,' said Sylvia Jones.

Mason's jaw dropped open and, as he stood, cut lengths of rope dropped from him and pooled around his feet.

'You knew?' was all he could say.

'Of course I did, but I couldn't tell you directly.'

'Why not?'

'They'll have a code of silence or some such rigamarole against talking to strangers,' Lugg said bitterly. 'They always do in these backward communities.'

'The Covenant,' said Mason, his face lighting up. 'You were keeping to the Covenant.'

'We are all descendants of the Covenanters who returned from America.'

'So can we call you Silence now?'

'I suppose so. Sylvia draws less attention' – she glared at Lugg – 'from strangers.'

'And Ethel is more commonplace than Ethelreda,' said Mary Ann.

'We had no wish to draw attention to ourselves, now that we were all gathered back here.'

'I don't understand.' Mason shook his head. 'Gathered here after nearly three hundred years? For what?'

'Excuse me!' shouted Lugg, loudly enough to have cleared a pub on a busy Saturday night. 'I hate to interrupt this 'istory lesson, but whoever it was clocked you and tied you up, where are they now?'

'The old woman – Ethelreda – and Joshua Jarmin, they took the dog when the other two men, Barly and Bugg, arrived and told them about the boat.'

'Barly and Bugg?' Lugg could not keep the scorn out of his voice. 'Sounds like a dodgy firm of solicitors. And what's a dog doing in all this?'

'And what's this about a boat?' asked Mary Ann Allen.

Lugg turned on her with a smug, self-satisfied smile.

'Oh, that'll be 'is nibs, Albert Campion. He's leading the seaborne invasion.'

Mr Campion was crouching in the wheelhouse of the *Jocasta* beside Tom Trybull, only the tops of their heads and eyes showing. Constable Siegfried was completely out of sight, down in the cabin, sniffing the fittings and fixtures for clues.

Trybull had cut the engine and allowed the *Jocasta* to drift into the narrow terminus of Worm Creek on the incoming tide. Here the boat fitted so snugly into the channel that Campion could see the mud under an inch of scummy seawater on either side. He thought of the yacht as being the cork squeezed into the neck of a bottle, but Trybull had urged him to think of it as a lock on a canal. When the water under the keel, perhaps six feet of it at full tide, was drained away as the tide turned, the *Jocasta* would drop lower until she had a wall of mud on either side of her and the trick would be to reverse out of that canyon before the keel lodged itself in the muddy floor. Francis Jarrold, either drunk or disabled by rabies, had misjudged the tides badly and effectively run the *Jocasta* aground, although still, ironically, some distance from solid ground.

'Here they come,' said Campion. 'We're drawing quite an audience – well, at least by Wicken standards.'

'Three men, an old woman and a dog,' said Trybull. 'Looks like you were right, it's all about dogs.'

'Partly about dogs,' said Campion. 'Wasn't there a Sherlock Holmes story about the dog who didn't bark in the night? I remember thinking that was terribly clever when I read it as a boy.'

'I was never a fan myself. When I was a kid I much preferred Arthur Ransome's books.'

'We went to the same school, you know, though not at the same time, of course. I suppose he sparked your love of messing about in boats.'

'You could say that, I suppose. Did Conan Doyle inspire your career as a detective?'

'Oh, I'd hardly call it a *career*.' Campion smiled broadly. 'It's been more a lifelong hobby fraught with disasters, like pottery. No matter how good you think you are, there is always a jug or a vase which suddenly goes wobbly on you and spins off the potter's wheel and showers you with wet clay. And talking of wet clay, why haven't that angry village mob sunk up to their armpits in it?'

As the approaching party weaved its way steadily towards the creek, it did not present the traditional fairy-tale image of a torch-carrying, pitchfork-wielding mob, although disgruntled villagers they probably were.

'I know those three men,' said Trybull, 'and they know me.'

'Then keep your head down for the moment. I'd like to keep you, and Siegfried, as my surprise weapons.'

'They were hanging around when Inspector Hankin and I were called out to Jarrold's body by Doc Fathoms. Surly buggers. They didn't have much to say for themselves, but I took statements anyway. One of them, Jarmin, had a bit of an attitude, you could tell.'

'You mean he didn't like policemen?'

'Don't think he liked anybody much, anybody not from Wicken that is. The other two, George Bugg and Bob Barly, they never said a word without a cue from Jarmin. They're all following that old woman with the dog. I'm not sure who she is.'

'I think,' said Campion, 'that is Mrs Worskitt, but I'm going on second-hand reports having only met the husband. My son had something of a brush with her and said she was quite formidable. She didn't walk especially softly, but she carried a big stick.'

Trybull frowned, not recognizing the reference. 'She seems to be the leader now. I mean, really leading them, into the mud.'

Their welcoming committee, if such it was, had halted on the edge of the marsh. The last two men in the column broke ranks slightly and bent over to retrieve something from behind a clump of marram grass. It looked like a plank to Campion, which the two men picked up front and back and carried at hip height. In single file the column stepped from the marsh grasses and on to Dengie Flat proper, though with the incoming tide now covering the mud, they gave the impression that they were walking on water. Campion noticed that all were wearing rubber boots, but were moving with a careful, deliberate tread. Only the dog, tongue lolling with excitement, seemed determined to splash through the water like a toddler unable to resist a large rain puddle.

'You're right, Sergeant, she's guiding them, showing them a safe path across the mud, though goodness knows how she's doing it,' said Campion. 'Do you know Venice, Sergeant?'

'Can't say I do, sir,' said Trybull, rather bewildered by the older man's change of tack.

'You'd love it. Everybody gets about by boat there. They have to because the streets are always flooded, but when Venice started up, it rose up out of the mud. The first Venetians were refugees who made a home on the mudbanks and islands in the lagoon there. Naturally in those days there were lots of invasions going on, and when the Lombards – I think it was the Lombards, though it could have been the Franks – moved into northern Italy, they tried to invade Venice, or what was to become Venice. Legend has it that the invaders were met on the edge of the mudbanks by a wizened old woman who advised them that the safest way to cross was *sempre diritto*, or "straight ahead". Foolishly they trusted her, went straight on and sank into the ooze. Moral of the story: never trust an old woman to lead you across a muddy swamp. Except here, apparently, where wizened old women seem to know exactly where to put their feet.'

'If they get close enough,' said Trybull, 'they can use that plank to get on deck. You think that's how they did business with Jarrold?'

'I think that's very possible. In the meantime, I think you should keep Constable Siegfried company below while I prepare to repel borders.'

'How do you propose to do that?'

'You may know them, but I don't, so the first and only polite thing to do is to introduce myself.'

Mason flexed his arms, rolled his shoulders and stretched his triceps, as if limbering up for an athletic event on the walk round to Silence Jones's house.

'You'll need gumboots if you're going out on the flats,' she had told them, and Lugg, who had spent a good thirty minutes that morning shining his brogues, agreed but with a caveat.

'Where are you going to find Wellingtons to fit my plates of meat? And this big old Yank here must be the same size if not bigger. Everything's supposed to be bigger in America, ain't it?'

'You might be surprised,' said Silence as she opened her front door. 'Everyone in Wicken keeps spare pairs for people who get stuck on the flats, mostly birdwatchers and ramblers, or when there's a neap tide. Quite often we find them washed up on the mud. I've got quite a collection and, anyway, how do you know you wouldn't fit a pair of mine? I think you've got quite dainty feet. Now come in quietly so we don't wake Frank.'

'Frank?' asked Mason softly.

'Husband of the woman who duffed you up, so they tell me. He was round here having a haircut and it fair tired him out.'

'A haircut?'

'Yes,' said Silence Jones, opening a cupboard under the stairs, 'I do a spot of hairdressing on the side – only for the neighbours, though.'

'Do you keep the hair?'

Lugg looked amazed at Mason's question, but Silence Jones took it with a serene innocence.

'Yes, I do, but not for the reason you think.' She began to fling rubber boots out of the cupboard. 'Here we are, first come, first served. Find the best fit.'

Lugg went down on one knee and began to undo a shoelace. Mason knelt beside him and did the same, wobbling slightly as Lugg's bulk leaned against him and Lugg whispered in his right ear. 'What's all that about hair?'

Lugg's idea of a confidential whisper, however, meant that in practical terms his voice carried to virtually the next postal district. Silence Jones certainly heard the question as Lugg turned from the cupboard with a Wellington boot in each hand and saved Mason the embarrassment of being caught talking in class.

'Mr Clay seems to think,' she said in the voice of the teacher who was never angry, just very disappointed at a pupil's behaviour, 'that I stuff little rag dolls with human hair as part of a witch's spell or curse.'

'Well, do yer?' Lugg asked reasonably.

'I do not! I do exactly the opposite! When I cut my neighbours' hair I gather it up and burn the excess, so that it cannot be used in any other ritual. I keep only what I need to make my reflections, not voodoo dolls. Their purpose is to warn people, tell them to be careful, perhaps bring them good luck.'

'Sounds like witchcraft to me,' said Lugg defiantly.

'We call it Merrywick round here, though that's just our word for it.'

'Yes, well, other people may call it some'fink else if they've a mind to.' Lugg's gaze dropped to what Miss Jones was holding. 'In the meantime, are those size twelve by any chance?'

Bizarrely, although they were not a matching pair, both boots were, and Lugg quickly claimed them, leaving Mason, who turned out to be the one with dainty feet, to appropriate a pair of Miss Jones's own bright red Wellingtons which Lugg referred to as 'dress Wellies'.

Suitably booted, with trousers tucked in, Lugg assumed operational command. 'Right, ladies, you two stay here while me and Mason go and see what's happening out there in Smuggler's Cove or whatever you call it.'

'Worm Creek,' said Silence Jones, 'and it's not a cove, it's just a gash in the mud, and it's dangerous out there.'

'So I 'ear, which is why Mrs Allen here will ring this number if anything unfortunate should happen.' Lugg took a business card from the pocket of his waistcoat and offered it to Mary Ann. 'That's Albert's London number, but the one scribbled on the back is a direct line to a Commander Luke at Scotland Yard. In the meantime, keep an eye on the old chap in the front room.'

'Frank Worskitt is neither a problem nor a threat,' said Silence Jones.

'His wife is,' said Mason, now on his feet and stamping them down into the red boots he had been assigned.

'Yes, she is. You should be wary of her.'

Mason touched his left temple, which had extended outwards in an egg-shaped bulge. 'I have good reason to be very wary of her, but I'm not sure what her plan is. She seemed obsessed with getting rid of a dog, Octavia Polley's dog.'

'She hid it in the chapel, didn't she?' said Mary Ann Allen. 'I saw the Polleys the other night, heading that way. I thought it was odd, they're not chapel folk.'

'Nobody in Wicken is really, apart from Frank; and don't worry about him, I made him a cup of my special herbal tea after his haircut. He'll sleep for a couple of hours yet.'

'So you saw this coming, did you?' asked Mason, asserting himself.

Silence Jones looked at the young American, her eyebrows raised in surprise and not a little admiration. 'I think you're finally beginning to understand, Mr Clay.'

'We ain't got time for this, Mason,' insisted Lugg, 'so grab your bucket and spade and let's get down to the beach. We don't want to miss the show.'

'There will be a show?'

'If Albert Campion's issuing the invitations, there's going to be a show.'

Mr Campion strode along the deck of the *Jocasta* feeling slightly overdressed. His borrowed waterproofs were more suited to the rugged Norwegian bosun of a fishing trawler caught with full nets in a Force 10 storm off the Faroe Islands, rather than a thin, white-haired elderly English gentleman standing on the polished deck of a totally immobile motor yacht stationary in what, to those unaware of the existence of Worm Creek, would appear to be no more than two inches of water.

It would have been far more appropriate, he thought, for him to have been kitted out in white flannels, a blazer with suitably impressive yacht club badge and a white captain's hat with gold braid. He could then have greeted the visitors with a cheery 'Ahoy there!' and while a loudhailer might have looked impressive, it would have been surplus to requirements, as his audience was close enough now for him to distinguish facial features.

Across the watery flats and the marsh bordering the land, they had presented a curious, slightly ominous sight. As they got closer, the fact that they appeared to be walking on water was almost mystical and the figures took on a supernatural sheen. No, up close, they were recognizable as very human, though far from friendly. An angry village mob indeed, two of them toting a length of wood which could be used as a gangplank to allow the pirates to board.

Dusk was approaching and Mr Campion tried to calculate whether that was in his favour or not. Unless they really did have supernatural powers, the marauding villagers would surely want to be back on dry land before dark. Their careful progress across marsh, mud and water had been impressive but at night would be suicidal. Alternatively, they might see the yacht as safe footing and therefore be more determined than ever to capture her as a prize.

Campion could, of course, instruct Trybull to put the engine in reverse and pull the boat back off the flats and into deeper water. Once the tide turned, he would have to do that anyway, to avoid the *Jocasta* sinking lower as Worm Creek emptied until she became embedded in the mud. Then their voyage would end just as Francis Jarrold's had.

When in doubt, outnumbered and with the elements against you, Campion reasoned, there was only one possible course of action: confrontation.

'Please allow me to introduce myself,' he declaimed loudly, causing the advancing column to come to a halt. 'My name is Albert Campion. I am unfamiliar to you, but this vessel is not, is it? What a splendid dog, by the way. It's a Basenji, I believe? A strange breed and one that would have fooled Sherlock Holmes: the dog that *couldn't* bark in the night.'

'What business do you have here?' challenged the old woman, clearly identifying herself as the pirate queen.

'I could say I came here for the golden beaches, the donkey rides and the funfair, but was misinformed. As it happens, I am here because of Francis Jarrold, late of this parish I believe, a man called Timms, also late, and a dog called Robespierre. If any of those names rings a bell, then we might have a profitable conversation.'

He was too far away to be sure, but he imagined the old woman's eyes lighting up at the word 'profitable'.

'The owner of that there boat owes us some money.'

The woman stared hard at Campion. He felt a distinct chill which could not be attributed to the slight breeze coming off the sea.

'I doubt that very much. You may think that the skipper of the *Jocasta* owed you something, but he is no longer with us as, I suspect, you very well know.'

The woman raised her walking stick and pointed it at Campion like a pistol. 'I know full well who the owner of that fancy boat is and she can afford to pay her debts.'

Mr Campion steeled himself, determined to contain his surprise at the woman's statement. Slowly he took off his spectacles and fumbled in the pocket of his waterproof trousers for his handkerchief. As he polished the large round lenses, he looked out over the damp landscape – or should that be mudscape? – as though seeing it for the first time. He decided it was time to stop trying to play chess with the woman and be more aggressive.

'You must be Mrs Worskitt,' he said, replacing his glasses and staring hard at her, defying her to deny it. It was an old lawyer's trick, but where lawyers rarely ask questions to which they do not already know the answers, Campion was guessing.

'What if I am?'

It had been a good guess and had struck home. 'And your gang comprises Messrs Jarmin, Bugg and Barly, whose fame, I would suggest, has recently spread as far as London's West End.'

The woman lowered her walking stick but remained immobile, seawater swirling around her boots. The three men closed ranks in single file behind her, their eyes also fixed on Campion and the yacht, with Jarmin towering head and shoulders above Mrs Worskitt's wizened face.

'I'm afraid the dog and I have not been introduced,' Campion said calmly, 'but I always seem to be meeting dogs when I come to Wicken, which is odd for a place with a reputation for not having any.'

Campion saw Jarmin lean forward and whisper into Mrs Worskitt's ear. He had no doubt that he was the subject matter.

'The last one I met I had to return to his owner after the poor beast had been shipwrecked on these very mudflats. Am I expected to see this one home as well?'

'How much?' said Mrs Worskitt.

'I'm sorry, what?'

'How much for the mutt?'

She jerked on the rope lead, pulling Pickles closer and then flicking out her left foot into his side. It was not an excessively violent kick, but the dog cowered and pawed at the water.

'Are you trying to sell me that dog, madam? I'm afraid I am not in the market for stolen goods.'

'Ain't stolen.' The woman's voice was shrill. 'We haven't been paid what we's due and somebody has to pay up.'

Campion feigned a sudden surprise revelation. 'Oh, I see, there was some sort of landing fee involved, a sort of import tax, you might say. Francis Jarrold wasn't in any position to pay his dues, so I suppose Mr Timms was the man with the wallet. I should say the late Mr Timms, who was murdered in his office yesterday. The murderer, or murderers, robbed him while they were at it and got away with a substantial amount of cash. Is there still a balance outstanding?'

Mr Campion had no idea how much had actually been taken from Timmy Timms and was merely trying to provoke a reaction. He got one, though not quite the one he expected.

Ethel Worskitt swivelled on her hips and lashed out with her walking stick, hitting an astonished Joshua Jarmin on the right kneecap with such force that Campion heard the blow land with a *crack*. Jarmin's leg gave way under him and he keeled over, landing shoulder first in a splash of water and a swirl of mud. If her sudden attack was surprising, what then happened to Jarmin was truly shocking. Immediately on making contact with the muddy surface, Jarmin began to sink. An arm extended to break his fall had disappeared under the surface, and as he struggled to right himself he seemed only to be falling backwards. The expression of pure terror on his face signified that he knew the dangers of leaving, even only by a few inches, the path down which Ethel Worskitt had led them.

Campion instinctively grabbed the handrail of the *Jocasta* and gripped it tightly. Vaulting over it to launch a dramatic rescue was out of the question for a man of his age, and racing across the treacherous mudflat could clearly be lethal, even though the distance was no more than twenty feet. He was doubtful if he could even throw one of the yacht's lifebelts that far, but then, with horror, realized it might not be necessary.

Standing over the struggling, splashing form of Joshua Jarmin, Ethel Worskitt calmly raised her walking stick again, but this time she used it like a gentle rapier rather than a swinging club. Placing the end of the stick somewhere on Jarmin's upper chest or lower neck and then straightening her arm, she pushed Jarmin deeper into the mud.

Campion stared as if hypnotized, not quite believing what he was seeing. The scene was outlandish, almost as stylized as a piece of Kabuki theatre and just as incomprehensible to the naïve Western tourist visiting Japan. It was, Campion decided, a ritual punishment rather than the execution he had feared, though the thought brought him little comfort as he knew he was powerless to intervene.

What was most unsettling of all was that Jarmin, who was clearly burly enough to bat away the stick – and indeed the old woman pinning him down – seemed to be accepting his fate. He did not cry out or curse his assailant, and he may well have known not to try and fight the pull of the ooze which lapped around him. The acceptance of his fate in utter silence was the most disturbing aspect.

The tableau on the mudflat dissolved when the Worskitt woman withdrew her walking stick and flicked it, almost like a stage magician's wand, as a signal to Barly and Bugg. Taking their cue, they laid down the plank they were carrying and, with one standing on one end, the other tiptoed along its length until he was close enough to grab Jarmin's hand and pull him upright until he too stood on the plank, his clothes dripping and plastered with filth. He did not look at Ethel Worskitt, but kept his eyes fixed on his boots; not that the woman seemed to have any further interest in him, for she had turned back to the yacht and to Campion.

'Are you going to give us what we're owed for this dog?' she shouted, yanking on the Basenji's lead again.

Mr Campion snapped himself into action, determined not to be intimidated by this awful woman and her thuggish army. 'Madam, I have no intention of supplementing your ill-gotten gains. That dog is not yours to sell. I believe it belongs to a theatrical gentleman called Geoffrey Clegg, and it is only in your possession as a result of several criminal acts including murder. I refuse to become complicit in such activities and I intend to see you held to account for them.'

'You talk too much and you know too much and if you won't give us what we're owed, we'll come and take it.'

It was a clear and present threat and the woman lost no time in carrying it out, waving her troops forward, pointing exactly where they should put their feet with her stick.

Barly and Bugg picked up the plank and laid it where the women directed, then began to cross on it with a wet and bedraggled Jarmin bringing up the rear.

Mr Campion did a quick calculation and realized that a younger and fitter man could easily jump from the end of the plank and on to the deck of the *Jocasta*, and the three men approaching were all younger and fitter than himself.

He stood to attention and puffed out his chest before shouting out over the bleak desolation of Dengie Flat, a landscape empty of other human habitation.

'I give you fair warning that if you trespass on board this boat I will have to call the police!'

Lugg and Mason Lowell reached the end of the Wicken track and looked out over marsh and mud to the distant drama, which appeared to involve a stationary yacht, low in the water, being boarded by a group of figures who had walked over water to get to it.

'Strewth!' exhaled Lugg in admiration. 'That's a good magic trick.'

'Not magic,' said Mason, 'Merrywick.'

Mary Ann Allen, remembering her medical background, insisted on checking the condition of Frank Worskitt, who was still splayed in the armchair where he had rested after the alarums and excursions of having his hair cut. He was exactly where Silence Jones had left him, snoring gently, his weather-beaten face the very image of a Renaissance angel, albeit a very old angel who had enjoyed an extensive night on the heavenly tiles.

Noticing the empty cup and saucer on the small coffee table next to his chair, Mary Ann picked up the drained cup and sniffed it.

'Frank always liked a measure or two of rum in his tea,' said Silence Jones, 'purely for medicinal purposes.'

'I thought Methodists didn't drink.'

'They don't, at least not in front of their wives, which is why old Frank liked regular haircuts. When I realized there could be trouble in the chapel, I slipped an additional something into his usual tipple; it was herbal and not dangerous. He should sleep for another hour at least, but I thought it best to keep him out of the way. He has no idea what Ethelreda gets up to.'

'You think Ethel's behind what happened to Mr Lugg's American friend?'

'Ethel's behind most things in Wicken.'

'So what is she doing out on the flats?'

'I'm not sure, but we might be able to see from upstairs. My bedroom looks out over towards Worm Creek.'

Mary Ann followed Silence upstairs and into her bedroom. Her frisson of excitement was less to do with that afternoon's events in Wicken, and more that she finally had an invitation to enter this previously inaccessible sanctum. As an experience it was both exhilarating and disappointing: exhilarating in that she realized her own wardrobe was at least a decade more fashionable than Miss Jones's, and disappointing in that the only evidence of her sewing skills were in some tasteful home-made cushions on her bed, embroidered with miniature roses.

The view from the bedroom's sash window was an expansive one over the flat, featureless terrain of marsh and Dengie Flat. Even in the faltering afternoon light they could see small figures out on the flats, clustered around the mast of a sailboat.

'Look, there's your friend and that charming American,' said Silence, jabbing a forefinger against the windowpane, indicating Lugg and Mason who had left the single-lane track and were stepping cautiously across the marsh.

'That's really dangerous, isn't it?'

'They'll be all right on the marsh if they're careful, but if they try and go out on the mudflats while the tide's in, that's foolhardy.'

'How did Ethel and her gang get all the way out there?'

'Ethelreda has spent twenty years walking those flats so she knows where the firm footing is. I've seen her every day, sometimes twice a day, out there with her walking stick, testing the ground and memorizing the safest pathways. She's not really lame, you know, and she may tell those idiots who take orders from her that it's using her second sight or that it's Merrywick, but really she has been mapping those flats in her mind for years.'

'But why?' asked Mary Ann.

'So she could lead people out to Worm Creek to meet a boat.'

'But boats don't come to Wicken.'

'Not unless they're invited.'

'Did everyone know this except me?'

'You are not Wicken,' said Silence solemnly, 'and neither is Frank Worskitt. Goodness knows what Ethel told him she was doing out on the flats but, knowing Ethel, I don't think Frank ever dared question her too closely.'

'But everybody else here knew about this?'

'More or less.'

'Even Richard Polley?'

It was Mary Ann's turn to jab a finger against the glass to point out that Richard Polley, smartly turned out in tweed jacket and a trilby with a feather in the brim, was marching down the track with a military air, passing Silence Jones's front gate.

'Yes, Richard knew, and the business with the dog, it was all for his sister . . .'

'Why is he carrying a shotgun?' asked Mary Ann.

EIGHTEEN
Quickmud

Mr Campion took a half-step backwards and surveyed the deck of the *Jocasta* to see how much room he had for manoeuvre. It was immediately clear the answer was not much, as there was a boom or a mast or some other such sailing regalia, plus the roof and small skylights of the cabin, all cluttering the deck and reducing the space available for a decent sword fight.

Which was just as well, as he did not have sword, or indeed a personal weapon of any kind. He made sure the advancing mob could see this by holding his arms out as if crucified to prove he had nothing to hide. Meanwhile the mob – if one could call three men and an old woman a mob, and he was pretty sure that in early Victorian times that had been a big enough gathering to merit transportation for life and possibly a cavalry charge – was advancing over the mud with almost military precision.

With Ethel Worskitt directing operations, the two men, Barly and Bugg, would place their trusty plank down in the water and they would advance across the mud, with a limping, bedraggled Jarmin bringing up the rear. Campion estimated that they had only to move the plank two more lengths and they would be near enough to step easily on to the yacht without having to jump.

'I have to ask,' he addressed them, boosted by a mental image of a soapbox politician haranguing a crowd, 'just what exactly you intend to get out of your assault on this fine craft? I am addressing you, madam, as I presume your foot soldiers do not speak except at your command.'

Ethel Worskitt glared at this strangely dressed elderly man – clearly from a class she had never had dealings with – and a spasm of doubt squirmed across her face, but she did not alter her steady tread across the plank towards the yacht.

'We want what's owed us, then we want you gone. Too many snoopers in Wicken.'

'I am well aware that the residents of Wicken value their privacy, for it is a close-knit community I am told; perhaps too close-knit to be healthy.'

'What do the likes of you know about the likes of us?'

'I have heard it said that the only book you'll find in Wicken is a Bible.'

'And what's wrong with that?'

'Absolutely nothing, but in view of what you are attempting, a copy of the Piracy Act 1837 might have been more useful.'

'What you talking about? You be cracked, you be.'

'That, or something similar, has been said many times in the past, but I did not set out on this voyage without first consulting the law, and boarding a vessel without permission and with intent to commit robbery or even murder is, I assure you, an act of piracy. It is also just about the only crime you can still be hanged for in this wonderfully liberal country of ours.'

The reaction of the advancing Bugg and Barly, who clearly registered the word 'hanged', showed that they had been listening to Campion's filibuster ramblings, though he doubted they had registered the irony of a filibuster about piracy when the word itself probably derived from the Elizabethan 'flibutor', a fast 'fly boat' used by pirates to chase and rob passing treasure ships. Neither of those two broad-shouldered, grim-faced toughs seemed likely to be lexicographers or cruciverbalists, a word Campion had learned from a charming man he had met in an Oxford pub where both were doing *The Times* crossword, and they were by now frighteningly close to the starboard side rail of the *Jocasta.*

'We ain't pirates,' shouted Ethel Worskitt, 'we're here for what we're owed. Fair recompense for work done.'

Campion backed away to the port side rail, until it connected with the back of his knees and he could go no further. Now only the beam of the yacht separated him from those trying to board the yacht. The yacht, squeezed into the narrow terminus of Worm Creek, wasn't going anywhere.

Although he could, from his new position, see only the top of her head, Mr Campion continued with their loud dialogue, which must have been audible over a considerable portion of Dengie Flat to the north and Ray Sand to the south; not that there was anyone for miles to listen in on their conversation, other than the small but select audience that Campion had brought with him.

'It's a technicality, I suppose,' he said, trying to keep the nerves out of his voice as Bugg and Barly both loomed over the starboard handrail, 'but it might not actually be piracy, so how does smuggling sound? Or extortion? For which crime are you actually owed money?'

'The crime isn't ours if we're the ones being diddled.'

'An interesting turn of logic, madam, but I seem to be the one being threatened, and yet I haven't diddled you or anyone else I can think of – the Inland Revenue excepted, of course.'

'Fancy talk, fancy man, but you took that soppy poodle that Jarrold brought over before we got a chance to get our commission.'

'From Timmy Timms, I presume,' said Campion, concentrating on the two men now reaching for the handrail, 'or Charles Wyndham as he was known in Tillingham. He was here when Jarrold's body was found but the dog had already been apprehended by someone else, hadn't it? So, what – did Timms refuse to pay the dog's fare from France? Is that why you sent your bully boys up to London?'

'To get our due,' the old woman shouted, though Campion could no longer see her for the two burly figures now on deck, 'and to warn him off. Since you turned up we've had nothing but snoopers sniffing around Wicken. We'll show you how we deal with snoopers.'

Barly and Bugg now had their feet on deck and a mud-caked, dripping Joshua Jarmin was clambering over the rail behind them. Any one of them could have come to grips with Campion with a village fete hop, skip and a jump. It was a long time since he had faced such odds unarmed, and his enemies sharing the deck of a yacht effectively locked in a world of swirling water and greedy mud had left him nowhere to run. There was only one course of action open to him.

'Constable Siegfried!' he shouted. 'I could really use some help out here!'

'I'm going to check on Octavia,' said Mary Ann Allen.

'I'll come with you,' said Silence Jones, pulling on a cardigan.

'It's not like Richard to leave her alone and I've never seen him with a gun before.'

'No, you won't. You stay here with Frank; you know him better than I do. When he comes round, he'll need a familiar face to explain what's happened to Ethel.'

'What do you think is going to happen to Ethel?

'How should I know?' Mary Ann looked Miss Jones in the eye. 'You're the one supposed to have the second sight or third eye or whatever you call it. But if you ask me, it's not going to end well for her.'

Lugg and Mason Lowell picked their way through the marsh as carefully as if crossing a minefield, even though the more daunting traverse of the mudflats covered by the eddying tide lay ahead of them. In the distance they could see the *Jocasta* and the figures milling around it but, apart from the mast, there was no visible outline of a boat, the bulk of the yacht being cocooned in the canyon of Worm Creek, so the whole scene had a dreamlike quality, as if the whole drama was being played out by figures moving *on* the surface of the sea.

With nothing but a vast, dirty grey mirror of North Sea beyond that makeshift stage, all semblance of land behind them, and the dying light, it was almost as if they had stepped from one familiar world into another, stranger one, full of odd sounds and smells. Every step they took was accompanied by a squelching, plopping sound and the distinct whiff of rotting vegetation.

'Stick to the clumps of grass,' said Mason, lengthening his stride. 'The footing will be firmer.'

Lugg, already lagging two yards behind the young American, concentrated nervously on placing his feet where his companion had, vainly trying to adjust for the weight difference between them.

'That lot of 'ooligans got out there somehow,' he wheezed, balancing on one foot while carefully placing the other. 'They must know a path through this mess. You're from the Wild West – can't you track them, follow their trail?'

'I'm not playing Tonto to your Lone Ranger.' Mason spoke without turning round. 'I'm a junior college professor, not an Indian scout.'

'Well, they didn't just float out there, did they?' moaned Lugg. 'Or can they really walk on water?'

'Nobody walks on water, they just know where to put their feet,' said Mason. 'They live here; they know this place, probably know every piece of reed and scrub grass.'

'It ain't exactly the sort of place you go for an afternoon stroll, though, is it?'

Even as he spoke, Lugg became aware, out of the corner of his left eye, of a figure walking sure-footedly over the marsh in parallel, not more than three yards away. It was a man he had never seen before, but from the cut of his tweed jacket, the gold watch and chain straddling a moleskin waistcoat (Lugg had a sharp eye for such details) and the fact that he carried a broken shotgun in the crook of his arm, it was clear he was a gentleman – or at least someone trying to be one.

'Afternoon,' said Lugg politely.

The man smiled a thin smile and nodded but did not break stride.

'Mr Polley! What are you doing here?' said Mason, mouth open and eyes wide in surprise.

'I've come to put a stop to all this,' said Richard Polley. 'It has already gone too far. I am sorry you were treated so roughly, Mr Clay. That was unforgiveable, but so was the treatment of my sister. I'm afraid Ethel's house of corruption is collapsing around her ears and causing her to react in a very unstable way. She must be stopped.'

From across the marsh and the mud, carried on the incoming sea breeze, came the faint but distinctive sound of a scream, causing Polley and Mason to turn their heads sharply in the direction of Worm Creek.

While their attention was occupied, Lugg hopped from tussock to tussock of marram grass with a daintiness that belied the fact that he was on anything but a firm footing, and brought himself to a halt face-to-face with Richard Polley.

'We 'aven't been properly introduced,' said Lugg, offering a handshake. 'My name's Lugg.'

Richard Polley, even in such a bizarre geographical location, walking over marsh and mud directly, to all intents and purposes, into the North Sea, could not resist the call of good manners.

He transferred the shotgun to his left arm and held out his right hand in the ritual of greeting.

Lugg took the offered palm firmly in his right paw and then delivered a powerful and precise left-handed short jab to Richard Polley's nose.

Before Mr Polley slumped to the ground, his legs turned to jelly, Lugg caught the falling shotgun.

Mr Campion had been determined to remember everything in detail in the remote possibility that he might be called upon to testify in a civil case for damages, or, more likely, speak at a medal-giving ceremony to mark the bravery of Police Constable Siegfried.

The dog had emerged from *Jocasta's* wheelhouse and torn across the cabin roof in a blizzard of black fur and flashing teeth. It was doubtful whether Robert Barly fully realized what was happening; it was his misfortune to be the nearest figure threatening Mr Campion and he had just made the cataclysmic mistake of pulling a long-bladed knife from the sleeve of his jacket. This, clearly, in Constable Siegfried's appealing brown eyes, made him a suitable target, and after being cooped up in the cabin while villainy, his senses told him, was in the air, he was coiled and ready to spring into action.

And spring he did, launching himself like a rocket with his jaws open, and then clamping on to Bob Barly's knife-wielding arm. The velocity of the dog's impact took Barly off his feet, and beast and man crashed into an equally startled George Bugg, all three sprawling across the deck. Siegfried was almost instantly back up on all four of his feet, his teeth still embedded in Barly's arm.

Joshua Jarmin, still dripping water and mud – and seeing his two companions being unceremoniously bowled over – froze with one leg half over the port rail, and Campion, delicately edging sideways along the starboard rail, away from the fracas, saw his eyes flick to the knife Barly had dropped.

'Don't you even think that, Josh Jarmin,' thundered Trybull, emerging from the wheelhouse, resplendent in his sergeant's uniform and peaked cap. 'You harm that dog and I'll see you in Chelmsford Prison. No, I'll let him take your throat out, *then* I'll see you in Chelmsford Prison.'

'Sergeant Trybull,' said Campion loudly over the howling of Bob Barly, 'how good to see you, though I think I had everything under control.'

'So I heard. Siggy – leave!'

The dog obeyed the command almost instantly, but not before a perfunctory snap at George Bugg's face as the man struggled to his feet.

'Siggy – sit! And you three, don't you move.'

The dog sat, keeping the three men under close scrutiny as Trybull moved to stand next to Campion.

'Are you all right, sir?'

'I'm fine, Sergeant. They didn't get close enough to lay a glove on me. I was actually quite surprised that they got as close as they did, across the mud.'

'If I hadn't seen it myself, I wouldn't have believed it. I've never heard of anyone crossing the Dengie Flat like that, or any other way come to think of it. Nobody would have thought of Worm Creek as a smuggler's cove.' He braced his feet apart and addressed the three men huddling together under the watchful eyes and sparking canines of PC Siegfried. 'Regular occurrence, was it? Meeting Francis Jarrold here and taking off contraband? What was he trading in – booze, duty-free fags, drugs?'

'I suspect it was somewhat less commercial,' said Campion, when the three men refused to speak. 'Dogs – or perhaps other pets – belonging to the rich, famous and incredibly stupid who insisted on taking their darling animals with them when they went to the Continent but couldn't stand the thought of leaving them in quarantine for a month when they returned. The Ministry of Agriculture has been getting very hot under the collar about the importation of mammals which might bring rabies into this country, and there's been new legislation this year. Jarrold was used to smuggling back Dame Jocasta's dog, so why not a few more on the side? The irony is that it was Jarrold himself who ended up bringing rabies ashore.'

'He was bewitched!' blurted Bob Barly, clutching his arm and glancing nervously at the Alsatian in case his outburst would provoke another attack.

'Shut it, Bob,' growled Jarmin.

'Jarrold's last trip didn't go to plan, did it?' said Campion.

'He made an unscheduled landing because he wasn't thinking straight. Timmy Timms wasn't here to meet him, was he? He would take the dogs off your hands and pay you for getting them ashore, except it went wrong that night because of Jarrold's erratic behaviour.'

'He was actin' pure stupid,' Barly confessed to the police dog, who remained stoically unimpressed. Mr Campion, rather flippantly, noted the Essex pronunciation of 'stoopid'.

'From his log and the way he ran the *Jocasta* aground, he was certainly deranged. He let the dogs out of their cages as well. Such a partner was a liability. Is that why you finished him off out there on the mud?'

'We had nothing to do with that,' snapped George Bugg, speaking for the first time.

'No, I don't think you did,' said Mr Campion, 'but you did go up to London and do for Timmy Timms, didn't you? And, for your information, the young chap you knocked senseless as you made your escape was my son. He has inherited the family's lack of brainy matter and so when somebody threatens to reduce it even more, I take exception.'

'I think it is time,' said Sergeant Trybull formally, 'for these three coves to realize they are under arrest.'

'I agree,' said Campion, 'and that knife on the deck there is probably a murder weapon, and will be of great interest to Scotland Yard.'

'Then I'll get Constable Siegfried to escort these three below. We can hold them in the cabin.'

'Four,' said Campion almost distractedly. 'We mustn't forget Mrs . . .'

As if hearing her cue, Mrs Worskitt made sure she was in no danger of being forgotten. 'What're you lumps doin' up there? Stop yer argefy and get on with it!'

It was Joshua Jarmin, still half on, half off the deck, who turned and shouted back at her. 'There's a policeman here, one that knows me.'

'And one that's going to see you locked up for good if you don't do something about him. Get rid of the incomers! Show 'em the mud then get that boat out of there and sink it.'

The three Wicken men exchanged nervous glances and, on the

other side of the deck, so too did Campion and Trybull. Only Constable Siegfried, seated between the two opposing teams but facing the forces of disorder rather than law, seemed anything but distressed at the old woman's screeching, although his tail began to sweep the deck in a slow, impatient way.

'Now don't do anything hasty, you fellows,' said Trybull, puffing out his chest and folding his arms to better display the sergeant's stripes on his uniform's sleeves, at the same time moving in front of Campion to shield him.

'Do it, or you'll answer to me!' shouted Ethel Worskitt.

Joshua Jarmin swung a leg over the port rail, planted both feet on the deck and looked at Trybull almost apologetically.

'We ain't got no choice,' he said, then launched himself towards the policeman just as Bob Barly went into a crouch and scooped up the knife he had dropped earlier.

'Why did you have to hit him?' Mason asked without slowing his erratic progress, hopping from one clump of marsh grass to the next.

'I wanted to borrow his shotgun and didn't have time to ask politely,' Lugg answered, some ten yards behind him. He himself had left Richard Polley sitting on his backside in the grass, holding a bunched handkerchief against his nose.

'We might need it,' Mason conceded, realizing he had reached the edge of the marsh and his boots were now splashing in the thin layer of seawater covering the mudflat. 'There's quite a ruckus going on over there.'

They were still too far away to make out what was being said, or shouted, distinctly, but that there was a ruckus – and Lugg decided he liked that word – taking place on the yacht there was no doubt, with several figures on deck now involved, one of them barking. To add to the unreality of the scene, a diminutive old woman with a small dog on a lead was walking on water and conducting the ruckus by waving a walking stick like a demented conductor trying to hold an electrified baton.

'Watch your step,' warned Mason. 'The going's pretty soft from here on in.'

'Can you see how they did it? Are there any footprints?'

'Not in this muck.'

Mason tested the footing slowly; each time he pulled a boot from the mud, it came out with a sucking *plop*.

'You'd better stay here,' he said. 'It won't take your weight.'

'Don't be cheeky, you young pup. There's four of them out there and together they weigh three times what I do.' He caught Mason's raised eyebrow. 'All right then, twice as much as me. Point is: if they can walk on water, why can't we?'

'Lend me your shoulder,' said Mason.

As Lugg drew near, Mason stretched out an arm to anchor himself while he lifted one foot and then the other to remove his boots and socks and roll up his trousers above the ankle. Then he pulled off his jacket and handed it to a bemused Lugg.

'On Harkers Island, I saw horses walking on water,' he said with a boyish grin, 'so why can't I? Horses are pretty dumb and I'm pretty smart. I reckon the answer is speed. Get across the mud before it knows I'm coming.'

Lugg swung Mason's jacket over his left shoulder and raised the shotgun to his right. 'Best of luck with that, chum, but it might be a bit of amusement for that lot playing pirates.' He settled the butt of the shotgun against the jowls of his cheek.

'What are you doing?' Mason asked, wriggling his toes in the cold mud to get the feel of the terrain.

'Me?' said Lugg innocently. 'I'm getting their attention.'

The three attackers were bunched so close together that when the police dog leapt at them, Mr Campion thought that Constable Siegfried alone would subdue them. A high-pitched canine yelp of pain indicated that he might need some help, and it was quickly forthcoming as Sergeant Trybull entered the fray.

Before he threw himself forward across the decking, he hissed at Campion. 'Get to the back of the boat. If they take me down, get in the dinghy and fetch help.'

At least, thought Campion, he had instructed him to go and get help, though from exactly where was unclear. He had not been told to simply run away, yet that would in fact be exactly what he would be doing. The advice was eminently sensible if unpalatable. He was a seventy-one-year-old man, physically fit but nowhere near as capable of rough-housing as he had been twenty years ago or, to be absolutely honest, forty years. His most formidable strength and main means of self-defence – his wits – had proved ineffective in the face of the strange, possessed brutality which now confronted him.

He knew the worthy Trybull was correct, he was a liability in a fight, and so – with a heavy heart and the taste of acid in his mouth – he sidestepped towards the stern as the policeman put down his head and charged.

The mêlée on the deck was a close-quarter confusion of punches, kicks, animal growls and grunts of pain. As far as Campion could tell as he backed away, cursing himself not as a coward but for being useless, the dog's jaws had locked on the forearm wielding the knife, though not before it had struck home somewhere as the blade was dripping blood.

Trybull landed a good right cross on the side of Jarmin's head, though the man stayed on his feet, and then Trybull himself took a boot in the stomach from George Bugg. The policeman continued to swing his fists at two opponents while the dog savaged Bob Barly's arms and, standing on its hind legs, used its front paws in Barly's chest to push the man off balance.

Campion's crab-like sideways shuffle had brought him to within touching distance of the rope securing the inflatable dinghy to the stern rail. The dinghy was floating at the same level as the deck, so all he had to do was untie it and step over the rail. It was hardly a difficult move and required little physical strength or effort, but an intense sense of shame prevented him from abandoning ship in such a way, and his hand hovered over the bowline knot securing the line to the dinghy.

He had no weapon and could not match the assailants in strength or technique, though he might distract them long enough for Trybull and the dog to gain the upper hand, or at least save themselves more punishment, if he could surprise them by attacking from the rear.

He crept around the wheelhouse and started down the port side, but he had taken only two strides before he realized he was now in full view of Ethel Worskitt, only a few yards to his right, doing a sort of angry jig in the mud and water. She raised her stick and pointed it at Campion while screaming the warning, 'Watch out, Josh, he's behind you!'

Mr Campion had never felt less like a pantomime villain, and certainly no threat to Jarmin, who either did not hear, or ignored Mrs Worskitt's warning, as he was busy trying to hold Sergeant Trybull in a bear-hug while George Bugg punched the sergeant in the stomach. All three of the combatants were struggling to keep their balance as Bob Barly and Constable Siegfried thrashed around their feet, locked in mortal combat.

Campion was now close enough to smell the stench of mud coming off Jarmin, yet still had no idea how to disable the man and thus help Tom Trybull. His frustration at his own weakness mounted. He was a ridiculous figure, he decided, so why not act ridiculously?

He removed his spectacles, slipped them into a jacket pocket, stepped up and tapped Jarmin on the shoulder, then adopted the classic 'fists up' boxing stance and said, 'Marquis of Queensbury Rules?'

That Jarmin was surprised was clear. That he was willing to turn to face the challenge from a new opponent was doubtful, but he relaxed enough for Trybull to wrestle free of his grip and head-butt George Bugg.

Mr Campion was, however, saved the inevitable humiliation of a close-quarter scrap with a younger and far more proficient fighter when the unmistakable sound of a gunshot boomed across the mudflats and the battle on the *Jocasta*'s deck was brought to an abrupt halt.

Campion knew it was a shotgun, and that it had been fired from distance or aimed deliberately high, because he felt tiny lead pellets of shot falling on his head and saw them bouncing off the deck. Jarmin and Bugg also recognized the sound immediately and paused in their exertions, but Bob Barly continued to roll around the deck with an angry Alsatian that was determined to exact revenge for the gash on his flank which had matted the fur with blood.

Automatically Campion tore his gaze away from the mayhem on deck to search for the source of the potshot somebody had taken at them. He was not altogether surprised to see, across the wet mud at the edge of the marsh, that the gunman was Lugg. Even without his spectacles, that orbital shape was easily identified.

What was unexpected and so surprising that he fumbled his glasses from his pocket and jammed them on his face, was the head-down figure of Mason Lowell charging like a Camargue bull across the Dengie Flat, splashing his way towards the *Jocasta*. Ethel Worskitt had seen him too, backed, it seemed, by a fat man with a gun, and clearly did not relish a confrontation.

The old woman flung away her walking stick and dropped the rope which restrained the Basenji, giving it a swift kick on the hindquarters to urge it towards the onrushing Mason. It was possible that she hoped the American would be diverted by the plight of the dog, which began to splash in erratic circles, happy to be off the rope lead but terrified by the unnatural surroundings of seawater and glutinous mud.

Ethel did not wait to see whether Mason took the bait. She turned and began to run with remarkable agility across the mudflat, diagonally away from Worm Creek in the general direction of nothing, except the advancing dusk and the North Sea.

The arrival of Mason on – and the departure of Mrs Worskitt from – the scene brought an end to hostilities on board the *Jocasta*, though for different reasons. The confidence of the defenders was boosted enormously by the prospect of reinforcements, while the marauding men from Wicken stared listlessly in the opposite direction at the retreating figure of Ethel Worskitt.

'She's leaving,' said Joshua Jarmin under his breath, so quietly that only Campion heard.

'You guys need a hand?' Mason hailed them.

He had made it to the plank lying across the mud and was toe-and-heeling his way along its length, arms outstretched for balance. In his right hand he held the rope lead of the Basenji, which seemed happy enough to splash alongside him. With his mud-splattered shirt and sodden trousers rolled up above the ankles and bare feet as black as shiny coal, he looked as if might be auditioning for an existential slapstick silent comedy about a would-be tightrope walker.

'Come aboard, Mason, but hang on to that little dog.'

'Don't worry about Siggy,' said Trybull, his fingers through the police dog's collar. 'He only goes for human flesh.'

As he spoke, Trybull reached out and took the long, thin knife from Bob Barly's limp grip. The dog never took his eyes off the arm that had wielded it.

Mr Campion studied the three men who, only a minute before, had been intent on doing him, and an English policeman, serious physical harm. The gunshot had startled them for sure, but the realization that Ethel Worskitt was abandoning them seemed to have drained the aggression out of them. Now they were watching her diminutive figure, jerking like a puppet as she splashed clumsily across the flats.

Mason climbed on board, the Basenji tucked under one muscular arm, then dropped unceremoniously on to the deck, shedding water and mud. The dog shook himself thoroughly and gave a whimper of interest at the presence of Constable Siegfried who, being a professional officer of the law, totally ignored the smaller hound and concentrated on the three humans he clearly regarded as prisoners, if not dinner.

'You got things under control here?' Mason asked.

'I think so,' said Campion. 'This, by the way, is Sergeant Trybull of Essex Police and he is currently restraining Police Constable Siegfried from ripping out the throats of these gentlemen form Wicken. I suspect you might know of them.'

'I surely do,' said Mason, clenching his fists, 'and I have a score to settle with one of them.'

'That can wait. The fight's gone out of them, it seems; but now you're here you can keep an eye on these reprobates while the sergeant gets on the radio and summons help.'

'What about her?' He indicated the fleeing figure of Mrs Worskitt. 'I could go and get her.'

'How?'

'The rubber dinghy you're towing – I could skim over the mud in that. Rowing was my sport in college.'

'How admirable,' said Campion, distracted, 'but your proposal, even if practical, now sadly seems to be redundant.'

All six men on the *Jocasta* now stared in horror at the shrinking figure of Ethel Worskitt who was a hundred yards from the boat, flapping and splashing her way in – roughly – a northeasterly direction until, suddenly, she wasn't.

One moment she was there, the next she had gone.

She did not cry out as the mud took her.

NINETEEN
Silence Is Broken

Lugg's greatest regret as he stood on guard where the marsh met the mud was that he did not have a camera to record Mr Campion's return to dry land. It was not, Mason would say later, Washington crossing the Delaware – a reference which flew freely over the fat man's head – but he agreed that it must have been quite a sight.

A short conference of war had taken place on the *Jocasta* in the uneasy truce following the sudden and shocking disappearance of Ethel Worskitt, which had left the three Wicken men stunned and listless, almost as if they were puppets with their strings cut; which, in a way, thought Campion, they were. All propensity to violence having drained from them in an instant, they no longer posed an immediate threat and had accepted their mutation from combatant to prisoner.

Dusk was upon them and darkness not far behind. Trybull was also keeping one eye on the tide and the need to reverse the yacht out of Worm Creek and back into open water to avoid spending an uncomfortable night on the mudflats. There was also the need to relieve Siegfried of the guard duty he had automatically assumed and to have the wound in his flank seen to, although he was suffering it stoically, while displaying bared teeth to Bob Barly to show it had not been forgotten.

Trybull had made radio contact with a fast police launch based in Southend and had arranged a rendezvous off Foulness Point whereby Siegfried could be transferred and examined by a vet. At the same time he requested a police presence in Wicken as a matter of urgency, only to be told that police cars had already been despatched from Burnham following a request from a Commander Luke of Scotland Yard, who was in turn responding to a telephone call from Wicken itself.

Campion nodded approvingly, even as Trybull wondered

whether answering 999 calls from remote parts of Essex really was the optimum use of such a senior policeman's time, and then proposed his own plan of action. If Trybull was confident he could handle the yacht on his own, and Campion admitted he was himself of little practical use, then he and Mason would escort their three prisoners to what passed for dry land in this part of the county. The fight had gone out of the Wicken men and they would have no wish to be left stranded on the mud after dark. They were all aware, anyway, that they would be under the watchful eye, and shotgun, of Lugg.

Trybull, although tempted to enquire what a 'Lugg' was, asked how Campion would accomplish this, even with the aid of his latest American ally, who was taking a childish pleasure in flexing his feet to squeeze the mud out from between his toes. He also reminded him that he might have to transport an orphaned Basenji, who was currently happily scurrying around the deck discovering a whole new world of interesting smells, much to the disdain of Constable Siegfried, who remained firmly on duty.

Mason had given him the idea, Campion explained, when he had offered to go to the rescue of Ethel Worskitt. They would use the dinghy, if the sergeant could spare it, and Mason was sure he could row it to cross the mudflat to the relatively more solid marsh, with Lugg providing covering fire if necessary. Campion himself intended to be purely a passenger, as befitted a man of his age and status.

'You can have the inflatable,' agreed Trybull, 'if this young chap thinks he can skim it over the mud, because there won't be any depth of water for rowing.'

'I reckon I can do a decent job of punting and slide it over there,' said Mason with a cheeky grin. 'We could always put Pickles in a harness and get him to pull us across.'

'Pickles?' asked Campion. 'What a ridiculous name for a Basenji – for any dog. His name is actually Barney,' the dog pricked up his ears in agreement, 'which isn't much better, I admit, but whatever he's called, he is not a beast of burden. They, on the other hand, are.'

Thus the sight which Lugg observed, a sight made almost mystical by the fading light reflecting weakly on the water, was of the three Wicken men trudging in a line through the mud, often stumbling or sinking into it, and towing by means of a rope over their shoulders a bright orange rubber dinghy. The dinghy was bouncing along, clearly disturbing the water's surface if not exactly creating a bow wave, its propulsion aided by the unmistakable figure of Mason Lowell kneeling in the stern, both arms swinging in unison to plunge a short rowing paddle into the mud, wrench it out and then return it. From a distance he looked like a diminutive gondolier, but because he was tall, if he stood as a real gondolier would, the paddle would not reach the surface. Mason's weight at the back and the strain on the tow rope on the front meant that the dinghy was riding at an angle, its nose in the air, clear of the water and mud. As befitted his status as a very important passenger, Mr Campion was sitting regally upright in the prow, clutching to his chest a small furry animal with perked-up ears and a flopping tongue.

If he could not photograph it, Lugg wanted to absorb the sight in every detail, from Mason's furious work-rate in the stern to the comical way the three men acting as dray horses attempted to stay upright on clearly treacherous footing. He was surprised that Campion had not fashioned some sort of whip to crack over the men's heads with an accompanying shout of 'Mush! Mush!'

Lugg's slightly sadistic reverie was disturbed by a voice behind him.

'What have you done to Richard, Mr Lugg?'

'Oo?' grunted the fat man, turning to find Mary Ann Allen crouching beside Richard Polley, who was still seated in the marram grass where Lugg had left him. She was cradling his head with an arm and, although he still held a handkerchief to his face, the bleeding seemed to have stopped.

'Oh, 'im,' said Lugg, implying that he had quite forgotten any encounter with the man. 'I needed his shotgun.' He hefted the weapon to prove his case. 'Don't suppose he's got any more shells on him, has he?'

'What do you want a shotgun for?'

'Crowd control,' sniffed Lugg. 'More to the point, what did *he* want one for?'

Richard Polley said something to Mary Ann which Lugg could not catch, then allowed her to help him to his feet.

'That man,' he said, pointing unsteadily out over the watery flats, 'he's bringing Pickles back.'

'That's Albert Campion,' Lugg informed him, 'dog-catcher to the crowned 'eads of Europe being just one of his many professions. That your mutt out there on the water-splash? The one with four legs, I mean. The white-haired elderly gent wearing glasses is mine.'

'My sister's dog actually,' said Polley. 'She's adopted it and is very fond of it.'

He dug into a blazer pocket, produced two fresh twelve-bore shells and handed them over to Lugg, who grunted his appreciation, broke the shotgun and replaced the spent cartridge.

'Give Octavia a wave to show you're all right, Richard,' said Mary Ann. 'I brought her with me but I had to leave her chair at the end of the lane. I couldn't bring it out here.'

Polley turned and waved back in the direction of Wicken. There, at the end of the track, above the level of the marsh, a figure wrapped in blankets sitting in a wheelchair returned his wave.

'Strewth!' exclaimed Lugg. 'We'll have the entire population of Wicken out here soon. Is there anybody left in the place?'

'Silence is looking after Frank Worskitt,' said Mary Ann, 'and I told Leonora Jarmin and Modesty Barly to stay inside and lock their doors until the police arrived.'

'You rang the number I gave you? Good girl.'

'It might take a while for them to get here, but Leonora and Modesty will stay indoors if they think Ethel is on the warpath.'

'Well, she ain't any more, if that was her who went down like the *Titanic* out there, once she found she couldn't walk on water no more.'

'She never could,' said Polley. 'She just wanted us to think she could.'

On reaching the marsh, the three men of Wicken, wet, stinking and filthy, collapsed to their knees. The raft they had been pulling slid to a halt, allowing Mr Campion to step imperiously on to a large tussock of marram grass. He dropped the dog he had been nursing to the ground, but held on to the lead as the Basenji strained forward, ears pricked and tail wagging, even treating the onlookers to its own version of a bark of greeting – a strange, yodel-like warble – when it clearly recognized Richard Polley.

Mason jumped from the dinghy, put his hands in the small of his back and stretched his upper body in an impressive arc.

'Call that rowing?' said Lugg.

'I think he did splendidly,' said Campion. 'In fact, I'm going to put him up for a Rowing Blue from my old Cambridge college. Like most American reinforcements, his arrival out there was a little late, but very welcome. Now I suppose we must contact the authorities.'

He turned and looked out to Worm Creek where the *Jocasta*'s mast, the only part of the yacht visible now the tide was turning, was moving seaward as Trybull navigated the channel in reverse.

'The rozzers are on their way,' said Lugg.

'I'm guessing we have Miss Allen here to thank for that.'

'She went to the top,' said Lugg with admiration, 'and rang Charlie Luke direct.'

'Well done, and I see you've picked up a new patient.'

'This is Richard Polley,' said Mary Ann, 'who had a bit of an accident as he rushed here to help Mr Lugg.'

Campion regarded the blood-spattered front of Polley's shirt and the vivid blue bruising around his nose and eyes, then looked askance at Lugg, who had assumed a false expression of innocence which would not have fooled a jury of benevolent angels for half a second.

'The dog seems to know you, Mr Polley,' he said as the Basenji pulled the rope lead taut.

'He was found wandering the marsh and my sister adopted him. If possible, she'd like to say goodbye to him,' said Polley, indicating the figure in the wheelchair on the raised roadway.

Campion offered him the rope. 'Would you be able to look after Barney for a while, perhaps a few days, until we can get things sorted out?'

Polley's face broke into a broad smile, then a wince, as painful muscles around the nose came into play. 'Delighted to. Come on, Pickles.'

'That dog will be getting a split personality,' said Campion as the dog trotted away happily with Richard Polley.

'The Covenanters had a thing about not having pets, so his sister had him hidden in the chapel,' said Mason, hopping on one leg to put his borrowed boots back on. 'I found him there, then they found me and locked me in.'

'A good breed of dog to hide, the non-barking kind,' mused Campion, 'and it might be a good idea to lock these three in the chapel until Luke's minions arrive.'

'Doubtful, as in the course of my rescue, the doors got sort of damaged.'

Campion looked at Lugg again. 'You have been busy, haven't you? As you've got the gun, you can stand guard.'

'As long as somebody brings me a mug of cocoa,' moaned the fat man. 'You can't do guard duty without cocoa.' He waved the shotgun barrel above the heads of the kneeling Wicken men. 'Up you get, you lot, let's be 'aving you, quick march in line. Cor blimey, you're all in a bit of a state. I reckon they'll have to hose you off before they let you in the back of a police car.'

Lugg's three prisoners were indeed a sorry sight, smeared from head to foot in mud and dripping water. Jarmin was limping on one leg and Barly clutching the arm on which Constable Siegfried had chewed across his chest.

'We might need your medical skills, Miss Allen,' said Campion. 'One of these reprobates tangled with a police dog who found him rather tasty, and Mr Jarmin here was clouted on the knee by Mrs Worskitt. Which reminds me . . .'

Campion returned to the rubber dinghy and from it retrieved Ethel Worskitt's walking stick, pointing the end at Mary Ann.

'I saw this floating by our little pleasure craft out there where Ethel dropped it and scooped it up. You see, I think this is a murder weapon. I saw the way Ethel used it on Jarmin there once she'd knocked him off his feet. She used it to push him deeper into the mud and I think that's what she did to Francis Jarrold, only Francis was face-down when she did, and he didn't get back up. Do tell Dr Fathoms that I think I have an explanation for the small round mark he found on the back of Jarrold's neck. My guess is that it was caused by the end of this stick, and – once that's confirmed – I will insist he gets recognition for spotting it.'

'He will appreciate that, thank you.'

'You can also tell him that Wicken will have no further need of witch bottles.'

'Because the wicked witch is dead?'

'Well,' said Campion thoughtfully, 'the wicked one is dead. For the others, I cannot vouch. Now, where can we go to dry off' – he glanced at Mason's mud-spattered clothes – 'and get cleaned up?'

'I left my shoes at Silence Jones's house,' said the American.

'She won't mind us going round to hers,' said Mary Ann. 'In fact, she's probably dying to know what went on out here.'

'What makes you think she didn't see all this unfolding before it actually happened?' Campion said mischievously. 'Was her third eye not working?'

Silence Jones certainly seemed to be expecting them, meeting the damp and bedraggled party at her front door, all the time straining her neck to see Lugg, throwing his considerable weight into the role of Prisoners' Escort, marching Josh Jarmin, Bob Barly and George Bugg into the chapel next door at gunpoint.

'A successful outcome according to the Polleys,' she greeted Mason cheerfully. 'Octavia is over the moon that you got her dog back. They've just taken Pickles home.'

'It was never her dog,' said Mr Campion, 'as you knew all along, but she is reunited with it for the moment.'

Mason Lowell, sensing a chill in the air not due to his wet clothes, intervened. 'Miss Jones, this is Albert Campion, who has been acting as a kind of mentor to me here in England and is our commander-in-chief, as you might say.'

'But I would not,' said Campion, 'because such authority usually comes with great responsibility, and I would not sleep at night if I thought I was responsible for what has gone on in Wicken.'

Miss Jones regarded Campion with a mixture of surprise and suspicion. He was, she thought, a little older than herself, but still retaining a distinct boyish charm under that shock of white hair and behind those ridiculously large tortoiseshell glasses. His bizarre, mud-splattered clothes gave the impression of a drunken fisherman who had got dressed in the dark, yet he carried them with a straight-faced conviction that defied comment.

'I understand you have Frank Worskitt here,' he said while being scrutinized, 'whom I have met before and who hopefully will remember me. I need to speak to him.'

'To break the news about Ethel,' said Silence, nodding her head.

'May I see him?'

'He's gone with the Polleys, last house on the lane. They will look after him. All things considered, he took the fact of Ethel's passing better than one could have reasonably expected. He was always telling her that it was dangerous to go out on the mud.'

'How did he know about Ethel?'

'I told him,' said Miss Jones as they locked eyes.

It was Campion who broke the stare, his eyes flicking to the upstairs windows of Abigail Cottage. 'You saw from the bedroom window?'

Silence jutted her jaw. 'No, I just knew.'

'Then I think we'd better come in if we may,' said Mr Campion politely. 'We need to talk.'

After giving Mason a towel and ordering him upstairs to the bathroom to clean himself, Miss Jones showed Campion into her front room, switched on the lights, drew the curtains and announced that she would be making tea. Mary Ann Allen offered to help her and take a mug of cocoa round to Mr Lugg, as requested, and Mr Campion thought it a splendid notion 'to keep the troops happy', but in reality was glad of the prospect of having Silence Jones to himself.

She returned bearing a tray loaded with the implements of tea for three and placed it on the backless chair previously employed for barbering services. She laid out three cups on saucers, poured milk into two of them and began to pour from a large floral-pattern teapot.

As she poured, both she and Campion heard the creaking of floorboards from above and the traverse of footsteps.

'That will be my American friend,' said Campion. 'Checking the view from the bedroom window.'

'But it's dark outside.'

'He will discover that for himself, eventually.' Campion smiled. 'But he is, as I am, curious as to how much you saw of what went on out there on the flats this evening. The light would not have been good and it's quite a distance to Worm Creek.'

'I told you, I saw nothing from that window.'

'But you did see something . . . somehow.'

'I saw . . . felt . . . Mrs Worskitt go into the mud and I knew she would not survive. The Wicken men out there knew it too and did nothing to save her. But I cannot be a witness for you, Mr Campion.'

'I don't want you to be one, Miss Jones. I took the precaution of bringing one of my own along in the form of the police sergeant who skippered the *Jocasta*, and I had another policeman with me, but he was more a bodyguard than a witness. The police may wish to take a statement from you, but I doubt very much you would be called upon to act as a witness. Except to me, that is, for I am unbearably curious about all things Wicken.'

'Sugar?' she asked, offering cup and saucer.

'No, thank you, just as it comes.'

'I haven't slipped anything into the teapot, apart from tea, that is.'

'Why ever should I think you had? Surely your third eye tells you that I can be trusted, am completely gullible and will believe anything you tell me.'

'So you know.'

Mr Campion shrugged his shoulders but was careful not to spill his tea. 'I have done some research and my wife has too. It was finding a witch's bottle which sparked our interest and then those little reflection dolls kept turning up, and by then I was involved in the goings-on in Wicken.'

Silence Jones remained silent and sipped her tea, observing Campion over the rim of her cup.

'Would it help if I went first?' he asked. 'If I laid my tarot cards on the table, so to speak?'

'Perhaps it might, though I resent the implication of tarot cards. That would imply we are fairground charlatans.'

'No doubt you will enlighten me . . . us.'

He paused as a drier and mostly presentable Mason entered the room and took a seat and a cup as directed.

'I think,' said the woman after a considered pause, 'you should tell me what you know, or think you know of Wicken.'

'Very well,' said Campion, crossing his long legs, which resulted in an awkward squeaking from his fisherman's over-trousers, 'mine is something of a shaggy dog story, quite literally.

'I came to Wicken to retrieve a missing dog and discovered a shipwreck, a dead body, and evidence to suggest that a second dog had survived the shipwreck and that the skipper, the late

Francis Jarrold, had been taking precautions against witchcraft. Numerous little hand-sewn idols or dolls, which go by the name of reflections, started to appear, and coincidentally – and I am not a big fan of coincidences – our American friend here arrives with stories of seventeenth-century Covenanters from Wicken. My interest was, shall we say, piqued. So I consulted various experts in London and my wife did the same in Cambridge.'

Miss Jones carefully replaced her cup and saucer on the tray. 'And did you reach a conclusion?'

'Two, actually. Firstly, that Francis Jarrold was making regular trips across the Channel, carrying the pets of the rich and famous and offloading them in Wicken to avoid quarantine regulations, a business for which he must have had assistants in Wicken. So far, so criminal, especially when it resulted in the murder of Timothy Timms, who was, I believe, the paymaster for the enterprise. But, as I say, this was criminal activity, no witchcraft was involved. That was the second conclusion I came to.'

'I don't follow,' Mason intervened.

'I'm sorry, my boy, I know you were set on the idea. The reflections, the witches' bottles, the link with Salem in 1692, there being thirteen families signed to the Billericay Covenant, the number traditionally required for a coven of witches; it all pointed that way, but it wasn't ever really witchcraft, it was wicken.'

'We're in Wicken,' said Mason, confused.

'Not the place – the belief, the *practice* of wicken. It might be a sort of magic, but it would be going too far to call it a religion, I feel.' Campion looked quizzically at Miss Jones.

'You are correct,' she said demurely. 'It is a belief in the ability to see into the future, which some call having a third eye. Seeing, of course, is not the same as understanding, or being able to avoid the future, but it can, when not abused, give shape and purpose to a life.'

'And the signatories of the Billericay Covenant were all believers in wicken?'

'Yes, they were, and they all came from here. There was an enclave of believers and they felt threatened by the political and religious upheavals of the 1690s, and not by the famous Essex witch trials, which were earlier in the century. They would still be a folk memory, though, and so it would have been a nasty shock to land in Salem only to find witch trials taking place.'

'You denied all knowledge of Salem when I interviewed you,' blustered Mason.

'That was an interview?'

Campion could not but admire Miss Jones's skill with a polite put-down.

'I did not deny everything, Mr Clay. Living in a house called Abigail Cottage made that impossible, but there was no reason to reveal all our secrets.'

'I'm surprised you couldn't use your third eye to see that Mason here is also totally harmless,' Campion said slyly, 'and my colleague, Mr Lugg, would be very interested in any predictions you might have for the football pools.'

'Wicken doesn't work like that – it can't be called upon to order. It's a feeling, a shared feeling, and those who have it share the same premonitions. Group decisions are taken for the good of the group, making it a rather democratic and harmonious way to live. When those Billericay Covenanters crossed to the New World and landed in Salem, they sensed immediately that life there with their peculiar gifts would be anything but harmonious, and so the thirteen families who had the wicken persuaded the *Abigail* to sail on down to Harkers Island.'

'You told me you had never heard of Harkers Island!' Mason moaned.

'I am sorry I lied to you about that, but I was telling the truth when I said I had no *written* proof that I was related to the Henry and Silence Jones who were Covenanters.'

'And among those who came back.'

'True. According to the stories I was told as a child, roughly half the families who were landed on Harkers hated the place immediately. They had a bad feeling about it, saw bad things coming, and those people trusted their feelings. Perhaps it reminded them too much of the Dengie Peninsula when they had been expecting a richer, more pleasant land.'

'Who was their leader?'

'The story goes that Abendigo Lux was the leading Covenanter.'

'I knew it!'

'And it was he who persuaded the captain of the *Abigail* to bring back those who preferred to return to England.'

Campion raised his teacup to make his point. 'May I ask how he persuaded Captain Waudby – yes, Mason, I was paying attention – to sail all those extra miles down the East Coast and then back to England? I am guessing that the Covenanters had bought one-way passages, not return tickets.'

'I think he must have had a very forceful personality – after all, he most likely persuaded them all to up sticks and leave Essex, and then half of them followed him back here.'

'Would you say he intimidated Captain Waubdy; perhaps he had some sort of fear hold over him?'

'A "fear hold",' said Miss Jones quietly. 'That's a quaint way of putting it, but you could be right. I know what you're thinking.'

In his short acquaintance with Mr Campion, Mason thought that few people had ever said that to him with any accuracy, but as Silence continued, Campion nodded along in agreement.

'You're thinking that Abendigo Lux could exert some sort of wicken power over the captain and, indeed, over the Covenanters. A power which may well be thought of as witchcraft. What's more, you think Ethel Worskitt, his direct descendant, also had that power over those of us here in Wicken.'

'Well, did she?'

'She certainly thought she did.'

'And that's why Miss Allen's house had several witches' bottles, because the previous owners were Jarrolds. Francis Jarrold continued with the insurance policy with one on the *Jocasta* and at least one in his digs in Brightlingsea. Jarrold clearly knew about the forces of wicken, but was he himself a participant, if that's the right word?'

'His mother's grandmother was a Jarmin, but wicken senses are not always inherited, at least not directly, and Francis had no particular power that I was aware of. He moved away a long time ago and the power is always strongest when several of us are together.'

'And a remarkable number of you do seem to be together here in Wicken. Nothing unusual for the seventeenth century but rather odd for the twentieth. So how did that come about? Please don't say coincidence.'

'Oh, it certainly wasn't coincidence – it was a deliberate

gathering of the clans, as you might say. We received the calling: come back to Wicken or end up lying by the wall. That was the message, the sense, the feeling, which drew us together, and it was Ethel Worskitt who sent that message out, calling us home. Perhaps she was a witch after all.'

'Calling you home?' queried Campion.

'Have you not noticed – I think Mr Clay has – that the average age of the residents of Wicken is rather advanced? There are no young couples here, and only Leonora Jarmin and Modesty Barly are, if one is being generous, of child-bearing age, though neither has shown any inclination to do so. Octavia Polley has been in a wheelchair for years since a riding accident as a girl and her brother never married, and neither did I. Ethelreda Lux married Frank Worskitt when she was thirty and he was at least fifty.'

'So she was not anticipating motherhood?' Campion asked. 'I'm sure it would have been biologically possible.'

'She didn't marry him to bear his children – she married him because of the house and the chapel.'

'I wondered about the chapel from the start,' said Campion, ignoring the quizzical look he was getting from Mason. 'It seemed odd that the cult of wicken, if I may call it that, had taken to Methodism as its religion of choice.'

'It was a case of hiding in plain sight,' said Silence Jones. 'Our small, rather peculiar community without a church would stand out as very unusual in Victorian times, but a remote Methodist chapel would not raise any suspicion. Plus, we have to be buried somewhere, and that's what attracted Ethelreda to Frank and the Worskitts, who were stalwart chapel-goers.'

Campion raised a forefinger, making a point. 'I distinctly remember when I met Frank Worskitt, he said his wife was an "incomer" from Shoeburyness.'

'She was. The Covenanter families may have all come back to Wicken, but they didn't all stay here. Over the years they dispersed. My own family lived in London, as did the Polleys. Abraham Lux was living in Shoeburyness when he joined the army in 1914. Ethelreda would have been about 14 when he was killed in action, and then her mother followed in the Spanish flu epidemic in 1919. It was only when she married Frank that she moved to Wicken and began to gather the Covenanters.'

'Gather them?'

'Call them home might be a better way of putting it; at least that's how she saw it. Of course, some of the Covenanter families were already here, such as the Buggs and the Barlys, who seemed to inter-marry at every given opportunity. When non-Covenanter families died out or moved out, Ethel persuaded Covenanters to move in. Joshua Jarmin, who had married one of Bob Barly's sisters, bought the cottage where the Bloomfields had lived, and when the Hankinses' house at the end of the lane came up for sale, Richard and Octavia Polley moved in. To be frank, there was never a queue of potential buyers wanting to move here. The exception being Francis Jarrold's old home, the bungalow next door, which Mary Ann Allen and her husband bought. By that time, I think Ethel had run out of fellow believers to entice here.'

'Are you saying that the woman deliberately populated Wicken with followers of wicken? How did she find them and how did she persuade them to come here?'

'Who knows how she found them? Perhaps they found her, answering some sort of calling. She seemed to have no trouble attracting the men of the Covenant, though there must be many female descendants out in the world, their name changed by marriage, who could trace a bloodline back to the passengers on the *Abigail*. But then, men always were more easily influenced by the wicken.'

'But what could Wicken – the place – offer them?' asked Campion. 'What was in it for them to move here?'

'Two things.' Silence Jones put her hands in her lap, sat up straight, and looked Campion squarely in the face, demanding his full attention. 'The first was the chance to be with their own kind, with people who shared the same feelings, the same visions, the same forebodings about the future. To be with people for whom the strangest sensations were commonplace and not to be feared, people who understood the beliefs which had bound the Covenanters together.

'The second was they would be guaranteed a place in the chapel's graveyard and thus avoid the terrible fate of being left *lying by the wall*, dead but unburied and among strangers. She was offering them a place to come and die.'

TWENTY
Curtain Calls

Mason allowed Lugg to drive the hire car back to London that night, bowing to the fat man's superior knowledge of the capital's byroads after dark and having decided that one more illegality, added to what he had experienced and witnessed that day, would count for little.

Lulled by the flashing of neon streetlights, Mason's head soon slumped on to his chest and, had he been awake, he would have thanked Lugg for making him fasten his seat belt after Campion had explained that Americans regarded such impositions by government as an assault on their inalienable rights.

Campion himself dozed fitfully until Lugg's infallible internal clock told him closing time was approaching and that perhaps a detour to a 'nice little boozer' in Bethnal Green was called for.

Mr Campion, risking mutiny, reminded him that Mason did not drink and that he deserved a better reward for his exertions out on the Dengie Flat. The better course of action was to head for Bottle Street with all speed.

Once there, Campion was immediately on the telephone to The Dorchester, requesting a room for the night and an emergency supper for four from whatever the kitchens had to hand. When Mason queried why supper for four, Campion merely stated the obvious, that Lugg was hungry. He then threw some clean clothes from his London wardrobe into an overnight bag and led his two guests out on to the street, conscious of the faint aroma of stagnant mud which still came off his American guest, and hoping that it might secure them a private table.

It was almost noon the next day that Campion sauntered back to the Bottle Street flat to find his companions in shirtsleeves at a table where they had clearly done battle with a makeshift breakfast, diligently scouring the pages of every national newspaper.

'Not a peep,' said a disgruntled Lugg. 'You'd have thought the *Express* would have gone with "Mayhem on the Marshes" or similar.'

'Don't get above yourself, old fruit – your time in the headlines is yet to come,' Campion told him. 'I am rather thankful that Charlie Luke seems to be keeping a lid on things, but as I have to ring him, I'll register your complaint that you are being denied your fair share of publicity.'

Lugg winked at Mason Lowell across the table. 'This'll be good. Nothing beats a good argument with a policeman first thing in the morning to get the blood pumping. Takes years off yer.'

'Ignore him, Mason,' said Campion as he dialled a familiar number. 'We are way past first thing in the morning and Charles is an old family friend. Oh, hello, Commander Luke, please. This is Albert Campion, but I am happy to wait.'

He did not have to wait long.

'Albert? What's this all about? I've had some very confused reports about a large bald gentleman waving a shotgun around the Essex marshes, and more than a few hints about witchcraft and voodoo dolls. Ring any bells?'

'Oh, come on, Charlie, a voodoo doll of Lugg? There aren't that many pins in Savile Row. What's the actual score?'

'Well, there's not much good news, I'm afraid,' Luke said down the telephone, 'if you're a rate-payer in Wicken that is. And wherever Wicken is, it's three rate-payers short this morning. I've got Messrs Jarmin, Bugg and Barly in custody for the Timms murder and the assault on Rupert.'

'I think you'll find Barly was the knife man, but all three went there looking for trouble.'

'They're also being questioned about an assault on an Essex police sergeant and possible involvement in smuggling animals across the Channel in contravention of the quarantine regulations.'

'That should be enough to be going on with,' observed Campion.

'Which reminds me, I should tell you that the gendarmerie across the water have come up with a little nugget about the late Francis Jarrold and his regular trips to Honfleur.'

'Really? Do tell.'

'It seems he was quite well known to the local *flics*, mainly through his drinking habits, but also because he was very chummy with a chap who ran what I understand is called a puppy farm – unlicensed, of course. All sorts of nasty things went on there, and Jarrold was thought to have a line in exporting dogs – without a proper pedigree or vaccinations – to England. A few weeks ago, the place was shut down when rabies was reported there. Jarrold could have got bitten while there; the timing seems to fit.'

'Oh good, that lets Barney and Robespierre off the hook.'

'What?'

'Nothing, Charlie, nothing important. Otherwise, everything quiet on the Wicken front?'

'Well, the top bods in Essex Police are a bit miffed about me throwing my weight around, but they'll get over it, and there will have to be an inquest on the Worskitt woman, though nobody thinks the body will ever be recovered. And one other casualty: the husband. It seems that when the penny dropped that his wife had gone for good, the poor chap had a bit of a stroke and he's likely to spend the rest of his days in a nursing home. He was ninety-five, you know, so he'd had a good run. He's in hospital in Southend at the moment, but they can't find any family to contact to let them know.'

'Poor chap,' said Campion. 'I don't think there was any immediate family, and his near neighbours – well, I think they might know already.'

'You'll have to fill me in on the goings-on out there, but only after you've given a full statement to the Essex boys. I will also need to get Rupert in to see if he can identify any of the thugs from the Timms murder.'

'You know where we live, Charles, and we are all, as ever, at your disposal.'

'Hah!'

'What was that?'

'That was Lugg, Charles, agreeing to do his civic duty.'

Mr Campion's next telephone call was to his son to see whether he had recovered enough to act as a chauffeur that afternoon and give his aged father a lift out to Brightlingsea in Essex to where he had carelessly left his own car.

Rupert was naturally willing to help, but felt he was in no condition to drive any distance due to occasional dizzy spells and blurred vision, possibly due to delayed concussion.

'Pull yourself together, boy!' snapped Mr Campion in his best headmasterly voice. 'You were beaten up and thrown down a flight of stairs, that's all. It's not as if you have a hangover from a night on the tiles with Lugg!'

Rupert laughed, admitted that he wasn't quite *hors de combat*, but said it might be wiser if Perdita drove them, then they could both hear a first-hand account of what had happened out at Wicken.

Campion agreed immediately on condition that he was not distracting his daughter-in-law from a rehearsal or an important audition. When Rupert replied that was not the case, his tone told Campion that it might be a sensitive subject and that Perdita, like Rupert and the vast majority of actors registered with Equity, was currently 'resting'.

And so, sitting in the passenger seat of their bright red Mini Cooper, with Rupert huddled in the back seat, Campion gave a running commentary on the fate and misfortunes of the residents of Wicken over the past forty-eight hours. He shared Rupert's opinion, formed on one brief encounter, of Ethel Worskitt, and he answered multiple questions from Perdita with enthusiasm on the grounds that he was likely to be similarly questioned by Amanda when she returned home, and it was always better to get one's story straight before the serious interrogation took place.

They were beyond Chelmsford before Perdita asked the question she had been itching to pose since they left London. 'So was Ethelreda really a witch?'

'I am in no position to judge,' said Campion.

'Well, she certainly scared me,' Rupert said into the rear-view mirror.

'Me too, and I think she assumed she had supernatural power over the other Covenanters, but you have to remember that wicken is not witchcraft. There are no spells or incantations, and certainly no dancing naked round a bonfire at midnight; it's far too cold out on the marshes for that.'

'But she had some sort of hold over them, even if it wasn't a spell?'

'Definitely, though it varied. The thing about wicken is that it's a shared sixth sense. They all felt it and they knew it was stronger when they were together, but certain members of the group felt less loyalty to the faith than others. Silence Jones for one. She respected it as a gift, but she was never in thrall to Ethel. Richard and Octavia Polley, I think, were easily bullied, and then you have Jarmin, Bugg and Barly who were completely under her influence and, essentially, her foot soldiers. They were the ones who did all the heavy lifting to help Jarrold in his smuggling activities.'

'Until it went wrong.'

'Yes, for all their combined "third eyes", no one in Wicken could predict that Jarrold would run the *Jocasta* aground and let his two passengers loose on the mudflats, but the poor fellow had rabies and wasn't thinking straight.'

'That sounds a horrible way to go,' said Perdita.

'It was,' Campion agreed, though he had spared her his thoughts on how Ethel Worskitt had administered the *coup de grâce*.

'But could it have been worth it? I mean, pet smuggling doesn't sound to be a particularly lucrative sort of crime.'

'You may be surprised how much the rich and famous will pay to avoid being shackled by the rules we mere mortals have to live by, but I don't think Ethel was trying to amass an illegal fortune. She was simply setting a bit aside, creating a funeral fund.'

'A funeral fund?'

'Look at the population of Wicken, or rather those descended from the Covenanters. What did they have in common?'

'Apart from this so-called "third eye",' offered Rupert, 'nothing except they were all old fogies, you know, Pop – your age.'

'True, and thank you for that,' said Campion through gritted teeth.

'None of them had children,' said Perdita, 'and none seemed especially well off.'

'Both excellent observations,' Campion said pointedly, 'and what preys on the mind of the elderly even more than the disrespect of ungrateful children? Their funerals. Where they are to be buried and who will pay for it. The physical resting place was taken care of thanks to Frank Worskitt's connections with the chapel and, according to Silence Jones, Ethel had established a Funeral Fund for the faithful, making payments into it from their ill-gotten gains. It was administered by a solicitor called Thurman in, of all places, Billericay.

'You see, Ethel was obsessed with the original Billericay Covenant and the way it had kept those with the gift of wicken safe and together. I think, as a descendant of Abendigo Lux, she saw herself as the protector of the Covenant, which bound their ancestors together. If she could not lead them in life, she would look after them in death.'

'How bizarre,' said Perdita, 'so the profits from smuggling dogs went into this fund?'

'That and any other spare cash that was earned in the village was paid as a sort of tax. It seems to have been a very co-operative venture, almost like one of those Christmas Clubs they have up north, or a benevolent society.'

'The whole scheme sounds gruesome to me, but at least the dogs survived to live happily ever after.'

'Yes,' said Mr Campion, 'I think they did.'

The Jaguar was where Campion had left it in Brightlingsea, but under the windscreen wiper was an official notice announcing 'Police Aware' which, Campion suspected, had been thoughtfully placed by Sergeant Trybull.

He walked down to the moorings on the hard, partly to show Rupert and Perdita the *Jocasta* and partly to reassure himself it was safely back where it belonged. There was no sign of Trybull, who was almost certainly chained to a desk somewhere typing out a report on the events at Wicken and the somewhat unofficial roles played by himself and Constable Siegfried.

Perdita wanted to climb on board what she described as 'the doggy slave ship', but Campion forbade it as the cabin and hatches would be locked – and officially, he presumed, the yacht had been taken into police custody.

At the sailing club, he left a bag containing the jacket and waterproofs he had borrowed, along with the note of thanks he had written before leaving London. The old salt on duty there, wearing a striped jersey and a Breton cap, was probably more a tourist attraction than an official harbour master, but he promised to make sure Tom Trybull got the bag.

'Thank you for the lift. Now you two head back to town and I'll shoot off home,' he told the younger Campions. 'Have to get the place tidy before your mother gets back.'

Perdita, dragging her feet, looked longingly down the line of yachts clinking at rest on their moorings along the River Colne and took in a deep breath.

'This is rather a lovely place,' she said, squeezing Rupert's hand. 'We should get a boat. I've always fancied messing about in boats, as Ratty said to Mole.'

'Be careful what you wish for,' said Mr Campion. 'It can be a very dangerous pastime.'

Lady Amanda returned from what her husband called her 'military liaisons' in Scotland the following day and duly demanded a full briefing on her husband's activities during her absence. Mr Campion politely demurred, saying that he would much prefer to hear of Amanda's sojourn in Lossiemouth testing top-secret jet engines, but he knew resistance was futile and provided an unexpurgated account of his adventures with wicken and in Wicken.

His wife listened patiently, all her observations being succinct and intelligent, as was to be expected, and only mildly scolded him for not insisting that she return from Scotland immediately to nurse Rupert after the assault in Timmy Timms's office.

That evening, while Mr Campion was out on his pre-dinner stroll across the fields, Amanda checked her watch, calculated the time difference and placed a transatlantic telephone call.

'Professor Luger? My name is Amanda Campion. I understand you knew my husband during the war . . .'

Two weeks after the 'disturbances on the Dengie Peninsula' as Mr Campion now referred to them, the Campions decamped for London for a short break, the official excuse being to see off Mason Lowell from the airport on his return flight to America and to reclaim the Bottle Street flat.

They stayed at The Dorchester – Amanda had insisted, calling it Mr Campion's 'emergency bachelor pad' – and, having reserved a table for a farewell dinner, she had disappeared on a shopping trip, leaving her husband to his own devices, although she had a good idea what those might entail.

This time, Mr Campion did telephone ahead before taking a black cab to Dame Jocasta Upcott's Chelsea home, where the door was opened almost immediately by the statuesque Verbena who was on the cusp of taking Robespierre for a walk.

The dog, straining on his leash and his tail threatening to damage the wood panelling in the hallway, greeted Campion like an old friend. Verbena did not, saying simply that he was expected and to go on in.

Dame Jocasta was dressed in a navy-blue satin dress set off by a lengthy string of pearls, her hair done to perfection as was her make-up, although Campion doubted it was for his benefit.

'To what do I owe the pleasure, Mr Campion?'

'I am afraid it won't be a pleasure, Dame Jocasta. I'm here to give you a severe telling-off.'

'Well you certainly have a grimness about you, the look of the theatre critic about to give me a bad review.'

'Oh, I doubt anything I can say would hurt you as much as that, or perhaps you've already seen it coming.'

'I have no idea what you are talking about, so please get to the point. I am expecting some newspaper people this afternoon to interview me about a new production. Please say what you have to say, admonish me if you must, loose your slings and arrows if you must, but please get on with it.'

'Some weeks ago, you sent me to a place called Wicken to rescue your dog,' Campion began, though with little hope of cracking Dame Jocasta's defensive shell. 'Which I did.'

'And I thanked you for it.'

'I had no idea at the time that I was complicit in a crime.'

'A *crime*?' The protested innocence was convincing but then, she was an accomplished actress.

'The avoidance of the animal quarantine regulations, not just for your own pet, but for those of your society friends – at a price, of course. It became a nice little sideline for the residents of Wicken, a perfect place to land contraband unseen with a willing workforce happy to co-operate, but you were well aware of that, weren't you?'

'I really cannot think what you are driving at. Francis Jarrold worked for me, that was true, and he may have indulged in questionable activities with Timmy Timms, but I can hardly be held responsible.'

'I think you can and should. It was you who spent every summer in France, you who gave society parties there, you who would know those English visitors who, with one of the stupidest traits of Englishness, could not bear to be parted from their lapdogs. Timms, acting as middleman, was just trying to please you. It is something I hear agents are supposed to do but rarely satisfy their clients.'

Dame Jocasta remained impassive, impenetrable.

'Are the newspaper reporters you are expecting aware that Timms was murdered by men from Wicken, or of your peculiar connection to the place?'

There was a narrowing of the eyes which Campion took as a definite chink in her armour plate.

'I don't know what you mean.'

'You chose Wicken, not Francis Jarrold, who had no love for the place. You chose Wicken because you knew it was populated by Covenanters.'

'I have no idea what a Covenanter is.'

The dame really was giving a convincing performance.

'My wife thinks you do. You see, it was her idea to ring an old friend in America, an academic, who has studied the population of a place called Harkers Island in North Carolina. It shares a history with Wicken and, indeed, the practice or belief in *wicken*, a sort of shared telepathy and ability to see into the future, which is often confused with witchcraft.

'My wife, being of a suspicious nature, began to uproot your family tree. It wasn't difficult, as you are a very public person, indeed a person who is about to be interviewed by the press. Perhaps they might be interested in the fact that your great-grandmother Almira met your great-grandfather, a British naval captain, while he was on a goodwill visit to a place called Morehead City in North Carolina, which is not far from Harkers Island.

'Captain Upcott arranged passage for Almira back to England, where they were married. As far as I am aware, she never went back to Harkers Island, because that's where she was born and her maiden name was Whybrow. I am told you still have relatives there.'

'What do you want?'

'Very little, actually. You should make a list for the police of all the pet-loving friends you have helped with your stupid cross-Channel ferry service and be prepared for some bad publicity when the inquest on Jarrold reports and the trial of Timmy Timms's killers begins. Other than that, I would keep a low profile from now on, starting this afternoon.

'I think you would be well-advised to cancel those newspaper reporters. Tell them you've been taken suddenly ill. A mild touch of rabies, perhaps?'

The great leading lady glared at Campion but remained silent.

Campion counted it as a victory.

At exactly the same time that Mr Campion was confronting one of the country's leading theatrical divas, Perdita was in Shepherd's Bush about to storm another bastion of the artistic establishment.

Wearing a wide-legged denim jumpsuit, clumpy wooden heels which added two inches to her height and huge square sunglasses, she had no problem persuading a BBC commissionaire that she had an appointment with Geoffrey Clegg, the renowned director in one of the old drill halls in the shadow of Television Centre, now used as a rehearsal room. Geoffrey Clegg, it seemed, was renowned for attracting young, female visitors such as her.

The great man was busy rehearsing a knife fight between two very nervous youths, who were waving blunted daggers at each other with as much menace as if they had been comparing knitting needles. If anything, the great director seemed to welcome the distraction of Perdita's unexpected arrival, though of course he could not show it.

'We're not doing auditions today, darling, just a few technicals. Go find one of the production assistants,' he said, dismissing her, but not before his eyes had given her a thorough going-over.

'I'm not here for an audition, Geoffrey, *darling*. I'm here to tell you you're not getting your dog back.'

Clegg gave her his full attention after casually waving the two knife fighters to take a break.

'You've found Barney?'

'Yes, Barney has been found and is safe and well, but no thanks to you trying to smuggle the poor thing back into the country in a cage on a boat which ran aground on the Essex marshes. Goodness knows how frightened the poor beast must have been, abandoned in the dark like that.'

'I had—'

'Luckily for you,' Perdita turned up the volume, 'he was taken in by a kind old lady, a disabled old lady, and the long and short of it is that he's now called Pickles and you're not getting him back.'

'But I was told by . . .' Clegg stopped himself but could do nothing to halt Perdita's righteous anger.

'Your friend Jocasta Upcott, I know. Probably said she had a foolproof way of smuggling your precious pet back to England – well, it went badly wrong this time and people died . . . one of them your agent.'

'Ah yes, poor Timmy.'

'Finding a new agent could be your main problem because you'll get off lightly from this business, as long as you accept that Barney isn't coming home.'

'Timmy said he'd sent some young chap out to look for him,' said Clegg, trying, unsuccessfully, to break Perdita's flow.

'I know, it was an impressionable young actor who was promised a part in *The Duchess of Malfi* if he found the dog; the only thing was that nobody had heard of any such production, and when he went to remonstrate with Timms, he got attacked by Timms's killers.'

'Well, I am doing something with *The Duchess of Malfi*, but it was a secret project until the day before yesterday. Nobody knew about it, apart from Timmy, of course.'

'So you are doing the play?'

'Not the Webster play, my own film script of the real *Duchess of Malfi*, Giovanna D'Aragona, married at twelve, a pregnant widow at nineteen, secretly married one of her stewards, had two children by him before going on the run from angry brothers. Chased across Renaissance Italy, pregnant again, she was caught and taken back to Amalfi and then she and the kids disappeared, presumed murdered. I see it as a *film noir*, except in colour, done in modern dress as a Mafia thriller. Location shooting in Amalfi, Ancona and Siena.'

'It sounds . . . exciting,' said Perdita, unable to restrain herself.

'It will be an all-action piece and my Giovanna won't be a meek little pawn, she'll be an independent, strong-willed woman who wants to be liberated from the men who oppress her. Her rebellion is doomed, of course, but she goes down fighting.' The great director leaned back to appraise Perdita once again. 'You seem to have the swank and the cockiness I'm looking for. Have you ever done any acting?'

Dinner for the four Campions, Lugg and Mason Lowell was a jolly affair with only two uncomfortable silences. The first was when Amanda asked Rupert if he had any acting work in the pipeline and he had to resort to the actors' mantra that the right role had not yet come along, but something was bound to turn up. Only Mr Campion noticed that, at that moment, Perdita went unusually quiet and began to play nervously with her napkin.

The second silence was when Mason, true to his convictions, refused all offers of cocktails, wines and *digestifs* and insisted on a large bottle of mineral water to see him through the evening. The expression of horror which crossed Lugg's face every time a glass was poured made no fewer than three waiters ask him if everything was all right with his meal.

Mason made a speech with grace and charm, thanking his hosts profusely for their generosity and, looking at Lugg, mentorship. He had enough material for two doctoral theses, possibly a book and it had all been a wonderful adventure.

Around ten p.m. Mr Campion agreed that it had been an exhausting adventure and he and Amanda were retiring for the night. The younger members of the party were encouraged to carry on the party – he was sure Lugg would as well – and they would all rendezvous the next day at Heathrow to see Mason's flight depart.

It was only when, the next day, Mason had disappeared, staggering slightly, under the sign saying International Departures, that Mr Campion confided in his wife.

'Mason looks bloody awful. I didn't know he was frightened of flying, but he looks as if he's going to be sick.'

'The poor boy could hardly speak,' said Amanda. 'He must be terrified.'

'Nothing to do with flying,' said Rupert and, next to him, Lugg took a step backwards into the throng of well-wishers waving goodbye to departing loved ones.

'What happened after your mother and I called it a night?'

'Lugg and Mason didn't. Lugg took him on a pub crawl of several historic hostelries.'

'But Mason doesn't drink,' Campion pointed out.

'He doesn't drink beer, wines or spirits,' said Lugg, innocently perusing the terminal building's ceiling. 'He never said anything about cider.'

'But in America, cider is just apple juice. Mason wouldn't know that over here it was alcoholic.'

'He does now,' said Lugg.

AUTHOR NOTE

I would like to thank Andrew Cocks for attempting to teach me the rudiments of sailing across Swatchways and Spitways and, through Ostara Publishing, for the chance to bring some of the work of Pip Youngman Carter back into print.

The book Rupert is trying to study in chapter one, *America's Wealth* by Peter d'Alroy Jones, was published in Britain as *The Consumer Society: A History of American Capitalism*. It is very good.

The aphorism (Once is happenstance . . .) that Campion remembers in chapter two, comes from *Goldfinger* by Ian Fleming, which Mr Campion read and thoroughly enjoyed in 1959.

The Dengie Peninsula did indeed prove a good place to film Dr Who, as it featured in the 1972 episode, *Carnival of Monsters*. While I have tried to be faithful to the actual geography, the location of where Wicken would be, if it existed, is somewhere near the large, present-day wind farm. I am grateful, as always, for the cartographic skills of Roger Johnson, who has joined in the deception.

Just as a matter of interest, the map is based on the one on the rear endpapers of Highways and Byways in Essex by Clifford Bax (Macmillan, 1939), with details adapted from the late 1950s' one-inch OS map and elsewhere.

Harkers Island in North Carolina exists and its native residents do speak in a distinctive English accent, though it is derived from the regional speech patterns of Norfolk rather than Essex. Other than that geographical discrepancy, what happened to Rupert Campion there happened to me – more or less.

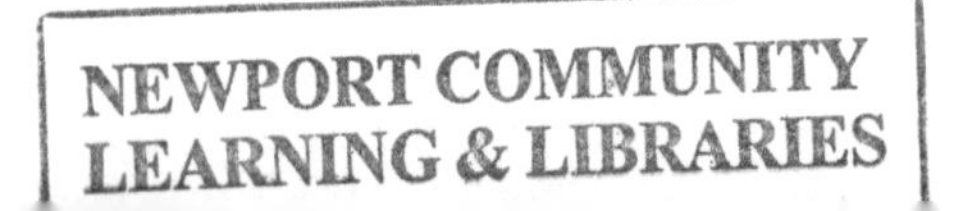